THE
NIGHTINGALE
LEGACY

THE NIGHTINGALE LEGACY

Catherine Coulter

G. P. PUTNAM'S SONS · NEW YORK

G. P. Putnam's Sons
Publishers Since 1838
200 Madison Avenue
New York, NY 10016

Library of Congress Cataloging-in-Publication Data

Coulter, Catherine.
The Nightingale legacy/Catherine Coulter.
p.   cm.
ISBN 0-399-13970-2
I. Title
PS3553.0843N54   1995   94-5840 CIP
813′.54—dc20

Printed in the United States of America
1   2   3   4   5   6   7   8   9   10

This book is printed on acid-free paper.
∞

To Sarah and Gordon Wean

Very good friends who suit each other
perfectly. You both suit me perfectly too.
Let's hear it for the BVI and Captain
Tim's political philosophy. Thanks for
being so bright, so funny, so very dear,
and so magnificent underwater. All the
best until our brutal next word game.

THE
NIGHTINGALE
LEGACY

1

St. Agnes Head, Cornwall
August 1814

Frederic North Nightingale looked down at the huddled woman at his feet. She was bowed in on herself, her knees drawn nearly to her chest, her arms over her head, as if she'd tried to protect herself as she fell from the cliff above. Her once stylish pale blue muslin gown was ripped violently beneath her arms, the bodice and skirt stained and filthy. One blue slipper dangled from twisted and torn ribbons from her right foot.

He came down to his knees beside her and gently pulled her stiff arms away from her head. It was difficult. She'd been dead for some time, at least eighteen hours, for her muscles were beginning to slacken again, the rigor lessening. He lightly pressed his fingers to her dirty neck, where the collar of her gown was ripped away. He didn't know why he was feeling for a pulse, perhaps he was hoping for a miracle, but of course, there was no beat, just cold flesh and death.

Her pale blue eyes stared up at him, not calm with acceptance, but bulging with the terror, with the knowledge that death was here and this was her last instant of life. Even though he'd seen too many men die in battle or after battle from infection, this touched him differently. She wasn't a soldier wielding a sword or a musket. She was a woman, thus frail by a man's standards, helpless in the face of a fall as violent as this one. He closed her eyes then pressed against her jaw to close her mouth, open wide on a last scream. It wouldn't close, and her terror was there to see if not to hear. It would remain there until she was no more than stripped white bone.

He rose slowly and stepped back, not too far back or else he'd go careening off the narrow ledge into the Irish Sea some forty feet below. The smell of the salt water was strong, the sound of the waves striking against the ageless tumbled black rocks was loud, but the rhythmic tumult was still curiously soothing to him. It had been since he'd been a boy, bent on escape.

She was no stranger to him. It had taken him a moment to recognize her, but he'd soon realized it was Eleanor Penrose, the widow of the now long-dead Squire Josiah Penrose of Scrilady Hall, just three miles or so north, very near the Trevaunance Cove. He'd known her since she'd arrived in the area from somewhere in Dorset and married the squire when North had been a boy of ten years or so. He remembered her as a laughing young woman with big breasts and a bigger smile, her soft brown hair falling in ringlets around her face that bounced about when she jested and poked the staid squire in his ribs, drawing a tortured smile even from that pinched mouth. And now she was dead, drawn in like a baby on a narrow ledge. He told himself she must have fallen. It was a tragic accident, surely that was all that it was, but he knew in his belly that it wasn't possible. Eleanor Penrose knew this land as well as he did. She wouldn't have been strolling out here by herself, far from home, and simply slip and fall over the cliff. How had it happened?

He made his way slowly back up the cliff, some thirty feet to the top, his fingers fitting into the familiar handholds, his feet slipping only twice. He pulled himself over the top onto the barren jagged edge of St. Agnes Head, rose and looked down as he dusted off his breeches. From this height she again became the patch of bright blue that had caught his attention and drawn him down in the first place.

Suddenly a clod of loose earth crumbled beneath his booted feet. He jerked back, arms flailing. His heart thudded madly until he was back a good three feet from the cliff edge. Perhaps that was what had happened to Eleanor Penrose. She'd walked too close to the edge and the ground had simply given beneath her and she'd not fallen all the way to the spuming waves below but onto that protruding ledge instead. And it had been enough to kill her. He dropped to his knees and examined the ground. Only the chunk he'd just dislodged seemed to have broken off. He just looked at the ground, then down at the ledge, barely visible from his vantage point. He rose and dusted off his hands.

North strode to his bay gelding, Treetop, a horse that stood over seventeen hands high and thus his name, who was standing motionless, watching his master's approach. Treetop didn't even look up at the flock of lapwings that wheeled low over them. A dragonfly lighted on his rump and he gently waved his tail. North would have to ride to see the magistrate. Then he realized he was the magistrate. This wasn't the army, no sergeants to do what he told them to do, no rules or protocols. "Well," he said as he swung easily onto Tree's broad back, "let's ride to get Dr. Treath. He should look at her before we move her. Do you think she fell?"

Tree didn't snort but he did fling his mighty head from side to side.

North said slowly as he looked back at the cliff where she'd gone over, shading the brilliant noontime sun from his eyes with his hand, "I don't think she did either. I think some son of a bitch killed her."

"Lord Chilton! Good God, my boy, when did you return? It's been over a year since you've come home. Just here for your father's funeral, then back again to the interminable war that's finally over, thank God. Now all our fine English lads can come home again. Come in, come in. You always did knock at my surgery entrance, eh?"

Dr. Treath, tall and straight as a sapling under a bright sun, and slender as a boy of eighteen, and as smart a man as North had ever known, pumped his hand and ushered him through his small surgery replete with its shining metal instruments and cabinets filled with carefully labeled bottles. There was a mortar and pestle on the scrubbed table just beneath the cabinets. He led North into the drawing room of Perth Cottage, a cozy, warm room with a fireplace at one end, too much furniture throughout and messy with strewn newspapers and journals and now empty cups on every surface that, North remembered, had held tea liberally laced with smuggled French brandy.

North smiled, remembering that when he was a boy Dr. Treath had seemed a giant of a man. The doctor was very tall, but now that North was a man full grown, Treath's height no longer seemed so extraordinary. Of course, North was bred from a line of tall men, of a height to intimidate if they were of a mind to do so.

Dr. Treath's smile was warm and welcoming.

"It has been a long time, sir. But now I'm home again, to stay this time."

"Sit down, North. Tea? A brandy?"

"No, sir. Actually I'm here as the magistrate to tell you that I just found Eleanor Penrose on that outcropping ledge beneath St. Agnes Head. She's dead, and has been for some time, at least a day, for her limbs were still rigid but were relaxing again."

Dr. Benjamin Treath became rigid as Lot's wife, becoming pale and paler still until his face was as white as his modest white cravat. He suddenly looked immeasurably older, all the vitality sucked out of him in that single instant, then, just as quickly, he was shaking his head. "No," he said, "no, that can't be right. You've forgotten what Eleanor looked like. No, not Eleanor. It's some other woman who resembles her. I'm sorry for the other woman but it isn't Eleanor, it can't be Eleanor. Tell me you've made a mistake, North."

"I'm sorry, sir, but it was Eleanor Penrose."

But Dr. Treath was still shaking his head, violently now, his eyes darkening, his pallor more marked. "Dead, you say? No, North, you're mistaken. I just dined with her two evenings ago. She was in fine fettle, laughing as she always does, you remember that, don't you? We ate oysters at Scrilady Hall and the candlelight was very soft and she laughed at my stories about the Navy, particularly the one about how we stole that bag of lemons from a Dutch ship in the Caribbean near St. Thomas because our men had scurvy. No, no, North, you're wrong, you must be wrong. I can't let Eleanor be dead."

Damnation, North thought. "I'm sorry, sir, truly. Yes, she's dead."

Benjamin Treath turned away and walked slowly to the French doors at the back of the sitting room that gave onto a small enclosed garden, flowering wildly now in middle August, roses interlaced with bougainvillea and hydrangeas, the colors vivid reds and pinks and yellows. One old sessile oak tree was so thick, its heavy leafed branches covered one entire corner of the garden, and its trunk was wrapped round and round with ivy. Blue agrion damselflies hovered over the ivy, making it appear to shimmer and shift in the lazy sunlight. North heard the croak of a bush cricket.

Dr. Treath just stood there, his shoulders rising and falling quickly, and North realized he was fighting down tears. "I'm very sorry, sir. I didn't know you and Mrs. Penrose were close. You must come with me, sir. Also, there's something more you must know."

Dr. Treath turned slowly to face him. "She's dead, you say. What else is there? Come, North, what is it?"

"I don't think she just fell from the cliff. I think someone pushed her. I didn't examine her or touch her except to feel for her pulse. You should do that."

"Yes," Dr. Treath said at last. "Yes, I'll come. Wait, what did you say? Someone pushed her? No, that's not possible. Everyone liked Eleanor, everyone. Oh Jesus. Yes, I'll come." He called out, "Bess! Come down, please. I must go out. Jack Marley is coming soon. Bess? Hurry, woman."

Bess Treath appeared suddenly in the doorway of the sitting room, out of breath, her hand clutched to her chest. She was a tall woman, slender, with hair darker even than North's. There was a great resemblance between brother and sister. She saw North, quickly curtsied, and said with pleasure, "My lord, you're home. How like your papa you look, but then all Nightingale men resemble each other from father to son and so it's always been, at least that's what Mrs. Freely says and what her mother before her said. Oh dear, something's wrong, isn't it? Why are you going out, Benjie? What has happened? Someone at Mount Hawke is ill?"

Dr. Treath just looked at her, actually beyond her, gone from Perth Cottage, from his sister and North, who stood at his side. He shook his head, as if to give himself direction. "Jack Marley has a boil on his neck. See to it if you want to, if not, then tell him to come back. Be sure to use the carbolic liberally to clean him up first. He never washes his neck, you know."

"Yes, I know, Benjie. I'll deal with him."

North said only, "There's been an accident, Miss Treath. We must go now."

"An accident? What happened? What's wrong, Benjie?"

Dr. Treath just kept shaking his head. He pushed past his sister, head down, North following.

2

Honeymead Manor, South Downs
September 1814

She was shivering. The house was quickly becoming as damp as it was bone cold. Even her wool stockings felt damp. For the past two days it had alternately rained thick sheets of gray, then slowed a bit to mist and drizzle, but regardless, the temperature had plummeted, making everyone miserable, including the brindle house cat and Mrs. Tailstrop's flat-nosed pug, Lucy, who wouldn't stop her whining. Mrs. Tailstrop carried the mutt about wrapped in a wool blanket.

She shivered again. Lord, it was cold. It was either the two Honeymead resident ghosts moving about, chilling every corner they touched, or just plain cheapness on the part of Roland Ffalkes, her guardian.

No guessing on that one. The ghosts didn't stand a chance. They were probably cold too. They'd been utterly silent since Ffalkes's arrival three days before, not even scaring the cat so his tail fluffed out ten times its usual size. Not that they came about all that much now, only once or twice a year, making pictures shake and tumble off the walls, and sending the house-maids shrieking from the kitchen when bowls of milk tipped over unaccountably into their laps, all to remind the residents that there were things that couldn't be explained in the South Downs *Gazette*.

Whenever Mr. Ffalkes visited her, he took over. It made her furious. Honeymead Manor was her parents' house and thus now her house. It was her wood and her fireplaces, yet he told the servants not to lay fires until November. His tone suggested that they personally were somehow out to cheat him. It was a pity the ghosts never did a thing untoward whenever he was here, damn them.

"Ah," Mrs. Tailstrop would say to her whenever she chanced to complain about it, nodding her head like a wise woman instructing a neophyte without much hope of success, not an ounce of sympathy in her voice, "it is always so with men. What they wish to have we must give them. They're the masters of their castles. It's their right. One must adjust, dear. You really must try to learn."

Nonsense, Caroline always said. This was *her* castle, not his. Mrs. Tailstrop would just pat her hand in a way that told her quite clearly that she hadn't a notion of the way things were, and would say, "Now, my dear child, you will learn one day, when you have a husband. If you don't learn to properly obey, then your husband won't be pleased with you and that, I can promise you, since I was myself once blessed with a dear husband, can be most unpleasant."

A husband. Fat chance of that, Caroline had decided two years before on her seventeenth birthday, and she hadn't changed her mind. Her teeth began to chatter.

She walked into the Flower Room, a room named for the immense splashes of red roses on stark-white wallpaper at least sixty years old and peeling, in search of warmth and found the grate empty of fire or ashes or even raw wood, and knew that her guardian had struck even here where neighbors would have tea when they were visiting. Why was he such a cheap fellow? It was her money, wasn't it? Why did he care how much wood she burned? Why did he always refuse to allow her to refurbish the aging settees and chairs and draperies? Why did he refuse to buy the bay mare Sir Roger had offered to sell her? Why did he permit her to own only a rickety old gig that was on its last wheels and a sweet old mare who would have surely lost to the tortoise had there been a race? And, good Lord, the tenants. Their cottages were in sore need of repair. They needed new plows and more seed.

Nothing had been done since her father had died. She felt deep guilt even though there was nothing she could do about his nipfarthing ways.

But much as she tried to deny it, even to herself, she well knew why he hadn't spent anything. He wanted her money for himself, and he saw any expenditure on her, her lands, her manor, as an utter waste. Well, her money wouldn't fall into his hands. He would soon see that she meant business.

She hugged herself, slapping her arms with her hands, then shook her head. It was absurd, ridiculous. She walked quickly outside. The sun had just broken through the thick overhanging gray clouds.

She stood on the narrow front steps of the manor, drew in a deep breath, and raised her face to the sky. She should have eaten her breakfast out here on the front steps rather than shivering like a loon in that dark, cold breakfast parlor that her guardian had refused to refurbish although it had needed it five decades before. But tomorrow it would be over. She could do exactly as she pleased after tomorrow.

Tomorrow she would be nineteen. Nineteen was the magic age her father had chosen to give her her freedom.

Freedom or marriage. There was no contest. Oh yes, she would marry one day when she was a toothless old biddy, and her husband would be a handsome young man whose job it would be to jollify her final years on this earth. And then she would reward him, depending on the success of his efforts. A good trade, certainly.

Tomorrow she would tell Mr. Ffalkes what she thought of him. She would call him cheap and niggardly and she would order that fires be set immediately, in every room, even in the great fireplace in the very old entrance hall that could easily roast an ox. Then she would kick him out. After tomorrow she would never have to see him or his wretched pointy-eared son again, a young man she liked when she didn't want to smack him for being such a weak sod whenever he chanced to displease his father, which was often, at least when they visited Honeymead Manor.

"Dear Miss Derwent-Jones."

She turned, frowning as she always did whenever Mr. Ffalkes addressed her with such hideous formality, which he did every time he saw her. She managed to erase the frown, striking a cool smile that she'd managed to cultivate during the past two years, exactly two years on the morrow it would be when he'd hauled Owen to Honeymead Manor to woo her. She'd known Owen all her life, and even liked him upon occasion, but that visit started them off in a horrid new direction, their childhood well and truly gone. Ah, what a tortuous drama they'd played, more like a comedy many times.

The father was a pompous ass, his son a weakling, a young man who would never be allowed to become a man until his father shucked off his mortal coil. But Owen was nice for all that, in a bewildered sort of way, despite his wretched father. Mr. Ffalkes and Owen had been here only three days and she'd wanted to strike her guardian down with the fireplace poker after only twenty minutes. They'd come for her birthday, Mr. Ffalkes had announced, rubbing his hands together as he looked about the entrance hall that had been built by the Countess of Shrewsbury herself in 1587 or thereabouts. Owen would have been utterly distressed if he'd missed her birthday, his fond father had continued, beaming down at her, his eyes cold as his mouth smiled. Owen had stood there, his ears sticking out from his head, and said nothing, as usual. Yes, the indulgent father had said, slanting a sideways look at the son, dear Owen was so fond of his cousin, so very devoted and concerned with her future and her happiness. Ah, then he'd gone on, laughing now, all fond tolerance, how Owen rhapsodized about her beautiful golden hair (actually it was a neat brown with perhaps a few strands of blond, cooked lighter under the summer sun) and her brilliant violet eyes—plain green her eyes were, if one were intent on reporting but a nodule of truth. On and on it went, until he'd gotten to her teeth. Then he'd failed utterly, finally comparing her teeth to the white cliffs of Dover, and that had made her laugh for she'd expected flawless pearls at the very least, but he'd run out of poetic nonsense and had to fall back on a geological formation.

She realized then that she'd been standing there, just staring at him. She shook herself, trying to remember if he'd said anything else.

"Hello, Mr. Ffalkes," she said, her own smile every bit as frigidly warm as his. "The sun is finally shining. Perhaps the manor will warm up in a couple of weeks if the warm weather holds."

"Perhaps, but it isn't important. I expect you were woolgathering, dear Miss Derwent-Jones. Well, that's what one expects from charming young ladies, isn't it? You are up and about quite early for a young miss who spent a late night in—dare I say it?—romantic sylvan pursuits? It's only just now eight o'clock."

"Is this a law of nature I've not heard about? A young lady is supposed to stay in bed all day after evening jollity?" She thought fondly of that eager young man she would marry when she was a doddering old crone leaning on a cane.

"You jest as usual, my dear. You are forever jesting with me, a charming part of your character, I would say, if I were at all charmed by such things. Owen is charmed by your repertoire of jests, but he is young and has no discrimination in such matters. Now, I should say, from my own experience, that young ladies don't have the stamina or the, er, vigor, to remain up at all hours as you were last night."

"I retired at nine-thirty, sir."

"Did you, now? But I thought you and Owen were strolling in the gardens and—"

"Perhaps Owen was strolling, sir. Perhaps he was comparing the roses to crimson velvet draperies or to red blood drops from a cut finger, though I don't see how he could have done that since it was quite dark last night and drizzling most of the time. Ah, you don't recall, do you? You were busily drinking my father's brandy, toasting yourself in front of the only fireplace that was lit, Mrs. Tailstrop hovering over you offering crumpets. No, last night, sir, there wasn't a single star to be rhapsodized over. Actually, Owen doesn't care for flowers at all. They make him sneeze. As for myself, I was in my bed dreaming birthday dreams. I have been dreaming them for some time now."

"Oh," he said, confounded and, she knew, doubtless angry at his son for letting her escape his net, also doubtless angry because it was true, he had been swilling her father's brandy with Mrs. Tailstrop nodding agreeably at whatever came out of his mouth. That, she'd told Caroline many times, was one of a lady's prime duties—to listen and nod and smile and offer food and drink. It was a litany that always drove Caroline quite mad.

She looked at Mr. Ffalkes from beneath her lashes. He still looked on the angry side, and also a bit uncertain of how to proceed. Oh yes, Caroline could just imagine the detailed instructions he'd forced down his son's skinny throat to seduce her, and Owen had let his sire down. He cleared his throat and said, all calm and charm, "As for your birthday, dear Miss Derwent-Jones, I had thought to have just the immediate family here for a luncheon for you."

She didn't care if she spent her birthday on the moon. She nodded. "That's fine, sir. It's a pity that I have no more immediate family in the area."

"Owen and I will be most attentive to you. I believe Owen has bought you a birthday present that—dare I say it?—could perhaps also double as an engagement present?"

He'd come out into the open at last. She was nonplussed for a moment, but just for a moment. She smiled widely at him. "How very kind of Owen, but I believe it's too soon for that, sir. Mr. Duncan has, of course, proposed, but we decided to wait until next month to announce our betrothal. We will wed at Christmas. No, I couldn't possibly accept a present from Owen until Mr. Duncan and I have announced our engagement formally."

"*Mr. Duncan!* Who the devil is this Mr. Duncan?"

He looked as if he would expire from apoplexy, his face all red and puffy. It pleased her enormously. She could practically see him falling down the front steps of the manor, flailing and foaming at the mouth in his rage. "Why, sir, he's a neighbor. I call him my own dear squire. Duncan is a local name, here for hundreds of years. We have been close for the past three years. Such a handsome gentleman he is, a very strong chin and ears that lie flat to his head. Yes, sir, we plan to marry and join our properties."

"You have never mentioned this man to me, dear Miss Derwent-Jones. Indeed, I have never heard of a Mr. Duncan. This is not what I want and you well know it. I will speak to Mrs. Tailstrop about this. I will tell her what I think of her wardenship."

"You were not often here, sir, until two years ago when you came so very often Mrs. Tailstrop thought we should keep fresh sheets on your bed. I hadn't thought of Mrs. Tailstrop as a warden. Still, what does it really matter now? To be honest, when you were here all the time, I tended to keep dear Mr. Duncan away."

"Owen was nearly always with me. You were with him a great deal of the time."

"Fresh sheets for Owen as well, sir."

"Your humor lists like a sinking boat, dear Miss Derwent-Jones. I have noticed that you have even grown more fully into this humor of yours just in the past few days. Mrs. Tailstrop tells me you have become more amusing by the year, but I informed her that it was her duty to curtail this eccentric habit of yours. Young ladies are to be demure and modest. How else will they attach a husband?"

"I managed it quite easily. Don't forget Mr. Duncan."

"So you say, so you say. Now, I would that you strive to answer me cleanly and directly."

"A wit should be a wit for all occasions. I'm distressed that you disapprove. Very well, sir. What would you like to know?"

"I would like to know about this Duncan fellow. I would like to meet him and ascertain his intentions toward you. You will be a rich young lady come tomorrow and I want to convince myself that he isn't a fortune hunter. Indeed, I insist upon meeting him. This evening, for dinner. It is only fair to Owen, don't you think? Even frivolous young ladies should strive for a modicum of sensitivity and goodwill toward young men who are truly in love with them."

Owen in love with her? She and Owen were like two bored dogs who would eye each other and yawn. Not only did her fatuous guardian dislike her humor—her only weapon against him—he believed her stupid and ineffectual, which perhaps she was, for after all there weren't any fires in any of the fireplaces, were there?

"I don't know if Mr. Duncan will be free for dinner this evening."

"You know, dear Miss Derwent-Jones, I cannot, in good conscience, allow you to enter into an alliance that I haven't approved. It would be against your best interests. I wouldn't be fulfilling my responsibility toward you. Indeed, there is a clause in your father's will that allows my discretion in the matter of your marriage. I naturally hadn't thought of it until now since I believed you and Owen would make a match of it."

She stared at him. No, she couldn't believe it, wouldn't believe it. She managed to keep her outrage behind her tongue and said, "I didn't know of any stipulations about my marriage, sir, or my lack of marriage. Actually, before I met Mr. Duncan, I hadn't planned to marry at all. I would like to see my father's will."

"Certainly, Miss Derwent-Jones." There was no *dear* this time, which was an improvement. "However, I hardly expect a young lady to understand it. There are legal terms that would surely confound a lady's faculties."

"I will contrive to raise my level of wit, sir, just for the occasion."

He looked at her as if he would like to strike her, and that pleased her, for surely she would like to stick a knife between his ribs. "Shall I read this part of my father's will right now, sir?"

"Unfortunately your father's will is in my office, in London. It will require some time for me to write to my clerk and more time for him to send it here to Honeymead Manor."

"I see," she said, and was very afraid that she did indeed see.

"In brief, your father wanted my approval of any suitor to your hand, Miss Derwent-Jones. If I refuse my approval then I am to continue as your guardian until you reach twenty-five or find a gentleman of whom I do approve."

"Very well, sir, you force me to admit to another wretched jest. There is no Mr. Duncan. There is no man I wish to marry. Therefore, sir, tomorrow, on my nineteenth birthday, I come into my parents' money—all of it—and you, sir, are no longer snapping the whip over my head."

"I thought as much," Mr. Ffalkes said, and she knew then he'd out-maneuvered her. He'd lied about that stipulation in her father's will, and she'd fallen for it. Then he struck a conciliatory pose, his palms upward. "You and I shouldn't be adversaries, my dear. Indeed, I have much admired you since you became such a lovely young woman. As has my son. Now, it's true that you will come into your fortune tomorrow. However, it is also true that I will continue as your trustee until you wed."

"And just what are a trustee's duties as opposed to a guardian's?"

"As a trustee, I will advise you on investments, oversee all legal matters, grant you a sufficient allowance to meet your needs, see to your continued well-being. I was your father's cousin, Miss Derwent-Jones. He trusted me to care for you, to see you well placed. I am pleased there is no Mr. Duncan. Men aren't always what they seem, you know. No, you don't know, do you? You have been protected, sheltered from gentlemen who would take advantage of your innocence. I will continue to protect you, Miss Derwent-Jones."

Just as he'd protected her by sending her to Chudleigh's Young Ladies' Academy in Nottingham, whence she'd managed to escape only three years before. She'd believed a convent couldn't be more stifling, more deadening than the echoing chambers at Chudleigh's, with all its giggling girls with naught on their minds but the dancing master's dimples. The mistresses had been so unrelenting in their quest to make every single girl just like every other single girl, all of them to be stupid but somehow charming to men, to nod and pretend to listen until their brains quite froze through, and to stitch samplers until death would thankfully overtake them, after, naturally, they'd produced a suitable number of surviving offspring.

Thus when she'd been sixteen, she'd come down with something akin to the plague that had scared even the headmistress, Miss Beemis, into near incontinence. She'd been packed quickly back to Honeymead Manor and dear Mrs. Tailstrop. The spots, made from walnut dye mixed with a thick gray clay and smashed oak leaves until it resembled oozing boils, had finally washed off.

"Yes," Mr. Ffalkes continued, "I will continue to guide you. Perhaps you will be content to remain here at Honeymead Manor, Miss Derwent-Jones. Owen much loves the country."

"I doubt that, Mr. Ffalkes. I doubt that very much."

"That Owen loves the country? Of a certainty he does."

She said nothing. She turned and walked back into the manor. Tomorrow she would shriek at him to her heart's content and then she would order him off her property.

It was Morna, the upstairs maid, who grabbed her sleeve, placed her finger over her lips, and hissed in her ear, "Come, miss, quickly, quickly!" She'd been running after Morna in a flash down the long first-floor hallway to the small estate room tucked at the rear of the manor, a quite ugly chamber that she avoided because it reminded her of too many men grown tedious and dull over the generations, all of them pondering and brooding in this room, doubtless worried about their groats.

The door wasn't quite closed. Morna nodded to her and gently shoved her closer. It was then she heard Owen's voice low and clear. "Please listen to me, Father. I know you want me to marry her. You've wanted it all along, but just listen to me this once. Caroline isn't an easy girl. She's stubborn. She is well used to doing just as she pleases. She doesn't dislike me but she thinks me a fool. She won't agree to marry me. I've told you that again and again. She won't change toward me."

"Yes," Mr. Ffalkes said finally. "You have mucked it right and proper, Owen."

She stopped cold and leaned against the crack in the door. She could hear Morna breathing rapidly behind her.

"I can't very well rape her," Owen said, sounding as petulant and sulky as a child, as he always did around his father.

"Why the devil not?"

There was complete silence, then Owen said slowly, "She is very strong. You know her well enough by now. She tries to jest her way out of things, but I know that if she had to, she'd fight me and I would have to hurt her, even tie her down to get it done."

"And?"

"And what, sir? I don't even know if I could manage to do it."

"You mean to tell me that my only son would be unable to perform his manly duty?"

"It would be touch and go."

"You have disappointed me, Owen. On the other hand, you are quite right. She's a spoiled, arrogant bitch, a haughty creature who needs to learn who is master here. She distrusts me and thus she distrusts you. It's a pity, but there's no hope for it then." She heard Mr. Ffalkes draw in a deep breath. "Very well, I will take her. She will marry me."

"Good God, sir, Caroline as my stepmother? She's not even nineteen!"

"She is a grown woman. Many girls have babes by the time they are her age."

"That's frightening. She's not even motherly. She's younger than I am. She's very strong, sir."

"So am I. What's more, my son, I would enjoy that particular manly duty. I am not too old to perform it. I should delight in performing it again and again on her. I am also more crafty than she will ever be. She tried to outsmart me just this morning, but I turned it all about on her and left her looking like a fool. Don't worry. She will be at my mercy. I will tie her down with no compunction at all. I will take her until she agrees to wed me and then I will take her until she is with child. Yes, that is the way it will be. Then she'll be quite motherly, you'll see, my boy. Should you like a little half brother?"

"I don't know, sir. Can't you just give her the inheritance and we'll leave?"

"No, I cannot. I won't. I need that money, Owen. I've kept her fortune wonderfully intact, all legal and right and tight, waiting for her damned birthday. Now that it's nearly here you expect me to turn tail and leave? Don't you want that new hunter Bittington is selling? Yes, I can see well enough that you do. Well then, boy, if you can't get it done, then I must do it. Enough now."

It was more than enough. She turned, realizing that Morna was standing there, just staring at her, her face flushed with anger. Caroline had never seen Morna angry in her life. She nodded, took Morna's hand, and ran back up the stairs. She would have to leave, there was no other option now. Mrs. Tailstrop wouldn't do a thing. It was Mr. Ffalkes who paid her salary. She was on her own. The money would be hers regardless of whether she was here at Honeymead Manor or in Russia. But would she be safe from Mr. Ffalkes when she returned to claim her inheritance?

What she needed was a gun. Barring a gun, she needed a man who was ruthless and smarter than Mr. Ffalkes and would agree to protect her with his life, given enough of her money.

Where was Mr. Duncan when she needed him?

3

The downstairs clock began its twelve long, deep strokes that resounded throughout the manor. Over the years the booming strikes had become simply night sounds that didn't rouse anyone, even Mrs. Tailstrop's annoying pug Lucy. Except this night Caroline was wide awake, listening, waiting, wound as tightly as that clock, only she couldn't toll or chime or make any noise at all.

When Mr. Ffalkes finally came into view in the entrance hall below, she slipped away from her hidey-hole behind a statue of Aristotle at the top of the landing and ran back into her bedchamber, carefully locking the door. She stood there, silent as the night sky, waiting, waiting. Soon she heard his heavy footfalls coming down the long corridor, closer and closer. He stopped. She could picture him reaching out his hand, but when the knob turned slowly, soundlessly, she jumped even though she'd expected it. She sucked in her breath and held herself very still. The knob turned again and again until he realized that the door was locked. She heard him curse. Then she heard nothing.

She could picture him just standing there, wondering what to do. She knew he wasn't stupid; he'd do something. He knocked, several quiet knocks, saying, his voice as smooth as the seedless strawberry jam Cook made just that morning, "Dear Miss Derwent-Jones? It is I, my dear, do let me in. I must speak to you. It's about your inheritance, and a serious matter. Let me in. Come now, let's have no fuss about this. It really is to your advantage to speak to me."

Ha, she thought. Letting him into her bedchamber would be like welcoming Napoleon to Whitehall. She said absolutely nothing, just waited, her face pressed to the door, waiting for him to go away, which he did after several more moments that seemed to stretch longer than the time her mother had wrapped a string around the doorknob to pull one of Caroline's baby teeth many years before.

Finally, she thought, finally he had given up. She forced herself to stay still for another five minutes, surely enough time for him to be in his bedchamber, three rooms down the corridor, and prepare himself for bed. Then she pulled her valise from beneath her bed, pulled on stout walking boots, and slung her blue velvet cloak over her shoulders. Very slowly she turned the key in the lock, then just as slowly turned the knob. The door opened slowly. She slipped through and stared up and down the corridor. She saw nothing but shadows, night shadows she'd known all her life.

She turned and walked quickly toward the central staircase, her boots making not a single sound. When an arm went around her, jerking her back, she opened her mouth to scream, but then a big palm was flattened against her teeth and she knew he'd again outsmarted her. She felt his hot breath against her ear, felt his arm tighten hard across her ribs, squeezing the breath from her.

"Now, you little bitch, not a sound from you. You believed you'd dupe me, did you? No one beats me, no one, certainly not an arrogant little girl. Now, you and I will take a walk. We will celebrate your birthday, fear not, and my gift to you will be my seed. You will like being married to me, Miss Derwent-Jones, and if you don't, well, I will have your money and it won't matter. I do suggest that you not struggle, that you accept your future, for it is upon you, yes it is."

She bit down hard on his hand. She heard him suck in his breath, felt a moment of sheer pleasure, until he whirled her about and struck her jaw hard with his fist. She crumbled where she stood.

The throbbing pain in her jaw brought her back. Her eyes opened and she blinked. There was only the flame from one small candle on a rickety wooden table near her. The rest of the chamber was in darkness. She tried to sit up but realized quickly enough that her hands were tied above her head to the slats of a narrow bed that didn't smell too clean.

"Well, you're awake. I didn't mean to hit you so hard, but you deserved it. Think of it as a lesson, one that will be repeated whenever you fail to obey me with proper dispatch and eagerness. Your jaw isn't broken, I've already felt it. Now, my dear, you are nineteen years old. You have come into your inheritance and you will shortly marry. What do you think?"

"I think you're quite mad."

"Then you can spend a lot of time on your knees praying our children won't inherit the madness. Ah, yes, there will be children, my dear, as many as I can plant in your belly. I plan to keep you pregnant. A big belly tends to keep a woman lumbering along slowly, all her attention on the babe, on all her little aches and pains. It keeps her silent. Who knows? After birthing a good dozen children perhaps you'll turn into a model wife. I doubt it, but who can say for sure?"

"Where did you get that idiot bit of wisdom?"

He just smiled and sat down beside her on the narrow bed. She froze and he saw it and smiled more widely. "I know you're afraid, though you'll try your best not to show it to me. You're like your father in that. I remember when we were boys how he led the rest of us into trouble that made his parents' hair rise off their necks, but he tried desperately never to show fear; he scoffed at any of us who did. So I know you're terrified, no use in your trying to hide it. Scream and cry if you like. I care not. Actually it would add spice to our proceedings. No one will hear you. No one will come to your aid. Now, shall we get on with our fleshly revels?"

"I think you'd best wait a moment, Mr. Ffalkes."

"My name is Roland. Since you will be my wife shortly, I think it appropriate for you to call me by my given name. I now give you my permission to do so."

"I will call you fool. No, old fool. That surely fits you the best."

He struck her cheek with his open palm. The sharp, stinging heat of the blow made her gasp, but even that she managed to hold in. No, she wouldn't show him fear, but dear God it was difficult, so very difficult.

"Now, I see that you're silent again. Women should be silent, you know." He rose then and she realized he was wearing only a dressing gown. It was a royal blue brocade with heavily stitched cuffs, and he'd belted it around his fat stomach. He pulled on the belt and the dressing gown parted. His belly was whiter than a nun's wimple, hard and protruding. Lower, there were tufts of grayish-brown hair, and embedded in that hair was his man's sex. She thought she'd gag.

She stared at his sex, at the thin legs. She didn't gag. She laughed. At first the laughter sounded forced and strangled with fear, but then she got it right and laughed and laughed. Soon she was choking on her laughter, seeing him now standing there rigid, the thick vein throbbing in his neck, his face tightening, becoming florid.

"You," she gasped on her laughter. She couldn't point at him so she jerked her chin toward him. "That thing—it is so pitiful. You're pitiful, and you're fat as a stoat. You're an old man, this is ridiculous." And she kept laughing.

He lunged at her then, throwing himself atop her, his weight crushing her down into the thin mattress.

"You bitch, you damned bitch. Close your mouth. Shut your damned mouth!" He straddled her, then struck her once and then again. He was panting hard and now she was silent. She wished she could insult him more, but words were beyond her now, far, far beyond. He ripped the bodice of her gown to her waist. He stared down at her chemise, then very slowly he ran the end of his blunt finger along the top of her breasts. "Very nice," he said. "You're doubtless a virgin. I haven't had a virgin since Owen's mother over twenty-five years ago. How very quiet you are now, my dear Miss Derwent-Jones, or should I now call you Caroline? I hate your name, but I will make do. There was a girl, you see, and her name was Caroline, and she wouldn't have me. She wanted your father. Ah, the triangles of life. He loved your mother, so that was the end of Caroline's dreams. I wonder what your mother was thinking when she named you Caroline, for your dear father must have resisted. Perhaps the other Caroline believed your father had done it because he regretted not wedding her? A question with no answer. Ah, but that's neither here nor there, is it? Shall we continue, my dear?"

"Continue? That is nonsense and well you know it. I should better call you father or grandfather."

He slapped her again, not hard, just enough to make her head hit back against the thin pillow.

"Now, let's see the rest of you." He jerked the chemise to her waist, but didn't seem interested in looking at her breasts. She felt the cool night air on her flesh, saw his old hands on her, and wanted to scream with the horror of what she knew was going to happen to her. He got off her and stood looking down at her, then he nodded, as if deciding something, and stripped off the rest of her clothes.

"Very nice," he said, then shrugged out of his dressing gown.

She closed her eyes then, felt his hands on her belly, kneading her, stroking lightly over her pelvic bones, stretching his fingers over her, measuring her. "You'll bear many children before you die of it. My poor Ann died with her second, the babe with her, but it was only a daughter, of little use to me."

"If you rape me I will kill you."

His head jerked up. She was staring at him. She said again, "If you rape me I will kill you. Believe me for I am deadly serious. Know, too, that I will never wed you, never."

"Yes you will. There will be no choice. You will be ruined if you refuse. No one would speak to you. You would be a pariah, your child a bastard, spat upon by the world."

"I don't care. I will have my inheritance. You can't force me to wed you."

"Actually," he said slowly, "I can. Now, let's get it done." He began to stroke his hands over his sex, pulling on it, his head thrown back, his eyes closed.

She tugged on the bonds that were tight around her wrists. There was just a little give, not much, but enough so that she could twist and turn and loosen the rope even more. She heard his gasping for breath, but she didn't look at him. She'd retch if she did.

Then he was over her, shoving her legs up, and without thought, without hesitation, she brought her knees to her chest and kicked him in the groin as hard as she could. He toppled off her backward onto the floor, holding himself, crying and moaning, cursing her, but he was helpless, at least for the moment. Ah, but not for long.

She felt the slickness of her own blood on her wrists, but she continued to work and twist the ropes harder and faster. Oh, God, she had to hurry, if he got hold of himself before she was free . . . She wouldn't think of it, wouldn't consider it. Finally, with the slippery blood on her hands, she managed to ease a hand free. Then the other. He was sitting up now, still holding himself, still moaning.

"You damned bastard!"

She picked up the small wooden table and struck him hard over the head. The single candle went flying but she managed to catch it before it struck the dirty floor.

"Oh my God, what have you done?"

There was Owen, his hair sticking up on his head, barefoot, his shirt hastily tucked into a pair of breeches. He stared at her, then down at his father. "I told him not to try it with you," Owen said, not moving, sounding strangely pleased. "Good God, Caroline, you're naked." Surprisingly, he looked away from her down to his father, who was now lying on his side, his hands still cupping himself. He was unconscious. "My poor father. You did him in. I came to stop him, you know."

"Did you now?"

"Yes. But you didn't need me. I don't think you need anyone. I told him you were strong."

"I know. I heard you telling him. He isn't dead, although if I had a gun I would shoot him. Now, turn your back to me, Owen, I must dress."

It was quickly done, her cloak covering her ripped bodice.

"What are you going to do, Caroline?"

"What do you care, you spineless worm?"

"I'm not spineless. I was coming to save you. He'll come after you, Caroline. He won't stop. He needs the money. He will have you."

She gave him a long look, then tossed the rope to him. There was blood on the rope, her blood. "Tie him up, Owen, and I mean do a good job. If you don't, I'll hit him again on the head with this stool. Then I'll hit you and it will hurt."

Owen did as he was bid. Indeed, if she wasn't mistaken, he appeared to be enjoying it. Suddenly his father's eyes popped open and he looked up at his son, then at his bound wrists. "Owen, my dear boy, what have you done? Have you subdued that damned bitch? Untie me now, boy, quickly. Ah, a son shouldn't see his father unclothed. Give me my dressing gown."

"No, Owen, I will need that dressing gown. Your dear father in all his fat glory will cause a good deal of consternation, depending upon who comes here first, but that is just too bad. Yes, Mr. Ffalkes, I realize we're in the stables in a miserable storage room that hasn't seen the light of day for years. But it's good. I rather hope every servant at Honeymead Manor gets this treat. You may be certain that I'll leave the door wide open."

Mr. Ffalkes looked over at her, his eyes red with fury. "You damned bitch, you'll not get away with this. I'll have you and then you'll regret doing this."

She laughed. This time it wasn't clogged with fear. She laughed freely and for a nice long time. Then she looked over at Owen. She blinked then, for he was holding a pistol loose in his hand. Bless him, he *had* come to stop his father. But why had he pulled out that pistol now? Quick as a snake, she grabbed it from his hand and shoved him back.

She turned back to Mr. Ffalkes. She enjoyed having him at her feet. "You actually put a bed in this poor storage room. How enterprising of you. I thank you for it. Now, Owen, I will say this only once. You will go back to the manor. You will doubtless find my valise in my bedchamber. Fetch it and bring it back here. I will expect you in five minutes. If you don't come back or if you bring someone, I will shoot your father. Then I will come after you. I'm feeling very mean, Owen, believe me."

"She won't, Owen, she's a female, they have no appetite for killing, don't believe her—"

31

She raised the pistol, saw that it held two bullets, aimed it and fired. Mr. Ffalkes screamed. The bullet tore up the wooden floor not two inches from his slippered feet.

"Go, Owen, now!"

She turned and looked down at her erstwhile guardian. "I wonder, sir, if my finger were to slip, then who would be my trustee?"

"You'll not get away with this savagery, Miss Derwent-Jones. I'll send the Bow Street Runners after you. They'll haul you back here—"

"Why?"

"Why what, damn you?"

"Why would anyone—other than you, of course—want to haul me back here? I'm now nineteen and I will deal with you to gain my inheritance after I've settled into my new, ah, home."

"What home? You don't have another home. Where do you think you're going, you idiot girl?"

"You honestly think I would tell you? I would be an idiot if I did."

"It won't matter. I'll find you quickly enough, and then you'll be sorry."

"You sound like a child making silly threats," she said, staring down at him, "but you're not, are you. How I wish the pistol held three bullets."

Owen suddenly appeared in the doorway, holding her valise. He had also pulled on a pair of boots and a cloak. He'd pulled an old felt hat over his ears.

"Now, Owen, you and I are going to do a bit of riding." She turned to Mr. Ffalkes. "I'm taking your son as a hostage, sir. If you try anything, I will remove his right arm. Owen needs his right arm. He needs everything he's got. Even missing one part, he would be in bad shape. Do you understand, sir?"

Roland Ffalkes cursed.

"Father, really, you shouldn't speak so in front of a lady."

Caroline thought Mr. Ffalkes would expire in apoplexy right then, but he didn't.

Owen just shook his head and preceded Caroline from the storage room, the pistol aimed at his back.

• • •

Owen said nothing for a full two hours. They were riding along a country lane, the air dry, just a bit chilly, but very fresh from the rain of the past days, the silence absolute. He said at last, "I shouldn't have left my father lying there naked. The servants will find him and it will be awful, both for them and for him. He is not a pretty sight, Caroline."

"He struck my face several times. He was quite ready to rape me, Owen. Didn't he deserve something for that?"

"You kicked him in the groin. You're not a man, Caroline, so you wouldn't know what that does. It's really quite dreadful."

"Has a young lady kicked you there, Owen?"

"Oh no, one of my friends hit me with a ball when we were boys. How did you know to do that?"

"Actually, my mother taught me when I was quite young. You see, one of our maids had been raped and it made my mother furious. She said no female was ever too young to know how to protect herself. I believe she got all the details of the kicking technique from my father. After she taught me, he smiled at me and patted my head. He said, 'Now I've a little Amazon. It's good.' "

"It does draw a man up short. When I was hit, I thought I was going to die."

She grinned, even knowing he couldn't see it, for it was quite dark, save for the quarter moon that sliced through the trees onto the narrow lane. "I'm glad your father suffered. He isn't a nice man."

"What are you going to do? Where are you taking me?"

"You've been silent as a stick since we left Honeymead Manor, not deigning to say a word to me. Why the questions now?"

"It took me a while to think of what I wanted to say and in what order."

She believed him. He was Owen and it was the way he was. She was beginning to believe herself quite mad to have brought him along. If he tried to bolt, she knew she wouldn't shoot him. Good Lord, she hadn't even bound his hands. If he wanted to, he could kick his horse in the ribs and ride away from her right this minute.

"You and I, Owen, are going to Cornwall."

"Cornwall? I was there once, in St. Austell, and it was really quite backward. Why that godforsaken place?"

"My aunt lives there. I haven't seen her for three years now. She'll take me in. She was my mother's sister. Your dear father didn't allow me to leave Honeymead Manor, you know, so I was never able to visit her, nor, I add, was she supposed to visit me, but she just laughed at that and came to see me several times at Chudleigh's Young Ladies' Academy, that prison your father incarcerated me in for more years than I care to remember. Your father is really a toad, Owen."

"Do you have any idea how many days it will take us to reach Cornwall? What part of Cornwall?"

"We're already in New Forest, Owen. Only about three or maybe four days, I should say, maybe less. I won't tell you exactly where we're going. You might decide to escape me and tell your father. Now, we'll ride at night and rest during the day. I stole money from your father so I know we have enough."

"What will you do with me if we reach Cornwall unscathed?"

She appeared to ponder deeply. "I don't know yet, Owen. Perhaps with you as my hostage, your father will be more reasonable. Perhaps he will agree to sign all the papers—or whatever it is he has to do—to put me in possession of my fortune."

"He won't do it, Caroline."

"Then I'll begin to send him your body parts, Owen."

"You mean like a finger?"

"Yes, or a toe or an ear."

He said nothing more. He fell into a profound silence, saying after they'd skirted the town of Steepleford, "I never did want to marry you, Caroline. You're pretty and all that, but still, you're not what you're supposed to be."

"And what is that?"

"What do you mean 'what'? It's obvious. You weren't crying or begging or pleading or lying there like a dead martyr, like any modest young lady would do. I had come to save you and you didn't need me. You actually had the gall to hurt my father and he was just trying to do his manly duty."

"Manly duty? Is that what you call rape?"

"That's what he called it."

"Yes, I remember now. I overheard nearly all of your conversation in the estate room. If your father hadn't been so wily, I would have escaped, and he wouldn't be lying naked in the stable ready to terrify a stable hand."

"It quite alarms me to think that you will be my stepmother."

"I won't ever be anyone's stepmother, Owen."

"Yes you will. He will find you. The good Lord knows what he will do to me, but he'll marry you, Caroline, and there's nothing you can do about it." He spoke with such simple confidence that for a moment she felt her blood run cold. Then she realized Owen still saw his father as would a boy, not a man. "You know, Owen, perhaps this adventure will be good for both of us. You are my prisoner, that's true enough—don't forget you know I'm mean and strong—but maybe when we reach my aunt, you will see that the world is quite different without your father there to tell you what to say and what to do."

"He'll get you," was all that Owen said, and he sounded as fervent in his belief as a newly converted Christian. "And then you'll be my stepmother."

Both of them shuddered at the thought.

A thick raindrop fell on the top of Caroline's head. "Oh dear," she said, looking upward, "why can't anything ever be easy?"

"It's my father's doing."

4

It rained hard and cold the remainder of that night. Owen and Caroline were both miserable and soaked to the bone, but they'd kept riding throughout that first miserable night, stopping at inns to drink hot ale and dry their clothes in front of the taproom fire. It slowed them down considerably, but there was no hope for it. They stopped at the Black Hair Inn in Dorchester late the following morning to dry themselves and to sleep.

Finally, during the second evening it stopped raining. Caroline dressed quickly, walked to the small window in the bedchamber, and peered out. There were a few horses and a carriage in the yard, several men milling about, but it had stopped raining, thank the good Lord. She stretched her arms over her head. It was nearly eleven o'clock at night. She'd had a refreshing sleep and so had Owen, judging by the occasional snores that had awakened her. They had to get on their way. He was sleeping atop blankets on the floor beside her narrow bed. She lightly kicked him with her toe.

"Come on, Owen, wake up. It's late and we must get beyond Plymouth before we can rest again. It's stopped raining so it won't be so bad. Come on."

Owen rolled onto his back, opened his eyes, and stared up at her. He blinked. He moaned. She lowered the candle to see him more closely. His face was red and hot with fever.

She just stared down at him. He was ill, damn him, the sod had the nerve to be ill. "Owen, talk to me. Don't just lie there and moan, talk to me."

He sent her a blurry look. "I don't like this, Caroline. I don't feel well."

Oh dear, he sounded awful. She knelt down on the floor beside him and laid her palm against his forehead. He was ill, indeed, he was very ill. "Let me help you up and into my bed."

He wasn't all that large, but he was nearly limp and she had a good deal of difficulty dragging him into her bed. She covered him with every blanket in the bedchamber, then stood there, staring down at him, wondering what the devil she was going to do.

She couldn't leave him, but she wanted to. "Well, curse you, Owen. If I didn't know better I'd think you were doing this on purpose."

Owen moaned.

"Don't you dare tell me this is your father's doing."

Owen went still as the bedposts.

"Oh, I believe you're sick. You're not deceitful enough to make it up." She took herself downstairs of the Black Hair Inn. The stairs were dusty and narrow and there was very little light. She followed the boisterous male sounds coming from the taproom. She stuck her head in the dim, smoke-filled room and looked about for the owner. He was no taller than she was, round as a barrel, his middle covered with a huge white apron that had more ale stains on it than surely this one day could bring. He was standing near the fireplace speaking to a man who was sitting alone, his legs stretched out in front of him. She slipped into the low-ceilinged room and skirted the wooden tables, going toward the owner.

Suddenly the noise began to die away. Men were staring at her, silently at first, then she heard one fellow say, "Wot's this, Mackie?"

"Why, 'tis a little birdie, flown in to play wit' us. Clorie won't mind sharing us. Little birdie, come 'ere and we'll give ye a nice brown ale and a little tickle."

She didn't look at them, just kept her eyes on the owner, who was still speaking to the man.

A hand caught her dress and pulled her up short.

"'Ey, little 'oney, wot's yer 'urry? Mackie 'ere wants to giv' ye a drink right out o' 'is mug. Eh?"

She turned slowly, not at all frightened, for surely they were just men, common laborers here for a night of drink and companionship, like many of the men who worked on the tenant farms at Honeymead. She gave them a friendly smile. "No thank you, Mr. Mackie. I must speak to the owner, Mr. Tewksberry."

"Lawks, she called ye Mr. Mackie, jest like ye was somebody important."

"I am important, ye gull-brain. So, little 'oney, ye wants to speak to old Tewksberry, uh? Ho, that's a tale, it is, eh wot, Walt? Ye splitting yer take wi' 'im, little 'un?"

"I don't have a take, sir. Please let go of my gown."

Mr. Tewksberry finally looked up.

Walt didn't release her. She stood for an instant, uncertain, then she shrugged, gave Walt and Mackie an indulgent look, picked up his mug of ale, and drank down a goodly amount. It swirled and twisted all the way to her belly. Her eyes bugged out and she started to shake and cough. "Oh my God, what is that stuff? My insides don't know whether to burn or to freeze."

The men were laughing now, thumping their mugs on the tabletops. "Another fer the little birdie! 'Ey, Clorie, another fer our little friend."

"No, thank you. That was quite enough."

Mackie, utterly charmed by a female for the first time in a decade, pulled her down onto his lap. "I nev'r afore seen a little nit the size of ye drink down a whole pint afore. Give me a kiss, luv."

Caroline frowned at him, seeing the dim light of befuddlement in his eyes, the tufts of hair on his jaws he'd missed shaving, smelled the odors of the stable rising from his body and clothes. "Mr. Mackie, you must let me up. Thank you for the ale, but I've had quite enough. Indeed it was an experience I don't believe I care to repeat. Now, listen to me, my brother is ill and I must get a doctor for him. Won't you help me?"

"Yer brother is that little cove what 'as the weak chin and looks shifty?" Walt asked, leaning toward her.

"Yes, that's Owen. Where can I find a doctor? I'm dreadfully worried about him."

Mr. Tewksberry left the gentleman and strode over to them. He did not look pleased. At last, she thought, he would assist her with these misguided men. He nearly shouted in her ear, "Miss Smith, what is this about your brother being ill? Really, missie, your *brother?* I never believed him anything but a young gentleman you were fleecing something shameless. Let her go, Mackie, she's too smart for you and Walt and all the rest of you poor ignorant louts. Aye, smart she is, a strumpet who's under my roof to conduct bad business. I wouldn't doubt it if she hadn't taken the poor little man upstairs for all his groats, then is just pretending he's sick. Did you poison him, Miss Smith?"

She was utterly taken aback. He believed her a strumpet? Shameless? Her mind balked at other words.

"Don't wet yerself, Tewks. The little one 'ere ain't done nothing to 'urt ye or anyone else. Aye, the lad's 'er brother. Look ye, Tewks, she's right purty and he's a driveling little toff. 'E's got to be 'er brother."

"Now, listen to me, Mackie, she's nothing—"

"My good Tewksberry, what is all this?"

It was the gentleman who'd been sitting by himself near the fireplace. His voice was deep and calm and sounded vaguely amused. He wasn't an affliction to the eyes.

"Excuse me, my lord. It's this Young Person here. Claims the fellow upstairs is her brother and he's ill. She's—"

"Why do you disbelieve her?"

"Just look at her, my lord, sitting there on Mackie's lap just like she belongs, like she's quite used to doing that sort of thing. Just look at Clorinda over there, all huffy and in a great snit because this one's trying to steal all her clients. I don't want no trouble. Clorinda will tear her bleeding hair out and we'll have screaming and crying and my nerves can't abide that. Didn't you see her toss down that ale? What lady would toss down ale like that?"

"This lady would and did," Caroline said. "I never tasted it before and probably never shall again. It's very strong. Is there some law I don't know about that forbids females to taste ale?"

"Ha," said Mr. Tewksberry.

"So," the man who was a lordship said, "you're a Miss Smith?"

"Not really, but it seemed wise." She turned and smiled at Mackie. "You must let me go now, Mr. Mackie. I really must fetch a doctor for my brother. Also, I don't want Clorinda to tear my hair out."

"Clorie's a tough little bird and 'er temper ain't the nicest. Best let 'er up, Mackie."

"We'll git yer doctor fer ye, missie," Mackie announced. He lifted her easily and set her on her feet. He rose then and she realized he was the tallest man she'd ever seen in her life. She smiled up at him.

"Thank you, Mr. Mackie."

Mackie gave her a courtly bow, kissed her hand, and said, "Yer a sweet lass. Ye just stay 'ere and keep yer distance from Clorie." He then gave her another bow, this one a bit more graceful than the first since he'd had that practice. He roared at the other men and all of them lumbered after him from the taproom, like an obedient army troop.

"Now, see here, missie, I won't allow you to—"

"Please hold a moment, Mr. Tewksberry. I wish to speak to Miss Smith. Please fetch her a cup of tea and do tell Miss Clorinda that I will see to it that this young pigeon doesn't migrate into her territory." He turned to give her a vague smile. "Would you like to sit on my lap or would a chair do just as well?"

"You're not as big as Mr. Mackie. Perhaps you will drop me. I'd best have a chair."

He stared down at her a good long time. "You have a ready mouth," he said at last. "I haven't met a young lady in a very long time with such a ready mouth."

He ushered her over to his table by the fireplace. He held back a chair for her. "Do sit, ma'am. We won't take chances that I am too weak to hold you properly."

"Thank you, sir."

He sat down in his former chair and stretched out his legs toward the fireplace. He looked meditative, then he frowned. "How did you do that?"

"Do what?"

"Those men. They looked like a devil-may-care lot, well into their cups, but then this Mackie fellow is nearly on his knees to you vowing eternal devotion. How did you do it?"

"I really don't know. I liked them, nothing more, really. They reminded me of farm laborers where I live, just men, just drinking to ease their cares. They were very kind, once they realized it was the right thing to be."

"I daresay they aren't all that kind at all to lone females who wander into their preserve, but they were to you. Well, then let it remain a mystery. Ah, the weather then. The miserable night has become less miserable."

"Yes, but I just woke up so I really wouldn't know as of yet, but at least it's stopped raining. I do so hate riding in the rain, and it really slowed us down."

She clapped her hand over her mouth, her eyes wide on his face, looking like a loyal soldier who's just accidentally spilled all his military secrets to the enemy.

"If your brother is ill," he said, his voice dispassionate, "then you won't be riding anywhere tonight."

"We got soaked clear through all last night and this morning. I thought a good sleep would keep us healthy. Owen isn't all that sturdy."

"Owen has the weak chin?"

"So you heard Walt say that, did you? I suppose he does. I believe I will talk him into trying to grow a beard to cover it. What do you think?"

"I think that I must first take a long look at this weak chin before recommending hair."

"There will be no need of that, sir. When Mr. Mackie comes back with the doctor, why, he will quack Owen with some sort of tonic and we'll be on our way tomorrow again."

"May I ask where you are going, ma'am?"

"To Cornwall."

He waited, a dark brow raised in silent question.

"I would just as soon not reveal everything to you, sir. Indeed, I can't believe I already told you so very much. You're a complete stranger. I don't know you. You could be dangerous. You could have accomplices waiting outside the inn for a sign from you."

"Yes," he said. "All of those things."

He said nothing more, merely looked straight ahead into the glowing embers. He looked perfectly relaxed, perfectly at his ease. She had the feeling that it didn't matter to him if she were there or not. He would have looked and acted and felt just the same. She said, "You're alone, aren't you? There's no one waiting outside."

"Yes, I'm quite alone."

Then she heard herself say, "My name isn't Miss Smith."

Slowly he turned his head to look at her. "No," he said. "You said it wasn't."

"It's Jones."

He stared at her. Then he smiled. It was a small stretching of his mouth, then it became a real smile. Then he laughed.

That laugh sounded wonderful, and she heard herself saying without hesitation, "There's more to it than just Jones, but again, I don't think I would be wise to tell you. I really don't understand it. You aren't ordering me or asking me or pleading with me to tell you anything and yet I just open my mouth and everything comes out. It's very disconcerting. You are a dangerous man."

"Then it is just as well we stay with Smith, although Miss Smith isn't all that inspiring, but then again, neither is Miss Jones."

"Who are you, sir?"

"I? Why, I'm Chilton."

"What Chilton? What sort of Chilton? Mr. Tewksberry called you 'my lord.'"

"Yes, he did, therefore Lord Chilton fits me quite as well as my socks. I've been here a good half-dozen times. Tewksberry likes to have a gentleman occasionally grace his hearth. I believe he thought the *strumpet* on Mackie's lap might give me a disgust of his inn. He was quite ready and eager to grab your ear and haul you out into the night."

"Where are you going?"

"To London, actually. I have business matters to see to. But that can't interest you, Miss Smith. Now, here's your tea. Why don't you drink it in peace and I'll go see if your weak-chinned brother is still among the breathing."

"Oh, no!" She jumped to her feet, oversetting the teacup. She watched the tea flow over the side of the table onto her skirt.

"I beg your pardon, Miss Smith?"

"My brother wouldn't want to see you. You're a stranger, please, you might frighten him and he might have a seizure or something, so please, sir, don't—"

He sat again, looking calm and bored and really, truth be told, indifferent. "Tewksberry," he called out, "another cup of tea, please, and a cloth. Miss Smith has been attempting to launder her gown."

"Thank you," she said. He merely nodded, paying her no more attention. Again, she heard herself say with no hesitation at all, "It isn't really that my brother would have a seizure or faint at the sight of you, a strange man. It's just that he might spit out everything and that wouldn't be good."

"Just as you're spitting to me right now, Miss Smith?"

"Oh dear, perhaps I am but I don't want to. It's just that I must continually catch myself at the very verge of spitting. I don't understand it."

"Perhaps you're Catholic and I remind you of a priest from your childhood?"

"Oh no, not at all. Every priest I've ever seen looked pale from being indoors too much and, well, ineffectual, I'd say, like they're afraid to say exactly what they mean for fear of getting smashed."

"Where are you going in Cornwall? No, don't spit it right out, make me work for it a bit. I live in Cornwall, you see, and I was wondering if perhaps we would be neighbors one of these days."

"Work for it, sir."

"Very well. I live near Goonbell."

"You're making that up. Oh, thank you, Mr. Tewksberry. I'm sorry I spilled the tea. This smells delicious."

Mr. Tewksberry harrumphed, saw that Lord Chilton didn't look at all discomfited by the strumpet's presence, and managed a stingy smile. "I will keep Clorie away from you, miss," he said, "but she's not happy, no, she's not. She doesn't trust you an inch."

"I appreciate that, Mr. Tewksberry. Now, sir, Goonbell? That's an absurd name, surely you're making that up."

"I've been found out. Very well, then, I live near Playing Place, which is close by to Cripplesease."

She laughed and choked on her tea, spitting it out on her bodice. "Oh dear, look what you made me do."

"At least you're wet all over now, not just your skirt."

"Playing Place, what nonsense. Cripplesease, that's quite impossible."

"Twelveheads."

"I can't drink any more tea, else I might spit it on you and that would never do."

"Actually, one of those is the truth, or very nearly."

"Do you know where I come from, sir?"

He raised a black brow, saying nothing at all. Finally he spoke. "I wager that if I just sit here, you'll blurt it out momentarily."

"I come from Affpuddle."

"A lovely place. I spent several quite contented weeks there with my mistress, Mrs. Oddsbottle."

She gave it up, drank her tea, and just sat there, concentrating on keeping her mouth closed and listening for Mr. Mackie and the doctor.

"Yes, Isabella Oddsbottle. I did encourage her to have her name officially changed, but she refused, said she was quite fond of Isabella, it was her grandmother's name."

She refused to take the bait. As for Lord Chilton, he sat back in his chair, crossed his hands over his chest, and wondered at himself. He'd actually been speaking to a strange young lady—she was both unknown and eccentric—and he'd enjoyed himself thoroughly. He wondered what the devil she was up to. He didn't believe for a minute that the Owen upstairs lying sick was her brother.

Was she eloping with him?

He was content to wait. Oddly enough, he was interested in finding out exactly who she was and who Owen was. It was late, the taproom warm, the brandy settled smoothly in his belly. He fell asleep.

Caroline stared at him. He was asleep; the man had the gall to fall asleep right in front of her.

She heard the front door of the inn open, innumerable male voices all talking at the same time, and smiled. The gentleman wouldn't snooze for much longer, not with this approaching racket.

Mr. Mackie stood in the doorway of the taproom, bent down, naturally, since he was at least a foot taller than the portal.

"The bone masher, missie. Walt here smelled 'is breath but good and it didn't flatten 'im. 'E can walk a straight path too, thus Old Bones shouldn't kill yer brother."

"Thank God for that," Lord Chilton said, not looking up.

"'Is name's Dr. Tuckbucket."

"Oh no," she said, rising. "I wonder if he hails from Mumbles. I understand that most of the Tuckbuckets do."

She heard Lord Chilton chuckle as she left the taproom. Like his laugh, his chuckle sounded rusty.

A strange man, she thought, climbing up the narrow staircase after Dr. Tuckbucket, who did indeed appear to be walking without too much assistance from Mr. Mackie.

5

Owen had come down with a very bad cold, so bad, in fact, that Dr. Tuckbucket poured an entire bottle of his own special tonic down his throat while Caroline held him down and told him not to be such a coward while he was coughing and wheezing and telling her she was a shrew and too mean to get sick. Dr. Tuckbucket then told her in private that her brother was quite ill and must remain in bed for a good week.

She stared at him in consternation. "A week? Oh no, sir, that's quite impossible." She thought of Mr. Ffalkes, and said, "I haven't the funds to keep us here for a week."

"Pay me first, if you please, miss."

"Oh yes, of course. Are you sure, sir? An entire week?"

"We'll see, but it doesn't look hopeful. He's got a muddy look to him."

"He won't die, will he?"

"No, not if you nurse him and keep yourself away from Mackie's ale."

The thought of nursing Owen was appalling, but she managed to nod, saying in a voice as accepting as a prisoner just sentenced, "Give me all the instructions and the medicine, sir. I will take care of him."

Saying it and doing it, Caroline quickly learned, were two vastly different endeavors. Owen thrashed about all through the night, throwing off the covers; then the fever burned him from the inside out, and he began shivering and moaning when the fever turned his blood to ice in his veins.

By four in the morning, she was sitting in the single chair, her legs stretched out limply in front of her, her hair dangling in her face, feeling so tired she didn't want to move, just staring over at Owen, who had finally fallen into a blessed sleep, fitful, but blessed nonetheless.

"A hostage," she said. "I took you as a damned hostage and look what you've done to me."

He moaned and she forced herself to get up. She gently placed her palm on his forehead. He was cool to the touch, thank the good Lord. At least for now.

There was a light knock on the door. She froze, then shook her head at herself. There was no way Mr. Ffalkes could have any idea which way she'd come. No way at all. It must be Mr. Mackie. Actually, she thought, brightening, she could use a good swig of ale right now.

She opened the door. Lord Chilton stood there, dressed all in black, leaning against the door frame, as indolent as a cat sunning on a windowsill, his arms crossed negligently across his chest. He looked dark, dangerous, and brooding. He was giving her a look that was menacing. She smiled up at him. "It's nearly dawn. Why are you awake?"

He frowned at her and she smiled more widely. "You might as well come in. There is only one chair and I suppose you will demand to have it since you're a lord and I'm not."

"Since I'm a lord and thus am also a gentleman, I suppose I shall have to relinquish the chair to you. At least you're not demanding to sit in my lap again."

He looked darker and more menacing than ever, and she just smiled more widely at him. He grunted, walked to the bed, looked meditatively down at Owen, placed his palm against his cheek, then his forehead, felt the pulse in his throat, nodded, then sat down in the chair. "I'm tired," he said, leaning his head back, "and am not feeling at all like a gentleman. He's your brother, you can sit beside him."

She very nearly kicked his booted foot. Instead, she said, "What are you doing here? Owen hasn't made much noise in the past hour so I know he didn't awaken you."

"Strange as it must sound, both to me and to you, I woke up and found myself worrying. You two are such innocents. I suppose you're nursing your brother? All by yourself?"

"I don't think Clorie would be anxious to serve."

"No, probably not. Actually, she wanted to serve me."

"Oh really? Why, at such a late hour? You shouldn't drink so much, sir, surely it can't be good for you."

He opened his eyes and looked at her with such annoyance that she blinked. "Don't be a fool," was all he said, leaned his head back again, and closed his eyes.

Seeing as how the *gentleman* had taken the only chair, Caroline sat on the edge of Owen's bed.

He said in a slow, lazy voice, "This chamber is an abomination. It's small and airless. It smells of fever. If you don't want dear brother Owen to speedily dispatch himself to heavenly climes, I suggest that you ask Tewksberry for a larger room."

"I can't afford it."

He sighed. "I thought not. Who the hell are you?"

"I'm not Prudence, that's for sure. I won't tell you my name. I won't be that stupid, although I'm so tired I can't begin to remember what I said two minutes ago."

"If you are indiscreet I will tell you so."

"Thank you. What are you doing here? You're just taking your ease, treating me like a halfwit, not doing a single helpful thing."

"All true." He opened his eyes. "You look like hell. Actually you're looking exactly as I would imagine a Prudence to look."

"You can call me Rosemary. It's my second name."

"Thank God for that."

"I don't like to be rude, Lord Chilton, but why don't you take yourself back to your own bedchamber?"

He rose swiftly from the chair, pulled a key from his pocket, and handed it to her. "Here, take it. It's number seven just down the hall on the right. It's the best bedchamber in this cursed inn. Go get some sleep. I'll see to brother Owen for a while."

"Are you serious?"

"Dead serious, just as you'll be if you don't get some rest. Go now while my good nature is still floating on top."

"He should remain asleep for another couple of hours. Then he must have more water. Dr. Tuckbucket said to pour water down him as if he were a thirsty camel."

"Where's the chamber pot?"

She stared at him.

"If he drinks like a camel he will want to relieve himself. Hadn't you thought of that, Rosemary? No, I can't say it. Let's leave it at Miss Smith." He sighed, a man sorely tried. "I see that you haven't performed that particular duty for him, nor had you even thought of it."

"Oh dear, the chamber pot's under the bed."

He just nodded and motioned toward the door. "Go to bed, Miss Smith."

She left him there, shaking her head, wondering what sort of man he was. She wondered what her aunt Ellie would say when she heard of this mad adventure. She prayed devoutly that the adventure would end at Aunt Ellie's doorstep and not in a gaol somewhere because she didn't have enough money to pay her shot. And there was Owen, poor Owen, who couldn't help it that he'd become ill. But why couldn't he have waited? Just until they'd reached Cornwall. She had this inescapable feeling that Mr. Ffalkes would find them. She just knew it.

She slept for a good six hours in Lord Chilton's soft feather mattress tester bed. It was he who woke her, his fingertip lightly smoothing over her eyebrows. What an odd feeling it was, and strangely soothing, and also, somehow terribly improper, she knew that, but still, it felt so interesting she said nothing, just sighed. The fingertip stopped and dropped away.

"You're awake, Miss Smith. Come, open your eyes. It's nearly noon and I have begged and pleaded with Miss Clorinda to feed you luncheon and not tear your fair hair out. It was difficult since you are in my bed and she knows it and has drawn her own conclusions based on your sitting on Mackie's lap last night after tripping down his ale."

She wished he'd stroke his fingertips over her eyebrows some more. She opened her eyes and looked up at him. He was leaning down, not more than a few inches from her face.

"Your eyes are very, very dark," she said. "Not black, but certainly not brown either. Were your parents Moors?"

"No, but my mother was part Irish, I heard it said. I am told that my eyes are even darker than hers, strange surely. Other than the eyes, I am my father's son, at least my person is. For the rest of it, I pray devoutly each morning that—" He paused and frowned at her. "I didn't mean to say that. How odd of me."

She raised her hand and lightly traced her own fingertip over his dark brows, first one, then the other. He didn't move, just looked down at her, his expression unreadable.

"How is Owen?"

"He is complaining. A good sign."

She dropped her hand and lightly pushed at his shoulder. He straightened, then rose. She sat up and stretched. "The gall of him, complaining and whining. He gets ill, forcing us to stop our journey, and then he complains about it, as if it's my fault, and the good Lord knows it isn't."

"He's just a man, Miss Smith."

"A boy who will grow into a man. If he's complaining now, just wait another five years."

Again, he chuckled, still a rusty sound, but it pleased her that she had made him chuckle. She smiled up at him, stretched once more, and got out of his bed. She felt about for her slippers and slipped into them, drawing up her leg to tie the ribbons about her ankles.

"You are strangely at your ease around me, a gentleman, Miss Smith. Showing me your ankles even. I am not used to such bounty from young ladies."

"Don't look then. With you standing there, how else am I to tie my slippers?"

"A good point. Come now, let's go downstairs and have luncheon. Owen has Miss Clorinda to attend him. I venture to say he'll soon be feverish for quite another reason."

"What would that be? Oh no, she's not feeding him wine or beef or heavy things like that, is she?"

"No, Miss Smith, she is giving him gruel with a dollop of honey on top."

"Excellent, don't worry me like that again. Oh dear, my hair."

He handed her a comb with a dark hair in it and pointed to the small mirror atop the bed table. He stood by the door, his arms folded over his chest, watching her while she smoothed out the tangles, then splashed water on her face from the pitcher beside the mirror. He watched her lightly pat her cheeks with a soft towel.

He'd watched only one other lady perform her toilette. He'd been so very young, a babe, really, but the picture of her in his mind for just a brief instant made pain slice through him even though her face was an indistinct shadow in his mind. He remembered humming, a smile, a very lovely smile, and it was given to him, from her. He turned away, opened the door, and walked into the narrow dusty hallway.

"Come along, Miss Smith."

It was midnight. Three days they'd been here at the Black Hair Inn. Strangely enough, Lord Chilton had remained as well, saying only when she commented on it, "I am being amused for the moment." Nothing more, just that, and she'd wanted to hit him, for it sounded like she and Owen were oddities for his entertainment. Still, she was very grateful for his presence. Without him, she just knew that Mr. Tewksberry would have tossed her and Owen out on their respective ears.

She knew Mr. Ffalkes was coming, she just knew it, so when there was a knock on the bedroom door at midnight, she didn't rise, didn't say a single word. The door flew open, crashed against the wall, and Mr. Ffalkes strode into Lord Chilton's former bedchamber, given over two days ago to Owen.

"Ah!"

"Good evening, Mr. Ffalkes. How did you find us?"

"Find you, damn your eyes, you stupid—"

"I pray you to keep your voice down, sir. Your son is still ill and is now sleeping."

Mr. Ffalkes grunted at that, but did look at his son curled up beneath a mountain of blankets. "What's wrong with him?"

"We were riding an entire night in the rain. He came down with a cold. He is improving and should be quite recovered by the end of the week."

"You take my son hostage and then you try to kill him?"

"Hostage? A lady take a gentleman *hostage?*"

Mr. Ffalkes whirled about at the intruder's voice. He saw a nobleman, no doubt about it in his mind. He could spot a nobleman from two miles away, damn their arrogance, their supercilious attitudes, their drawling voices that made resentment boil in him, for surely he should have been born on a richer blanket, like his cousin, that damned sod of a knight, who was, at least, now long dead.

"Yes," Caroline said. "I'm surprised Owen hasn't told you, but I suppose he wanted to protect me. I did take him as my hostage, and he must have seen himself honor-bound to keep quiet in that role. This is his father, Mr. Roland Ffalkes. Sir, this is Lord Chilton."

"So, you're her father."

"What?"

"Well, if Owen is her brother, then a paternal conclusion rather jumps to the fore, does it not?"

Mr. Ffalkes drew himself up. He looked rather formidable in his dark cloak and his boots. "I am her betrothed," he said, "not that it is any of your business, Lord Chilton."

"Oh no, it's none of my business at all, though you do seem a trifle old for the young lady. May I inquire why your son is her hostage?"

"He is not her hostage, that is nonsense. He is a man. No, you may not inquire about anything. You are intruding. You may leave now, sir."

"You are not my betrothed," Caroline said, rising. "Just stop this nonsense, Mr. Ffalkes. Lord Chilton, this man was my guardian until I became nineteen last week. He tried to force me to marry Owen, but that was ridiculous, then he was going to rape me and force me to marry himself instead. I got away and took Owen with me as a hostage. Then," she added, looking over at Owen, who was awake now, the covers pulled nearly to his eyes, staring at his father like a boy who has just been caught stealing his father's money, "Owen got ill."

"I see," Chilton said.

"Leave now, sir," Mr. Ffalkes said.

"How did you find us?"

Mr. Ffalkes looked at his son as he said, "It rained a lot. Every inn you stopped at remembered you. Also, I had five men out searching for the direction you took."

"I'll just wager you paid them with my money, didn't you, you bloody thief? "

"It would seem to me, sir," Chilton said, seeing that Miss Smith was now alarmingly red in the face and holding a fire poker in her left hand snuggled in her skirts, "that since Miss Smith here—"

"Smith? What is this idiocy? Smith? Her name is Derwent-Jones and I am her betrothed. I believe we will be wed before we leave here."

"—that Miss Derwent-Jones is of age, thus if she doesn't want to marry you, she doesn't have to."

"Naturally she does. Her reputation is in shreds. She has no reputation unless I marry her and repair it."

"I would rather marry Owen!"

There was whimpering from the bed.

"Hush, my boy, I won't saddle you with her. I'll saddle myself and regret it doubtless, but it will be done."

North Nightingale, Lord Chilton, looked from Mr. Ffalkes, who didn't look to be all that bad a man, but did look to be stubborn as a stoat and perfectly ready to do anything to gain what he wanted, to Miss Derwent-Jones, who was ready to raise that poker and strike Mr. Ffalkes on the head, to the whimpering Owen, whose eyes were now tightly closed above the line of blankets, and said, "Do you know, Mr. Ffalkes, that Miss Derwent-Jones has been sleeping in my bed for the past three nights? Did you also know that I invariably awaken her in the morning, my fingertips smoothing over her eyebrows? Do you know how much I enjoy watching her comb her hair and bathe?"

Mr. Ffalkes just stared at him.

Caroline could only stare at him. He'd told the exact truth. It sounded like she was a strumpet. She understood that he was trying to save her from Mr. Ffalkes.

"I want my inheritance, Mr. Ffalkes. I want you to sign over the papers to me right this minute. I want what is mine by right."

"Nothing is really yours, my girl. You're naught but a female and thus are incapable of dealing with your own affairs. Your father was a fool to leave things thusly. No, you will have a husband—I—and I will deal with everything, including you and my son. I will even accept you though you've consorted with this man whilst your poor cousin Owen was here suffering by himself."

"Surely this is a melodrama," North said to the fireplace. "A very bad melodrama, much like the one in London last March where this young man was convinced his love had betrayed him and thus went on a rampage and killed a goat by mistake and—"

"That is enough, sir!"

"Actually," North said gently, "it's 'my lord.' Contrive not to forget your manners, else I will have to challenge you to a duel and wound you and then both you and Owen would be laid up side by side, complaining."

"Arrogant young puppy."

"Now, that is just fine, so long as you identify me after your string of descriptive words."

Caroline stared at the two men, drew herself up, and said, "Mr. Ffalkes, now that you're here, you will take over Owen's care. I'm leaving. Lord Chilton, thank you for your assistance. I very much appreciate it."

"You're not going anywhere, my girl!" Mr. Ffalkes grabbed her arm as she walked past him and jerked her about. North watched transfixed as she raised the poker and struck Mr. Ffalkes hard on his shoulder.

He yowled, releasing her. "You damned bitch, I'll—"

She hit him again on his other shoulder, then threw the poker to the floor. She dusted her hands, picked up her valise, and began to pile her clothes into it.

"You've killed me."

"No," she said, not looking at him, "but I wish I had. Leave me alone, Mr. Ffalkes. I will have my solicitor contact you."

She picked up her cloak and strode from the bedchamber. Mr. Ffalkes made to go after her, but Owen, emerging from beneath his fortress of blankets, said, "No, Father, do let her go. She won't wed me and she won't wed you. She doesn't care about her reputation. Please, Father, give her her money. End it now and let's go home."

"I won't give her a bloody sou, and you, you faithless sniveling hound, I will see that you suffer for the muddle you've made of everything."

"Muddle? Father, I became ill. If I hadn't become ill, then you would never have found us."

"Don't be a fool, Owen. I know where she's going. To her aunt Ellie in Cornwall, in a godforsaken place called Trevellas. If I hadn't found the two of you here, I would have continued on there. It's better I found you here, though, for that blasted woman would have tried to protect her."

North felt as if he'd been kicked in the gut. Trevellas? Aunt Ellie? For an instant he felt lightheaded, then a searing pain went through him, a pain that would be her pain very soon.

"It has been quite an experience," North said to Mr. Ffalkes. He nodded to Owen, who said unexpectedly and with a good deal of liking, "Thank you, North, for taking care of me. I hope I will see you again. Perhaps you can teach me more strategy at piquet."

"Humph," said his father.

"Perhaps," North said. "Good-bye, Owen, Mr. Ffalkes."

Mr. Ffalkes gave him a cold bow, saying nothing. He turned to his son and said, "You will remain here, Owen, and keep yourself warm, though how you can bear all those blankets is beyond me. I'm going after Miss Derwent-Jones. She won't get far. She won't bring me low this time. I will handle things. I am a man and I am devious and I will see to it."

And North thought as he walked down the corridor, *Like hell you will.*

6

North stared at Tewksberry, feeling a bolt of deep admiration, and tried to keep himself from laughing out loud.

"Aye, my lord, you might just look that disgusted, for that little strum—er, miss, left and without paying her shot, just as I said. What am I to do?"

He should have known, North thought, yes, he should have known. Well, and why should she have to pay for Owen, her hostage? *Hostage.* He fought again to control his laughter. She'd taken a man hostage. He just shrugged and said, "Her father is upstairs right now with her brother. His name is Mr. Roland Ffalkes. Quite naturally he will cover what's owing."

"But why did she fly off like a bird out of its cage if her father's come?"

"It seems," North said, leaning forward, all confidences, "that Mr. Ffalkes's wife, Mathilda, eloped with a German footman. The daughter took the mother's part and ran away too, the brother coming with her. She dislikes the father thoroughly. You'll see he's rather a nasty sort."

"Ah," said Tewksberry. "Ah, so that's the way of it. A footman, eh? German, you say? Poor little mite."

North nodded solemnly, paid his own bill, nodded to Mr. Tewksberry, and left the inn. He walked out into the inn yard, lightly slapping his riding crop against his thigh. The morning was overcast and would prove to be warm.

Rain threatened, but then again, rain always threatened in England, particularly here on the southwest coast. He called to one of the stable lads to bring out Treetop, who was probably so bored with his inactivity he'd race like the wind. He had to catch up with her and he doubted it would take him very long at all. Treetop was a magnificent beast, fleet and strong.

The boy saluted and bobbed, then ran into the large ramshackle stable set off to the side of the inn. He returned in very short order, red in the face, his eyes darting about frantically in search of help, of which there was none.

"Yer 'orse is gone, milord."

"I beg your pardon? It's the bay gelding with the two white socks."

"I know, milord, but Sparkie says the young lady took Treetop and left 'er own 'orse fer ye—a brave old mare, full in the shoulders, but not a goer, milord, iffen ye ken what I mean."

He shouldn't be surprised, he thought, this time curses rather than amusement bubbling up. She'd done in Mr. Ffalkes and now she'd done him in as well, and with little effort on her part. She'd doubtless eyed Treetop and known she'd make better time with that superb beast carrying her than her own mare, who looked like she'd been eating her head off since they'd arrived here. She looked sleepy and lazy.

"Well, you old nag, what do you say?"

The old nag gave him a bored look.

"That bad, is it? No choice, sorry. Shall we find your mistress? It seems she's misplaced herself along with my horse."

Within minutes he'd found the note scribbled on a small bit of foolscap stuck in one of the leather saddle folds. He read:

Lord Chilton:

Do forgive me for taking your horse, but I don't want Mr. Ffalkes to catch up with me. I would have to shoot him this time. I will return your horse to you, I swear. Wherever I go I will ask about Goonbell.

yr. servant
Caroline Derwent-Jones

Within five more minutes he was on his way back to Cornwall. So much for London, his man of business, his charming mistress, Judith, who was also an actress, who wouldn't remain faithful to him or any other man if memorizing her lines depended on it. He sighed. Well, Judith was a bit slow in her thinking even if she chattered all the time. He remembered one evening he'd just crested in his pleasure when she'd said in a chirpy voice, "How I would love to play Desdemona, my lord. Can't you just see me in a long blond wig—yellow blond—and Iago would do me in and my handsome Moor would strangle me and then regret it so deeply that he would arrange my lovely self against the covers and the pillow and then kill himself in his anguish and—"

He'd groaned, his fingers itching to go around her damned throat. He realized now that he was perilously close to laughing aloud remembering the ridiculous matter. He'd believed Judith incredibly skilled, which she was, but stupid, which hadn't mattered. Her incessant chatter had grated, but somehow it paled when she caressed him and kissed him and . . . Damnation, now he was riding after that damned chit who had stolen his horse. Treetop had never known a sidesaddle before. He hoped he wouldn't find her in a ditch somewhere with a broken neck.

He didn't find her at all. She must be an excellent rider, for Treetop could be a handful even for him. For a stranger? For a female stranger who had the gall to put a sidesaddle on his massive back?

Unlike Miss Derwent-Jones, he didn't have to hide himself during the day, and whatever else she was, stupid wasn't it. He knew she'd continue the same habit of sleeping during the day and riding only at night. Thus, he rode through Exeter on to Bovey Tracy, rested for several hours in a copse of maple trees beside the road, then rode in one long spurt to Liskeard. He put up at the Naked Goose Inn and slept for six straight hours. He was off again at six o'clock in the morning.

The weather had held, thank heaven for that, and he'd made excellent time. He might be riding a horse he would disdain in any other circumstance, but he found that the mare did have grit and a good deal of endurance. It never occurred to him to sell her or leave her at an inn and rent another horse. No, even though he didn't know her name, he quite liked her. Toward the end of that first long day, just as he was growing near to Liskeard, he'd named her Regina, for that's what she'd become. "It's just a temporary name," he told her, patting down her fat neck, "just until we find that damned mistress of yours. If she survives the meeting with me, why then, you can return to her and to your old name."

When he'd come out of the Naked Goose Inn in Liskeard early the following morning, he knew she'd seen him coming, for her head went up and she whinnied at him, nodding her head. Then when he'd reached her, she'd butted her head against his hand.

"You're quite the seductress, aren't you, Reggie? Have a carrot, old girl, then we'll be on our way." He stroked her soft muzzle, fed her until he swore she was grinning at him, then mounted and off they went, all the way to St. Agnes today.

He wondered what he would do when he met Caroline Derwent-Jones again. It wasn't going to be pleasant, telling her that someone had killed her aunt. He wondered what he would do when Mr. Ffalkes came here to get her. He sighed. He didn't want to be involved with this girl, with her bravado and her innocence, ah, and he couldn't forget that her ready wit had made him laugh at least twice, had made him resort to wit and conversation that had come rather easily and made him not at all uncomfortable. He'd felt a bit like he'd felt at Chase Park with the Wyndhams, a temporary feeling at best, this liking and comfort he'd found with Marcus and his bride, Duchess, and their servants, who were better friends than most people gained in a lifetime. No, he'd left Yorkshire, deeming it time for him to return to Cornwall, to face those demons that awaited him there, finally, to take over his birthright, for he'd become

Viscount Chilton fifteen months earlier upon the unexpected death of his father.

Above all, though, he'd wanted his solitude. He did better alone. He had his dogs, his horses, his house that was vast and empty save for the few servants who had lived their lives there, it seemed, knowing nothing else save the Nightingales.

No, he didn't want to deal with Miss Derwent-Jones again. Once was quite enough. He didn't want to admire her delicious little ears or those nicely arched eyebrows of hers that he'd smoothed down with his fingertips each time he'd awakened her, or that long graceful neck, save to close his fingers around it and squeeze. Most of all, he didn't want to be the one to tell her that her aunt was dead, murdered, stabbed in the back, and thrown over the ledge at St. Agnes Head.

He rode directly to his estate, Mount Hawke, looming high and stark atop a gently rising hill above the village of the same name, the protector of those villagers since the time Henry VIII had chopped off Katherine Howard's pretty head. Indeed, the estate records showed that the great doors were affixed to Mount Hawke on the exact day of her beheading.

He hated the bloody mausoleum, more a square-built castle really, with four towers that weren't good for anything, large drafty staircases and corridors, stone floors that echoed footsteps as if an army were marching through, cold as the devil those bloody floors were, save where his ancestors along about one hundred years later had thrown down thick Turkey carpets. It was built all of mellow gray stone quarried nearby at Baldhu, and still quite beautiful if one were objective, which North wasn't. And the pile belonged to him and he was supposed to cherish it, since it had passed from father to son in an unbroken chain for nearly three hundred and fifty years, quite a feat in itself, the continuous propagation of male after male. It was impressive, he admitted, in a rather foreboding, menacing sort of way, standing tall atop its own private hill, casting its shadow over the slopes of the hill and the town below.

It was nearly dark when he rode up the wide carriage drive that made deep curves back and forth many times so the ascent wouldn't be too steep before reaching the great black iron gates. Since there was no more threat of invading armies or invading neighbors, comfort was the thing. He imagined that when it was built, it looked like a clumsy helmet sitting atop a naked man's head, all impressive and isolated and alone.

Tom O'Laddy, the Nightingale gatekeeper for longer than North had been alive, greeted him with a huge grin, showing the empty space that should have held his front teeth, the result of a fight he'd won. He sighed, then fainted dead away. O'Laddy was a man of ale and jests. Too much ale, and he was a man of violence.

"Ho, my lord! 'Tis home ye are. 'Twere a short trip to Lunnon, eh? Foul place, Lunnon. Mr. Coombe and Mr. Tregeagle weren't expecting ye fer another fortnight."

"Good evening, Tom. Yes, I can see you're wondering where Treetop is, but this sweet old girl is Reggie and she's really quite a surprise, lots of heart. How's your nephew?"

"He's still on the weak side, my lord, but Mr. Polgrain sends the lad some of his special broth every day and thus he's on the mend."

"Excellent. Next time tell him not to fall out of his boat and nearly drown himself."

"Aye, my lord, the boy's properly learnt his lesson. Actually, it was that little nit of a blacksmith's daughter who'd pushed him out of the boat. It seems he was making advances and she didn't like it."

North grunted, at least he tried to, but a smile came up instead.

He rode through the great gates and still upward, the carriage path growing even wider now as it neared that monstrous edifice that had tried over the past nearly three centuries to become more a home than a fortress, and he supposed it had succeeded. There had even once been a drawbridge, considered in the enlightened sixteenth century to be quite unnecessary, but that drawbridge had saved Mount Hawke from Oliver Cromwell's Roundhead soldiers in the bloody civil war in the next century. Long since, the wide deep gully had been filled in and an orchard planted, now thick with apple trees, rippling down the sides of the slopes, beautiful, really.

Men, he thought, as he pulled Reggie to a gentle halt and looked upward at the massive rising blocks of gray stone that went up and up until they seemed to reach the dark skies themselves on overcast days. Men must fight and conquer or die trying. They couldn't seem to content themselves with what they had even if it was really quite sufficient. He himself had been a soldier, and it had been his goal to stop Napoleon, at least that's what he continually told himself. Truth be told, he liked a good fight. He liked to test himself, his strength, his wits on any and all opponents. He supposed he would have done very well in medieval times. With Napoleon tucked away on Elba he couldn't imagine any more war on such a scale. Sometimes it depressed him. He knew it depressed his friend Marcus Wyndham, as well. And now Marcus was well married and running his own estate, just as North would now do as well. He marveled at the ways of life.

He rode Reggie to the magnificent Mount Hawke stable, a long brick building with tack rooms, large stalls, hay bins, everything his obsessive great-grandfather could think of. He dismounted Reggie, waved to Pa-Dou, and waited until the frail old man had come to take the mare's reins.

He chatted with old Pa-Dou, watching in amazement. Hard to believe his arthritic gnarled fingers could so skillfully handle the horses' reins and saddles.

Tomorrow he would go to Goonbell. He found himself grinning as he clasped the huge brass knocker and slammed it against the oak door. Goonbell. Good Lord, what if instead of Mount Hawke—surely a name that sounded rather splendid—he lived in Mount Goonbell overlooking the village of Goonbell.

He was chuckling when Coombe, his butler and his father's butler before him, opened the doors to him and blinked to see his master actually laughing.

North eyed the astonished Coombe, realized the reason for his astonishment, and said, "I was just thinking how odd it would sound were we called Mount Goonbell, and not Mount Hawke. It both amuses and terrifies."

Coombe appeared to ponder this for a moment, then said, "Surely laughter is too strong a reaction to such an unfortunate thought, my lord."

North grunted.

"Much better," Coombe said. "Welcome home, my lord, though I can't imagine why you're here two weeks sooner than we expected you to be here."

She hadn't yet arrived in Goonbell and he knew this was where she would come, at the very least to find out how to reach Scrilady Hall. He asked the fishermen, who knew everything about everyone, and the innkeeper, Mrs. Freely, who outdid the fishermen. No Miss Derwent-Jones.

He sighed and remounted Reggie. It took him only thirty minutes to reach Scrilady Hall, just outside of Trevellas, no more than a half mile from the sea.

There were three servants in residence at the seasoned red-brick manor house set amid charmingly wild bougainvilleas and roses and jasmine. It was a lovely house and now, he supposed, it belonged to Miss Derwent-Jones, though he wasn't certain of that.

But it was here she would come, eventually.

He was greeted by Dr. Benjamin Treath, who was showing an unknown gentleman about the house.

"Ah, my boy, do come in. What are you doing here?"

North only nodded, not yet ready to say anything.

"This is Mr. Brogan, a solicitor who is here to make an inventory of everything so that Squire Penrose's will can be executed."

"I see," North said. "When do you expect Miss Derwent-Jones to arrive, Mr. Brogan?"

There was nothing more than a rapid blinking of Mr. Brogan's large brown eyes to give away his surprise.

He merely fastened his eyes on a point just beyond North's left shoulder and said, "I hadn't realized, my lord, that you were so intimate with the family. Indeed, there is Miss Derwent-Jones and there is a Mr. Penrose— obviously on the squire's side of the family—who is the only other family member standing to inherit. Mr. Bennett Penrose has been here in the area on and off over the past five or so years. Of course I can really say no more about it until I've read the will to the two aforementioned individuals."

"Commendable," North said. He turned to Dr. Treath. "Are you all right, sir?"

"Yes, but it's difficult, North, very difficult. Nothing more has come to light since you left for your trip to London. Ah, you weren't gone for very long."

"No, not long at all. I assume you wrote to Miss Derwent-Jones, Mr. Brogan?"

Again Mr. Brogan gave no sign of surprise. "Yes, some weeks ago. I don't know why I haven't heard from her, but one must suppose that she will arrive shortly. If she doesn't arrive by the end of the week, I will write again. The post isn't all that reliable."

"Yes, you are probably right."

"You are acquainted with the lady, my lord?"

"Yes," North said.

"But how? I don't understand any of this, my lord."

"It's a rather involved tale, Mr. Brogan. Why don't we wait for Miss Derwent-Jones."

Mrs. Trebaw, the housekeeper, served them tea and cakes in the drawing room. Conversation was pleasant. North took his leave some minutes later, before Dr. Treath or Mr. Brogan could inquire how the devil he had met Miss Derwent-Jones, why he was here, and what the hell he wanted.

It appeared that Miss Derwent-Jones would be greeted by a solicitor and Dr. Treath when she arrived. She didn't need him there to tell her that some madman had killed her aunt. He tried to believe it, but didn't really.

But Miss Derwent-Jones didn't go to Scrilady Hall.

At ten o'clock the following night, Coombe lightly knocked on North's library door. He cleared his throat as he entered, looked over North's right shoulder at the shadowed mantel, upon which sat a very old clock made in Hamburg that was just quietly striking the tenth of its strokes.

"Yes, Coombe?"

"My lord, this is difficult and unusual and not at all what we are used to. There's a *Young Lady* here to see you. It is dreadfully late, and she looks quite in a state, and I was on the point of telling her to peddle her wares elsewhere when she drew this pistol on me and demanded to see you."

7

North was past him in a moment, striding quickly into the long narrow entrance hall. She was standing there by the front door, her head bent, her shoulders slumped, the single valise sitting by her left foot. She was wearing her cloak, dreadfully wrinkled and soiled now, but had pulled the hood back. Her hair was coiled around her head in thick loose braids, now coming loose, trailing tendrils of lazily curling hair over her shoulders. Hanging limp in her right hand was the infamous pistol.

At that moment, she raised her head. It wasn't fatigue he saw. It was pain, raw and deep, and fear.

"Miss Derwent-Jones," he said, striding toward her. "God, I'm sorry, so very sorry."

She gulped, he saw it, and she gulped again. Then he held out his arms, something entirely unplanned, something that didn't quite seem as odd as it should have, and she threw herself against him. For several moments, she was rigid, her hands fisted against his chest. The pistol fell from her fingers and skittered over the smooth marble of the entrance hall. Then suddenly, she began to sob, deep rending sobs that shook her entire body. She seemed to collapse against him, all the fight, all the bravado swept away by her grief and her shock.

His arms went around her and he pulled her close, stroking his hands over her hair, trying to soothe her, comfort her, saying nonsense really, rocking her against him.

She raised her head finally, pulling back a bit from him. "You knew," she said. "You knew and you didn't say anything to me."

"No, there was no chance. You left rather hurriedly."

"She's dead, Lord Chilton. No, not just dead, somebody killed her. I can't—"

He lightly touched his fingertip to her lips. "Hush, you're exhausted. Come into the library and warm yourself. A bit of brandy and some food will help. Come now."

Coombe said from just behind North, his voice disapproving as North's father's would become just before . . . No, he wouldn't think about that now. "I will bring refreshments, my lord, though I doubt Mr. Polgrain has much of anything in the kitchen."

"Thank you, Coombe. Bring what you have. Now, Miss Derwent-Jones, come with me."

He watched her take off her cloak, fold it ever so slowly and carefully, as if she was trying to get a hold of herself. Then she placed it over the back of a chair. She sighed, but still didn't look at him. He watched her smooth the folds of the cloak several times without, he suspected, even realizing what she was doing. He watched her walk to the fireplace, place another log on the fire, stir it up a bit, then reach her hands toward the flames. She was utterly silent, utterly still. She didn't seem at all like the same girl he'd met such a short time before who'd been sitting on Mackie's lap, all smiles and magic, downing that ale and coughing until her face turned crimson. He quietly closed the library doors to keep in the warmth, then turned, wondering what to say. She'd run away from her guardian to come to her aunt Ellie, only to find tragedy beyond what she could have ever imagined.

He remained silent, just watching her stand there in front of the fireplace, until Coombe brought in a single tray that held an old silver teapot that had more dents in its sides than Major Denny of the Twelfth Lincolnshire

Infantry had pox marks dug into his still-handsome face. The cups and saucers were so old and chipped, surely they should have been given to the poor fifty years before. As for the food, there were two slices of bread that surely had a bit of mold around the edges, a cup of clotted Cornish cream that was more yellow than white, and a single scone that looked as if it could be used as a weapon. He looked hard at Coombe, who just shrugged helplessly, not meeting his eyes. North held his tongue. The last thing his guest needed at this moment was to hear him yelling at his butler.

He poured them each a cup of tea, unable to offer her lemon, milk, or sugar, since there wasn't any on the tray.

"Thank you," she said, and gratefully sipped the hot tea. She sputtered, coughed, then quickly pressed a napkin to her mouth. "Oh dear, I'm sorry, it's just that the tea, well it's rather got big fists, and—"

North took a gingerly sip and thought his tongue would fall off. The tea was stronger than a storm wind blowing off the Irish Sea and tasted as brackish as the drinking water on his majesty's ships. Fists indeed.

"I'm sorry," he said, and took the cup from her. "Just rest here a moment. I'll fetch something else for you." He wanted to go to the kitchen, line up every pair of buttocks, and kick them all soundly, but decided he didn't want to leave her alone, at least not yet. She looked white and lost and battered down. He fetched her a brandy from the sideboard. "Here, this will warm you much better than my cook's notion of tea."

She sipped it slowly. She'd obviously learned from Mackie's ale. He watched color gradually come back into her face. "It's good. Not quite so serious a kick as Mr. Mackie's ale, which is a relief. Actually it's not so serious as that tea either. I've never had brandy before."

"Think of it as medicine," he said. "Would you care for the scone?"

She eyed the thing on the tray, looked up at him in bewilderment, which made him vow to kick every one of them harder than he'd planned just five minutes before, then slowly shook her head. "No, I'm not hungry, but thank you."

He stared off toward the fire for a moment, then said, "I wanted to be the one to tell you, but I had no idea when you would arrive or where you would go first. I did ride to Scrilady Hall, but the solicitor was there, a Mr. Brogan, and I don't think I was all that welcome. I'm sorry about your aunt. I liked Eleanor Penrose very much. She first came here when I was a boy of only ten. She was very popular."

"Not with everyone, it appears."

Tears welled up again but he held his place, not moving, saying nothing.

"Mrs. Freely at the inn in Goonbell said you were the one who had found her."

"Yes. Listen, Miss Derwent-Jones, you're very tired. It's too late for you to go to Scrilady Hall. You will remain here tonight and I will escort you there on the morrow."

To his pleasure, she gave him a crooked smile. "Can one drink brandy for breakfast?"

He smiled, such a strange feeling, really. "The breakfast tea will be wonderful, I promise you. I will have a small cozy chat with Cook about recipes and such."

"I thought your butler would slam the doors in my face. I'm sorry I threatened him with the pistol but I didn't know what else to do."

"He deserved it. He will survive the shock. As to his behavior, all I can say is that there hasn't been a lady in Mount Hawke in many more years than they've been alive. I suppose that he and Cook didn't quite know what to make of things."

"Evidently she didn't want me here either."

"He, actually. Mr. Polgrain is my cook."

He saw that she was weaving where she sat, and rose. "Excuse me a moment, Miss Derwent-Jones. I must inform Tregeagle to prepare a bed-chamber for you."

"Does Tregeagle wear skirts?"

"No, it's Mr. Augustus Tregeagle. As I said, it is a very long time since a female has been here. It's a house of men only."

"Oh. I'm sorry. It must be very difficult for you."

"Actually not," he said shortly, then smiled to soften it, and again, that smile came easily, too easily, and he thought, Well, fancy that, she feels sorry for me because I don't have females roaming my corridors, females sniffing the air to make certain it's sweet enough for their tender nostrils, females clucking over sheets with but small rents in them and worrying incessantly over how black the fireplaces are, and here I am smiling at her about it. He wanted to tell her he was grateful that God had spared him that; indeed, it was a fine thing for other men like his friend Marcus Wyndham, but not for him, but he held his peace. He found himself smiling at her again, and here she was very nearly asleep and not even noticing she was the recipient of a rare occurrence, for him at any rate.

He left her there, slumped down in the chair close to the blazing fireplace, to find Tregeagle. He hoped Tregeagle, a man with more waving white hair than a man should have at his age, and a handsome face that many men would kill to have, wouldn't be too far under the kitchen table from the quantities of Goonbell ale he consumed nightly, that he wouldn't now know the difference between clean sheets and a chamber pot.

It seemed Tregeagle wasn't drinking Goonbell ale at all. He was, in fact, in close conversation with Coombe and Polgrain, standing by the wooden counter, watching Polgrain wipe away stray crumbs from an already very clean surface. Tregeagle stood tall and straight and lean as he'd been as a young man. North stood in the doorway watching men who'd known him since he was a boy, since he'd come to live here at the age of five, to be exact, then cleared his throat loudly, hearty curses hovering on his tongue.

"Ah, my lord," Coombe said, his voice as smarmy as a tinker's who'd just sold all his hair potions to a bald man. He hurried forward, wiping his hands on Polgrain's apron as he passed him. "Was everything satisfactory?"

"No, it wasn't, as all of you well know. However, we will speak of your collective lapse on the morrow. Tregeagle, I need a bedchamber for our guest."

"But, my lord, there isn't a bedchamber!"

"Don't be an ass, Coombe. This house is larger than the village. There are at least two dozen bedchambers, damn your stubborn hide."

"That is all very well and good, my lord," Tregeagle said, drawing to his full five foot eleven inches, meant to intimidate, but didn't, not North in any case, "but Mr. Coombe is right. We have fed the Young Lady. We have given her sufficient succor. But to have her remain here? Unheard of, my lord, not possible. This is a gentleman's establishment. Our reputation would be—"

"*Our* reputation? What bloody nonsense is this? No, be quiet and listen to me. She is Mrs. Eleanor Penrose's niece. She just found out her aunt was murdered."

"Oh, dear," said Mr. Coombe, "she didn't tell me that, just aimed that pistol at me and looked mean. I thought her quite mad, my lord."

"It is a pity, certainly," said Tregeagle. "Such news would be enough to lead to female hysteria, which I understand is more prevalent among their sex than even we could guess."

"Surely she would be happier at Scrilady Hall," Polgrain said. "There are women who would see to her and comfort her. Also, I hear they have excellent food there."

"It would have to be better than what you offered her," North said. "Jesus, Polgrain, I could have thrown that scone at you and killed you dead—it was like a damned stone. Now, enough of this or I'll begin to believe you're nothing but a dried-up old trio of misogynists. Never mind, I already believe it, but hear this. Miss Derwent-Jones is very young. If she didn't know me, she wouldn't have anyone. She's exhausted and needs a good night's sleep. It's too late to take her to Scrilady Hall. See to it, Tregeagle, and no more muttering behind your damned teeth."

"Certainly, my lord," Tregeagle said at his most stately. "I think I will make up the Autumn Chamber."

"It's too dark, too chilly," said North, thankful he knew which bedchamber it was. "She would catch an inflammation of the lung were she to have to sleep in there. It also needs airing."

The three men looked at each other. Coombe said slowly, "If she became ill, she could be here for a very long time."

North nodded, saying, "Quite true. If you put her in a poorly aired bedchamber, one that's damp to boot, she might very well become ill. Very ill. Then she would be here for a very long time, possibly a longer time than Coombe believes."

"A pertinent observation, my lord," Coombe said, cleared his throat, and added, "I think the Pink Oval Room would be best. She's a female, after all, and everyone knows that pink goes well with the peculiar temperament of their sex."

"That would be appropriate," said Mr. Tregeagle after some deliberation. "The windows were open all day yesterday since our new maid, Timmy, was cleaning in there—for practice, you understand, my lord—and it wasn't raining. Yes, that will be fine, Coombe."

North just shook his head at them. He was grateful actually that they'd welcomed him back, since Mount Hawke had basically been theirs since his father had died. He wondered if they would have kept the doors locked in his face had he been a female. It seemed a distinct possibility, given their behavior toward Miss Derwent-Jones. It was a good thing she was leaving in the morning, otherwise they might poison her.

He nodded, aware that Coombe and Tregeagle were both looking at him, supposedly for his approval, which seemed silly since they obviously did exactly what they liked, but he said, "The Pink Oval Room would be quite nice, or at least it had better be."

She was sound asleep when he carried her upstairs to the lovely corner room that overlooked an apple orchard, planted more than fifty years before. His mouth watered at the thought of those fat apples, nearly ripe now, so many of them, enough for the villagers throughout the winter. The trees gracefully covered the sloping land that fell away from the castle nearly to the bottom, where the land flattened out and there was a narrow thread of a stream that wound about over three acres of Mount Hawke land.

The room had once belonged to a female, to which female, he had no idea. He didn't know who had furnished it in the soft pink and cream colors. He supposed that women had lived here at least a few years at a time, since male heirs had continued to be born and inherit Mount Hawke. But he hadn't lived here with his mother, only his father and his grandfather. Had his mother ever visited Mount Hawke? He shook his head, shoving the brief memory and the elusive pain it brought far back. No, there had been no woman living at Mount Hawke in this century.

The furnishings were frayed, for they were old, but all was clean and polished. Everything smelled like lemon and wax. Although he hated this stone mausoleum, he appreciated the care everyone had taken of it. Timmy, the new maid, had done quite an acceptable job. A household of men wasn't at all a bad thing, that is, until they were called upon to exhibit good manners to a passing female.

He removed only her scuffed boots. There was a hole in her stocking on the outside of her left foot. The skin was reddened and chafed. He didn't like the looks of it. He covered her and snuffed out the single candle.

Coombe was waiting outside the Pink Oval Room. "Is the young lady all right, my lord?"

"She's asleep. We'll see just how all right she is tomorrow."

"The, er, chamber, my lord, it showed Mount Hawke to advantage?"

"Yes, the maid, Timmy, did a fine job. Oh yes, Coombe, you will ensure that the breakfast Polgrain serves tomorrow is magnificent. You will ensure that the dishes used don't have a single crack and that they're sparkling clean. There will be a spotless tablecloth on the table. There will be linen napkins. Do you quite understand me?"

"Aye, my lord. Of a certainty. We are not stupid. Since she is leaving immediately after breakfast, we have determined it our duty to see that her young lady's stomach is well filled for her journey to where she belongs."

And just where, North wondered, did she belong? He wondered when Mr. Roland Ffalkes would be arriving, for arrive he would, doubtless with poor Owen in tow. He supposed that since she was young and a female and didn't know the way of things in this man's world, it was up to him to see that she was protected from her erstwhile guardian. What it was he would do, he hadn't the faintest idea.

He quietly closed the door. He was frowning. Coombe said, "You require my services, my lord?"

"Oh no. It's just that she's—no, it's nothing of importance, really. Good night, Coombe."

"Good night, my lord. We will survive this."

"Survive what? The temporary visitation of one single female?"

"You forget that she was armed, my lord."

"Go to bed, Coombe."

"She looked vicious, my lord. She could have shot me."

"You deserve to be shot. Go to bed."

"Yes, my lord."

When he awoke in the dark of the night to a terrified scream, he thought for an instant he was back at the battle of Toulouse, surrounded with cannon belching death at them, and French soldiers shooting madly, piercing flesh with the deadly bayonets, men who had nothing left to die for but glory— surely nonsense to want to die with your guts exploding out of you as you screamed away your life—and for Napoleon, a man who deserved to write himself into history, but without any more deaths for his doomed cause. He could still hear the French soldiers shouting, *La gloire! La gloire!*" Even when their comrades dropped dead beside them or in front of them and they had to step over their bodies, they kept up their shouts, over and over again, *"La gloire! La gloire!"*

He sat bolt upright in his bed utterly disoriented. There was another scream, then another. It was a female scream, not a man's scream, not a soldier's scream. A woman? Here? At Mount Hawke? He got his wits in order as he shoveled his hands through his hair.

Yes, the girl who'd taken poor Owen hostage and stolen North's horse, the girl who had turned up on his doorstep frightened and in tears and exhausted and he'd given her tea that could have felled a field ox and offered her a scone that could have felled the same ox if the tea hadn't done the job. He raced out of his bedchamber, pulling on his dressing gown as he ran.

8

H e turned the knob, slammed into the door at the same time, and
hurtled into the dark bedchamber.

"Miss Derwent-Jones—Caroline!"

He heard her breathing, harsh and deep, and he didn't think, just rushed
to the bed. There was faint moonlight coming through the far window, just a
sliver of light really, but it was enough for him to see her sitting up in bed,
stiff as the bedpost. She was staring straight ahead, seemingly at the soft
pink lacquered armoire opposite the canopied bed.

"What the hell is going on? Did you have a nightmare?"

He grabbed her without really thinking about why he did it or if it was
even necessary, for she was here, obviously frightened, breathing as if she'd
run all the way from Mount Hawke village to the castle. He pulled her
against him and held her tightly, rubbing his big hands up and down her
back, feeling the smooth softness of her beneath her clothing.

She eased against him, slipping her arms around his back, and said in a
whisper against his shoulder, "I'm glad you came bursting in here. You see,
there's someone lurking behind the armoire."

"What?"

Her mouth touched his neck. She whispered again, "There's someone behind the armoire. I think it's a man. I woke up and he was just standing there, staring down at me, breathing really hard. I screeched and he kind of gulped and hissed like a snake who knew his time was up, and ran back there."

He gently pushed her away, saying quietly, "Stay down and don't move." He rose slowly, his eyes now adjusted to the shadowed bedchamber. He looked toward the armoire. Nothing. No sign of movement. No shadow that shouldn't be there. He saw that there was space behind the armoire where someone could hide. A man? In her room? It seemed impossible, but nonetheless, he strode to the blasted armoire, grabbed the handles, and gave a violent pull. The armoire tilted toward him. He released it and watched it teeter back.

A yell. A man's yell.

"Come out, you bugger! Now, damn you!"

It wasn't a man who crawled from behind the armoire. It was Timmy, the maid, all of twelve years old, violent red hair, barely a patch of white skin showing through all the freckles on his face. Right now, he looked terrified, his mouth hanging open, ready to yell or scream or cry out in pain if the armoire were to fall on him.

North took a step back, crossed his arms over his chest, and stared down at the maid. "May I ask why you're here in a lady's bedchamber in the middle of the night?"

"I just cleaned this bedchamber, milord."

"That's very good. Why are you here now?"

Timmy the maid looked wildly about for help. There was none to be seen. He said, his eyes on his shoes, "The girl's wot's in bed over there near to broke me eardrums, milord, with 'er shrieks." He lightly hit the heel of his hand against the side of his head to emphasize his words. "Loudest shrieks I ever 'eard from a girl, near to kilt me."

"I believe I asked you a question, Timmy. Also, if she shrieked it's because you scared the blasted, er, stuffing out of her."

The boy looked up at his lordship, knew doom was near, and struggled to his feet and stared down at them. He just stood there, head down, waiting for punishment that would surely be bad, given what he'd done. Hadn't he heard enough stories about his lordship's father, that old geezer who had taken his cane to McBride's backside when he just happened to say something about the weather and that dark cloud that always seemed to mill over his lordship's head?

"I jest wanted to see 'er, milord, nuthin' more, jest see 'er. I 'eard she was purty as them fat-tailed peacocks an' I wanted to see 'er."

"You what? Good God, boy, she's just a girl, a female like any other female who lives around here. What the devil do you mean you wanted to see her? What the devil do you mean she looks like a fat-tailed peacock?"

Caroline said from just behind North, "He was standing over me, holding this candle. It was the heat from the candle that woke me up and perhaps the shadowy light."

Timmy sucked in his breath, craning around North so he could see her. "Cor'," he breathed out reverently, "I 'ad to see 'er, milord. She's so beautiful, like an angel, like a princess, like a, er, not really like a peacock's tail."

"That's quite enough," North said, sounding utterly revolted. "She's just a female, nothing at all out of the ordinary. Now, you scared the very devil out of this angel and princess and peacock's tail. What the blasted devil am I to do with you?"

"An angel, you say?" Caroline asked, crowding North out of the way.

"Aye, miss. Yer 'air's jest like spun gold, an' so bleedin' thick and smooth and jest like silk an'—"

She turned to North. "Surely what he did isn't so bad, my lord."

"You're only saying that because he's flattering you shamelessly. Angel, ha! Go look in the mirror, Caroline, you're a fright, an utter mess, your hair's about your head like sticks and hay straws and—"

"That's quite enough, North. Be quiet." She leaned toward Timmy, who, for the first time since being caught, had a gleam of hope in his very green slanted eyes. "Why did you really come in here, Timmy?"

He threw in his hand, hoping for a bit of pity from a female, for surely there wouldn't be any from his lordship. "It were Mr. Coombe, miss. I 'eard him telling Mr. Tregeagle that you 'ad a gun, that ye'd pointed the thing at 'im, shocked to 'is slippers, 'e were. My pa's gun is broke and 'e needs it when 'is snares don't work. Me brothers 'n sisters are hungry, ye see, and they need food."

"You were going to steal my pistol?"

He nodded his head.

"I see," she said. Then she shrugged and smiled. "Very well. It sounds as if your pa has far more need of it than I do. However, there is a very bad man who is going to come after me. He wants me to marry him so he can have my money. I might have to shoot him to save myself. Let me take care of him and then I will give you the gun. All right, Timmy?"

"Won't 'is lordship take care o' ye, miss? Won't 'is lordship pop the bad man's cork?"

"No, it's up to me to do any popping necessary. Now, after I take complete care of him I'll give you the gun. What do you say, Timmy?"

"Oh, miss, that's wunnerful, my pa'll be grunting with the greatness of yer beauty and yer bounty and—"

"Put a cork in it, Timmy," North said. "May I ask why you didn't come to me?"

"Mr. Coombe says we're never to bother ye, milord. Yer a lordship wot likes 'is solitude and privacy, that's wot Mr. Coombe says. Mr. Tregeagle says no one ever bothers a Nightingale gentleman, it jest ain't done. Thus, it's true. Ain't nobody to bother ye, milord. Mr. Coombe says we're all to protect ye and that means keeping meddlesome folk away from ye, like female meddlesome folk."

"I'm bothered now. Because of you I was jerked out of a very pleasant dream and forced to—"

"That's enough, my lord. Timmy has apologized. All is well now."

"Go to bed, Timmy," North said, giving it up. "You and I will speak more of this tomorrow. Good night."

Timmy nodded solemnly to North and gave Caroline a cocky smile. North said nothing until the boy had walked through the door and out of the bedchamber. He turned slowly to look down at her. "Your scream did scare the devil out of me."

"I'm sorry. Timmy nearly scared me into old age. Your hair's sticking up. It looks quite nice."

He smoothed down his hair, then said, "That's silly. Now, about you. Why, you're a bloody angel, a precious princess, your beauty makes the seas recede, you are a fat-tailed peacock, in short, a—"

She laughed, actually laughed, and lightly punched his arm. "Oh, do stop before I laugh myself silly. Goodness, what a debacle. I'm sorry for awakening you, but he did scare me quite witless." She looked down and said blankly, "You took off my boots."

"Yes, but nothing else, as you know, since you're not standing there naked as the statue in one of the east wing recesses. Timmy got closer to you than I did. Your left stocking has a hole in it and you've rubbed a blister. It doesn't look good. Do see to it in the morning."

"All right. You called me Caroline."

"Miss Derwent-Jones seemed a bit excessive when I was throwing myself headfirst into your bedchamber to save you from a dragon or a thief or that dastardly Mr. Ffalkes."

"It's all right. You can call me Caroline. I like the way you say it. It's deep and dark and really quite exciting. It thrilled me to my female toes."

"You think that, do you? Very well. Perhaps we haven't known each other all that long, but I daresay our experiences have gone a long way to breaking down formality between us. You may call me North, though you already did, didn't you?"

"North what?"

"Actually, it's Frederic North Nightingale, Baron Penrith, Viscount Chilton, nothing more really. It took my ancestors long enough to gain anything at all. When my long-ago ancestor became Viscount Chilton and built Mount Hawke, he changed the name of the village down below to that name."

"What was the name before he changed it?"

He found himself giving her a slow, drawing smile. "Would you believe it was called Pigeon's Foot?"

"No, I won't. Come, what was it?"

He just shrugged.

She looked very thoughtful for a long time. Then she looked up at him, smiled, and said, "North Nightingale. That's a lovely name. It's very romantic. Did your mother select it?"

"I strongly doubt it."

"Then your father was a romantic."

He said nothing. The silence hardened between them, not a good comfortable sort of silence, but one that was fraught with dark undercurrents. What sort of undercurrents, she had no clue. She said quickly, "Thank you for coming to my rescue so quickly. You were here in a veritable instant."

"You're welcome. Come back to bed."

He helped her climb onto the dais, then into bed. He pulled the covers to her chin, then tucked them securely around her shoulders, as if he were her father or an uncle, or someone who looked at her as one would a child. It was both galling and comforting.

"You know, Caroline, I will see that Mr. Ffalkes doesn't do foul things to your fair person."

"That's nice of you, North, but I really can see to myself. I did before and I will again."

"That's fine," he said mildly. "But don't think I'm going to walk away from you. I will continue to keep an eye out for him. He will come, you know."

A thick tendril of hair had fallen over her forehead and he smoothed it back. He lightly cupped her cheek in his palm, then smiled down at her. He then smoothed her eyebrows with his fingertips. It was soothing, it moved something deep inside her. Suddenly, without warning, she burst into tears.

North froze over her, feeling more helpless than he ever had in his life. He sat beside her, fidgeting a moment, then pulled her up against his chest. "It's all right," he said against her hair, rocking her back and forth against him. "It's going to be fine, I promise you. I didn't mean to frighten you with the talk of Ffalkes."

"No, no, it's not him," she said, her voice low and liquid with tears. "He's a worm, nothing more. I'll kill him if I have to. I'm sorry. It's when you pulled the covers up—the way you did it—it was like my mother did it. And you pushed back my hair and patted my cheek and smoothed my eyebrows.

So very long ago. When I was a little girl. So long ago." She cried harder and he just held her now, feeling the loneliness in her, and now there was more pain and tragedy she had to face. Again, she pulled back, sniffed, and said, "Forgive me for wetting you down. So silly of me. I don't cry, really, not at all, because it's a vast waste of time."

"Don't be a fool, Caroline. Tears cleanse the mind and the body and make us see the sense of things. Life is chaos, you know. It's only right that we cry now and then. It brings things back into proper perspective."

She was silent. Then she said on a sigh, "You're right. There doesn't seem to be any way to halt memories when they hit you just right. They simply overwhelm you. But still, I thank you, North."

"Are you all right now?"

"Quite all right, thank you."

This time he didn't pull the covers back up, just left them at her waist when he laid her back down again. He did, however, lightly pat her cheek; why, he didn't know.

After he had left her, closing the door quietly behind him, Caroline rose and removed her gown. It was hopelessly wrinkled and she didn't have another one. She smoothed it the best she could and laid it over the back of a chair. She lay down again on her back, her arms crossed under her head. She felt tears stinging her eyes and closed them tightly. Just the way he'd tucked those covers just under her chin, it had broken her, brought back her mother, whose face she couldn't begin to picture anymore in her mind. And those memories didn't really matter, not in the face of Aunt Ellie's murder. Who could have killed her? Nothing seemed to make any sense anymore, particularly when she was lying in bed in the house of a gentleman she'd met barely a week before.

What was she going to do?

She knew she looked a fright, but at least she was fairly clean. She'd awakened to find a bowl of still-warm water on the round commode table. She'd stripped off her underclothes and scrubbed herself. Four days without a proper bath was too many. She wished the phantom servant who'd brought the bowl had brought instead a regular tub for her to bathe in. However, after the greeting she'd been given the previous night, she supposed a bowl of warm water was quite a concession all in all.

She walked slowly down the grand staircase, wide enough for at least three ladies dressed in full regalia to walk side by side. There was an immense chandelier that hung from the floor above down two floors to come to a stop some twelve feet above the entrance hall. It looked to have quite a lot of gold in its ornately curved holders that were not only sparkling clean but held candles that gleamed so brightly they looked as if they'd even been polished.

She stopped a moment on the staircase, looking around her. It was a magnificent old house. No, rather, she supposed it was more of a castle that had been reshaped in the direction of a huge manor house over the centuries. But it was still a castle with a castle's grandeur. Its cavernous entrance hall, which must have been built many centuries before the great hall, was long and narrow, but narrow only in the sense that it wasn't as wide as an average manor house. She'd never seen its like before. She felt something quite odd as she gazed about her, a sort of recognition, a sort of wistful longing, which surely couldn't be right. She shook her head, but the feeling didn't go away as she continued looking around her.

The walls of the vast entranceway below were very nearly covered with portraits of men—no women, just men—and they seemed to stretch back well into the sixteenth century. She looked more closely. No, there were no women at all. How very odd.

Why weren't there any paintings of women? Surely women had to have given birth to all of those men, and they were, she imagined, legitimate. Surely they had lived here at least part of the time. It was very strange.

"Good morning."

Her host stood at the foot of the stairs dressed in buckskins, beautifully polished Hessians, and a white lawn shirt open at the neck and covered with a pale brown coat. For the first time she looked at him as a man and he looked quite lovely. His dark hair was long, too long for fashion, but on him, here in the wilds of Cornwall, master of a huge edifice that would be a castle until time itself came to its end, it looked just right. It surprised her to realize that he was quite handsome. It was also disconcerting. She saw him suddenly holding her while she'd cried—both times, like a blubbering ninny—then she saw him leaning over her, tucking her into bed.

"Er, hello," she said.

"Did you bathe your foot?"

"My foot? I bathed all of me, though there was but a small basin of water. Not that I'm complaining, North, it was really quite thoughtful. Was it Timmy the maid who brought me the water?"

He waved away her question. "Your stocking is torn and your foot is abraded, obviously from rubbing against your boot for many days. Did you bathe it? How bad is it?"

"Oh. It does hurt a bit. There wasn't anything I could do about it. You see, I had to leave my valise in Dorchester. What I'm wearing is all I have, torn stocking and all."

He frowned at her, saying finally, "It won't do." He turned and shouted, "Tregeagle! Come here immediately!"

He turned back to her, his frown in place, saying nothing until Tregeagle appeared. She was interested to see this housekeeper who had put her in a very nice bedchamber. When he appeared, she nearly gasped out loud. He was quite tall and quite the most beautiful older man she'd ever seen. He looked like the *beau idéal* of a grandfather: a head of full silver hair, very clear blue eyes, and a face with clean lines and angles. This lovely older man was the housekeeper? This was surely a very strange household. She said, "Thank you for my lovely room, Tregeagle. Also, I appreciated the warm water."

"It should have been hot," Tregeagle said. He bowed briefly in her general direction, then said, "My lord?"

"Bring me ointment for a raw blister and some clean cloths for bandages. And a basin of very hot water. In the library. Now."

"Yes, my lord, but it is an odd request. May I inquire—"

"No, just do it."

"Yes, my lord. Miss." He gave her but a curt nod, turned, and walked slowly and with the stateliness of a bishop toward the back of the house.

He expected her to tell him to leave her be—to turn into a horrified maiden on him—which, he supposed would be natural enough since she was young and a maiden, and she was here in his home without chaperon, but instead she said, "Your home is beautiful. It's incredible, actually. A real live castle that so many people have put their stamp on, so many changes, softening, I guess I'd say. It makes me just want to sit here on the steps and let it settle into my bones."

He merely cocked a dark brow, saying nothing.

"What is the family crest?"

"Well, it isn't a nightingale bird, if that's what you're thinking. It's two lions fighting each other with crossed swords behind them. Again, the Nightingale motto doesn't have a thing to do with any nightingale bird, rather it says simply, *Virtue appears like an oak.*"

"That's neither wildly romantic nor strikingly profound."

"I know. I'm disappointed as well. Maybe that was all my long-ago ancestor could think of when he decided he wouldn't have a thing to do with a damned nightingale bird."

"You said it was two fighting lions with crossed swords. Where's an oak?"

"In the background somewhere."

"Well, at least you've got a family crest and a motto. Indeed, you're very lucky. My home—Honeymead Manor—is quite nice, but nothing out of the ordinary, a manor house no more than sixty years old, no family crest or motto either, but here"—she drew a deep breath and looked toward the very old suit of armor that resided in the far corner next to a mammoth fireplace whose inside was black from fires at least a century old—"but here, it's magic. It's wonderful."

"Thank you."

It was her turn to frown at him, which she did.

"Ah, Tregeagle, all my doctor's implements. Ah, some bascilicum powder as well. Place them on my desk in the library, if you please. Now, Caroline, come with me."

"Caroline?" Tregeagle turned in some surprise to his master. "My lord, you called the Young Person by her first name. It's a nice name, even though it is on the common side, but it's still her given name, and thus it isn't appropriate that you make such easy use of it. She only arrived last night and she will be leaving right after she has breakfast. Surely her last name would be more appropriate."

She could but stare. As for her host, he flushed, looking ready to wrap his hands around his housekeeper's throat, but at the last moment he managed to gain control over himself. "Thank you, Tregeagle, for your observation, which was quite the thing to say if you want me to break your damned neck. Go away. See to the breakfast. Tell Polgrain we will eat in ten minutes. Ah, Tregeagle—"

"Yes, my lord?"

"Don't forget, the food will be heaven-sent."

"Yes, my lord."

She looked after the retreating housekeeper. When he'd finally seen himself out of the library, she said in some wonder to North, "He is like one of my schoolmistresses at Chudleigh's Young Ladies' Academy. She couldn't bear the girls, not really, but at least she tried to hide it just a little bit. I don't understand, North. There are no portraits of ladies. Perhaps all their portraits are kept in a special ladies' gallery, but even if that's true, it's still very strange. Another thing, all your servants are men. You told me it was a household of men last night. It's obvious they don't want any female here. Why?"

"Forget it. It's nothing to concern you. Actually it's none of your business. Now, sit down and put your left foot up on that hassock."

"I can see to my blister myself, North. It's not like it's on my back and I can't reach it."

"Be quiet and sit down."

She did. He came down on his knees in front of her, unlaced her boot and slipped it off her foot. She'd wadded a handkerchief against the side of her foot. He recognized it as one of his own, his initials elegantly embroidered on it—a gift from his old tutor—and wondered where she'd gotten it. He pulled it free of the blister. Beneath, the flesh was raw and inflamed. In his army years he'd seen too many men with such minor abrasions like this who'd died in a delirium of fever. He studied the blister. There were no angry red lines radiating out from the sore like spokes from the center of a wheel. That was something at least.

"Hold still. This won't feel all that good in the beginning." That was an understatement, she thought, as he ripped the remainder of her stocking up to her ankle and dipped her foot into the basin of hot water. She nearly rose right out of the chair.

"Hold still, the pain will lessen."

"It better," she said between gritted teeth, "else I will shriek and then your servants will doubtless come running in here and shoot me."

"No, I doubt they'd do that. Too messy, too noisy. They'd just see that you were clubbed over the head and buried in the garden."

"Wonderful," she said, and began to relax, at least until he lifted her foot again and began to wash it thoroughly. "Perhaps they'd consider just deporting me. I've always wanted to visit Botany Bay."

"Come now, Caroline, I know it hurts, just hold on a little while longer. There, all clean. Now, some of my fine French brandy—no, don't try to escape. I know it burns—"

Her fingers were white clutching the arms of the chair, her teeth gritted against the pain. She looked ready to scream, but managed instead to say calmly enough, "Burns, my lord? Let me tell you, North Nightingale, burning is but a small part of the agony. It's ghastly, it's stretching my bravery—"

"Don't whine. There, all done. Now, just a bit of the bascilicum powder."

He was gentle, she'd give him that. She hadn't realized her foot was quite so bad. She gripped the arms of the chair as hard as she could when he began to wrap her foot in some white linen strips.

"I'll never get my boot back on," she said, observing the thick white bandage covering the top half of her foot.

"No boot or slipper. Indeed, you will walk as little as possible for a good week. After you're settled in at Scrilady Hall, Dr. Treath can look at it. All right?"

She looked down at his dark head, at his equally tanned hands holding her foot. This was all very strange, she thought, wondering why, during the past minutes, she hadn't thought once of her situation, of her aunt Ellie, dead, of herself, now completely alone.

It was there, of course, and she felt that wretched bowing pain again.

"Does it still hurt?"

"No, thank you, North."

"All right," he said, rising. "Let's go have some breakfast. Then I'll take you to Scrilady Hall."

And there, she thought, she'd wait for her former guardian to come, and she knew he would come. It was obvious Mr. Ffalkes needed money badly, and she was the only pullet about for him to pluck. Yes, she'd think about him just as she would about who killed her aunt Ellie. Tears came again, stupid useless tears. She simply turned away, trying very hard not to sniff.

He said nothing, bless him, merely waited until she got control, then led her to the breakfast room. Let him think it was her foot that pained her, that was better than his pity.

9

She tried to feel just a very small pinch, just the veriest dollop of compassion for the young man who was seated before the blazing fire in the drawing room of Scrilady Hall, his head down, his hands loosely clasped together between his knees, but she couldn't find it. She drew on a sorely depleted store of patience. It wasn't easy because, truth be told, she wanted to smack him.

"Cousin Bennett," she said, limping toward him. "I know it's difficult for you. It's difficult for me as well. Come have some tea now. It will make you feel better. Mr. Brogan is here to speak to us about Aunt Ellie's will."

"Who cares about her bloody will?" Bennett said, not looking up at her. "I want to see my uncle's will. That's the important one, not *hers.*"

"Why? Your uncle died five years ago, or something like that. He left all his possessions to his wife, Aunt Eleanor."

"I don't believe it now. I never believed it. I'm his only male heir; he would have left everything to me. I know she must have changed it, hired Mr. Brogan to change it, probably became his mistress so he would do what she wanted."

Her patience was dwindling at a rapid pace. She said sharply, "If you believed that, then why didn't you act at the time?"

"I was only twenty-three when he died. Who would have believed me? I had no money, no important friends. It was that damned widow they believed. She was a strumpet, did you know that? I'll wager she even slept with Mr. Brogan, who has the look of one of those damned little Cornish piskeys—all wizened and old. I'll wager he lives in a tree trunk and not a house."

"Yes, and no doubt he thrashes corn on moonlit nights. Now, mind your tongue, Bennett. Just be quiet. Stop acting like a fool. Why are you sitting there shivering? It's not the dead of winter, it's not snowing. Goodness, it's not at all cold."

"It's cold enough in this damned savage backwater," he said, finally turning to look at her, then rising. "God, how I hate this place and all the barren savage cliffs and those wretched ugly tin mines. This is the most desolate spot on the face of the earth. I hate it, do you hear me?"

"I think it's the most beautiful place on earth, Bennett, so you see, your opinion is just one. Also, tin has been mined here for centuries, even back before the Romans came. The mines provide jobs. Stop being so critical, Bennett."

"I still don't understand what happened to your foot or how you got here or why you don't have any clothes, and why there's no female with you to act as chaperon. Another thing, Viscount Chilton brought you here. I remember he has the very devil of a reputation. Dark and brooding, like some Byronic hero, and all the local maids swooned over him, but he just looked withdrawn and mean and black-browed. How do you know him? It's all quite improper, Caroline."

"It's a very long story and doubtless it would bore you since all you want to talk about is how you think you've been cheated and how much you hate Cornwall. No, don't say any more, Bennett. Mr. Brogan is here. Shortly we'll know what's in Aunt Ellie's will. You're in it, else you wouldn't have been invited here. Come now and strive for a modicum of manners."

"Easy for you to say," he said under his breath, but she still heard him, frowned, but held her peace.

Cousin Bennett was a very handsome man who had the nicest smile, with hair as blond as an angel's and lovely eyes as blue as the heavens themselves. However, as their acquaintance had deepened the day before—it took only about thirty minutes—he began to show his true feelings, and they were angry and resentful. She looked at him now, his lower lip sullen, and wanted to kick him. For all she knew, Aunt Ellie had left him everything. After all, Caroline was already an heiress and didn't need Scrilady Hall or any more groats, and Aunt Ellie had known that.

However, it was not to be. Mr. Brogan, pale from spending too many years inside an office, patted his grizzled hair and motioned for the two of them to be seated. "Eleanor Penrose's will is quite short and to the point, at least at the beginning," he said, untying the slender ribbon and smoothing out the document. "She had me prepare this will only two years ago. After some bequests to the Penrose servants and several local charities in Trevellas, the remainder of her money goes to you, Miss Derwent-Jones, and it is a sizable amount."

"No," Bennett howled, and jumped from his chair. "All her money—my uncle's money—to Caroline? I won't accept it. I will fight this, I will—"

"Do sit down, Mr. Penrose. There is much more in Mrs. Penrose's will, but I will leave this instant if you don't control yourself."

Bennett flung himself back into the chair and looked as if he would kill both Mr. Brogan and Caroline.

"Now," Mr. Brogan said, clearing his throat, "your aunt had me write down this explanation exactly. He set his glasses on his nose, lifted the paper, and read:

My dearest niece:

I look forward to the day when you will come to Cornwall and live with me. When you become nineteen, I will come fetch you from that awful man Mr. Ffalkes. He will have no more hold over you. Together, my love, we will make Scrilady Hall a home again, filled with laughter and fun and parties. Never forget that I've loved you through the years and wanted only the best for you.

Your loving aunt
Eleanor Penrose

Caroline couldn't help it. She lowered her head and let the tears roll down her cheeks and drip on the back of her hands, clasped in her lap.

"Miss Derwent-Jones, naturally your aunt assumed you would be coming here to live with her until you married. As I said, she wrote the will when you were seventeen and she decided to write you the letter as if she would pass away at that time, because doing it that way, she told me, it would sound as if it came from her heart, which it did."

He looked up then and saw that she was crying. "Oh dear, I'm so very sorry, Miss Derwent-Jones. Forgive me. This is all such a shock for you, such a tragedy—"

"What about me?"

"Huh? Oh, Mr. Penrose. Why don't we discuss it once Miss Derwent-Jones has composed herself? This is naturally quite upsetting to her."

"Why? She's got all the money."

Caroline rubbed the back of her hand over her eyes, blew her nose on her aunt's handkerchief, and said, "It's all right, Mr. Brogan. Forgive me. It's just hearing her letter, it's like she's here, talking to me."

"I understand. Your aunt was a fine lady. You wish to continue?"

"Yes, certainly."

"Very well." Mr. Brogan set his glasses back onto his nose and perused the paper in his hands. "Now, the will becomes complicated and for the both of you, extremely unusual, perhaps startling.

"I suppose the best way to explain it is to tell you that Eleanor Penrose was a strong woman, yet a very compassionate woman, a woman who felt that money carried with it responsibilities toward those less fortunate than herself."

"I am certainly to be considered less fortunate than my uncle's blasted widow."

"Mr. Penrose, you will hold your tongue," Mr. Brogan said with unaccustomed heat. "Now, Mrs. Penrose was a lady of standing in the area, and beyond that, she had begun working many hours with young girls who had become pregnant out of wedlock. These girls had invariably been seduced or even raped by their employers or their employers' sons and thus cast out even by their own families and left with nothing. She saved them, brought them here, and put them in a small house in St. Agnes. She and Dr. Treath had become close during the past couple of years. One reason I suppose is that she brought him a steady supply of patients."

It was an attempt at a jest, and Caroline forced herself to smile. Mr. Brogan had tried. He cleared his throat and continued. "After the young girls gave birth, Eleanor would help them do whatever it was they themselves wished. If they chose to keep the children, she would see that they obtained positions that would make that possible. If not, then the children were adopted."

"What utter nonsense," Bennett Penrose said, rising to pace to and fro in front of the desk. "A pack of silly young girls who couldn't keep their legs together—what the devil does this have to do with me? With us? Seduced by their employers, you say? You mean their betters? What's wrong with that? It's their fault for getting pregnant, it's a witless thing to do. As for the rest of it, why—"

"Be quiet, Bennett," Caroline said, rising and limping to stare him right in his eyes. "You will shut your damned mouth or I will hit you, I swear it. Maybe I'll even shoot you. I'm quite a good shot, you know."

"No, don't get violent on me. Just listen, none of this has anything to do with us, Caroline."

Mr. Brogan's cheeks flushed red, but he managed to say calmly enough, "Actually it does, Mr. Bennett. Mrs. Penrose bequeathed Scrilady Hall, all the lands, the tin mines, everything, to the both of you. However—"

Bennett Penrose whirled around, quite an athletic movement for such a languid young man, his face now scarlet with rage. "What? That's just more of her bloody nonsense! She gives Caroline all the money and leaves me with half a house, half the income from the rents and the tin mines, half the servants, half of the damned furniture?"

"That's not quite right, Mr. Penrose. Actually, the two of you will be joint trustees of Scrilady Hall, the tin mines, the farms, and any other income that could accrue from other sources. Scrilady Hall will become a refuge for these young girls. Eleanor Penrose hoped you would take an interest and provide not only a home for them, but also training so they would be able to make something of themselves after they'd birthed their children. She knew there were sufficient funds for the upkeep of Scrilady Hall from the rents and the three tin mines."

Bennett Penrose could only stand there in front of the desk and stare at Mr. Brogan. He looked incredulous and revolted; he looked nearly to the point of violence. "You say that I'm to live here with Caroline and with a passel of bloody fat-bellied young girls? Common little baggages who can't speak English, are budding whores, who will whine that they'd been forced by the very gentlemen who employed them, and will drop bastards about the place? This is idiocy and my aunt must have been crazy as a loon when she prepared this damned will. I won't allow it to stand, Mr. Brogan. I'm not twenty-three anymore and without resources or friends. I will contest this absurd will."

"I'll just bet you have no more important friends now than you did when you were twenty-three."

"By God, you get everything and you have the gall to snarl at me. Damn you, Caroline, I won't put up with this, I won't."

"Do calm yourself, Mr. Penrose. This comes as something of a shock, I can see that. Be seated, sir, and remember you're a gentleman. What do you think, Miss Derwent-Jones?"

Caroline looked from Bennett's furious face to Mr. Brogan's impassive one. She knew she was red in the face, knew she wanted to smack Bennett, but she drew a deep breath and brought herself to the point of it all. She said, "I've never known a young girl who got pregnant. It must be frightening. How many pregnant girls are there currently, sir?"

"There are only three at present. They currently reside in a small cottage in St. Agnes under the nominal aegis of the vicar, Mr. Plumberry. He, er, was never very enthusiastic about your aunt's project, but I suppose he felt it his Christian duty to agree with Mrs. Penrose's scheme since he was also the recipient of a good deal of bounty himself from your aunt. I assume that the bounty assisted him in doing his duty. The girls are mightily upset by Mrs. Penrose's death. Dr. Treath tells me that one of them, only fourteen years old, hasn't stopped crying since it happened. She looked upon Eleanor Penrose as a saint."

Caroline rose slowly. She looked down at her bandaged foot, which had still throbbed when she'd poured brandy over it the previous night before she'd gone to bed. She smoothed her gown with her hands. She remembered all too starkly that awful night when Mr. Ffalkes would have raped her if she hadn't managed to get her hands free, if she hadn't managed to kick him in the groin. If he'd succeeded, why then, she could have ended up pregnant. It was a terrifying thought. Girls were very, very vulnerable, particularly comely girls in the employ of dishonorable men. Finally, she turned to Bennett Penrose and said, "Listen, Bennett, let's stop the bickering. You must agree that whatever a person wants to do with his or her money should be that person's decision. I know nothing about being a trustee to anyone, much less to girls who are in such a situation. But this is what Aunt Eleanor wanted. You and I will be in charge, Bennett. I think we should give it a try."

"You're just a bloody simpering little saint, aren't you, Caroline? Just a moment ago you were a damned shrew, squawking and railing at me. You make me ill." He gave a furious look to Mr. Brogan and strode from the drawing room.

"He isn't a very pleasant man," Mr. Brogan said as he straightened his papers. "I knew him as a boy. He hasn't improved."

"He had what I believe are called expectations, sir. Do you know, Mr. Brogan, why Aunt Eleanor left her estate in such a way?"

"I believe, Miss Derwent-Jones, that Eleanor felt Bennett could be salvaged. I strongly disagreed with her assessment, but it was a belief she held about most of her fellow men, despite the obvious rottenness of the individual under discussion. Bennett was always borrowing money from her after his uncle died, not that he ever did anything productive with any money she gave him. I think she hoped with a challenge he just might become a better person, perhaps even grow up, perhaps even learn responsibility. It probably isn't fair to you, but she thought you could be of help to Bennett, direct him, perhaps, make him do the right thing. She had a great deal of faith in you, and respect for you."

Caroline just stared at him. "But how could she possibly know that I would be willing to give it a try? How could she know that I wasn't a silly little twit who would wring her hands and whine?"

Mr. Brogan unhooked his glasses from behind his ears and polished them with his handkerchief. "She told me you had your father's sense of justice and your mother's forthrightness. She said you had your own stubborn streak that should carry you through any unpleasantness."

Caroline sighed. "I don't want to disappoint her, truly, Mr. Brogan, but this is a great responsibility and there are others involved in all this as well." She thought of Mr. Ffalkes, always in the back of her mind. She thought of Owen, then of Bennett Penrose. "Perhaps we should include ill-mannered wastrels in amongst our pregnant girls. Provide them training and counseling."

Mr. Brogan, for the very first time, actually smiled at her. "Excellent," he said. "This is just excellent."

"You think so, do you?"

Caroline convinced Mr. Brogan to remain for lunch, though when she saw what Mrs. Trebaw, the Scrilady housekeeper, brought in from the kitchen, she wasn't so certain it was such a good idea. But Mr. Brogan said, rubbing his hands together, "Ah, stargazey pie, how very delightful."

Caroline stared at the huge round pie, stared even harder at the pilchard heads sticking out of the sides, eyes open.

Mr. Brogan grinned at her. "The Cornish are a very thrifty people, Miss Derwent-Jones. It's wasteful, you see, to cover the inedible pilchard head with crust, thus they're all left to stick out. On the other hand, if one cuts off the heads, then all the oil is lost and thus doesn't soak into the meat."

She ate the crust, unable not to keep eyeing that damned pilchard head.

Dr. Treath appeared after luncheon, and Caroline, realizing quickly that Dr. Treath had been more than just a friend of her aunt's, asked him to stay. He looked at her foot, questioned her closely, then, satisfied, patted her knee and said, "Very well, I know you want to speak to Everett here. If I can be of some assistance to Ellie's niece, it would be my pleasure."

She drew a deep breath. "I need all the help I can get, Dr. Treath." She told them about Mr. Ffalkes, what he'd tried to do, how she'd taken Owen hostage and he'd been too bewildered to realize he could have ridden away at any time. She told them about North Nightingale and how he'd helped her when Owen had fallen ill at the inn in Dorchester. "Finally," she said, aware that they were staring at her as hard as she'd been staring at those glassy-eyed pilchard heads, "I don't doubt that Mr. Ffalkes will be coming here to Cornwall. He needs money. He wants mine. He said he would be able to make me marry him. I need your help, gentlemen."

There came a quiet voice from the drawing room door, "And mine as well, Caroline."

She turned, giving North a dazzling smile. She jumped up from her chair and limped over to him. If he was surprised at her enthusiastic greeting, he didn't show it. He took her hand and raised her fingers to his lips. She rushed into speech when his warm mouth touched her flesh. "Ah, North, you've come to visit. Do come in. How much did you hear me telling Mr. Brogan and Dr. Treath?"

"Enough. Well, gentlemen, what do you think? Shall we hire an assassin to go blow off Mr. Ffalkes's head?"

"Yes," said Dr. Treath. "He sounds like a thoroughly disagreeable fellow."

"I've never heard of such a thing," Mr. Brogan said. "That mangy, miserable man. To think that he was her father's cousin and look what he's tried to do."

"I should like to lock him in Mount Hawke's dungeon," Dr. Treath said. "Let him rot there for several weeks and I daresay he will learn his lesson."

"We can put Mr. Bennett Penrose with him," Mr. Brogan said. "It's possible they'd kill each other."

North assisted Caroline back to her chair. "How is your foot?"

"It's just fine, thank you."

"You did an excellent job, my boy," Dr. Treath said. "There's no more swelling and it's healing nicely now."

The three men now contemplated their hostess's bandaged foot, and Caroline, looking from one to the other, took a deep breath and said, "Mr. Brogan, would you please be my solicitor? Would you please get all my funds and trusts and whatever from Mr. Ffalkes? I'm of age now and surely I should have control of my own inheritance."

"He told you he was your trustee?"

"Yes."

"He probably lied," North said. "Don't worry, Caroline. Mr. Brogan can get everything started. Sir, if necessary, you can work with my solicitor in London. Caroline, in the meantime, you won't be alone. If Mr. Ffalkes shows his face, he'll surely be sorry for it."

"I do hope he doesn't bring poor Owen into it," she said. "Owen does mean well."

"If he does, why then, you can take him hostage again," North said. "Now, ma'am, if Dr. Treath says it's all right, I'm taking you for a ride. You look as pale as that white wall over there."

Her eyes lit up. "I'd love that. Oh dear, I don't have riding clothes."

Dr. Treath gently cleared his throat. "Your dear aunt loved to ride. Her clothes won't fit you exactly since she was larger than you are, but doubtless you can make do until you can have your clothes sent here. There's a royal blue that is beautiful, with small brass buttons on the jacket and gold epaulets on the shoulders."

She saw his eyes were misted with tears and quickly rose. "Thank you, sir. I'm sure it will fit me just fine."

It didn't, but North, who just stared at her bosom, said only, "I'd say that your aunt was a woman greatly endowed."

Then he grinned at her, and she thought him the most beautiful man in the whole world.

10

Caroline wanted to ride to St. Agnes Head. When they neared the stark sweep of land that lay between the village of St. Agnes and the high coast cliffs, she threw back her head and breathed in the salty air. It was savagely beautiful here, a place like none other she'd ever seen or imagined. She felt as if she'd come home, surely odd since she'd never before been to Cornwall, but nonetheless, she felt the mystical pull of it, the magical agelessness. She looked northward toward St. Agnes Beach, an immense half-circle of sand with barren cliffs rising above it. She thought of her aunt, who had probably ridden here so many times, admired the beauty of it, and died here, in this beautiful, uncivilized spot. She wondered what her aunt's last thoughts were, wondered if she'd fought the person who killed her. She closed her eyes a moment against the bright sunlight overhead and let the pain deep within swell and be recognized, and she let herself willingly suffer it.

Then North said in a prosaic voice, "Let's pull up here, Caroline. I don't trust the earth after that hard rain last night."

She was wearing only one riding boot, one of her aunt Ellie's, and even though the leather was soft, it still pinched her toes. Her left foot was bandaged. He took her arm and helped her to the edge of the cliff.

"Down below is a narrow ledge some two feet wide." His voice was utterly emotionless and for that she was grateful. "I had ridden here and was just standing on this spot, looking south toward St. Ives, and I happened to see this odd splash of color. I called out but there was no answer, so I climbed down and there she was."

Caroline was silent, trying to see what he had seen through his words, but she couldn't. Her aunt was dead and she would never see her again. She sighed and turned away. Suddenly there was a burst of wind that whistled through the thick rock slabs and blew her riding skirt flat against her. She turned about and let the sting of the salty air slap harshly against her face, and yet it felt deeply satisfying, the feel of the air and the sound of the waves striking hard against the barren black rocks below. She breathed in the warm scent of the heather and scurvy grass that grew in profusion amid all the barren rocks and down the cliffs, poking out in wild tufts through craggy boulders as old as the earth itself. Lower down on the cliff face grew sea lavender, orange lichen, and green algae, flourishing in the face of the spewing, turbulent sea. There was so much vibrant color, such an abundant variety of plants, so much life in this seemingly bleak and barren spot. Such a harshly stunning place. Overhead flew the beautiful sleek kittiwake, fulmars swinging into flight beside them. She fancied she saw several puffins landed on a jutting rock, nestling down into a spray of buttercups.

Such an unlikely place for violence and death.

She turned to look up at North. "What happened to her horse?"

"I don't know. I hadn't thought about it. Jesus, I'm the bloody magistrate and I didn't even think about her damned horse."

"Her horse doubtless went back to Scrilady Hall. I'll ask Robin, the head stable lad, indeed, now that I think about it, he's the only stable lad."

"I'll ask him when we return."

He sounded like an army commander, all stiff and aloof and colder than the winter wind off the Irish Sea because he'd missed something potentially important and was furious at himself because of it.

She only nodded, then said, "If she was already dead when she was pushed off the cliff, it doesn't seem possible that she would have landed on that ledge."

"I know. It took effort to grab at something to break her fall. There are several bushes protruding out of the rocks there. She must have landed on the bushes and managed to grab one."

She ran her tongue over her dry lips, trying desperately to keep hold of herself. Her aunt Ellie didn't need her weeping all over the ground; she needed someone to find out who had killed her. "That means then that she was still alive when she was pushed over and tried to save herself."

"Yes, it seems likely. But she was very weak. I don't think she suffered long, Caroline."

She was silent a moment, the words stuck in her throat. Finally, she said, "I must know, North. How did she die, exactly?"

"She was stabbed in the back."

"Who could have done such a thing? I mean, there's Mr. Ffalkes and he's a bad man, a desperate man, but even he wouldn't stab someone in the back and shove them over a cliff—that's evil, North."

"Evil," he repeated quietly. "Random evil or a great hatred or simple greed, Caroline."

"Do you think anyone could have hated my aunt that much?"

"I don't know. As for greed, you are the heir, Caroline, so that isn't the answer. You weren't here."

"Evil," she said. "Great evil."

He frowned down at her for a moment, then said, "I've hired a local man to help me. Oddly enough, he's a former pickpocket, but a smart fellow nonetheless. Sir Rafael Carstairs, a former ship captain and now a neighbor, swears by him, told me he helped him solve a mystery down near St. Austell and saved his hide as well. You'll like him—his name is Flash Savory."

"Flash, I assume, refers to the speed with which he picked pockets?"

"I would imagine so."

She looked back out over the sea. "Dr. Treath was very fond of my aunt."

"Yes, when I rode to see him immediately after I found your aunt, he was in shock, his grief palpable. I felt very sorry for him. His sister, Bess, has been taking very good care of him, I hear."

"Here's something you'll not credit. Bennett Penrose told me my aunt was a strumpet and that she'd probably even had Mr. Brogan for a lover so he'd cook up a fake will."

"A wastrel's disappointment. Do you think he'll cause trouble?"

"I don't know. Right now he simply can't credit what Aunt Eleanor has requested that he and I do together."

"And what is that?"

"We're to be the trustees of Scrilady Hall, a refuge for pregnant unwed girls."

"Oh my God." He stared down at her, both appalled and fascinated.

"Well, yes, it's difficult, but there it is. There are currently three girls in this condition, living in St. Agnes, under the vicar's eye."

"I'll wager that old fool thinks they'll go out and corrupt the village."

"I haven't yet met Mr. Plumberry. Is he truly a fool?"

"You should have heard his eulogy for your aunt. If there were ghosts, then your aunt will come back and give him endless grief. He said things like . . . 'Even though she was a lady, she was still an endearing creature. Even though she took in loose and worthless females, she still had a kindness that couldn't be dismissed.' "

"I will stuff his scepter down his throat."

To North's surprise, he laughed. "The scepter is quite large."

"It sounds like his mouth is even larger."

"I still can't get over your aunt asking you—who are barely nineteen—to be in charge of pregnant girls."

"Evidently they're not just any pregnant unwed girls. They're girls who were seduced or raped by their employers. Girls with no father or brother to protect them are very vulnerable, North. And when the family is poor, I imagine protection is but a word bandied about, with no real meaning."

"A lady surely shouldn't know this side of life."

"Why ever not? Aunt Ellie did. She helped. I'll try to help too. There's little enough any one person can do, unfortunately. I doubt I'll be able to count much on Bennett."

He sighed, raised his hand, then lowered it. "You are so very young, Caroline."

She grinned at that. "Come now, North, nineteen is a grand old age. I was told often enough by Mrs. Tailstrop—she was my nominal chaperon at Honeymead Manor—that a girl who reached my advanced years was very nearly on the shelf and it was fortunate I had money to make myself more acceptable."

"Shelf—what an odd word."

"It is, isn't it? Should I feel like a jar of preserves, perhaps? Or a poultry dish? Or perhaps an oatmeal bowl?"

"Well, forget that nonsense. You're just fine as you are, quite acceptable."

"How old are you, North?"

"Twenty-five."

"Goodness, you are indeed on that infamous shelf."

"It doesn't apply to men."

"That seems hardly fair, does it? But I suppose it does make some sense. I've noticed that men appear to need more seasoning than women do. Poor Owen, he's but two years younger than you, yet I would say he needs many more years of ripening to make him remotely acceptable. You, my lord, on the other hand, are just right."

"My seasonings are all at the right levels?"

"Yes, and like a summer peach, you're of a perfect ripeness."

He smiled at her but didn't say anything, just stood shoulder to shoulder with her and looked out over the Irish Sea for a good long time. Finally, he said, not turning to look at her, "Look to your left down the coast. That's St. Ives with all the bright cottages climbing up the cliffs and all the fishing boats there in the harbor. At low tide, the boats are sitting on wet sand. It's a strange sight. Beyond is Trevose Head. Here on the north coast, everything is rugged and savage, any trees that survive are bowed and stunted from the harsh storm winds off the Irish Sea. It's very different from the southern coast, where you can sit beneath a palm tree, enjoy a balmy breeze, and read poetry to your ladylove." He paused a moment, then said thoughtfully, "I don't recall having spoken like this to a female in a very long time. Other than exchanging inane remarks about the weather, taking her to—well, never mind that. What I mean is that somehow, for whatever reason, I seem to talk to you, and it's easy and pleasurable. Actually, I haven't smiled with a female in a very long time either. There was the Duchess, of course—she's my friend Marcus Wyndham's new wife, and a very fine woman—but even with her—" He broke off, shaking his head, obviously, at least to her, very confused and uncertain about himself. "You're different, I suppose."

"I don't understand. You never acted as though you didn't want to be around me. I thought you quite witty from the moment I met you. Then you added kindness. And you're a very handsome man, North. Don't you like women?"

He looked momentarily shocked, then realized she had no idea what she'd intimated. It didn't occur to him to soften what was the truth for him. "Women are vital, but quite unnecessary for a man's daily contentment."

"That sounded like a litany, something drummed into your head from your earliest boyhood. So you don't like women. Bennett said you have a bad reputation, that you were dark and brooding and dangerous, but still took your pleasure with local maidens whenever it pleased you to do so."

"What a fool this Penrose fellow must be. Remind me to plant my fivers squarely in his paltry mouth when I meet him. Unlike poor Owen, does this one have a chin? Just a small one, huh? Now, about women. I like women well enough. As I said, they're vital. A man must have a woman to, ah, ease himself."

"That sounds very odd, North. It sounds like you think all women are alike, that they're all interchangeable. Does that mean that I should think of you the same way I think of Mr. Ffalkes or poor Owen or that sniveling Bennett, whose character would improve if he were coshed every day?"

"It's not that you're all interchangeable, it's just that I have never before felt the need . . . Ah, enough of this, it's very improper. Now, you shouldn't even be with me since you have no chaperon. On the other hand, I would just as soon stay close until Mr. Ffalkes makes his move, and I know he will. He's a desperate man and you're the only lifeboat around to save him from his sea of debt."

"Are you dark and brooding and dangerous, North?"

"Do you think I am?"

"Yes, it's possible. You certainly do adapt to the role with ease. Bennett said you looked like a wild Byronic hero, and that's true enough. But you've been wonderful to me, so I'll accept all sides of you. If you want to go off with your hounds and brood on the moors, why, it's your business. A person should be allowed to develop like a rich tapestry with all sorts of vivid colors and different moods and settings, some harsh, some gentle."

"Perhaps," he said, looking at her closely now because no woman had ever before spoken thusly to him. Of course, he'd never before been alone so long with a woman and not making love to her. He said, "Tell me, Caroline, how do you know I have hounds? When you were with me, they were all in their enclosure. As I recall they weren't even howling at the moon."

"I overheard Mr. Tregeagle say something about their food to Mr. Polgrain. He called them 'bloody proper pigs.' "

"Ah. I guess they are. Tell me something else, Caroline. What dark secrets are you hiding?" He stared down into her open, quite lovely face, those remarkable deep-green eyes of hers, bright with humor, mischief, and intelligence. Ah, and so much curiosity and interest in everything. No, she wasn't interchangeable with any other woman, and for a brief moment it scared him quite to his toes. Then, without warning, in his mind's eye he saw his father yelling at him, his face mottled red with his fury, with his interminable impatience, his bitterness, his rage. No, he wouldn't think of his father. He raised his hand to smooth back a thick tendril of rich chestnut hair that had come loose from its coil at the back of her neck. As he tucked the hair behind her ear, he said, his voice low and dark and smooth, "No, you don't have any secrets, do you? You're open and sweet and remarkably kindhearted, given the guardian who's plagued you for how many years."

"Mr. Ffalkes was my guardian since I was eleven years old. I don't think I like to be called sweet. It sounds like a fat pug who lies about waiting to be scratched on the belly."

"You're too trusting, Caroline, out here on this windblown promontory with a black-souled devil like myself. Much too trusting. Oh damnation, give me your mouth."

He leaned down and kissed her lightly on her closed lips. She was too surprised to move, just stared up at him, her head slightly tilted to the side in question. For a moment, his fingers caressed her cheeks, her ears, her throat.

"Sorry," he said, stepping back from her. "I must contrive to remember I'm a gentleman and a gentleman doesn't take advantage of a lady."

Caroline stared up at him in blank surprise. She touched her fingertips to her mouth, now looking thoughtful. "Actually, you just took me by surprise. Perhaps you could do that again? I think it might be very nice. It might be more to my advantage than to yours."

"Stop it. Come, let's ride northward and I'll show you a hidden walkway down to the beach."

Roland Ffalkes knocked on the immense griffin-head brass knocker of Scrilady Hall at six o'clock the following evening.

Caroline was quite alone, save for two servants and Mrs. Trebaw, the housekeeper. It was Mrs. Trebaw who appeared in the doorway of the small breakfast room where Caroline was eating her dinner in isolated splendor, Bennett having ridden to Goonbell to drink himself into a stupor at Mrs. Freely's Pilchard Head Inn.

"Begging your pardon, Miss Caroline, but a Mr. Roland Ffalkes is here. He said he was your guardian and sort of your cousin and uncle, and he's most anxious to see you. Shall I show him in?"

But she didn't have to, for he'd followed her, now standing behind Mrs. Trebaw, looking confident, hale, and hearty as a stoat.

Caroline knew a moment of sheer terror. Then she slowly rose from her chair. "Mrs. Trebaw, listen to me carefully. I want you to have Robin fetch Lord Chilton right now. Don't tarry."

"Oh, I don't think that will be necessary, Mrs. Trebaw," Mr. Ffalkes said easily, coming into the breakfast room now, a comfortable smile on his mouth. "You see, dear ma'am, my ward and I have had a disagreement. I am here to mend fences, so to speak."

"How do you manage to dredge up a smile? It nearly looks sincere. Never mind. Do it, Mrs. Trebaw. This man is a criminal. He is not my guardian. Have Lord Chilton fetched immediately."

Mrs. Trebaw, looking perplexed and just a bit frightened, hurried away.

"It won't matter, Caroline," Roland Ffalkes said, looking briefly after the fleeing housekeeper. "If Lord Chilton even bothers to tear himself away from his own amusements at Mount Hawke, he will arrive only to find you gone. Are you ready, my dear?"

"Go to the devil, Mr. Ffalkes. This is my home. You will leave now. I have nothing to say to you. My solicitor will be in touch with you. You are no longer my guardian. You are nothing to me, nothing at all. No, I take that back. You are a thoroughly wretched memory. Now, get out."

He laughed and walked to the rectangular table, after quietly closing the door behind him. The room was small and square and there was no other exit. She picked up a knife beside her plate. "Keep your distance, sir, or I'll skewer you, and enjoy it immensely."

"I doubt it, Caroline. You caught me by surprise last time, but not again. Be easy, my dear. Accept me, for you really have no other choice."

She watched him calmly pull a large white handkerchief from his pocket. From his other pocket he withdrew a vial of clear liquid. She watched him liberally douse the handkerchief with the clear liquid.

She stared at that vial, the liquid within as clear as water. "What is that?"

He merely smiled at her and came around the table. "Put the knife down, Caroline."

"No, I won't. I'm not going to faint or weep. Believe me, Mr. Ffalkes, I'll stab you and I don't care if the knife isn't all that sharp. I'm very strong, I'll get it shoved in you nice and deep and then I'll turn it. Such a pity I left my pistol upstairs in my bedchamber, but this will gullet you just as well. I mean it, Mr. Ffalkes, go away from here."

He was six feet from her. He didn't pause in his confident stride toward her, the soaked handkerchief held toward her in his right hand. Suddenly, he tilted one of the heavy mahogany chairs and shoved it hard and fast, so it teetered madly, right at her. She tried to move out of the way, but it struck her arm. She grabbed her arm because the pain was numbing. In the next instant, he was on her, slamming the wet handkerchief against her face with one hand, his other hand clutching the nape of her neck, holding her still.

She felt his hot breath on her face. "That's it, my dear, struggle like a wild thing, it will go all that much faster." She tried to stab him with the knife, but the fumes, strangely sweet, were filling her nostrils, her throat, her brain. She felt herself growing faint and weak, all her coordination falling away from her. She felt floppy, her muscles lax and useless. She raised the knife, only to feel her fingers release it. She heard it drop to the wooden floor. She tried to free herself, but she couldn't. The last thing she saw was his face hard with satisfaction above hers. "Yes, that's it, Caroline. Breathe deeply. It's chloroform and it will keep you quiet for a very long time."

She tried one last time to twist away from him, but she couldn't. His face blurred above hers. She saw his smile, heard him say from a great distance, "I did wonder how long it would take before I got you alone. Not long at all."

She heard him laugh. Then she didn't hear or see anything at all.

North couldn't remember being so frightened before in his life. Treetop ate up the ground between Mount Hawke and Scrilady Hall, but he knew in his gut that Ffalkes had come because he'd been watching and had known she'd be alone, without even that idiot Bennett Penrose there to give her protection, and Penrose had been told never to leave her side if other men weren't about, namely him. He'd wanted to dine with her this evening, but one of his mares was foaling and she was having a hard time of it and he was fond of Spring Rain and so he'd remained to help her. And now this, dammit.

Caroline was tough, she was resourceful. For a girl, she was strong. He knew that, just as he knew she wouldn't faint helplessly away in the face of adversity, but he also knew that Ffalkes wouldn't take any chances with her, not this time he wouldn't. No, he'd arrived prepared and North knew in his gut that he'd succeed. His blood ran cold.

He outstripped poor Robin in a matter of minutes, his body bent low over Treetop's neck, urging his bay to go faster and faster. When he arrived at Scrilady Hall, Mrs. Trebaw was standing in the open door, wringing her hands on her black bombazine skirts, pale as a hoary frost of November.

"He took her, my lord! Beyond wicked, he is. I never would have believed it, but he came in and took her. Oh dear, oh dear, I couldn't stop him and I tried. He just shoved me out of the way."

North pulled Treetop next to the Scrilady Hall steps, but he didn't dismount. "How did he take her?"

"She could have been dead, my lord. He was carrying her and her head was flopping back over his arm. He had a carriage. I tried to stop him, my lord, please I swear that I did, but as I said, he just pushed me away and said it was none of my business. The two maids were of no help at all, hysterical, both of the silly girls. He had a man driving the carriage. They went northward, toward Newquay."

"I want you to have Robin fetch Dr. Treath as soon as he gets here and tell him the same thing you told me. Have him go to Mount Hawke and wait for me. It's all right, Mrs. Trebaw, I'll get her back."

Jesus, what if . . . No, he wouldn't let himself think about all the awful things Ffalkes could do to her. He had to turn his energies to following the quite clear carriage wheels. It had rained during the afternoon and the wheel marks were nice and deep. At least this was one advantage Ffalkes hadn't counted on him having. But he had to ride Treetop more slowly than he would have liked. Would Ffalkes rape her in the carriage? While she was unconscious? He had no doubt that somehow he'd managed to knock her out. No, she wasn't dead, that would defeat Ffalkes's purpose.

He kept his eyes on the wheel tracks. It would be dark in an hour; thank God he still had that much daylight left. Suddenly the wheel tracks veered away, going directly toward the narrow cliff road, more a path that was treacherous and surely too rutted and winding for a carriage. Something wasn't right. He stopped Treetop and dismounted. He was glad he'd stopped. It took him a while, for someone had taken a tree branch and swept it across the ground. He could almost feel the man's impatience, sweeping the branch over the hoof marks, believing it foolish and unnecessary. North looked very closely and was soon rewarded for his own diligence and the man's impatience. He saw the deep hoof marks. Three horses, one set of hooves deeper than the others, showing the horse was carrying more weight, which meant that Ffalkes was now carrying her. The bloody carriage was some sort of diversion.

Who was riding that other horse? It better not be that chinless Owen. And who was on the third horse? Doubtless both of the other horses carried hired villains, and that made North gnash his teeth with anger and worry.

He dug his heels into Treetop's belly. Within minutes, one set of horse's hooves veered away.

11

"She's waking up, guv."

"I'm relieved. I didn't know how much to give her. That damned apothecary was so drunk he didn't even realize what I was buying. I could have killed her and that would have gained me nothing at all."

"She's a purty little bite."

"She's too tall, her breasts aren't large enough, she has a bitch's mouth, but I suppose, when her mouth is properly closed, her face is all right."

"I've been awatchin' 'er breathe, guv, and 'er titties seem jest fine to me. As fer 'er face, lordie, she's a luv, and ever so soft-lookin'. Jest look at them eyebrows of 'ers, all nice and arched and dark as 'er eyelashes. Aye, guv, she's a sweet little bite."

"Shut up. I want to make that cottage before dark."

The scruffy young man with thick black eyebrows that met in a straight line over his eyes, whose name was Trimmer, shut his mouth for the simple reason that the rich old cove wot 'ired him 'ad the groats and thus the power. Poor little girl. What was he going to do with her? But Trimmer knew what he was going to do. He wondered if he would be allowed to enjoy himself with the delicious little piece after the old guv had her. But all that trouble just to plow a single female's little belly? It seemed beyond strange to Trimmer. Females could be had cheap, so why this bleedin' drama?

Caroline looked up at Roland Ffalkes's chin above the folds of his black coat and cravat. There was a tuft of whiskers he'd missed shaving. He was holding her close and she felt the smooth motion of the horse beneath her. She'd lost and she felt the return of the terror she'd felt when he'd first walked into her breakfast room.

She said very slowly, her voice and brain still slurred from the fumes from the soaked handkerchief, "Where are you taking me?"

"Ah, awake, are you? Hello, Caroline. No protector for you now, my dear. Just your dear soon-to-be husband and a very harsh young individual who won't be as kind to you as I am if provoked, so I beg you to remember your manners."

"When you're through admiring the sound of your own voice, tell me where you're taking me."

"Still so mouthy, so full of swagger so unbecoming the gentle sex. I've never understood where you got this flippancy of yours. Your father was a quiet man, albeit a man of many moods. All he needed to make him content was a cause; anything would do: the corn laws, for example, the deportation of a miserable lout who stole a loaf of bread. He loved to smash his head against what couldn't ever be changed, all in the name of justice, which has never meant anything at all. As for your mother . . . that's it, that's where you get this damnable smart mouth of yours. She always said just what she wanted to say. But she never jested, not like you do. She could hurt a man just speaking her mind. Once, she went too far and I was just showing her how much I admired her, but . . . Ah, you needn't know what she was really like. Odd, isn't it? I tried to keep you alone, isolated, if you will, after you so cleverly got yourself away from the young ladies' academy. Mrs. Tailstrop was the most witless female of the appropriate level of quality I could find to live with you and be your chaperon. I believed you'd take to Owen because there was simply no one else. But you didn't. As for this pathetic jesting of yours, Caroline, you will get over the woeful tendency once you've been my wife for a while. I suggest that you try now for a bit of conciliation. I am perfectly willing to wed you before I take you to bed and relieve you of your precious virginity. Well?"

"Where are you taking me?"

He struck her cheek with his gloved hand.

"'Ey, guv! No need to belt the little bite!"

"Shut your face, Trimmer. Now, Caroline, will you wed me now or shall I rape you until you're with child?"

"I will never marry you, Mr. Ffalkes. You're old and ugly and a thoroughly bad man." He'd loosened his hold on her when he'd slapped her. Without thought to consequences, she raised her arm and struck him as hard as she could with the side of her hand into his throat. She shoved at him, trying to unseat him. He was frantically trying to slow the horse, trying to keep her securely held, trying to catch his breath, for he couldn't seem to suck in enough air, and that was frightening. Caroline didn't stop fighting. She struck him again on his ear and she knew the pain was bad, but still he held on to her and to the horse. He couldn't yet speak, just make furious gurgling noises.

"'Ey, missie! Ye can't do that, no ye can't!"

And now she had to contend with Trimmer. She yelled at him, "I will pay you more than this miserable old man! He has nothing, indeed, he'll probably kill you rather than pay you. That's why he wants me to marry him, he—"

The butt end of the pistol struck her left temple and she crumpled inward against him.

"Did ye kill 'er, guv?"

"No, naturally not. Jesus, it hurts to talk, the damned little bitch. She'll pay for that. It's nearly dark. I have to get her to that cottage. It's just through that patch of woods there."

"She's a lady born," said Trimmer. "I do wonder where she learned to do that. Fair to poked the edge of 'er hand through yer gullet, guv."

Suddenly, a deep, very smooth voice said from behind them, "I believe I will have the pleasure of finishing the job Caroline began, Ffalkes. No, gentlemen, I suggest that neither of you move a single knuckle of any finger. Mr. Ffalkes, you will very slowly dismount and lay Caroline on the ground over there on the grass. As for you, Trimmer, throw your gun and knife on the ground—surely a creature of your ilk would have a knife. Yes, of course you do."

"Now, listen, guv, there's things to speak about 'ere, don't ye think that—"

North very calmly fired, hitting Trimmer's right wrist as he brought up the gun, gleaming silver and stark in the dull evening light, and all primed to fire. "Do as I tell you or the next bullet will be through your bloody head. Yes, that's very good. Stop yowling, Trimmer, you'll live, if you're not stupid. Now, Ffalkes, it's your turn. Slowly, man, or I'll make you very sorry."

North felt Ffalkes's rage, his utter frustration, and it pleased him no end. He held his dueling pistol directly at Ffalkes's head as he dismounted clumsily, Caroline still unconscious in his arms.

"Ease her down gently, Ffalkes."

"I'll kill you for this, Chilton."

"I hope you may try, you dishonorable bastard. I've been picturing your wrinkled throat between my hands for the past hour."

"My neck isn't wrinkled."

North merely smiled coldly at him.

Once Caroline was on the ground, North said, "Now, Ffalkes, you and I are going to a very small, very smelly, and rodent-filled gaol in Goonbell."

"Look here, Chilton, it's your word against mine. You can't do a thing to me."

"You think not? Perhaps I forgot to mention that I'm the local magistrate. I rather believed transportation to Botany Bay might be just the thing for you. Might give you some character, though you're probably too bloody old to change."

"Damn you, I'm not old! I'll have her. If you think anyone will believe her, you must be mad. She's only a female. No one believes a female. I will simply say she became hysterical, that she begged me to elope with her and I—"

North interrupted smoothly, his voice deeper, darker now, but his rage well contained. "Trimmer, ride away now, and you'll wake up in your own bed with just a bandage around your scrawny wrist. Never let me see your face again."

But Trimmer didn't move. He was holding his bloody wrist, and he was still as a fence post. "I don't think so, guv," he said finally, and he was looking behind North.

"Please, Trimmer, not that old sharper's trick."

"Ain't no trick, m'lord. Now then, ye lay that popper o' yers on the ground. Ye be all right, Mr. Ffalkes?"

Another man. The third set of tracks. North felt fury at himself for his own stupidity. He hadn't taken sufficient care. He'd underestimated Ffalkes. He had scouted for the other tracks when he'd heard them talking, but he hadn't seen them. Hell and damnation.

"I'm quite pleased to see you, Treffek," Ffalkes said, rubbing his hands together. "Now, my lord, do as he says, put your gun on the ground. Excellent. Now, let me see to my little pigeon here."

At that moment, Caroline moaned. North was off Treetop's back in an instant and on his knees beside her, drawing her up into his arms. He lowered his face until his forehead was touching hers, and said very quietly, "Caroline, I'm so sorry, so very sorry."

She just looked up at him, trying to clear her head, then she smiled and lifted her fingers to touch his mouth, his jaw, his nose, and he jerked back. "North," she said, and pressed her face against his chest.

"Thank you, my lord," Ffalkes said. "You have just given me the perfect lever. I always forget how very stubborn she is, but now it won't matter. Treffek, tie up his lordship's wrists. Trimmer, stop your moaning. When Chilton is taken care of, we'll wrap your wrist in a handkerchief. Stop your damned whining, you gutless coward."

North had no choice. He set Caroline away from him, watched her trying desperately to gain control, but he knew the blow Ffalkes had dealt her must hurt a great deal.

"You wonder, don't you, my lord," Ffalkes said, as Treffek bound North's wrists. "You wonder where he was. Well, he was guarding the cottage and we're very nearly there. The gunshot brought him. Good man, Treffek. I'll see you well rewarded for this once the bitch here is married to me.

"Now, let's get to the cottage. Is the vicar there, Treffek?"

"Aye, sir, old Mr. Barhold arrived on the meanest little donkey I've ever seen, all 'uffin' and wheezin', and complainin' louder than a stoat gettin' its throat chopped, not that he can even put one together properly—but those guineas you put in his shiny black pocket will keep his mouth saying the marriage lines."

"I won't marry you," Caroline said. "Nothing you do to me will make me marry you."

He laughed, hauled her to her feet, and threw her over his shoulder. She fainted from the pain in her head.

Caroline opened her eyes to find herself not on the ground, not in North's arms, but in a small mean room, lying on a narrow filthy cot. An elderly man with a high shrill voice was speaking to Ffalkes, or trying to, his stammer worsening as his voice rose. North was bound to a chair in a shadowed corner opposite her. The two villains were standing by the door, their guns now both pointed at North.

"S-see here," the small elderly man was saying, "this is more than h-highly ir-r-regular, sir, this is im-impossible. The young lady is u-u-unconscious! She can't even s-say her lines. This s-special li-li-license is surely in order and a pretty pence you paid the Arch-arch-archbishop of Canterbury for it, b-but the wo-woman must respond, s-she—"

"She will," Ffalkes said, striding over to the narrow, quite smelly mattress where she was lying on her back, her eyes now tightly closed. "Caroline." He lightly slapped her cheeks. "Come on now, my dear, wake up. You don't want to miss your own wedding, now do you?"

She opened her eyes, felt more clear in her thinking than she had before, knew she could bear the pain, and said quite clearly, "I won't marry you, Mr. Ffalkes. Let me go."

"It sim-sim-simply w-won't d-do," the small elderly man said.

"Shush, Caroline. That is the vicar, Mr. Barhold. You wouldn't want him to get the wrong impression." Before she could yell to the vicar, Ffalkes lightly lay his finger over her lips. "Look over there in the corner, my dear.

It's Lord Chilton, and he doesn't look any too happy, does he? Now, here is the bargain I am offering you. If you wed me, I won't kill him. If you continue refusing me, I'll have Treffek put a bullet right through his mouth. And Treffek would, Caroline. He's the biggest knave I've ever met, and believe me, I've met many in my life. Just look at those black eyes of his, all dead and empty and colder than a winter in the Highlands of Scotland. Aye, he'll do anything for a groat."

North said quite clearly, "Whatever he's telling you, Caroline, it doesn't matter. Spit in his face."

Without hesitation, she spit in Ffalkes's face.

Ffalkes drew back, so furious he wanted to kill her. He raised his fist, his eyes glittering, then slowly, slowly, he lowered his arm. "No, I shan't let you goad me, not now, not when it is nearly done." Then he smiled and rose from the narrow bed. "Trimmer, take Mr. Barhold outside for just a moment. It isn't raining and the moon is shining quite in a very romantic fashion. I'll call you when we are ready for the ceremony."

"Mr. F-Ffalkes, I-I'm n-not certain—"

"Go, Mr. Barhold. My betrothed simply doesn't quite yet understand the complete extent of her good fortune. She will, very shortly."

Ffalkes waited until Trimmer and Mr. Barhold had closed the very old and flimsy front cottage door behind them.

He looked from North back to Caroline, even as he wiped his handkerchief over his cheek. "Now, Caroline, if you willingly wed with me, Lord Chilton here goes back to Mount Hawke and to his own pursuits. If you don't willingly wed me, Treffek will kill him here and we'll bury him so he'll never be found. Didn't someone kill your dear aunt? In Lord Chilton's case, there won't even be a body for anyone to find. Don't doubt me, Caroline. I need your money badly. I will do anything to get it. Now, will you have me for your husband in exchange for Lord Chilton's life?"

She looked at North, tears filling her eyes. She said clearly, with no hesitation, "I will marry you, but first I want to see Lord Chilton freed and away from here."

"Oh no, I don't trust you enough for that, my dear girl. You will just have to have faith in me."

Then she smiled and it was a mean, very malicious smile. "Very well, Mr. Ffalkes. I will marry you. If Lord Chilton isn't freed, unharmed, you will believe that I will kill you. It won't matter if I hang for it. It certainly won't matter to you because you'll be dead and rotting, the flesh falling from your old bones. Don't think Owen will cry over your worthless carcass, because he won't."

Ffalkes wanted to say something amusing perhaps, something to let her believe he didn't believe her for an instant, because, after all, she was only a girl. He thought of that exquisitely painful hack of her hand against his throat, he thought of that blow of hers to his groin. Would she kill him if he harmed her lover? Yes, he knew in that instant that she would, and yes, he knew Chilton was her lover as well. As for Owen, certainly his son would cry over him, but not for many years, yes, long into the future, when he would finally die in his bed, all comfortable and ready. He said, "So, you've moved very quickly, Lord Chilton. You met my betrothed just weeks ago and she is already your mistress. No, I didn't believe you'd taken her at that inn in Dorchester, though you did make me doubt for a while. But since she's arrived here, things have changed, and you have nestled between her legs, haven't you? Evidently you've done it well, for her devotion to you is quite charming, don't you think? And a surprise, I must admit. She's a deceitful little piece, all full of pride and that damnable arrogance and an independent streak that isn't at all proper, yet she seems willing to give any and everything for you. Yes, it's touching."

North couldn't believe his ears. He said nothing, he was simply too stunned by what she'd said and by Ffalkes's conclusions.

Ffalkes said now to Caroline, "It doesn't appear that his lordship shares your tender feelings, my dear, but no matter, they're all one-sided; it is women, you know, who spout all that romantic drivel. Men aren't touched by such nonsense, thank the wise Lord. They do what they have to do to have a woman part her legs, but after they've relieved themselves, they then return to what's important to them. Now, let's have the ceremony."

Trimmer brought in Mr. Barhold, who was very quiet now, his head bowed.

"You call yourself a man of God?" Caroline shouted at him. "You're naught but a sniveling pathetic excuse for a worm! You're a fraud!"

Very swiftly, and with a smile on his face, Ffalkes backhanded her. "No more, my dear. No more. Treffek, move a bit closer to his lordship. Show my lovely betrothed just how close to his divine maker his lordship is if she doesn't cooperate and keep her mouth properly shut."

"You will surely pay for that, Ffalkes," North said, his voice very low and deep.

Caroline was very afraid, not for herself, but for North. But he would be all right. She knew Ffalkes believed her. If he dared harm North, she would kill him, oh indeed she would. It occurred to her then to wonder how much longer she would be a wife before Mr. Ffalkes made himself a widower. He simply couldn't afford to let her live, could he? There should have been irony there, but she couldn't find it.

"All right," she said, swinging her legs to the floor and standing.

"Ho, guv," Trimmer said from the door. "Lookee who's 'ere! It's yer dear little boy wot was sick but is all full of piss now and—"

Trimmer dropped where he'd stood, falling forward into the cottage. Owen came in behind him, a gun in his hand.

"No, Father, don't start screaming at me again. You won't do any forcing with Caroline. It's over, all over. I won't let this continue."

"Owen," his father said, walking toward his son, but Owen knew his father well. He quickly moved to stand behind the vicar. "Don't try it, Father, else I'll shoot the vicar, then there won't be anyone to force Caroline to marry you."

"I-I'm a rec-rector," Mr. Barhold managed, "n-not a vicar. The bishop d-didn't think I c-could be a-a v-vicar with my ve-ve-very slight s-s-stammer."

"Now, lookee 'ere, boy, I got his shooter on 'is lordship and—"

"Shut up, you damned fool," Caroline shouted. She was on her feet now, weaving a bit, but she was walking quickly toward North, her eyes pinning Treffek. "Don't you dare hurt him, you bloody ass. It's all over. If you have a single brain in that ugly head of yours, you'll take Trimmer and leave."

"But me shooter, and the guv there promised me five guineas! Five guineas is more than enuf money fer four pints a night fer six months!"

"I'll give you six guineas, good for at least eight months. You may accompany me back to Scrilady Hall and I will give you six guineas tonight, no waiting, no killing anyone, no nothing."

"I'll make it seven, Treffek! Keep the gun against his lordship's mouth, do you hear me? Don't listen to this idiot girl here, don't listen to my idiot son, don't—"

"Very well," North said. "Now, Treffek, if you don't put down your shooter, if you don't release me, I swear to you that not a single pint of Mrs. Freely's best Goonbell ale will swill down your throat ever again."

Treffek looked closely at North. He sighed then and let the gun hang loosely at his side. "Sorry, guv," he said to Ffalkes, "but it do seem that all be against ye. Even yer son, and the good Lord knows a son is the last to defect from 'is pa. Maybe yer not such a lovin' pa and that's the trouble. Maybe yer even a bad man like the little bite said."

"Shut up, you bloody coward!"

"Now, guv, ain't no call to be callin' me names. This lordship 'ere, 'e's not a man to go again'; 'e's a bloody military man, I can tell, and 'e's tougher than those old boots of Trimmer's. Now, miss, I'll bring poor Trimmer here back to Scrilady Hall. Eight guineas, ye say?"

"No, you thief, six guineas, one more than Ffalkes was going to pay you."

"Yer a tough little bite," Treffek said, shaking his head, but taking it in stride. "I surely do like tough little bites." He picked Trimmer off the floor and threw him over his shoulder. He gave one last look at Ffalkes and left the cottage.

Caroline quickly untied North. He rubbed his wrists to get back the feeling as he said, "Owen, you have done well. Thank you for telling me what you knew. And thank you for saving the day, for save it you certainly did."

"I had to," Owen said to North. "I just had to. You and Caroline took care of me and, well—" He turned to Caroline. "You won't take me hostage again, will you?"

"No, Owen, I will give you anything you wish. Now, North, what do we do with Mr. Ffalkes here?"

"Well, this is the very first thing—" North calmly walked to Ffalkes and sent his fist hard into his jaw. Ffalkes moaned, grabbed his jaw, and fell backward on the filthy cot. He came up again and North struck him again, much harder this time. Mr. Ffalkes fell onto his back, limp and unconscious. "Sorry, Owen, but he struck Caroline twice. Actually he deserves much more. We will talk about it. Now, the rector."

"Well, he's just a worm when all's said and done, North, but—" She looked at him, a very startled expression on her face. She weaved where she stood, clapped her hand to her head, and collapsed on the filthy wooden cottage floor.

12

"My head hurts like the very devil."

"Sorry I couldn't prevent him from slamming that pistol butt on your temple. You scared the devil out of me when you fainted again in the cottage. You weren't supposed to do that. Just one faint per injury from now on, all right? Ah, but here you are awake and clear-eyed again. Do you always bounce back, Caroline? I would that you say yes. I don't want to be scared into an old man as of yet."

She looked embarrassed that she'd fainted, and he recognized it and laughed. "Don't be a ninny. I would have probably fainted dead away myself, just not a second time. A man would never swoon a second time. Men would have more consideration for a lady's feelings." He sobered quickly enough when she said in a voice that was surely too soft and warm, "You saved me. Thank you, North."

He said nothing, just gently felt the bump above her left temple. She tried to keep the moan behind her teeth, but couldn't quite manage it. "Shush, it's all right. Now, I'm going to carry you in front of me on Treetop. Actually, it was Owen who came through for us this time. Now, we'll take Mr. Ffalkes to Mount Hawke and let my bully boys be host to your former guardian until I decide what to do with him. They might not care for females, but they detest villains. I'm just not sure that they would consider Mr. Ffalkes a villain, since he was simply trying to rid the neighborhood of a Young Female Person."

"Lie to them, then maybe Mr. Polgrain will feed him some poison."

"Seems a good idea. Or maybe Timmy the maid can visit him in the middle of the night like he did you, and scare the evil out of him."

"Or Tregeagle can put him in with the hounds."

North laughed and eased her more closely into his arms once he was on Treetop's back. "Just lie still. We'll be home soon enough. Dr. Treath will be waiting for us."

She felt the pain in her head pulling at her and couldn't say anything. She just closed her eyes and pressed her face against his chest. He'd said *home.* It sounded marvelous to her.

Owen was downstairs in the Mount Hawke library swilling brandy, wondering exactly where Tregeagle and Polgrain and Coombe had put his father for the night. Probably someplace cold and damp and nasty, with rats and no candle. North had been very angry. Owen sighed over the events of the evening. He was depressed and wondered what the hell he was going to do, both with himself and with his father. He drank more brandy. Life didn't look particularly agreeable for either his father or for him at the moment.

Coombe watched the dejected young man a moment from the open doorway, then said, "Now, sir, don't fret yourself. Lord Chilton will see that everything will be done properly. His lordship owes you a debt. He will pay it and he will pay it well. He is a Nightingale and Nightingale men always pay their debts. Don't think of those soft white birds when you think of his lordship. No, all Nightingale men are tough, no softness anywhere in them. Now, as I was saying, they do pay their debts and they do a particularly fine job paying when the debt is one of honor. His lordship's grandfather and father were particularly to be trusted when the debt was one of honor. It was the other sorts of debts, ones that involved gambling—well, that's neither here nor there, is it? Besides, they're dead now, so who's to care?"

Who indeed, Owen wondered, as he stared at Coombe and drank more brandy, his father's parting curses ringing in his brain: ungrateful, unnatural wretch, worthless, disowned. There were more names, but thankfully he'd forgotten them. He shook his head and said, "I don't know, Coombe. I don't see a neat way out of this mess."

"Trust his lordship, sir."

"Do I have a choice?"

"None at all, sir. None at all. However, his current lordship, despite his lack of proper raising by the men of the house, does seem to know his duty and carry it out with a good deal of efficiency."

"What duty?" Owen asked, but Coombe merely shook his head and looked wise.

Upstairs in the Pink Oval Room, Dr. Treath touched the bump with fingers so gentle and so knowledgeable he could probably tell her what she was thinking just by touching her head. He nodded to his sister, Bess, then looked at North. "Concussion, my lord. No laudanum as yet. Keep her awake. Now, Caroline, how many fingers do you see?"

"You're waggling three fingers, Dr. Treath, and North is looking like a black thundercloud. Also, I'm here and still have most of my wits, so you can talk to me."

"His lordship looks a bit disordered, Caroline, thus it's better if I speak to him until he has himself together again. You scared the devil out of him when you vomited."

"I know and I'm sorry for it. It was the motion of riding Treetop that made me sick. I meant to ask you to stop but there wasn't time. Did I throw up on your boots, North?"

"No, you missed my boots by a good two inches. Just lie still. Would you like some barley water?"

"Oh yes."

If Dr. Treath thought the viscount was uncommonly tender with the young lady, he didn't remark upon it. No Viscount Chilton had been tender with a young lady in all the combined local memory, both present and historic, of folk hereabout. No, Nightingale men were a breed apart. He thought briefly of the young viscount's late father and shuddered. Jesus, all of it was highly irregular. He saw her eyelashes flutter closed and said sharply, "Caroline, wake up. I'm sorry, my child, but you must fight falling asleep. How many fingers now?"

"Five. I'm very sleepy, Dr. Treath. And I'm not a child. I'm nineteen and my inheritance is mine if only Mr. Ffalkes would just admit it or if he insists on marrying me for my money, then I'll shoot him, but I don't want to. I don't want to be hanged, at least not for a long time."

"Admirable," North said. "I'll see that she stays awake. Will you stay the night, sir?"

"I can't, my lord. Mrs. Treboggan will be birthing a child tonight. It won't be an easy birth. I must be with her and do what I can. If something happens, just send one of your men to me."

Tregeagle appeared in the doorway and cleared his throat. "My lord."

"Yes, man, what is it?"

"A villainous-looking young fellow is here demanding guineas."

"Ah, Treffek. Please give him the six guineas, Tregeagle, but not one pence more, mind, else Caroline won't be pleased with you. He'll probably whine or claim that the young miss promised him at least a hundred guineas. Be firm. Six guineas."

"He's quite good, Tregeagle," Caroline said, trying to focus her fading vision on the beautiful older housekeeper. "You'd best be on your toes."

Tregeagle ignored her, saying to North, "Yes, my lord. Er, how is this Young Person feeling, this one who is again in the Pink Oval Room?"

"She will be fine."

"If I may say, my lord, it is a pity she must needs be here so soon after she was here not a long enough time ago."

Caroline moaned from the bed.

"Go away, Tregeagle."

Dr. Treath called out, "Let's talk to Polgrain, Tregeagle, about what he's to make for her to eat."

"Perhaps, Dr. Treath, the Young Person will be fit enough to return to Scrilady Hall before Mr. Polgrain must prepare nourishment."

"Unlikely. Come, Tregeagle, be a sport." Dr. Treath turned to Caroline, gently patted her cheek, and smiled. "I see much of your aunt Eleanor in you. She was a very fine lady, and so jolly and—" His eyes filmed with tears. Caroline, who was simply trying to keep her eyes open, didn't consider her words really, just said with such gentleness that it was nearly his undoing, "I'm sorry, sir. You must have loved her very much."

"I still do," Dr. Treath said.

"I do too. I only wish I could have known her as well as you did."

North sat beside her bed after Dr. Treath and his sister left, his fingertips steepled, lightly tapping his chin. "Don't go to sleep."

"I won't. You're finger-drumming, North. What are you thinking?"

"That I'm going to break Bennett Penrose's nose, the irresponsible sod."

"Let Owen do it. If I'm not wrong, I'll wager that poor Owen is currently someplace chewing his fingernails, sunk in the depths of despair."

"You think Owen could deal with Bennett?"

She was silent for a moment, then said, "Yes, I do. Owen has shown me hitherto unplumbed depths. It is gratifying since it is unexpected. I do believe I have a plan. There are details I have to sort through and my head does hurt awfully bad."

"You can solve all their problems in the morning, then."

"What are we going to do with Mr. Ffalkes?"

North sighed. "Damned if I know. I hesitate to outright kill the bounder and I know that he would never survive deportation. Let him go again? He would simply try to steal you away, come hell or Satan. I must admit to some admiration for the man. He's tenacious as a hound I had as a boy whose name was Dogged."

"You're lying, North. Dogged? For a dog?"

"No, for a hound. He never gave up, that damned hound. Just like Mr. Ffalkes. He sees you as his salvation. He's beyond reason. I don't think he'll ever back down from this. It's almost as if he believes your money should rightfully be his. Now, Caroline, how many fingers am I tapping against this manly chin of mine?"

"All of them. You have very nice hands, North."

"Thank you. Would you like some more barley water?"

"That first batch from Polgrain tasted rather awful. Do you think he poisoned it?"

"If he did, he knows I'd shoot him. I know it was bad, I tasted it. This time I had Polgrain put some honey in this batch, until I approved it."

When Owen came into the Pink Oval Room the following morning, he was shuffling, his shoulders bowed, his head down.

"Bloody goodness, Owen, straighten up. Stop looking like a defeated dog or a nobleman ready to lay his head on the French block. That's it, shoulders back. Listen, now, I need you."

That brought his head up in an instant. "You need me, Caroline?"

"I certainly needed you last night and you saved the day, why not again?"

"Well, actually, North did—"

"North tried, but it was you who saved me, and North's hide as well. Stop shaking your head. You did save both of us. Stop acting modest. It doesn't become you. Now, I have a proposition for you."

"Something to do with my father?"

"No. We will discuss what to do with your father later today. This is just you, Owen, just you. Now listen."

Two hours later at Scrilady Hall, Owen tracked down his prey, namely Bennett Penrose, in the back gentleman's smoking room. He was sitting in a very large wing chair, as unmoving as a statue. Owen strode over to him, came to a halt directly in front of him, and came right to the point, for he'd rehearsed it over and over all the way from Mount Hawke.

"You shouldn't have left Caroline alone, Penrose. You were a fool and she could have been forced to marry my father."

Bennett Penrose had a hangover that could have felled a bull. He heard the man's words, but all he could do was moan and hold himself very still, and wish the fellow would go away.

"I repeat—"

Bennett raised his head, giving the man a pained look. He wasn't much of a man, no more really than a barely grown lad, no older than he had been when his uncle had died and he hadn't gotten any of his money. However, the fellow didn't look as if he were in a hurry to leave. He gave it up and said, "Don't bother repeating anything. Caroline can take care of herself. She is all right, isn't she, despite all that foolishness Mrs. Trebaw was whining about to me last night? Jesus, that damned girl gets herself into more trouble than I do, and that's saying a lot. Besides, she cheated me, so why should I care what happens to her? I am not her keeper, indeed, I am the keeper for three pregnant girls, curses on all their heads. By the way, who the devil are you?"

"I'm Caroline's cousin, Owen Ffalkes. I'm not my father's son. Well, I am but I don't want to marry Caroline. I will live here. I am her partner in administering the Penrose estate, and the tin mines, and in being a trustee to all the unfortunate females who will be shortly arriving."

Bennett moaned loudly. "Oh God, I can't take it. You've joined forces with Caroline?"

"Yes, I have. Leave if you don't like it. You will either help or you will take yourself off."

"You, my lad, have no say about anything." Bennett's hangover was receding as his anger rose. "Her damned aunt did this to me and now Caroline will follow in her footsteps. I've been cheated out of Scrilady Hall and all its rents. I don't even get a pence from any of the tin mines. It isn't fair. I was cheated. I won't have it. Just maybe what happened to Aunt Eleanor will happen to Caroline. Yes, that sounds just exactly right. I wouldn't mind seeing the little cheat who acts like a bloody saint on that cliff edge."

Owen, to his later disbelief and pride, leaned over Bennett Penrose, grabbed him by his loosely tied cravat, hauled him to his shaky feet, and planted his fist into his mouth. Bennett went limply to the floor. "If you speak like that again, I will throw you through the window. The bay window in the drawing room at the front of the hall."

Bennett didn't move, but he did manage to say through his sore mouth, "You will be sorry for that, you mangy little bastard."

"I'm not a bastard. Just ask my father. No, perhaps you'd best not. He's not particularly pleased with me at the moment. Indeed, I doubt he'll ever be pleased with me again. I've told you what's going to happen and now I must return to Mount Hawke. Oh dear, my father. It's all rather too much."

Owen made his way, shaking his head, past Mrs. Trebaw, out the quite lovely front door of Scrilady Hall.

"You are moving in, Mr. Ffalkes?"

Owen gave her a distracted nod. "Yes, probably tomorrow."

"And that horrid man who is your father?"

"Oh no, just I will be coming."

"And Miss Caroline?"

"She's still in bed; my father struck her on the head, but she'll probably be home shortly."

"It isn't good, sir, and you tell her that. Mount Hawke is a *man's* residence. No women have been allowed there forever and ever. She's there with no chaperon and she's a young lady. You speak to her, Mr. Ffalkes, yes, you speak to her and bring her home, else she'll be quite ruined. To a Nightingale man, ruining a lady doesn't mean anything, you tell her that."

"North isn't like that, Mrs. Trebaw."

She harrumphed. "That remains to be seen. But I doubt it. He's still a Nightingale man and they've all been alike forever and ever."

"I will tell her what you've said, but she will do just as she pleases; she always does."

"So did her aunt Eleanor," Mrs. Trebaw said, and sighed. "Do your best. Tell her the Nightingale men aren't to be trusted. Black-hearted devils, every last one of them. You wouldn't believe what the current viscount's father and grandfather did, but that's not important right now. Poor little girl." She shook her head and walked back into Scrilady Hall.

He didn't mean to do it, he really didn't, but she was lying there sleeping, looking so soft and inviting, that he simply didn't think, just sat down on the bed beside her, leaned down, and began kissing her. She had the softest mouth, he thought, just lightly running his tongue over her lips. So very soft and warm and . . .

Her mouth opened and North knew he had to stop, he simply had to while he could. Nightingale men were passionate, impatient, and a female couldn't stop them even if she wanted to once their lust was stirred, as his was right now with naught but a few kisses from a sleeping girl. Except now she wasn't asleep, her lips were parted, and she was kissing him back and it was beyond anything he could have imagined, beyond what he ever wanted to imagine, and thus refused to.

"No," he said into her warm mouth, and with the greatest effort imaginable, he pulled himself back. He just stared down at her, his eyes nearly black in his hunger, his hands fisting, then opening, again and again at his sides, to keep them off her.

"No," he said again, and he rose, stepping back from the bed where she was lying on her back, her breasts heaving slightly, from what, he wondered, and she was looking at him, and it was a wonderful look she was looking.

"That was nice, North," she said, and smiled at him. "I'm glad I woke up in time to kiss you back." She ran her fingertips over her lips and he just stared at those fingers and her lips and thought he'd die.

"You have the greenest eyes," he said, not meaning to but doing it nonetheless. "I thought they were kind of a gray-green, but that's not true. They're green, not hazel, but pure green. It's a nice color, like that hawthorn scrub that grows over near St. Erth."

"Thank you. Perhaps you could take me there and show me this scrub grass. Perhaps you could kiss me again, North. Perhaps my eyes will change color again."

He wasn't stupid. He took another step back. "No. Forgive me for attacking you and you were asleep, thus unable to say yea or nay."

"Yea."

"Be quiet, Caroline. You're still half asleep and don't know what you're saying."

"But I do know what I'm feeling and it's very nice. No one has ever kissed me before, North, just you. I never thought a man would stick his tongue into a woman's mouth. Is it the thing to do? Do all men do it?"

He stared at her, fascinated. "Yes."

"And you were licking my lips, like I was a good meal. It was quite enjoyable once I realized what was happening."

"Be quiet."

"Why? Can't I tell you what I wish?"

He shook his head. "Yes, certainly. But know that when it all comes down to what is proper and what isn't, I am still a man and you're still an unmarried, unchaperoned girl. You're in my house, under my protection. I will try my damnedest not to touch you again."

She sighed, looking more frustrated than North's Portuguese mistress had when he'd smiled blissfully up at her then fallen into an exhausted stupor after only an hour or two of the most perverse, enjoyable sex games he'd ever played in his life.

"You're a hard man, North Nightingale."

"You have no idea," he said, and turned away to sit down in a stiff-backed lady's chair from the previous century that groaned under his weight. "Now, how do you feel?"

She realized he had himself well away from her now. For the moment she would just have to accept it. When she had her full strength back again, he wouldn't get away from her so easily. She understood his gentleman's code. She was in his house, under his protection. He was being noble. She would allow him his spate of nobility, at least for the moment, at least until her head didn't feel like it would split from her neck. "I feel better than I did last night. Has Owen returned from Scrilady Hall yet?"

North grinned. "Not yet. I very much like your idea. You told me that Owen needed to get out from under his father's thumb. I'm wagering that his first thumbless assignment will be a success. Just consider his adversary."

She giggled, such a surprise and so very sweet. It locked his knees together. He tried not to respond to that giggle, but he did. He picked up a newspaper from the table beside the chair and read the same sentence five times.

"What are we going to do about Mr. Ffalkes?"

He slowly lowered the *Gazette*. "I've given this a lot of thought, sorted through every pro and con I can come up with." He drew a deep breath. "I think I'm going to have to kill him, Caroline."

To his utter astonishment, she said, "Oh dear, I was afraid of that. No, North, that isn't right. If he's to be killed, then I will do it. He's my problem, not yours."

North rose and began to pace. "Hell and damnation, you're a woman and you didn't shriek or clasp your hand to your palpitating bosom or whimper that killing is awful, and I'd go to the devil. No, you just said you'd do it. It's difficult for me, Caroline, to hear a female speak like that. The Duchess, maybe, but she has Marcus to contend with and he is a handful and a bastard and she loves him to distraction."

"You've said a lot there. Tell me, why is it difficult to hear a female speak like that, North? Like a man? Like a logical person? Isn't a woman allowed to be logical, to think things through and come up with solutions?"

He nodded and said, "No, it's outside anyone's experience. It isn't done. You're not what you should be, Caroline. Now, listen to me, and stop all this blather. Men don't necessarily like the thought of killing. Indeed, I hate the thought of killing a man just because he's so bloody stupid and stubborn and desperate. If you were only married, then Ffalkes couldn't—" He stopped, stared at her, an appalled look on his face, then, without another word, strode from her bedchamber, closing the door very quietly behind him.

"It's a wonderful idea," she whispered to the room with its early afternoon shadows beginning to gather in the corners.

It was five o'clock that same afternoon when Tregeagle admitted himself after three brief knocks and two long ones, the most warning, Caroline supposed, that she would ever get. He was carrying a heavy volume bound in dark brown moroccan leather. He brought it to the bed and very gently lowered it onto the cover beside her. It looked to weigh both their weights together.

Caroline eyed the tome, then eyed Tregeagle. "What is it? All the historical reasons why Young Female Persons shouldn't ever stay more than ten minutes at Mount Hawke?"

"Ten minutes pushes it," Tregeagle said, his eyes going to a spot beyond her right shoulder.

"What is this book?"

"His lordship thought you might be bored with your forced inactivity. He didn't wish to spend any more time with you, which is understandable since he's a Nightingale man. Thus, he asked me to fetch you up a book that might amuse you. This is what I have fetched. It is something in the way of a legend long in the keeping of the Nightingale family. All nonsense, of course, but perhaps it will pass the time until you are fit enough to take your leave of this residence."

"Thank you, Tregeagle. What is it?"

"Why, it's about King Mark of Cornwall and how he was buried here on Nightingale land with all sorts of treasure, and not in the south at Fowey, where most believe he lived and fought and died."

"What do you believe, Tregeagle?"

"Many Nightingale ancestors have been of a fanciful turn of mind."

"Including his current lordship?"

"His current lordship is too young and too long away from his home for me to yet cast a judgment. His years in the army doubtless affected his fancifulness. One will see in due time. At least he is now showing the good Nightingale sense to stay away from you, a female, who just happens, unfortunately, to be in his house."

"King Mark is very romantic. I know all about the legend."

He gave her a disgusted look. "Young Female Persons seem to think so. I do believe, though, that the Nightingale ancestors have felt drawn to the poor king since he was betrayed by his queen Isolde and his beloved nephew Tristan—" Tregeagle coughed behind a hastily raised hand and shook his head. "Read the entries, if it pleases you to do so. If I may add, you are looking quite fit, miss. Perhaps after a nourishing pilchard-head soup for your dinner, you will wish to take your leave on the morrow."

"Pilchard-head soup, you say, Tregeagle?"

He nodded, his chin going up.

"How very thoughtful of Polgrain. How did he know that was my favorite dish? Cook at Scrilady Hall introduced me to the delicious concoction. His lordship must have mentioned it to him. Thank him, Tregeagle. Goodness, with pilchard-head soup, I just might never leave Mount Hawke. Such an unexpected treat. I believe I feel a bit faint and weak just contemplating it."

Caroline touched her palm to her brow and tried to look frail and pale.

"Ah, but my poor head is beginning to pain me again. The weakness of limb, the frailty of my delicate constitution, the innate delicacy of my female person, why, it's positively——" She stopped at that for Tregeagle had turned remarkably pale.

He said, a guard to a prisoner who surely shouldn't be there, "I will leave you now, miss. Regain your strength. Perhaps you should walk a bit around the chamber. Perhaps you should sleep rather than engross yourself in that magnificent and interesting volume that is really drivel. King Mark indeed, sending his wretched nephew Tristan to Ireland to fetch him his wife, Isolde, who was a perfidious female as all females are, and just look what happened. The two of them drank a love potion prepared by Isolde's maid Brangien that had been intended for King Mark and his beautiful bride, and just see what came to pass. The nephew and his wife betrayed him and it is recorded that Isolde killed her maid so she wouldn't tell the king what had happened. Damnable betrayal, all of it. And that dear King Mark, he let them go. He didn't behead them or tear out their fingernails and break their bones—no, the precious noble king let them go, damned idiot."

"Yes, I suppose he was a fool, wasn't he? A real fool with no sense of justice."

He left quickly, giving her a ferocious frown, at a loss for words, for which she was justifiably proud, and she was left there grinning from ear to ear.

13

"Caroline, this is Flash Savory, the young man I told you about who helped Rafael Carstairs with some trouble down St. Austell way."

"Hello, Miss Caroline," Flash Savory said, and stuck out his hand.

He was a handsome young man, all golden, slender, and smiling. She found herself looking at his hand closely before shaking it. "Are you right-handed or left-handed, Mr. Savory, or both?"

He grinned down at her. "Both."

"Ah, that's fortunate. Either pocket, with incredible speed, I'd wager."

"Aye, true enough," he said cheerfully. "It was before the captain caught me with my fingers in his left pocket, and me with my fast left hand. Near to broke my wrist, he did, but now I'm as honest as that poor dead pilchard whose head is floating in that bowl and is fair to turning my stomach. Is that intended to be a special treat for your guests, Miss Caroline?"

Caroline shuddered.

"Dare I ask if you ate the rest of that pilchard, Caroline?" North asked, staring down at the fish head.

"The napkin must have slipped," Caroline said, and hastily covered the remains again. She'd grossly underestimated Polgrain or Tregeagle or

Coombe, or more likely, all of those female-hating fellows. Tregeagle had positively beamed at her when he'd brought the soup to her and lifted the silver lid for her inspection. It had been close, but she hadn't gagged, at least not in front of Tregeagle.

"Why would someone give you a pilchard broth?" Flash asked. "Are you bilious?"

"No, I don't believe so. However, there are some gentlemen who believe culinary torture just might relieve them of an unwanted presence, namely a female presence, namely me."

She smiled at North as she spoke, but he was frowning down at that damned bowl, now thankfully covered, then toward the door.

"North, is Flash here to discuss what happened to Aunt Eleanor?" It got North's attention off his minions, at least for the moment.

"Yes," he said. "I thought you might be studying your toenails by now in your boredom. I've told Flash everything I know. Now it's your turn."

He and Flash Savory sat near her bed. Flash gave her a white smile that would melt a maiden's objections quickly, Caroline thought, wanting just for an instant to smile back, but not being able to do it because she was hungry and she was also thinking of her aunt and how she hadn't been here to help her. No one had been, except the person who had hated her so much as to stab her in the back.

"I don't know anything, Flash. I wasn't here. I hadn't seen my aunt Eleanor for nearly three years. North took me to St. Agnes Head, to the spot where she was stabbed and pushed over the cliff. Did you discover what happened to her horse?"

"Yes," North said. "I checked with Robin at Scrilady Hall. It seems her horse never left the stable, so obviously she wasn't out riding and didn't meet her killer that way." He fidgeted a moment, then said, "I hadn't realized when I found your aunt that she wasn't wearing a riding habit, Caroline. I just didn't think of it. She was wearing a blue gown, but I just didn't make the connection in my mind that she wouldn't wear a gown out riding. Damnation, I was a damned man with no sense at all."

"I strongly doubt the fact that she was or wasn't riding her horse makes any difference, North."

"That's right, my lord," Flash said, nodding. "No use you batting yourself on the head. Miss Caroline is right. It makes no difference. Now, it seems to me that there are several possibilities that present themselves. The dear lady could have been in a carriage or gig with someone, and if that's the case it was most likely with someone she knew."

North said, "Yes, that's a strong possibility. I did speak to Mrs. Trebaw about the day I found your aunt, Caroline. She said Mrs. Penrose went riding every afternoon, just like clockwork. After you and I discussed her horse, Caroline, I spoke to her again, telling her that your aunt's horse hadn't left the stable. It seems then that your aunt must have gone for a walk that afternoon. She was fond of walking, Mrs. Trebaw said, and she went for walks like clockwork, if she wasn't riding, that is. As to someone coming to Scrilady Hall and taking her for a ride in a carriage, she just doesn't remember. It appears that's something she didn't do like clockwork. When you go back to Scrilady Hall, you should speak to her again, perhaps several more times, try to jog her memory. Also, once you're back at the hall and the mistress there, you will automatically have the confidence of the other servants, who wouldn't even look me in the face, just stood there, shuffling their feet and saying they didn't know anything."

"Nothing unusual in that," Flash said matter-of-factly. "Servants have to be very careful about whose bread they're seen buttering."

"I will," Caroline said. "So it seems that Aunt Eleanor met someone away from Scrilady Hall."

"Or she was going for a walk and was abducted by a stranger," North said. "But more likely, by someone she knew. Someone she liked, someone she trusted."

"Lots of possibilities," Flash agreed. "As I said. However, I now know lots of bully boys in Goonbell and Mount Hawke and Trevellas. I'll start nosing about, all subtle like, you know. The captain says I'm a quiet one with big ears, when it suits me to be so." He leaned toward the bed, his hands clasped between his knees. "Miss Caroline, do you think young Bennett Penrose could have killed your aunt?"

This was serious, dead serious. "I don't know. When I first met him I just saw him as a sulky little boy with a nasty mouth and no spine, although he's not a boy at all. He's really twenty-eight. I just don't know, Flash. When Mr. Brogan read her will, I know Bennett was furious at how things had been left. He was accusing Mr. Brogan of fakery, of being Aunt Eleanor's lover, of cooking up evil plots and vile things. To answer your question, I think he could, yes. His is not an admirable character."

"That's a good start, Flash. Find out where Mr. Bennett Penrose was when Eleanor Penrose was killed. If he was here in the area, then he goes to the head of the list and I will take great personal pleasure in sticking my face in his."

"If she was killed because of money," Caroline said, "then I should be there."

"You would be," North said coolly, "if you'd been in the neighborhood, but you weren't. I already mentioned that to you, but you were a bit under the weather at the time, as I recall." He rose. "Now, Caroline, I will speak personally to Polgrain and make certain he delivers you a dinner that won't frighten off your guests unless it's covered with a napkin. I'm sorry this happened, not surprised, but sorry."

She managed to smile despite the headache that was growing stronger by the moment. "It's all right, North. I find I'm looking forward to what your men will do next. I admire ingenuity and they've lots of it." She sighed. "I just wish there weren't malice in there as well."

"I say," Flash said. "What is that huge tome? The Nightingale family Bible, my lord?"

North was frowning at the massive tome. "No. What is it, Caroline?"

"It's your ancestors' writings on the belief that King Mark lived and died here at Mount Hawke and not at Fowey. I just started it. The first notes are by the fifth Baron Hawke, Donniger George Nightingale, who was also the first Viscount Chilton. He wrote his opinions back in the beginning of the last century. That would make him your great-grandfather, wouldn't it?"

"Yes, he was the first Viscount Chilton." North picked up the heavy volume and began paging through it. "I had no idea Great-Grandfather was such a lover of myth. He's written nearly half of this, and it's all in journal entries, something like a diary. Listen to this: 'Over near the abandoned Wheal Weffel, my young dairymaid Barney found a piece of gold jewelry wrapped in a faded and crumbling piece of brilliant gold cloth. He brought it to me, holding it as carefully as a father would his baby boy. It was a gold armlet, very, very old, and on it was etched *REX*. It belonged to King Mark, of that I'm certain. I will keep it safe for all eternity, and when I find his burial place here on Nightingale land, I will reunite it with that blessed noble king.' " North looked up. "Very interesting. Where the devil is this gold armlet that Great-Grandfather planned to keep for all eternity? I've never heard about it, never seen it."

"A dairymaid named Barney?" Flash said, laughing. "And your great-grandfather likened the boy's reverence to a father holding his baby boy? That sounds rather odd, my lord. However, I would like to see that gold armlet. I wonder how much I could sell it for in London."

Caroline laughed. "A goodly amount, I'd say. Oh yes, now there's a maid named Timmy. This is a house of men, and evidently it's been that way for many, many years. You're safe, Flash, you don't have to worry about being poisoned or terrified out of your wits on a dark night; you're the right sex."

She turned back to North, who was frowning over that huge book that his great-grandfather had filled with an alarming number of pages. She said, "If you're interested, I'll give you reports."

"I remember now," North said slowly, staring down at that huge book. "My father spoke of this when I was a small boy. He told me stories of King Mark to send me off to sleep at night, stories of how if men couldn't trust their beloved nephews, probably their best friends and their brothers as well, then civilization would crumble." He riffled through the rest of the pages. "It appears that my father wrote only an odd dozen pages. Tell me if he says anything earth-shattering, Caroline."

She nodded.

"I should prefer believing King Arthur was buried here," Flash said, peering over North's shoulder at the thick tome. "He was surely a more dashing fellow, more famous, what with old Merlin, and his round table and all. Just think, the Holy Grail could be buried on Nightingale land."

"You're right," Caroline said. "King Arthur is much more romantic. Not all that many people even know about poor old King Mark. What is this, North? You're looking skeptical. You're young enough to be converted. Perhaps in your doddering years you, too, will write about poor old Mark and how he's buried twenty feet beneath the apple trees down the east slope." She'd looked briefly through the immense number of journal entries, the philosophic meanderings, the occasional map and offered proof of King Mark's presence here, and had seen immediately that no women had penned a word or offered an idea about Arthur or anyone else. Of course, not many women were given credit for ever having an idea. Or, in the case of the Nightingales, the misogyny obviously went deeper, it had to go deeper, witness the aversion in which Coombe, Tregeagle, and Polgrain held her. As there were no portraits of a single woman she'd seen here at Mount Hawke, there were no writings either. Why? What the devil had happened? Of course it had something to do with betrayal. By North's great-grandmother? Goodness, if that were true, the Nightingale men had very, very long memories.

She looked up to see Flash studying her closely. "Do I still have the shadow of the pilchard head on my chin?"

"Oh no, Miss Caroline. Actually, I was thinking that the captain's wife, Lady Victoria, would enjoy meeting you. She gives the captain, er, Sir Rafael, fits, makes him yowl with rage, and he quite enjoys it."

"I should like to meet her," she said with little enthusiasm. She had more on her plate now than a vicar had on his collection plate in a church full of converts.

"Caroline," North said. "Flash will get on with it now and I'll see that your stomach doesn't shrivel into dust. I won't be long."

It wasn't Coombe or Polgrain or Tregeagle who delivered her dinner. It was North himself and it was obvious that he had overseen the preparation. There was enough baked pork for a good dozen feasters and at least a half-dozen other dishes, all covered with highly polished silver domes.

"Eat," he said, and sat down in his chair beside her bed. He waited until she'd forked some of the delicious flaky pork into her mouth before he said, "Rafael Carstairs was a ship captain, a spy, really, for our war office, doing all the harm he could to Napoleon on the seas. When he came home after it became known who he really was and what he was really doing, he was asked to destroy a revived Hell-fire club. You know the sort of thing— young men debauching to their hearts' content. He did destroy the club and was then knighted. He's an identical twin, and his brother is Baron Drago, and therein lies a tale for a long winter night. As for Rafael, however, Flash still calls him Captain. He's helping me with the tin mines here at Mount Hawke. Wheal David in particular needs many repairs. There's flooding from God knows where and I don't know what equipment I need to buy to stop it or where the flooding is even coming from. It's strange; it's very near to one of yours: Wheal Kitty, which is running smoothly as a damned carriage with new wheels."

"I've only spoken to my manager once, but he seems competent. His name is Mr. Peetree. Why don't you speak to him and see what he has to say?" North nodded and she forked down another bite of the most delicious buttery boiled potatoes. But she wondered about her own tin mines. Mr. Peetree had told her everything was dandy, but on the other hand, she was a female and thus perhaps he didn't believe her capable of understanding any problems the mines might be having. She frowned, resolving to speak to Mr. Peetree again.

"What are you frowning about? Does your head hurt?"

"Oh no, I was just remembering that I'm a female."

"Surely it can't be all that difficult to keep in mind."

She laughed. "You'd be surprised. Really, I was just now wondering if perhaps there are problems in my own tin mines from which Mr. Peetree is protecting me."

"If he has half a brain, he isn't."

"Thank you," she said, reached out her hand, saw him frown at it, and drew it back.

He kept frowning, down at his boots now. "Rafael Carstairs seems to love his wife. I heard them laughing when I was still outside. Then I saw him kissing her."

She swallowed, cocking her head to the side in question. "Why ever shouldn't he love his wife?"

North merely shrugged and looked put out with himself for having said anything. "Nothing. She's a woman, pretty, I suppose, but nothing out of the ordinary."

"Well, her captain obviously thinks her beyond the ordinary." She pushed a pile of peas into a small mound of potatoes and began mixing them together, saying, "Have you ever thought a woman beyond the ordinary, North?"

"No."

"You're very young yet, and a man. Perhaps you do need seasoning, perhaps even more ripening, before you're able to attach yourself properly to a lady."

"Perhaps, but doubtful. Is that what you believe Rafael Carstairs has done? Attached himself?"

"It sounds like it, according to Flash Savory. They sound as if they're much in love."

North grunted, saying only, "They probably haven't been married all that long."

"Not only are you not ripe, you're a cynic. It doesn't become you, North."

He only shrugged. "Your pregnant girls will be arriving at Scrilady Hall tomorrow."

"Coward," she said under her breath but not under enough. However, he didn't say anything. "Oh dear," she added, choking on the tender bite of baked pheasant she'd just swallowed. "My pregnant girls. Oh dear." She grabbed for a glass of water and drank deeply. She managed to catch her breath and wheeze out, "Oh, goodness, I must be there, North. I am feeling fine. Another night in this magnificent bed will see me fit as Mrs. Tailstrop's pug, Lucy, a repellent animal but healthy nonetheless."

"I'll have Dr. Treath come and check you over tomorrow morning."

"No, truly, I'm fine, North." She gave him a crooked smile. "Besides, all your male minions will be so happy to see the back of my skirts, they're likely to dance the waltz in the entrance hall. It's a sight I don't want to miss."

"It's possible. Very well, I'll see you home tomorrow morning."

"North?"

He turned and raised a dark eyebrow. His shining dark hair swung over his brow and onto his cheek and he looked as dangerous and brooding and as utterly fascinating as any gothic hero could ever look.

He looked magnificent and she said, "Perhaps you'd like to kiss me good night?"

14

H e flinched as if he'd been struck. The dark brooding hero was gone. In his place was a man who wanted to take flight immediately. He looked panicked. "No," he said. However, after just a moment of hesitation he quickly walked back to her. He leaned over, lightly took her chin in his palm, and brought her face upward. "Damnation," he said, his warm breath touching her flesh, "your mouth is delicious and soft and—" He kissed her then, teasing her with his tongue, caressing her mouth with his, lightly nipping at her lips, then licking where he'd nipped. He took her face between both his hands and sat down beside her. "This isn't a good idea," he said, and began kissing her again. "It's a wretched idea. Any idea that feels like this has to be not only bad, but dangerous as the Devil's right hand." His tongue glided over her bottom lip and the pressure deepened. She parted her lips to him and felt a jolt of sharp pleasure at the taste and feel of him in her mouth.

"Oh goodness," she said, then wrapped her arms around his back, pulling him down with all her strength.

He did try, he truly did, to pull himself off her, but before he knew it, he was lying his full length on top of her and he could feel her belly beneath him through the covers and her nightgown.

He was pushing at her, not meaning to, but unable to stop himself. His mouth was more insistent now and his hand went unerringly to her breast. It was the touch of her soft flesh through the light lawn nightgown, her woman's flesh fitting so perfectly into his hand that made him very nearly leap off the bed. He stood there over her, panting hard, his eyes nearly crossed with lust, knowing that if she weren't so damned innocent she'd look at him and see how desperately he wanted her, to take her now, with no more of kissing or caressing, just thrust himself into her and feel her closing around him and knowing, simply knowing, that it would be unlike anything he'd ever known in his life.

"You're leaving in the morning," he said, panting as if he'd just run a mile. "You must. I can't take this, I simply can't."

He strode away from her, not pausing even when she called out, "You're being a coward again, North. A bloody coward."

He slammed the door behind him.

Both Dr. Treath and his sister, Bess Treath, visited Caroline again the following morning. As before, Miss Treath sat off to one side, ready to assist her brother should he ask her to. He sat down beside Caroline, took her wrist between his fingers, and looked at his pocket watch.

"Excellent," he said after a bit. "Normal as can be. Let me see your eyes." He leaned closer and she felt his breath on her face, warm and minty. It didn't do at all what North's breath did to her. She just wished he'd finish. She closed her eyes then as he felt the bump on her head.

"That's going down as well. Do you have a headache this morning?"

"Oh no. I feel fine, truly."

She felt his hands lightly skimming over her throat to her shoulders. He leaned against her chest, listening to her heart.

"She looks fit, Benjamin."

Caroline opened her eyes to see Bess Treath standing over her next to her brother.

Dr. Treath smiled down at her, taking her hand in his as he did so. He squeezed her fingers. "She has the look of Eleanor, doesn't she, Bess?"

"Perhaps a bit. There's a goodly dollop of deviltry in those green eyes of hers, but Eleanor was different, so filled with fun and laughter and so very beautiful. Caroline will have to grow into her kind of beauty. Let her be herself."

Dr. Treath smiled. "She does have her own beauty, but there is a look of Eleanor about her, despite what you say." He rose, still looking down at Caroline. "His lordship tells me he's taking you to Scrilady Hall this morning if I agree to it. I do. You're fit again. However, I will come to see you tomorrow morning. No sense in taking any chances."

Bess Treath smiled down at her and gently shook her hand. "You are yourself, Miss Derwent-Jones. I hope you didn't take my words amiss. Your aunt was very special in her own right, particularly to my brother, as I'm sure you know. I will also see you tomorrow. Good luck with the sparrows."

"What sparrows?"

"The pregnant girls," Dr. Treath said. "My sister has an interesting sense of humor."

Caroline leaned back her head, watching the two of them leave beneath slitted eyes. Why hadn't North come up with Dr. Treath?

She asked him when he was assisting her down the great stairs of Mount Hawke. She didn't need the support, but she enjoyed the feel of his arm beneath her hand, the closeness of him. She wondered if he felt anything at all this morning or if men's lust was reserved only for the evening hours.

"I had other matters to attend to," he said only, not looking at her.

"What other matters?"

He did look at her then, stopping on the stairs. "I don't recall thinking it was any of your business. Prying doesn't become you, Caroline. Why do you ask?"

"It would seem to me that your male minions would demand that you monitor Dr. Treath so that you could assure them that I was fit as a stoat and ready to leave here within the hour."

"Ah, but that happened anyway. Just look, Caroline, all of them lined up to bid you a fond farewell. A pity they're not waltzing."

"I hope they all rot," she said under her breath, but he heard her and chuckled. It was a nice sound, that raw chuckle of his.

"Miss is leaving," Tregeagle announced when she hadn't yet even reached the bottom step.

"Yes," she called out, "but I'll be returning for dinner. Won't that be nice, Coombe?"

"I daresay it could be pleasant," Coombe said, "but I fear that Mr. Polgrain is beginning to suffer from a severe migraine. The good Lord knows what we'll be eating this evening. Perhaps you'd best wait, miss. Yes, you'd best favor Scrilady Hall with your custom this evening."

She laughed. They were really quite good, all of them. "Well, in any case, do tell Polgrain that even though I enjoyed the pilchard head thoroughly, my guests nearly vomited upon viewing it."

"Surely that is too stark a word, miss," Tregeagle said. "Far too vulgar for a Female Person to use. Perhaps *retch* is less offensive. Ah, look, I've opened the front door for you and there is Mr. Owen all ready to take you away from . . . to take you home."

She said nothing more, just walked beside North onto the wide, very worn front steps of Mount Hawke. Owen was dutifully standing beside an ancient gig, pulled by an equally ancient old cob.

"Goodness, Owen, where did you unearth that thing?"

"Good morning, North, Caroline. Mrs. Trebaw insisted you must be pampered, Caroline, thus this relic. I just hope the wheels don't fall off."

Caroline turned to North and laid her hand on his sleeve. "Thank you," she said simply. She wished she could tell Owen to take the ancient gig and drive it to London, anything to give her more time with North, but she said instead, "Will you come dine with us this evening?"

He shook his head and said, "Yes."

She smiled wickedly, lightly touched her fingers to his chin, then stood on her tiptoes and kissed his cheek, her tongue lightly touching his warm flesh. She said into his ear, "There, that should have Polgrain, Coombe, and the inimical Tregeagle in a dither for at least an hour."

He was breathing quickly, wanting her right this moment, here on the front steps, perhaps in the gig with her sitting on his legs, or bent over, leaning on the opposite seat of the gig, her petticoats thrown up about her head—good Lord, the gig didn't have an opposite seat. He was fast becoming a halfwit, a lust-sodden fool. North shook his head. He gave her the coldest look he could dredge up. "Damn you, Caroline, you did that on purpose."

"Yes, but it was so very nice, North. I will see you this evening. Now, I'm off to see that everything's in order for my pregnant ladies."

"Take care," he said. "Tonight, you and Owen and I will discuss what the devil to do with his damned father."

"Er, North," Owen said, drawing close. "Your men haven't kept him in a dungeon, have they?"

"No, Owen, he's in a small room up there in the east wing. He isn't happy, but on the other hand, he isn't free to go after Caroline again."

"If he saw Caroline kissing you then he must realize that all will soon be lost."

North jerked as if he'd been shot. "What the hell does that mean, Owen?"

"Why, the two of you, the way Caroline looks at you and she's always smiling when you're nearby and touching you whenever you're close enough to touch. And you, North, your eyes get all dark when she's about and you look at her like a man would at a meal when he hasn't eaten for a week, and well, it's very obvious to everyone that, well, that is—"

"Nothing is obvious to anyone," Caroline said. She firmly took Owen by the arm and led him to the gig. "Do you want to drive, Owen, or shall I?"

Owen was staring up at the east wing, his body suddenly as stiff and tense as a maiden aunt at a horse mating. "Oh dear, do you think he's watching us?"

"I hope so," she said, then grinned and kissed Owen lightly on his chin, and hugged him tightly for a moment. She gave him another kiss for good measure. There," she said with a good deal of satisfaction, "Let him think I'll be a bigamist."

"Caroline!"

"Oh goodness, Owen, don't be such a prissy prude. Now, let's go home."

Owen clicked the old nag forward and Caroline found herself looking back at Mount Hawke. North was still standing on the steps staring after her. She raised her hand and waved. He turned and strode back into the castle.

North hadn't really seen her, she thought. He was perhaps shortsighted, that was it. He hadn't seen her wave. She shivered then as she looked upward at the third floor of the east wing. Somehow she knew Mr. Ffalkes was there by the window, watching her, watching and waiting and planning.

Caroline looked at each of the three young women who were now her responsibility and hers alone. Only one of them was younger than she— Alice, only fourteen years old, her belly huge on her thin body. She was so very pale and frightened; if Caroline ever met up with the man who'd forced her, she was certain she'd kill him. She felt such fury for a moment that she held herself very still and very silent.

When she'd managed to control her rage, she said, "Would you like another biscuit, Alice?" This time, she was careful not to make any sudden movements. She'd already done that and poor Alice had nearly jumped out of her pregnant skin. "They're filled with currants and ever so delicious. Mrs. Trebaw thinks we need to fatten you up a bit."

"Thank you, Miss Caroline," Alice said, speaking slowly and very carefully. "They do look wun-wonderful." Even the girl's fingers were thin and so very white, the blue veins clear beneath her skin. She looked more fragile than the small Dresden shepherdess on the mantel.

Caroline turned to Evelyn, a girl now almost twenty who'd been seduced by the young gentleman of the house. When she'd become pregnant, the young gentleman had informed his fond mother that Evelyn was a wanton trollop, that she'd come into his bedchamber and climbed into his bed, and just look at what she'd tried to do: compromise him so he'd have to marry her. Of course, she'd been dismissed without a character. She'd not wanted to go back to her parents, which was understandable, since there were already eight children in the small house in Mousehole, and her father was mean when he drank, which was most of the time now. It had been then that Miss Eleanor had found her crying her eyes out in Penzance, there, alone, sitting on the beach, unmindful that the tide was coming in fast and edging closer to her slippered feet.

"Another cup of tea for you, Evelyn?"

"Thank you ever so much, Miss Caroline. It do be a treat. Rather I should say it is very nice of you to offer, very nice indeed, don't you agree, Miss Mary Patricia?"

"Most assuredly, Evelyn," said Miss Mary Patricia. "And the company is so very refined."

Caroline grinned at Miss Mary Patricia, no simple Mary for her. She had a good deal of presence for a young woman who was twenty-two years old and one of five daughters of a vicar who lived in Dorset. She'd been trained to be a governess, and on her first post with two very young, very spoiled children who had nearly killed her with misery, the master of the house, a Mr. Trenwith of East Looe, had caught her in the gardens at the back of the house and raped her. "One time," Miss Mary Patricia had said, "just one time, and here I was, my life in ruins, not knowing what to do, and this babe growing in my womb." Aunt Eleanor had found her in a taproom in Truro trying to get a job as a barmaid.

Caroline now handed Miss Mary Patricia a cup of tea and a small cucumber sandwich. It occurred to her then that Owen Ffalkes and Bennett Penrose, both in residence here at Scrilady Hall, were men. Men had done this to her three sparrows. No, she thought, frowning over the name Bess Treath had given them, they weren't sparrows. They were all individuals and she hoped they would all eventually be able to do what it was they wanted. No, not sparrows by any stretch of the mind.

She saw that Alice was trembling again. Perhaps she knew there were men in the house. Oh dear, what was she to do to reassure them? She knew there was no harm at all in Owen, but what about Bennett? He looked like an angel, true enough, but he was more like a Devil's familiar, never pleased with himself, and thus impossible for him to be pleased with others. Oh dear.

It was Alice who whispered, "I seen . . . that is, Miss Caroline, I *saw* a man. He's not old and he's handsome and seems to live here."

"It's the handsome ones," Evelyn said, nodding even as she patted Alice's thin hand. "Aye, the handsome ones who believe they're entitled to any woman and of course any woman would want them because they're handsome and that's that. Fools, the mangy fools. Now, don't you worry, Alice, Miss Caroline will take care of things."

Yes, she would, she thought. She would hit it head on. She smiled brightly at the three of them and said, "My cousin Owen Ffalkes does live here and he's very nice. My other cousin, Bennett Penrose, lives here also. He's the handsome one, and to be honest, he isn't very nice. However, I will speak to him. I won't allow you ever to wonder if you'll be safe here. None of you are to worry."

Evelyn laughed, a big hearty laugh, then patted her protruding belly. "Even a randy young man won't be interested in us until after we birth the babes. Take heart, Alice, no one will try to hurt you here. If afterward one of them tries it, I'll skewer him in the belly, maybe take a nip off the end of his little rod." She leaned down and pulled up her skirt to show the small knife strapped to her calf. "No more will I be helpless around one of them, er, *those* wretched snakes."

"Good idea," said Caroline. "I should have one. Thank you, Evelyn."

"I don't want to be helpless either," Alice said, then gasped. "I'm just so afraid."

"You're also a babe yourself," Miss Mary Patricia said, patting Alice's hand. "No wonder you're afraid. Nothing bad will ever happen to any of us again, will it, Miss Caroline?"

"No," Caroline said, "it won't, not if I can help it anyway." She thought about their arrival in the vicar's small gig, nearly all piled on top of one another, and that damned vicar had treated them like the dregs in his teacup, as if their being with child was all their fault.

He tried to protest their staying here at Scrilady Hall, with naught but a young girl to look after them, but she'd cut him off quickly, saying, "They will be happy here, I'll see to it."

"They don't deserve to be happy! You and your aunt, both of you looking at things the wrong way and—"

"Pray, what is the right way to look at this, vicar?"

"They were cast out. They should remain cast out. They sinned and were caught and have shamed all womankind and—"

Caroline had seen Alice's face then, all pale and drawn, and she was flinching as if the vicar's horrid words were actual blows. As for Evelyn, she had blood in her eye, her fists clenched at her sides. Miss Mary Patricia had her chin high in the air, holding herself aloof and apart, or at least trying to. Caroline had said quickly, "You will leave, Mr. Plumberry. Don't bother to return else I might shoot you."

"You're overwrought," said the vicar, taking a step toward her, his hand outstretched. "You poor child, you don't know what you're saying. All this grief, all this unexpected pressure, your dear aunt shouldn't have thrown this all at you, and—"

"Good-bye, vicar. Go away."

He'd left, but she knew he believed her nearly hysterical, just a weak woman unable to see the truth of things when they stared her in the face. She'd turned back to the three very pregnant females and said, "Welcome to Scrilady Hall. My name is Caroline Derwent-Jones. You are truly welcome here. Everything will be all right, I promise you."

But she wondered now how she'd be able to keep her promise. Alice looked less ill than she had, but there was such fear, such wariness in her pale blue eyes that it made Caroline want to howl at the unfairness of life. She'd been set upon by three young bloods near St. Ives and they'd raped her, all of them. As for Evelyn, she had a good deal of bravado, but she did have the sense to strap that knife to her calf. Smart girl. As for Miss Mary Patricia, she looked as calm as a nun at her morning prayers, but if Caroline looked closely enough, she could see the slight tremor in her white hands.

Caroline said now, "I think Evelyn's very smart. All women are vulnerable because we're weaker then most men. Unfortunately some men are vicious and have no honor. I myself was nearly raped by such a man, so I do understand something of what happened to you. I will have all of us fitted with knives. All right?"

Alice began to cry, her thin shoulders jerking.

Evelyn turned to her and said gently as she took her into her arms, "Hush now, my baby, hush. Miss Caroline will see that everything works out for you."

Miss Mary Patricia said thoughtfully, "I think I would prefer a gun. Do they make them small now, do you know, Miss Caroline?"

Caroline didn't hesitate. It was a brilliant idea. "Yes, they do. I can even have a small strap made for it to fasten to your leg. Is that what you wish?"

"Yes, thank you. Now, Alice," she continued in a matter-of-fact voice, "it's time for lessons. You and Evelyn have learned to speak very nicely, but there's still the reading, and you won't want to be ignorant girls, will you?"

"No, Miss Mary Patricia," Alice said, and heaved herself out of her chair.

"Can we read more of that spicy story written by that Mr. Voltaire fellow?"

"Certainly," said Miss Mary Patricia, rising gracefully to her feet. She said to Caroline, "Evelyn loves *Candide*."

Caroline rose as well. "I like it too. Now, let me get Mrs. Trebaw and we'll all go to your rooms. I hope you like them."

Miss Mary Patricia said, "It'll be better than the cramped single room we all shared in the vicar's attic after Miss Eleanor died and he insisted that the cottage be closed down. He said there was no reason to waste money on the likes of us."

"The vicar did that?" Caroline said. At their nods, she felt a lovely wash of anger. "I'll get him for that."

"I don't know if you need a knife," Evelyn said, and grinned impudently.

15

When Caroline was alone, Miss Mary Patricia giving lessons to Alice and Evelyn in the long-unused schoolroom at the top of Scrilady Hall, she sent Owen into Trevellas to find a small gun and two knives like the one Evelyn had.

"The women don't need weapons, Caroline," he said, utterly aghast. "Why, I'm here and you're here. You wouldn't let anyone hurt them."

"It's not that, Owen," she said patiently. "They feel frightened. Look what men did to them. If a knife or a gun makes them feel safer, they should have them. By the by, that second knife is for me. If I'd had one the last time your father got me, perhaps you wouldn't have had to go against your father. I also might have gulleted him, which is an excellent idea if you look at the problem in a certain light."

"He still is my father, Caroline."

She sighed. "I know, Owen, and I'm sorry for it. We'll think of something."

Owen's eyes lit up. "Maybe they'll shoot Bennett by mistake."

"Buy three pistols, then. Goodness, what an utterly fragrant thought. Where is he anyway?"

"In Goonbell, probably in Mrs. Freely's taproom drinking ale until it comes out his bloody ears."

"Just as well. Goodness, there's so much to be done. I know, Owen, you can go to the mines and find Mr. Peetree, the manager. Find out what's going on and then we can discuss it later. Ask him what he thinks about the flooding in North's tin mine, Wheal David. I do know that our mine, Wheal Kitty, is just fine. The two mines are very close. Ask him why this is happening at North's mine and not in ours. Also there's Wheal Daffel and Wheal Bealle. Do learn all you can about how they're run, the production, the equipment."

Owen turned pale. "But I don't know anything about tin mines, Caroline. I don't know what to say to him, truly, my father always did—"

"Owen, stop sniveling and acting like a nitwit. You saved both North and me. You proved yourself. Now, you will introduce yourself, explain that you're my partner, and that since we're new to the area and to tin mining, you need to learn about it. Find out if repairs are needed. As I said, ask what the production is. Ask what the wages are, oh goodness, Owen, just use your brain. You know what to do. Write down what he tells you. Oh, and be properly humble. We don't want to set anyone's back up."

He left and she would swear she heard him speaking aloud, saying, "Mr. Peetree, would you mind very much telling me what the mines' annual production is?"

She grinned, shook her head, hoping Owen wouldn't be that diffident, and headed for the stables. She needed to go to Trevellas to the seamstress. Yes, she'd do that before seeing her estate manager, Mr. Dumbarton. There were five farms on Penrose land and it was time she discovered what was needed. She wanted to meet her tenants. Also, her pregnant ladies needed clothes, damn that miserable vicar. Miss Mary Patricia had told her that the vicar's wife had sold the clothes Miss Eleanor had made for them. All they had was what they'd arrived wearing.

She rubbed Regina's nose—now back in her own stable where she belonged, despite her obvious affection for North—gave her a carrot, and watched as Robin, the one and only stable lad, saddled her. She wondered what she would do to the vicar.

"Excellent," she said, and let him toss her into the saddle. "Tell Mrs. Trebaw I'll be home in a couple of hours, hopefully with the seamstress in tow."

"Er, Miss Caroline."

"Yes, what is it, Robby?"

"The little girls what have their bellies filled—"

"Yes?"

He was flushing violently. "Er, if there's sumthin' I can do to help ye, jest ask."

"Thank you, I will. Just keep an eye on them when they're outside. Particularly the very young girl, Alice. She's very frightened. Be gentle, Robby."

She rode away from Scrilady Hall, looking back once over her shoulder at the lovely peach brick facade shining so cleanly beneath the noonday sun. She particularly loved the five gables and the four chimney stacks that rose a good twenty feet above the roof. It was her home now. There weren't, however, enough plants or trees around the house. That was another thing she had to do—speak to the gardener, whatever his name was. She grinned then. Perhaps she should hire a female gardener, perhaps she should make Scrilady Hall a household of women.

Oh goodness, she thought suddenly, there was Honeymead Manor and Mrs. Tailstrop. She would have to speak to North about having someone go there and take charge of things. He would know what had to be done. Odd, how she didn't even hesitate. North was there, in the back of her mind, always there, when he wasn't in the front of her mind, or standing in front of her or perhaps even kissing her or caressing her. "Oh goodness, Regina, I'm beginning to think that North Nightingale is always going to be there. And you, you lazy nag, you quite adore him, don't you, all because he changed your name. Regina! Ha, if I had any sense I'd call you Petunia again." North. Yes, he was always there. She thought about their dinner the previous evening. Only Owen was present, Bennett gone yet again to Goonbell to drink with his cronies. She would have given her new stockings to have Owen at least twenty miles away from Scrilady Hall.

But alas, he was there and would remain, but the evening had been full of fun and jesting and good food until they'd spoken of Mr. Ffalkes.

North had spooned a bite of almond blancmange into his mouth, savored the crisp flavor, then said, "Your father, Owen, is not a happy man. I spoke to him this afternoon. When he finished cursing me, cursing my antecedents, cursing Caroline and every friend she's ever had, he calmed down. I put it to him, Owen. I asked him what I should do with him since he had this obsession with Caroline. He claimed there was no more obsession. He said at last he knew he couldn't have her, or rather her money."

"Please don't speak as if I'm not here," Caroline said. "Do you believe him, North?"

"I don't believe him," Owen said, leaning forward, a glass of port between his hands. "My father is craftier than a moneylender in Bear Alley in London, and I've heard that they'd steal the gold from their grandmothers' teeth without her realizing it, and if they did realize it, they'd just conk them on the head and steal the teeth anyway. No, North, he hasn't given up."

"I tell you what, Owen. Why don't you travel to London and speak to your father's associates. Find out what his financial situation really is. In the meanwhile, I've already written instructions to my man in London to see to the transfer of Caroline's inheritance from your father's control, with Mr. Brogan's assistance."

When Owen finally took himself off, giving the two of them knowing looks and a silly grin, Caroline said to North, "He won't give up, North, Owen's right about that. He's more stubborn than a stoat and more determined than a bishop in a roomful of infidels." She stopped then and gazed up at him through her lashes. She swallowed. "Perhaps I should marry. As you said, that would be the best way to ensure that he wouldn't kidnap me again."

"I did say that, didn't I?"

"Would you marry me, North?"

He stared down at her, pale now and silent and very still.

"I'm probably very rich."

He still said nothing, merely looked at her, even more silent if that were possible.

"Do you find me so very unacceptable?"

He leaned down and kissed her. In an instant, she was against him, her arms around his back, holding herself tightly to him, on her tiptoes now, her mouth wild on his. "Don't stop," she said into his mouth, "please, North, don't stop. It feels so very nice."

"Nice?" he said, and kept kissing her. "Just *nice?*" He didn't want to, but his hands were stroking down her back, lower and lower until he cupped her buttocks and lifted her tightly against him. She froze against him, then he felt her shock disappear and now she was interested, feeling things she'd never felt before in her young life, and wanting more. Good Lord, she was full of passion, but she was innocent and now here he was, seducing her in her own home, his hands wild on her bottom, and he knew he had to stop. He didn't want to marry, even Caroline, even this girl he wanted more than he'd ever wanted a female. But that was lust, honest lust, and he could deal with that, but he couldn't deal with marriage. Not yet, not ever, probably, at least he couldn't deal with it the way his ancestors had done, beginning with his great-grandfather, and there were too many memories of his father's rage and anger, so clear in his mind right this instant, for the rages had begun when he'd been just a small boy, becoming bitter and uglier as North had grown older, fanned by his grandfather, who should have died years before he actually did because he was such a miserable old bastard. It had never stopped.

Then he felt her warm tongue touching his and thought he would spill his seed at that very moment.

He grabbed her arms and pulled them back. "No," he said, gasping for breath. "No, dammit. This has got to stop, Caroline. I don't want to marry you. I just want to bed you and that can't be. You're a lady, and when I manage to remember, I'm a gentleman. I'll take care of my lust with someone else, but not you, never you. I'll never shame you, Caroline, even though when I touch you I want to fling you to the floor and pull up your skirts and come down over you . . . Jesus, I've got to stop this. You're so bloody innocent and you haven't the faintest notion of what I'm even talking about.

"But dear God, I want to touch you and kiss you, every inch of you, in that soft crook behind your knees; I want to taste the soft flesh of your inner thighs. Ah, and to kiss your belly and lower, tasting you and feeling you quiver against my mouth, your thighs tightening, your hips lifting in my hands. Yes, I want all of that until you're screaming with need, but you don't even understand what I'm feeling, do you? Ah, the joys of innocence. You feel desire, but you don't know, Caroline, you can't know, what it's like for a man to want a woman, what it's like to know that you're soft and willing and would let me come into you. No, you can't begin to understand that. You don't even know what a man looks like, do you, Caroline? No, of course you don't. Well, we're not beautiful and white and soft like you. We're all hairy and hard and damned frightening when we want a woman because our sex . . . No, dammit, forget I said that, forget that's even a part of it. And no, I won't kiss you again, so close your damned mouth and keep your tongue behind your teeth. God, women, even ones as innocent as you are, know instinctively how to drive a man wild with lust. Just look at you, your lips apart, and I can see your tongue.

"Damnation, don't look at me like that. Stay away from me. I'm close to the edge, very close."

He gave her one last furious look, shook his head at himself, and strode out of the drawing room. Again, he slammed the door behind him.

"Well," she'd said to the empty room, "he does appear to feel strongly about this. I don't believe he's ever spoken so many words together since I've known him. Yes, North is a passionate man. And that is a good thing, I think."

She hadn't slept well, for he was there, the taste of him distant yet still heady in her mouth, the heat from his body still warming her, all of her, and that warmth was still with her, and the things he'd said. She tried to imagine each action and knew it wouldn't be as strange and embarrassing as it sounded, no, it would be magic with him. What had he meant when he'd said he'd frighten her, something about his sex. She sincerely hoped she'd find out.

She shook her head now, clicked Regina forward, and wondered if North would persist in this seemingly generational dislike of marriage. But his father had married, as had his grandfather and as had his great-grandfather. None of it made any sense.

Where was North's mother? Had she died birthing him?

16

Oh dear, she'd forgotten all about Dr. Treath coming to see her and her new charges. "You say that Miss Treath had tea with the ladies, Mrs. Trebaw?"

"Yes, Miss Caroline. She stayed on a bit after Dr. Treath gave each of them a look over. A very nice lady is Bess Treath. Never sharp or nasty or gossipy, if you know what I mean, no matter how low-born or high-born the patient is. Take our girls here, she was just as nice as can be. No turning up her nose; just like her brother in that respect. Never married, but seems content enough taking care of her brother, particularly after his young wife died so many years ago."

"I didn't know Dr. Treath had been married before."

"Oh yes, to a lovely young girl from St. Ives who died in childbed not a year after they were married. Ah well, there's no promise our lives will go well or even continue, is there?"

"No," Caroline said, "there isn't."

"One must act and not dither about. That's what I always told Mr. Trebaw, the dear man who never did act, just dithered and talked about acting, until he just up and died some seven years ago."

"I'm sorry, Mrs. Trebaw."

"It's been a long time now, Miss Caroline, a very long time. But don't you forget now, don't waste your days dithering. Life is more uncertain than a cup of milk that's sat on the windowsill in the afternoon sun."

"You're right," Caroline said. "Dear heavens, you're absolutely right."

"I told the same thing to your aunt Eleanor. I do believe soon after that she decided she was going to marry Dr. Treath. Poor dear lady."

Caroline just stared at her. "But he never said anything about proposing to her."

"I don't suppose he had the chance, oh, but he wanted to marry her, it was plain as a pikestaff for all to see. No one had a doubt about it in the world. Your poor aunt was killed soon after. Poor lady, so very fun she was and full of high spirits, never caring if the day was dreary or rainy, no, she gave life everything she had. Poor lady."

Caroline stared after Mrs. Trebaw as she walked quickly away, shouting at Dumpling, the cook's scullery, "Off you go now, Dumpling! No, don't spill that milk. Careful, girl! Arrgh, you deserve a clout for that!" She turned and said to Caroline, "Nice is nice, but I'll wager that even Bess Treath has clouted her maids in the ear now and again. Dumpling! You clumsy girl!"

Caroline went to the third floor, to the old nanny's large room where she'd ensconced the seamstress from Trevellas. Mrs. Wiggins would remain here for two weeks, sewing gowns for all of them. She was jolly and big-bosomed and had no taste at all. Thankfully, Miss Mary Patricia was blessed with exquisite taste, even managing quite skillfully to temper the overly exuberant wishes of Evelyn, and it was she who directed Mrs. Wiggins in the choice of materials for the three of them and the styles. Miss Mary Patricia also agreed to oversee the making of several gowns for Caroline.

She left Miss Mary Patricia and Evelyn arguing about a particularly vile shade of puce that Evelyn thought would be just beautiful on Miss Caroline. Caroline shook her head and left quickly. She went back downstairs and came face-to-face with Bennett Penrose.

"Good day, cousin," she said, and kept walking toward the small back room that she'd taken over as her workroom.

"I want to speak to you, Caroline."

She said over her shoulder, "Good. I want to speak to you as well. Come along, Bennett."

She knew he didn't like her sitting behind the desk, the sunlight behind her and thus in his eyes, but she didn't care.

"Our three ladies are here now, Bennett," she said without preamble. "You will be polite to all of them. You will be careful not to frighten them, particularly Alice, who is very young and very frightened of anyone who is male."

"Then why'd she toss up her skirts if she was frightened of men?"

"Bennett," she said, willing herself to patience, "Alice is fourteen years old. She was raped by three young men who were probably drunk. She is a child and now she is pregnant. You will be very, very careful around her."

Bennett looked contemptuous and shrugged. She wanted to smack him, but she said only, "Scrilady Hall is their refuge and now their home. They are safe here, from nastiness, from threat. Do you understand me?"

He only shrugged again.

"Bennett, you can move out if you wish."

"Where would I go? Would you give me money to leave, Caroline? You could, you know. I wouldn't relinquish my share of anything here, but if you gave me an income from all the money you inherited, then I would gladly be on my way."

It was a thought, a very good one, actually, but she knew her aunt had believed Bennett to be redeemable. More fool her aunt in this case, but Caroline supposed she had to give it a try. "No. Why don't you get work. You're not particularly stupid, just lazy."

"I'm a gentleman."

"Ah, that means then that you'll skulk and sulk about and drink yourself to death at Mrs. Freely's inn in Goonbell? I doubt North would consider that a proper gentleman's pursuits."

"He's got money. I don't have any."

"He didn't have any money until he came into the title. He was in the army, from the age of sixteen, doing something useful, earning his own keep."

"Napoleon's gone. There's no more reason to go into the army. Besides, I would have to have a commission. Would you give me the seven or eight hundred pounds to buy me one?"

She sighed. "What do you want to do, Bennett?"

He rose and walked to the long windows that gave onto a lovely enclosed garden. He said finally, "I want to marry an heiress."

Well, that was something. "How does one go about marrying an heiress?"

"There aren't any in this godforsaken area, that's for sure. No, I must go to London to find a rich cit's daughter. I'm of excellent breeding even though I don't have a title. Yes, all I need is capital and I will be married to an heiress within six months."

"So you want me to loan you the money? An investment in the hunt?"

"Yes," he said as he turned back to face her. "I venture to say that five thousand pounds would get the job done. I would give you, say, ten percent in return after a period of eight months. Perhaps then you would buy me out of my half of all this. God knows the last thing I want to do is take care of pregnant sluts. Is that acceptable to you?"

Caroline didn't know what to say, and that was odd because usually words tumbled merrily off her tongue. She could only stare at Bennett and wonder what kind of a man he was. She said finally, "I will think about this, Bennett. In the meanwhile, why don't you make yourself useful here."

"Doing what? Meeting with those damned boring farmers? Making repairs on their cottages? Should I force myself to listen to them talk of their meager crops that are always rotting in the fields from too much rain? Do you want me to sit down with Mr. Dumbarton and commiserate on having you here as mistress and not a man? You want me to enter stupid numbers in a ledger? Go spend my time in the tin mines, licking Peetree's boots, like you've got Owen doing? Oh yes, I saw him over at Wheal Kitty walking about with that damned manager, acting like a stupid schoolboy, all ears, looking ready to pant."

"If you married an heiress, Bennett, you would be expected to do something useful. If there's an estate, it would be your responsibility to see that it's well run. If your wife's family is in banking, for example, you would be expected to learn that job."

He shrugged. "I would hire an estate manager. As for banking, I would no more set foot into the city than I would go to America. I told you, Caroline, I'm a gentleman. Gentlemen aren't in trade."

She rose then and placed her hands palm down on the desktop. "You're a fool, Bennett, but I will think about this, though I can't imagine giving you the money to dupe some poor girl into marrying you."

"Then you'll never be rid of me, Caroline. This is my home now, just as it's yours. There are three pregnant little sluts just upstairs. After they've dropped their brats, why then, I can have my pick of them. Perhaps I won't be so bored after all." He turned and strolled from the room, whistling now as if he hadn't a care in the world.

Damn him. He was right. What was she going to do?

"All right, Caroline, what's going on? You look like you're ready to shoot somebody."

She was pacing back and forth in North's drawing room still so furious she was near to panting with it. "It's Bennett," she said, striving to keep her voice from shaking with rage, stopping just a moment, then resuming her pacing.

He drew up, now alarmingly rigid. "Did that mangy little bastard insult you?"

His harsh tone brought her up short. That would enrage him? If she were the one insulted? Ah, perhaps . . . She smiled at him, a big beautiful smile, and made North wish he'd kept his damned mouth shut. As for Caroline, it was strange, but suddenly her rage at Bennett had unaccountably dispersed like rain clouds. There was nothing but bright sunshine.

She said now, quite unconcerned, "No, he didn't insult me, not directly anyway. He wants five thousand pounds from me so he can go to London and catch himself an heiress for a wife. Then I can buy him out of his half of everything here, and there's got to be lots of money in it, naturally. Then he can continue a wastrel's life."

"That's not all of it, is it? That would just make you laugh, Caroline. Come on now, what else?"

"He said if I didn't give him the money, he'd wait until my ladies dropped their brats and then he'd have them himself. He called them sluts, acted like he'd be some sort of sultan with his own harem."

North found himself looking again at her heaving breasts. His fingers itched to touch her, to fondle her breasts, to hold them in his hands, to close his eyes while he felt her soft flesh. He shook himself and rose. "What do you want me to do about him?"

"Oh, it's not your problem, North. Forgive me, I was just so very angry and Regina came here without my even telling her where I wanted to go. What did you do to my mare, other than change her name? She dotes on you. It's quite revolting. I've fed her and loved her since she was foaled, yet all her loyalty lands on your lap after only a couple of days."

"You really should give Regina to me."

"No, I shan't. Why didn't Treetop fall in love with me? I treated him well, sang to him, as a matter of fact. No, he saw you and came running. He couldn't wait to get away from me. It's not fair."

"Call me magic," he said.

"All right, that's fair, but about the horses—"

"Caroline, just stop it."

She sighed. "Oh, you'll like this. Coombe nearly expired on the spot when he opened the door to find me standing there, flicking my riding crop against my boot, picturing it as Bennett's back."

"I can imagine," North said. "Now, Caroline, what do you want from me?"

She studied him, then said quietly, "I want you to hold me, just hold me, North, and then, perhaps, if that turns out satisfactorily, you could consider kissing me and caressing me with your hands like you did before. It was wonderful. I liked everything you did."

He shuddered and didn't move. His hands were clenched at his sides. "Go away, Caroline. I have business to attend to. I have no more time for any of

this. If you want me to kill Bennett, just ask. As for the other, go away. I'm
not at all interested in any of it."

"Oh no, I won't go away," she said, and walked to him. He stood rigid as a
stick but it didn't deter her. Mrs. Trebaw was right—life was too uncertain
to dither about. She stood on her tiptoes and kissed his mouth. She touched
her fingers to his chin, to his nose, to his dark eyebrows, smoothing them
lightly. "You are so beautiful, North. Please kiss me."

"Damn you," he said, "I'm a man. I'm not beautiful. I told you, men are
big and ungainly and—" and he kissed her. He tried not to touch her but that
didn't last long. Very quickly she was in his arms, his hands wild on her
back, clutching her tightly to him, then easing, only to cup her buttocks and
lift her against him. He was breathing hard, and his tongue was in her
mouth, touching her, tasting her, and he wanted, quite simply, to yell with
the pleasure of it.

"My lord."

He wanted to pull up her riding skirts, to feel the soft flesh of her thighs,
to billow her skirts and petticoats up around her chest, to have her naked to
the waist, her beautiful legs parted for him so he could . . .

"My lord!"

"Oh hell," he said into her mouth. He was shaking like a palsy sufferer,
so intent on what she was making him feel, on what he wanted to do to her,
on just having her now, here in the drawing room. Lord he wanted to touch
her flesh, feel the dampness of her, her need for him, kiss that delightful
smile off her mouth and bring on a moan instead.

"My lord, this is most inappropriate; it is unacceptable from everyone's
perspective. You must gather yourself together and pull yourself apart from
the Female Person. We have guests and they cannot be ignored."

Slowly, breathing deeply to regain a semblance of control, North eased
out of her hold. She was standing there, just staring up at him, and he saw
something in her green eyes that scared the devil out of him. He knew trust
when he saw it and it was there, deep and clear in her eyes, as clear as the
passion that was still burning brightly between them.

"Caroline," he said very quietly. "It's damnable and I'm sorry. Just hold
still. Try to keep upright. Can you manage it?"

She nodded, mute as a fig leaf.

North turned to Coombe. "You will leave immediately and close the door behind you. What guests?"

"It's Sir Rafael and Lady Victoria Carstairs, my lord."

North cursed very quietly and very fluently. "Tell them I will be with them shortly. Invite them to luncheon and take them to the dining room."

"Yes, my lord."

"Get out, Coombe, now."

"Yes, my lord."

North waited until the door closed, then he strode over to it and locked it. He turned to look at her, this young girl who made him feel things he'd never imagined to be possible, at least within himself. She was standing there, her arms at her sides, her breasts still heaving just a bit, her lips still slightly parted, and he wanted desperately to go back to her, to hold her against him, to kiss her and perhaps kiss her even more than another good dozen times, on her mouth, her throat, her breasts. She was wearing a jaunty green riding hat with a feather that curled about her face, a dark green that nearly matched her eyes. It was lurching to the right side. Tendrils of rich chestnut hair curled in tangles down her neck. She looked drunk. He wondered if he looked the same way. God, he had to get her away from him. He shook himself. "Caroline, I'm sorry."

"You keep saying that, North. It's quite unnecessary. You shouldn't be sorry, for I'm assuredly not, and since I'm the virgin here, the one whose experience amounts to what you choose to dole out, doesn't it seem that my wishes should count the most?"

"No, you haven't a whit of sense. A virgin is supposed to shriek with outrage and cross her hands over her bosom. A virgin is supposed to slap a man if he does what I just did to you . . . not moan and hold me like you'll die if I quit kissing you and caressing you and pressing your belly against me. . . . Oh, damn it all, Caroline, you're mad. Will you remain for lunch and meet our neighbors?"

"Certainly," she said, and tried to straighten her clothes. She walked to the mantel and tucked and patted her hair into place as she looked into the mirror. "How delightful of you to extend me an invitation."

"I don't want to," he said as he took her arm. "But I see no other choice. If you were to leave without introduction, they would believe you my mistress, a female of no importance at all. You're their neighbor as well. You must meet them."

"Yes," she said, giving him a grin that made him want to kiss her again and smack her at the same time. "I see that now, though I can't say that I would have understood anything so complicated a few minutes ago."

"Be quiet, Caroline."

Caroline left Mount Hawke in the middle afternoon. It had been drizzling lightly, but now it had stopped and a bit of sun was peeping through the still-lingering dark clouds. She rode Regina to St. Agnes Head. She dismounted and walked to the edge of the cliff. She stood there, just looking out over the choppy water, watching it crash against the black rocks below, spewing spray halfway up the cliff.

"Who did this to you, Aunt Eleanor?"

Regina nickered softly behind her.

She sighed and began to walk along the edge, careful to stay back from the earth that looked loose from the rainfall. She found a path some fifty yards up from where Aunt Eleanor had been shoved over the cliff. It was the huge beach North had showed her, shaped like a big quarter moon, the cliffs towering high behind it, stark and barren. Slowly, very carefully, she made her way down the narrow path. It was strewn with small rocks and some not so small, and some she had to lift out of the way. No one had walked this path in quite some time, probably not since summer, when local children came here to swim. It took her ten minutes to reach the beach below. The sand was wet with the incoming tide. It was dark and dirty-looking, particularly with no bright sun overhead to soften the colors. Driftwood and rocks strewed the beach, which was very long really and deep, curving into darkness beneath the cliff. She wondered how far back the beach extended under the cliff. Next time she should bring a candle and explore. The rock looked to be shale and sandstone, and that's why it had eroded so severely over time. She turned about and stared out at the sea. She imagined that at high tide most of the beach was covered in water, perhaps it went all the way to the cliff.

She sat down on a large black rock and hugged her knees to her chest, wrapping her arms around her legs. It was chilly, but not that chilly. It felt good. She looked at the waves rolling in, never the same, but always ending the same with the waves tossing themselves as far as they could reach on the beach, fanning out white and wispy into the sand, then withdrawing, again and again.

She didn't want to dither, she didn't want to just let life happen to her. She didn't want to be like Mr. Trebaw, who'd evidently not done very much. She wanted to be responsible for her life, to make decisions for herself. She didn't want life to get away from her and leave her wallowing in something she didn't want. But there was North, the man she wanted, and all he seemed to feel for her was his damnable lust and his wretched indifference, and even though she was fighting with all her might, it just didn't look hopeful. She sighed and hugged her knees closer to her chest. She watched a sand crab scuttle to and fro for a good long time before it sank under the sand. What was she to do? How to make North agree to make her the happiest woman on earth?

"I won't stand for this, Caroline. You scared the devil out of me, damn you."

17

She jumped, felt her heart slam against her chest in fear, but for only a moment. Surely he couldn't be all that indifferent, since he was here. She turned, smiling, and said, "Hello, North. I'm sorry I frightened you. I wanted to think and I came upon this path and came down to the beach. Remember, you showed it to me? Why are you here?"

He looked uncertain for a moment, then shrugged. "I don't know. I was out riding. I was going to visit Wheal David, then I just came here. When I saw Regina and didn't see you I thought you'd gone over the cliff. Don't ever scare me like that again, Caroline."

She smiled more widely. "I won't."

"See that you don't or I'll throttle you."

"All right," she said, still smiling, for she knew as well as he did that if he allowed himself to lace his fingers about her neck, he'd soon be kissing her.

"Stop it, Caroline."

She just shrugged and looked out over the dark water. "I liked the Carstaires. Lady Victoria wasn't at all ordinary. She's very pretty and very charming. Her husband adores her. He's very possibly nearly as handsome as you are, not as handsome, mind you, but nearly."

"She's also pregnant."

"Really? She's quite slender. How do you know that she's pregnant?"

He frowned at her. "You're a damned female, couldn't you tell?"

"Well, no. You're a damned man, so how did you know?"

His frown cleared and he said with a man's wonderful arrogance, "There's a look about her, a sort of radiance, and her husband was very careful when he touched her. It's really quite obvious." He looked thoughtful, then said, "I'd say she was about three months along."

"Goodness, I had no idea you were so observant, North. I needn't have bothered Dr. Treath at all. You could have simply looked at all my pregnant ladies and told them to do this and to do that. I'm very impressed."

He looked distinctly harassed. "Very well, you don't believe me. At least I tried. I heard Rafael tell her that he wouldn't caress her breasts no matter how much she wanted him to because he knew she was tender and he might hurt her. He told her to be patient, that Dr. Treath had told him that she would become less tender in a month or so. Then he would caress her all she wished. And then she said that she didn't think he would hurt her because he could be gentle when he wasn't dancing about the room, holding her with her legs wrapped around his . . . er, forget that. There, are you pleased now that you've pried it out of me?"

"I didn't realize that a woman's breasts got tender."

"Caroline! Dammit, control your mouth. That is highly improper, you shouldn't even know about—"

"Breasts? Being pregnant?"

"Be quiet. Now, what are you doing here?"

"Thinking."

"About your aunt?"

She shook her head, looking away from him at the encroaching tide that had just tumbled a huge splaying wave that finally flattened only two feet from the big rock where she sat. "No, I was thinking about you. I was thinking about how one should take charge of one's life. I was remembering how I was so very lonely for such a long time and how now there's so much for me to do that I scarce even have time now to remember that other life and that other Caroline."

He went still as the rock she was sitting on.

"That's quite a lot, Caroline. However, if you were thinking about me in all that morass, you will stop it now. I don't want you thinking about me, Caroline."

"Why not?"

"Because I'm simply not interested in you."

The lie was so blatantly false that she merely stared at him with as much fascination as she would study an aphid sitting atop a rose.

"Very well, you force me to be blunt again. I told you it was all lust. Well, it is. If you weren't so damned innocent, you'd be able to recognize lust for what it is. No, I take that back. You damned women, you want to wrap up a man in sentimental rot, you want him to ply you with flattery and roses and romance and spiritual intermingling."

"Then why did you come looking for me? Perhaps you wanted to make love to me? To assuage your lust?"

It was his turn to look toward the waves since one just missed spewing over the toe of his Hessian boot. He took a step back. "Rafael is assisting me with my tin mines. Wheal David is a mess and there are still no answers. I may have to close it down until we figure out what to do. However, Wheal Malcolm is doing well, so I will have as many of the men working over there as I can." He stopped a moment and sighed. "But there is still so much I need to learn."

"I as well. I sent Owen to begin his lessons with Mr. Peetree, my manager."

"Ah, good, so Owen will deal with the mines. It's not a lady's responsibility to get involved with them."

"Why ever not, North?"

"It's a man's sort of thing and well you know it. The miners are rough and tough and well used to danger since it's a part of their lives. It would distract them to have a woman prancing about the mine."

"That sounds like a mare trying to tempt a stallion. Would it interest you if I pranced?"

"You're so bloody beautiful it wouldn't matter if you crawled about with your head down."

Bloody beautiful. She liked the sound of that. She gave him another dazzling, very big smile. "Really, you truly believe I'm beautiful?"

"Shut up, Caroline. Which mines are now yours besides Wheal Kitty?"

"Wheal Daffel and Wheal Bealle."

"They're both good producers. According to Rafael, Wheal Kitty is the highest producer hereabouts, and this Mr. Peetree is a man to be trusted."

"That's a nice surprise. I have yet to speak to Owen, but I did tell him to learn all he could and not act like an idiot arrogant owner."

"He isn't going to London. There's no need."

"How do you know that?"

"He visited his father this morning and they spoke for quite a while. After Mr. Ffalkes ceased his loudest recriminations, Owen learned that his father is in very deep financial difficulty. He needs money very badly and saw you as his only salvation, thus his relentless pursuit of you."

"It's lovely to be wanted for one's money and not for oneself."

"This is real life, Caroline. Don't be a fool. Don't try to make me think you're at all cast down about Mr. Ffalkes's motives or that you're even surprised."

"Very well. So what are we going to do?" There, she thought, she'd said it. We, not just her alone. She waited, watching the encroaching waves come closer and closer. If North didn't pay attention, his lovely boots would shortly be splashed and likely ruined. A sea gull flew overhead, then finally landed on a black rock near Caroline. A peregrine falcon lazily tilted his wings toward the beach.

"I spoke to Mr. Ffalkes after Owen told me all that had passed between them." North stared down at his feet, then held out his hand to her. "Time for us to retreat."

She knew he didn't want to touch her, rather he wanted to touch her too much, all because of this lust of his, but she just smiled, placed her hand in his, and let him tug her gently off the rock. They walked slowly back toward the dark shadows beneath the towering cliffs.

"And what did he say?"

"He said he would get you and he swore that the third try would see him succeed."

She cursed, very colorfully and very loudly.

He stared at her, then threw back his head and laughed loud and deeply.

That laugh of his, it sounded wonderful. She said, "You're not at all dour and brooding, North. That laugh was very nice. I'd like to hear it more."

He was immediately silent, immediately frowning. "It shouldn't have happened. If I continue to laugh I shall have to inform Marcus Wyndham that he can no longer call me menacing and dark and dangerous."

"How very romantic. No, don't tell him anything. Dark and dangerous, hmmm?"

"Now you sound like Marcus's young cousins, Antonia and Fanny. They found me vastly romantic."

"North, what will we do about Mr. Ffalkes?"

He drew a very deep breath. "I guess you'll just have to marry someone."

"Someone, North?"

"That's right. Someone."

"Not you?"

"I'm not available."

She gave him a very long look, then sighed and smiled. She pulled away from him, back toward the path that led back up the cliff. She said over her shoulder, "Very well, I'll marry Owen. That way, Mr. Ffalkes can have my money and I won't have to worry about him shooting my husband so he can force me to marry him. Yes, Owen is the someone."

"Owen! Have you lost what few wits God gave you? He's a boy, he's barely got down on his chin. Damnation, he's barely got a chin. You would badger him to death within a week, Caroline. Already he's now under your thumb. He would have escaped his father to end up with you, the biggest female tyrant I've ever met. What's more, I like Owen. He doesn't deserve it."

"Well, then, how about Bennett Penrose? He has a chin. Indeed, he's quite lovely on the outside. He's three years older than you, so you can't claim he's a mere boy. He needs an heiress and I suppose I come close to being that. If Mr. Ffalkes were to shoot him to get me into widowhood, I shouldn't feel so terrible about it. What do you think, North?"

"Damn you, Caroline."

He strode to her, grabbed her upper arms, and shook her. She did absolutely nothing, just let him shake to his heart's content. At last he seemed to have stopped dithering. He stopped abruptly and in the very next instant, suddenly wild and urgent, he was kissing her, crushing her against him. She knew then, more surely than she knew anything in her entire life, that this man was the only one for her. Did that mean spiritual intermingling? Did this mean she would expect him to spout sentimental rot? She parted her lips and felt his warmth, tasted the sweet wine he'd had for lunch, felt his tongue lightly stroke hers.

At that moment, the sun broke through the clouds and they were bathed in fierce light. It felt odd, the heat of the sun overhead and the heat he was building deep inside her, beneath his hands, through her clothes.

This time she knew he wouldn't stop. She also knew she wouldn't stop him, not that she'd ever tried to stop him in the past. Come what may afterward, tomorrow, next week, she wanted this to happen. She wanted him and perhaps, just perhaps, he would sense the love she felt for him, the commitment she was offering to him.

Ah, she would give him laughter, surely there was nothing more seductive than laughter.

But he stopped cold, in the very next instant, dropped his arms from her, and stumbled back several steps.

"North?"

He looked at her as if he hated her. "Listen to me, Caroline, if I don't stop now, I won't. That's the truth of it. Do you want me to take your virginity here on a wet beach?"

She looked him squarely in his face. "Yes," she said. "I shouldn't mind where you made love with me. I just wish you'd get a grip on yourself and do it, North."

He stared at her and she could see he was trying to come up with more arguments, but it was obvious his own lust, his own full-blown need, was hampering his thinking. It was probably a good thing.

"Sand gets into everything," he said at last. "I made love to Emily Trevedor on a beach when I was fifteen, and I itched in very embarrassing parts for a good week afterward. Poor girl, I don't know how she dealt with the miserable sand."

Caroline laughed, she couldn't help it. "Oh, North, you are so wonderful. I don't care where you make love with me. I just want you so very much. I want you to teach me everything. I want you to show me how to please you and give you as much joy and excitement as you give to me."

He frowned at her, but said with some humor, "If you gave me any more excitement, I'd explode."

She cocked her head to one side in question.

"Men are excessively uncomplicated when it comes to sexual matters. Don't look at me like that. All right, Caroline Derwent-Jones. Just what the hell am I going to do with you?"

Here I go, Mrs. Trebaw, she thought, no more dithering, and said, "Marry me."

He plowed his fingers through his thick hair. He looked harassed. He looked distracted. "Damnation, I hadn't thought to marry anytime soon. I'm only twenty-five years old, my birthday isn't for four more months. I thought to marry when I was much older, say thirty-five or so, beget an heir and that would be that."

"Begetting an heir would be nice, North, but I think there are other things as well that would bring you pleasure and contentment and joy. Perhaps you could consider me being with you, laughing with you, discussing things with you—"

"Fighting with me, doubtless."

"Certainly. That's all a part of life. I can't believe I'd smash you under my female tyrant's thumb like you seem to think I'd do to Owen."

"Since when do you know so much about life?"

She was silent for just a moment. She didn't look at him, just said quietly, "I was very much alone for a good many years, and to be honest, I didn't know much of anything. I knew there was more, but I didn't know how to get it or even where to find it." She drew a deep breath and looked at him straightly. "Now I have so much. Now I have you, and it's wonderful to have someone to care about, someone to worry about, someone to trust. It's still very new to me, and if I offend you, please forgive me, for I do it out of ignorance.

"I think I grew up quite magically that night Mr. Ffalkes tried to rape me. I didn't learn all that much about life, but I did grow up. No, no, I'm not trying to get you to pity me, to soothe me. It's not that at all, North. It's just that I want to marry you. No other man, just you. I want to spend my life with you, no other man. I want very much to be with you forever. I'm a good sort, North, and I swear I'll try my best not to disappoint you, or pry when you want to be private, or beg you for flattery or romance or anything like that. I swear never to be maudlin."

He looked ready to stamp his boot into the sand. Instead, he plowed his fingers through his hair. "Why, for God's sake? You see me as your best protection against Ffalkes? If so that's nonsense. I'd kill the bugger before I married you for that reason."

"Oh no. I think I want to experience this lust business of yours for the next fifty years of my life." She walked to him then and was pleased when he didn't back up any more. She slipped her arms around his back and looked up at him. "I think you're the most wonderful man in the world, North."

He gave her a twisted smile. "What if I go off and brood on the moors with my hounds?"

"I'll have Polgrain pack you a hearty lunch and wave good-bye to you. And when you come home, I'll smile at you and kiss you and caress you until you forgot why ever you wanted to go to the moors in the first place."

"I'm used to being alone, Caroline, just as you were alone. The big difference was that I wanted to be alone. It's not the same thing—being alone and lonely. I knew people, knew all about them, and I decided I preferred keeping to myself. I left Mount Hawke when I was sixteen, I told you that. I had no one when I left here, and even now the number of men who are my close friends are very few. I'm not good being with people, Caroline, particularly women, at least women who are ladies."

"That isn't true at all." She went up on her tiptoes and kissed his mouth. "Why do you say you're not good with women?" She kissed him again and again, light nipping kisses, kisses he'd taught her. "You've always been wonderful with me. You make me laugh, you make me want to touch you and hold you and kiss you until I dwindle away into an old woman."

"I don't understand that either," he said, and began to return her kisses.

"You see," she said, then lightly slipped her tongue between his lips. "You see," she said again, her breath warm in his mouth, "I am the obvious woman for you. You should stop worrying about it, North. I am your fate. Take me because I most certainly want to be taken by you."

18

"Damnation," he said, and fell to his knees in front of her. She stood stock still, not understanding, just staring down at him.

"See if you can accept this, Caroline. If this shocks you to your little virgin toes, I'm sorry, but it's what I have wanted." Without another word, he pulled up her gown, her petticoats, her chemise. "Hold them up." She did, still staring down at him, still not understanding. She was naked in front of him and he just looked at her for a long moment, at the white thighs, strong and supple, and upward to the tight swirl of curls as richly chestnut as the hair on her head, and he reached out his fingers to touch her. "Spread your legs."

She gasped and spread her legs, balancing herself better. "Are you certain you want to do this, North? Look at me like this? It's very embarrassing, you know. No one has ever looked at my waist before."

"I'm not looking at your damned waist. I'm looking at where I'm going to caress you with my fingers and with my mouth. God, you're beautiful."

"North, but surely—"

His mouth touched her then as his fingers held her apart for him. Caroline froze, then, to her utter astonishment, she felt a tremor that shook her from her toes to her neck. Her knees buckled and she collapsed, her riding skirt and petticoats billowing out over him. She felt North's hands on her bottom as she landed on her back. He was over her then, on top of her, balanced above her on his elbows, looking down into her very dazed eyes.

"You're lovely," he said, and kissed her. Before she could clasp him around his back to keep him close, he was off her, standing there, staring down at her. Her skirts were up about her waist, her legs sprawled, and he smiled at her and held out his hand.

"I pictured you like this, your skirts all up about your chest and your belly naked. Yes, I pictured you very clearly. But let me tell you, Caroline, you're more beautiful here, now, in your white flesh, than you were even in my very imaginative mind. I like the white stockings and the black riding boots. It adds mystery. It's exotic. Come now, we're going home."

He pulled her up, then stood back, watching her straighten her clothes. Her hands were trembling and she was very, very silent.

"My God," he said, and laughed. "You're embarrassed. I've finally succeeded in getting you to close your mouth."

He grunted then, doubling over slightly when she rammed her fist into his belly.

He just grinned, rubbed his stomach, and said, "We'll wed next week, on Friday, all right? Will that give you sufficient time?"

She looked at him, saw the deviltry in his dark eyes, saw the amusement tugging at the corners of his beautiful mouth, and shook her head. "No, I would prefer Wednesday."

"You're a mouthy girl, Caroline, but it pleases me. We will compromise on Thursday. I have to find us a bishop, you know, and procure a license, since I don't think you want to post any banns."

"No, that takes a long time, doesn't it?"

"Four weeks, three of them where the vicar reads out the intent to marry in church. Too long, much too long. I want you in front of me naked so I can caress you again. Will you hold up your clothes for me again?"

"North!"

"It's nice to outdo you verbally, Caroline. I used to be quite content to sit in brooding silence, listening to others go on and on and laugh and tell jests, but now, with you, I find I quite enjoy reducing you to blushes and groans and little squeaks when I manage to shock you."

He grinned down at her, patted her face, and gave her his hand. "Come along, we have a lot to do. Careful now, this path isn't all that easy a climb."

It wasn't until late that same night that Caroline, tossing in her own bed, quite alone and hating it, realized that Mr. Ffalkes could quite easily kill North, widow her, and force her to marry him. But no, that was absurd. He would be hanged if he murdered anybody. She was becoming hysterical. Her mind had obviously been shoved off its proper track, what with those utterly delightful and very unexpected things North had done to her on the beach. She knew she was embarrassed, shocked to her toes, really, but it didn't prevent the warmth building low in her belly right now, just remembering how his mouth actually touched her, how his tongue licked her. Oh goodness. She wondered what would have happened if he hadn't stopped doing all those things with his hands and his mouth.

At Mount Hawke, North wasn't in his bed. He was standing in the library, his three minions facing him, all their faces mirroring the same emotion—disbelief, utter consternation, and denial.

"What the hell is going on here, damn you! I'm marrying Caroline Derwent-Jones. She will be Lady Chilton. She will be your mistress. You know her. You know she isn't rapacious, isn't looking to wed me for anything other than very warm feelings she nourishes for me. Do you want to know what she said about the three of you? Well, I'll tell you. She thought you were all immensely creative. She said she admired creativity and inventiveness."

"It's not exactly that, my lord," Tregeagle said, stepping forward. "Her rapaciousness, I mean."

"Then what the hell is it?"

"Here," Tregeagle said, and handed North a thin book bound in crimson leather. "Please, my lord, read this. You must. This decision you're making—"

"I've already made it," North said, but took the small volume. "What the devil is this?"

"We thought perhaps this is why you called all of us to see you," Tregeagle said. "Thus we deemed it best to be prepared. It's writings from your great-grandfather, your grandfather, and finally, your father."

"I see," North said with disgust. "Didn't they write enough about King Mark? Wasn't his damned betrayal enough for them? This is supposed to convince me to become as woman-hating as the rest of you lunatics? I can't help what my ancestors did, but listen to me, I have nothing to do with them, nothing at all. Now, get out of here, all of you. Caroline and I will be married next week, and if there's any hint of a dead pilchard in any dish you serve her, I'll gullet all of you. I'll send my bayonet through your bellies. I'll see that none of you ever breathe again."

"That is rather comprehensive, my lord," Coombe said. "No woman has lived here at Mount Hawke since your great-grandfather's time. Please, my lord, listen to us. It just isn't done."

"That's absurd."

"It's true what Mr. Coombe says," Tregeagle said. "Women aren't allowed here."

"They are now," North said. "Go on, now, get out, all of you."

Polgrain, Coombe, and Tregeagle slowly nodded and left the library. North stared after them, then just shook his head. He heard Tregeagle stop and looked up. "Please, my lord, read what the Nightingale men have written. It's all true. Truth casts a long shadow, particularly for Nightingale men."

"Damnation, all right, I'll read it, but it won't change anything."

"You never should have left when you were sixteen. You didn't learn the truth of things. You would have come to understand why—"

"You would have left too, Tregeagle, had my father been your father. That miserable bastard, he—" North shut up, and drew upon his control. "Go away, Tregeagle, just go away."

"Yes, my lord, but I really don't want to. All of us just seek to protect you, to nurture you in your privacy, here with us, alone and happy."

"Get out of here, you idiot."

"Yes, my lord."

Flash Savory faced Lord Chilton across his desk and said without preamble, "Bennett Penrose was here, skulking about in Goonbell some three weeks before Eleanor Penrose was murdered. He used his own name and added the name York. I imagine that's why you didn't learn much of anything when you initially looked into her death, my lord. Yes, old Bennett York was trying to be clever, but I found him out."

"Excellent, Flash. If he did kill her then it would be in hopes that she'd left him money, lots of it."

"That's right. I doubt he knew a thing about Miss Caroline, and if he did, I imagine that old Bennett—being such a man's man—thought no one could possibly leave any groats at all to a mere female."

"That could put Caroline in danger, but not for long. Once we're wedded, then all her money belongs to me. Then there'd be no motive for the little sod." North sat back in the high-backed leather chair and closed his eyes. "That still leaves Mr. Ffalkes. I can't say I want him living here at Mount Hawke for much longer, Flash."

"I say let him go, my lord. Once you and Miss Caroline are wed, just let him go. And you will ensure he knows that he would get his neck stretched on the gibbet if he killed you or if anything at all happened to you."

"You've given this a lot of thought, Flash."

"Aye, I venture to say nearly as much as you. Also I spoke to the captain. He said he'd be quite pleased to tell Mr. Ffalkes the facts of his new life."

North smiled at that. "It seems all goes forward then. We still don't have any evidence, however. That bloody knife—what did the killer do with it? Dr. Treath, once the poor man could speak about it, said he believed it to be just a regular knife, the sort one would find in any kitchen. Not a fishing or hunting knife, nothing out of the ordinary."

"I plan to visit Mr. Bennett Penrose's chamber this evening at Scrilady

Hall. Our boyo will be in Goonbell drinking with his cohorts again. I'll see what I can unearth. Also, my lord, I found out from Mrs. Freely, quite a talker she is, and—" Flash paused a moment and preened. "Aye, it's true, the ladies find me quite appetizing. Well, in any case, she told me that Mrs. Penrose wasn't the first lady to die under mysterious circumstances. There was another lady who was skewered with a knife some three years ago, by the name of Elizabeth Godolphin, the widow of a merchant who lived down near Perranporth. The lady had a goodly competence, but she wasn't rich, as Mrs. Eleanor was."

"Any other similarities?"

"Mrs. Freely said something about her seeing some gentleman, but she couldn't remember any more. She said she'd be seeing some of her friends who live there and she'd ask them about it."

"Good, we're gaining ground then."

"Congratulations on your marrying Miss Caroline, my lord. She's a fine girl, all full of spit and fire and mischief, and that mouth of hers, well, the captain told me she'd give you as many fits as Lady Victoria gives him."

North grunted. The thought of walking his hounds on the moors, however, didn't play such a large part in his scenario of daily life anymore.

"I'll also find out if our Bennett Penrose was here when the other lady was killed. It's my understanding he's been hereabouts throughout the years. The little bugger would have been about your age then, my lord. Maybe he was living off her, maybe . . . ah, well, we'll see."

At one o'clock that morning, North was propped up in his bed reading the slim volume Tregeagle had given him. Quite simply, he couldn't believe it. It was a house of men only, and certainly he'd wondered about that, but any questions when he'd been a boy had been dealt with harshly by his father. When he'd been a boy and asked about his mother, he'd been told she was a slut, a trollop, and she was dead, just as she deserved. He hadn't understood the words, but he'd well understood the rage, the bitterness. He'd not asked about his mother all that much past the age of five when he'd come to Mount Hawke with his father to live after his mother had died. He shook his head, leaned back, and closed his eyes. His father's written words were burned sharply in his mind: "Nightingale men don't suffer like other men, once they understand that they are different. I didn't believe my father's and his father's words, but now I do. By all the gods, they were right. At least I have the next generation Nightingale, the next Viscount Chilton, and that miserable slut is gone. All will be well. I will teach North, and pray God he will listen and believe me. There's no need for him to go through what I went through. He will beget his heir and quickly rid himself of the slut necessary to be the Nightingale vessel. He will be free. He won't suffer even a moment's anguish, like the rest of us. He *will* believe me."

Those words were written when North had been five years old. He tried desperately to remember that time, but all he could remember was screaming and shouting and crying, a woman crying. His mother? He didn't know. Then he'd come here. Then he'd been told that his mother was dead. And then there'd been the year upon year of misery and hatefulness and spite and utter gloom. What had happened?

He thumbed through his grandfather's and great-grandfather's writings, but didn't read them, just his father's, and the good lord knew, it was enough.

He was appalled.

"My lord."

"Yes, Tregeagle, what is it?"

"Er, my lord, did you read the tome we presented to you yesterday?"

North tossed down the quill and leaned back in his desk chair. He'd been writing an announcement to the *Gazette* and to the *Times* about his upcoming marriage to Miss Derwent-Jones. "Yes, I read part of it, the part my father wrote."

"I see," Tregeagle said, and waited hopefully, keeping quiet because he wasn't stupid.

"It sounded just like my father—all ranting and shrieking at the dishonor of the female species, pitying himself in a bottle of brandy, all rage and bitterness. Nothing new. However, even that worsened under the influence of my grandfather. I remember both of them as relentlessly cruel, sadistic men who hated everyone, and obviously lost what few wits were left to them."

"My lord, he was your father!"

"He was a filthy old bedlamite, Tregeagle! God, how I despised him. Now, that's quite enough. There will be a Countess of Chilton living at Mount Hawke beginning in four days' time. The first one in how long a time? You don't even answer that, do you?

"I realize I didn't live at Mount Hawke until I was five years old. My mother died and I was brought here. Why didn't she live here during her marriage to my father? Ah, not a word. No matter. What would I expect from you, my father's minion? Well, my countess won't be kept hidden away in London like a damned mistress, or ensconced on one of my moldering estates. This will be her home just as it is mine. If you can't accept that, Tregeagle, if any of you can't accept that, why then, you will all leave."

"My lord, we will remain to protect you, to see to your needs and your wishes."

North sighed. "I shouldn't have spoken to you like that. However, I will hear no more about it. Go away, I must finish with this task."

North watched his housekeeper slowly leave the small estate room. It was all nonsense, but the male minions believed every word, every assertion. It was amazing that they were so tied into the bitterness of the past.

Then he pictured Caroline's shocked yet quite interested expression when he'd had her hold up her own skirts and petticoats on the beach and he was touching her. He smiled and noticed that his hand shook a bit. He would protect her. All would be well. He would be a husband, something that simply hadn't occurred to him as being devoutly wished for, but he would have Caroline in his bed whenever he wanted her, and that was surely a fine thing. She was lovely, she seemed eager, and he wanted her more than he'd ever wanted a woman in his life. No more going without a woman or having to install a mistress or having an affair with a local lady, something he'd avoided like the plague in the past.

He realized then, at that moment, that part of his desire for solitude, an attitude so longstanding this was the first time he'd truly questioned it, came from the continuous bitterness and barely tamped-down rage spouted by his father, his distrust of people in general and women in particular. North had obviously taken the words to heart throughout his youth and simply turned himself away from the possibility of betrayal by believing he didn't need people. Unlike Caroline, he hadn't realized he was missing what life was all about. Unlike Caroline, he'd had to be pulled into joy and into the possibility of sadness and disappointment.

He would be Caroline's husband.

He would laugh for the rest of his life.

19

Caroline came bolt upright in her bed at the sound of a piercing scream. She threw back the covers, grabbed her dressing gown, and was into the corridor in the next moment.

There was another scream, only this one just a small cry, muffled, barely to be heard. Oh God, it was coming from Alice's bedchamber. She ran down the hall, stopped to catch her breath, and flung open the door.

There was a single candle lit, standing atop the small table beside Alice's bed. Alice wasn't alone. It wasn't a nightmare. It was Bennett and he was on top of her, shoving his belly against her, and Alice was struggling frantically.

Bennett drew back his hand and slapped her hard. "Shut up, you little slut, just shut up. If you didn't want this, you wouldn't have your belly filled with a brat. Shut up and give me what I want."

"No," Alice whimpered, and kept struggling.

"Bennett!"

He went utterly still. Slowly, he turned to face her. She was wearing a dressing gown, her hair was thick and wild around her face. He shook his head, not understanding. "Caroline? What are you doing here?"

"By God, you're drunk, you filthy pig. Get off her."

"Oh no, she's here and she's mine and you should have seen the looks she was giving me all day. She all but begged me to come to her tonight."

Caroline wished she had a gun, but since she didn't, she'd just have to make do.

She picked up a footstool, a very solid oak footstool, its surface covered with a lovely tapestry, lifted it high, and said quietly, "Bennett, I'm talking to you. Won't you turn this way now?"

"Go away, Caroline, unless you want me to take you next." No sooner were the words out of his mouth than Bennett froze. "No," he said, and jerked away from Alice, but he wasn't fast enough. "No, Caroline—"

She brought the footstool down on his head as hard as she could. She stepped back and watched him fall off Alice, who shoved at him to keep him from falling over her.

"Oh, Miss Caroline, I swear to you, I didn't ask him to come here, I promise, Oh, Miss—"

"Hush, Alice. Let me see if the damned bounder is dead." She knelt down and pressed her palm to his heart. "He's not, more's the pity," she said, looking up at Alice, who looked like the child she was, pale and drawn and shaking. "Did he force you, Alice?"

Alice shook her head, tendrils of light brown hair swirling about her thin face, come loose from her braid. "He just hit me and shoved himself at me."

"I heard your cry and came immediately."

"He didn't think I'd mind. He didn't think I'd scream, but I did, but he was too much in the fever to stop. He just kept calling me those horrible names, just like the vicar does."

"I know, I know," Caroline said. Sudden rage surged through her and she kicked Bennett in his ribs. She wished she had Mr. Plumberry there as well; she'd boot him but good. "There," she said, "that feels better." She stepped over Bennett's unconscious body and sat on the side of the bed, drawing Alice into her arms. "There, it's all right. I swear this won't happen again, I swear it. Do you want to kick him, Alice?"

Alice stopped crying. She became very still, then drew away from Caroline. "Kick him?"

"Yes, for what he tried to do to you."

Alice looked very worried, then, suddenly, she smiled. "Oh yes," she said. "Oh yes." She eased off the bed, stood over Bennett, then kicked him as hard as she could in his ribs.

"Do it again, Alice. He deserves it."

She kicked him again, and this time she said, "That were wunner . . . er, that *was wonderful,* Miss Caroline. I even hurt my foot kicking the bounder."

"By God, what's going on in here? Caroline!"

It was Owen. He'd been running so fast his dressing gown was still flapping about his bare legs. "Bennett! That bloody bastard, I'll—"

"You won't do a thing to him at the moment, Owen, so calm down. Thank you for coming so quickly. Ho, here's Evelyn and Miss Mary Patricia."

They'd come more slowly, their pregnant bellies keeping them at a walk.

"Oh goodness," Evelyn said, taking in the situation at a glance, "my little baby, oh dear."

"It's all right," Caroline said. "She'll be just fine. She just gave Bennett two very sturdy kicks in his miserable ribs. Yes, Alice will be fine. However, it seems advisable for Miss Mary Patricia to fetch you some warm milk to calm you down before you decide to kick the rest of us."

Alice giggled. Her would-be rapist was on the floor, yet she'd giggled. Caroline was so pleased she wanted to dance.

"Yes, an excellent idea, Miss Caroline," Miss Mary Patricia said.

"Owen, would you drag Bennett out of here and into his bedchamber? Oh dear, there's blood on his head. Do you think we should call Dr. Treath?"

Owen didn't think they should call anyone save the hangman, but Caroline, eyeing the flowing blood from the blow she'd struck him, shook her head. "Do go fetch Dr. Treath. The last thing we want is for Bennett to croak here at Scrilady Hall. After all, Owen, I was the one who hit him and therefore it would be I who would go to the gallows."

"Let him rot, Caroline."

"Let me kick him again, Miss Caroline," Alice said.

"We can't, more's the pity."

The two of them together dragged Bennett into his room and hefted him onto his bed. Caroline wrapped a folded cloth over the wound in his head and Owen quickly dressed. "I'll be back as soon as I can. If that bloody bastard wakes up, hit him again."

She grinned, but it was a sorry excuse for a grin. When Owen was gone, she left Bennett and returned to Alice. Both Evelyn and Miss Mary Patricia were petting and soothing her, giving her milk, stroking her hair, telling her how strong she was and how she'd gotten that miserable bastard but good.

"Is he dead, Miss Caroline?" Evelyn said.

"No he's not. Bennett is a sorry man and he's drunk and I hope he has the most horrid headache imaginable when he wakes up. Lord knows his ribs will hurt like the very devil. Now, don't worry anymore about this." But Caroline was worrying. If Bennett was here, then there was always the chance he'd try this again.

She shook her head. "I'm just relieved I heard you scream, Alice. It was a big one, thank God."

"But I didn't scream, not really, Miss Caroline, just cried out before he slapped his hand over my mouth."

Caroline stared at her. "But I heard you, clear as if you were in my bedchamber. I heard you, Alice. It was loud."

"No, miss, truly. I'm glad you did hear me, but I only sounded like a squeaky little mouse."

It was Bess Treath who told her how this was possible while Dr. Treath was stitching Bennett's head. "Eleanor told me about it," she said comfortably, gently daubing at the flow of blood while Dr. Treath drew his needle in and out of Bennett's scalp. Caroline didn't look.

"You see, there are several connecting passages behind the bedchambers. The major one connects Alice's bedchamber to yours. The chimney acts like a tunnel that exaggerates any and all sounds. It's not completely solid, you see, and gives onto the passageway."

"So I heard this god-awful scream but it was only Alice crying out."

"Exactly. I think the reason the two of those bedchambers connect up is because the grandfather of the former Squire Penrose had both a wife and a ladylove. He sent the wife off to London for a new wardrobe, so it's recounted, and while she was gone, he had the passageway built and his mistress installed as the governess. When the wife returned, she was none the wiser, and she was the proud possessor of some very nice clothes. At that time, it's said, her bedchamber was the one furthest down the east hall."

"Goodness, that's amazing."

Bess Treath laughed, even as she continued to clean up the blood from Bennett's head and face. "My own opinion is the wife found out exactly what her dear husband had done because every year after that, she went off to London and spent ever so much money on new clothes. Her husband said not a word."

Caroline joined in her laughter.

"Now, Bess, you have no idea if that's really true." Dr. Treath knotted off his stitches, patted Bennett's head, then began to bandage it. "It's one of those tales that's talked about on and off over the years, during cold winter evenings. Ah, he's waking up. Too bad he waited so long. I should have liked to have him suffer the needle just a bit, mind you."

"Benjie, what a thing for a physician to say."

"Well, the little drunkard deserves something for what he tried to do."

Bennett groaned and tried to pull away. Dr. Treath said, "Hold still, I'm nearly done. That's right, moan if you must, but don't move."

When it was over, Bennett looked up to see Caroline standing there close to his bed. "You," he said, even as he lightly touched his fingertips to his aching head, "you hit me with that footstool."

"If I'd had a gun I would have shot you, you miserable excuse for a man."

"Listen to me, Caroline, the little slut wanted it, she wanted me, she—"

Caroline picked up a footstool that sat in front of the wing chair in front of the fireplace and turned with it over her head. "Yes, Bennett?"

He eyed the footstool, then shrugged. "Believe what you will. Leave me alone. God, my ribs hurt like fire."

Dr. Treath didn't offer any laudanum. He merely told Bennett to remain in bed for several days. "No drinking and no wenching," he said. "If you do either, you'll be in danger of causing an infection, and an infection in the brain most often leads to death."

"That was well done," Caroline said to Dr. Treath when they were out in the corridor.

"Yes, it was," he said, and chuckled. "Now, Caroline, I want to examine you to see that you're all right."

"Me? I'm dandy, Dr. Treath. It's Alice you need to see to."

"I will after I've checked you over. Bess will go to Alice now and begin."

Bess merely smiled, nodded, and took herself off down the corridor to Alice's bedchamber.

"Now, my dear, come along."

When they reached her bedchamber, Dr. Treath told her to sit on the bed. He listened to her heart, but nothing more. Actually, he didn't really examine her at all. He straightened beside the bed and said without preamble, "This bothers me immensely, Caroline, as I'm sure it does you. Now, you and North are going to be married tomorrow. I don't think—"

She cut him off with her hand and with a smile. "Don't worry, Dr. Treath, I know what I'm going to do. You'll see. Incidentally, both Alice and I kicked Bennett in the ribs but good. I'm very pleased he hurts."

Then she laughed and hugged him, kissing his cheek. "Don't worry."

Bess Treath said from the door, "Alice is just fine. No cramping, just a bit of nervousness, natural, of course. Would you like to give her a tonic?"

"No, just a drop of laudanum in milk. That will send her right off to sleep."

After Bess and Benjamin Treath had left, Caroline, with a very awake Mrs. Trebaw at her heels, made certain the front door and all the first-floor windows were secured. "Of course, since Mr. Penrose lives here and has a latchkey, this is rather silly," Caroline said. "But it does make me feel better."

She sent Mrs. Trebaw to bed. She tucked Alice in and sent Miss Mary Patricia and Evelyn back to their bedchambers. She sighed deeply when she came into her bedchamber and quickly closed the door. She stretched and rubbed the back of her neck. She felt exhaustion pull at her. She began to untie the sash of her dressing gown when she heard a man's low voice say from behind her, "Please don't disrobe, Miss Caroline."

She whipped about and stared, clapping her hand over her heart. "Oh! I nearly jumped out of my skin! Flash Savory, how did you get in here?"

"Oh, I've been here for some time now. I didn't want to show myself because the good doctor just might not understand. I'm here to search Bennett's bedchamber. You coshed him, Caroline? Did I hear aright?"

"Yes, he was trying to rape Alice. She's only fourteen, Flash, only fourteen years old and she's with child. I had her kick him hard in the ribs. It made her feel better, gave her some power."

"That was very well done of you. Now, where's Owen?"

"Owen. Goodness, I sent him after Dr. Treath, but I forgot about him. He isn't here?"

"I didn't see him."

Caroline gave Flash a crooked smile. "I know where he is. In fact, we should be hearing—"

She paused, grinning, at the sound of men's voices.

"He fetched his lordship," Flash said. "Smart young man, that Owen. Your betrothed sounds on the ragged edge."

North was beyond ragged. He flung open the door to Caroline's bedchamber, saw her standing there in her dressing gown, her hair wild and loose about her face and down her back, and yelled, "What the holy hell are you doing, Caroline Derwent-Jones? Damnation, I can't leave you alone for an hour without you getting yourself into messes that will surely turn my hair gray before I'm thirty. Oh, you, Flash? What the devil are you doing in Caroline's bedchamber? You little bastard, if you have touched—"

Caroline laughed and walked right into him, wrapping her arms around his back. Actually, it took him a moment before he raised his arms and hugged her to him.

"It's all right, North. Everything's all right. I wish Owen had told me he was going to fetch you. I would have talked him out of it. But it's nice of you to come. Goodness, you're still breathing hard." She kissed him, there in front of Flash and Owen, a sweet kiss, a chaste kiss, but it went through him like lightning.

He took her arms in his hands and set her away from him. "Tell me what the hell happened here. And tell me what this smiling bastard is doing in your bedchamber."

"All right. Why don't we go downstairs and I'll pour you a brandy."

It required two brandies and many questions on North's part before he was satisfied. He stood there by the fireplace, frowning down at his boots, then said, "Let's go, Flash. We'll both search that bloody little sod's room. If we find something, we'll just dump him out the window."

"Sounds like a fine plan to me," Flash said. "The miserable bugger, trying to hurt that little girl."

"I'll help," Owen said.

"All right, Owen. Caroline, you go to bed. By God, we're getting married in six hours. I would appreciate my bride not snoring during the ceremony. Or after, as a matter of fact, at least until we've—"

"North!"

Flash Savory just grinned. "The captain is always trying to put Lady Victoria to the blush, and she yells at him and turns red and sometimes punches him in the belly."

"Hear that, North? Best be careful, you and your outrageous tongue."

"Ah, Caroline, you—"

"North, be quiet."

Flash, Owen, and North spent a good thirty minutes searching Bennett Penrose's bedchamber. There was no sound save for Bennett's snores, but Flash did find a small square box on top of which was a pair of Bennett's evening shoes. "Hi ho, what's this, I wonder?"

North took the box from him and opened it. "Letters," he said. "There are at least half a dozen letters here." He pulled one out and spread out the single piece of paper. "Bloody hell," he said, "you'll not believe this one." North cursed some more, stopped himself from stamping his booted feet on the floor in sheer frustration and disappointment.

Flash took the letter, read it, and sighed deeply. "Well, that more or less lets our boy off the hook, doesn't it?"

"Yes," North said. "Damnation, it shows he was in London for those days surrounding Eleanor Penrose's death, if this letter is to be believed, which I suppose it must."

"He was such a meaty suspect," Flash said. "I had pinned such hopes on him."

"Where do we go from here, my lord?"

"Home to bed, Flash. I'm getting married tomorrow."

20

Bishop Horton from Truro married Frederic North Nightingale, Baron Penrith and Viscount Chilton, to Miss Caroline Aiden Handerson Derwent-Jones, spinster, the following morning at precisely ten o'clock in the drawing room of Mount Hawke in a ceremony that lasted precisely eight and a half minutes. The final five and a half minutes of the ceremony took place with eyes closed. Bishop Horton prayed. He began with praise of the metaphorical wedding of Adam and Eve, came smoothly forward to the glory and the Christian purpose of the wedding currently under way, then moved onward to extend well into the future to North and Caroline's progeny, who would doubtless, if God so ordained, find as noble spouses as their ancestors had. Caroline found that she was getting confused between herself as an ancestor and some Chilton now long dead. Or was it someone long dead in the distant future?

When Bishop Horton decided he'd been as thorough as was pertinent to the proceedings, he beamed on Caroline and North, then asked if anyone would like to step forward to take exception to this blessed union. To everyone's relief, no one moved, including Mr. Ffalkes. After the bishop's final blessing, Caroline was beginning to feel less dazed at how the entire course of her life had been changed all in the space of three minutes of spoken instructions and the rest in a prayer that recounted and praised untold generations of marital bliss.

North kissed her after Bishop Horton closed his Bible and nodded to him. It was a very chaste kiss, over quickly.

Mount Hawke servants—male to the man—stood on one side of the drawing room, and the denizens from Scrilady Hall—female all, save the stable lad, Robin—stood on the other. There were locals there as well, the most notable amongst them Mrs. Freely, Mr. Peetree, the Treaths, Mr. Brogan, and the Carstairses. Mrs. Freely had spoken behind her hand discreetly, commenting on Caroline's gown, the lightness of her face powder, the speed with which the young couple were marrying, how the bride looked thin as a rail, which was a good thing, wasn't it? Both North and Caroline heard every word, as did every other guest.

Caroline was at least pleased with Mrs. Freely's opinions on her gown. It was a soft ivory satin that was simple and elegant, binding her beneath her breasts with a ribbon just a shade darker than the gown, and matching the ribbon and soft white burnet roses threaded through her chestnut hair, gleaming bright and clean in the clear sunlight pouring into the drawing room. The bodice was low and filled with an ivory linen chemisette. She didn't wear a veil over her face. She looked tall and slender, radiant and smiling, her eyes bright, the excitement clear whenever she looked at her husband.

"A love match," Victoria Carstairs said to her husband as she watched North turn away from his bride to begin accepting congratulations. "How lovely."

"More a lust match on North's part," Rafael Carstairs said. "His eyes nearly turn black when he looks at her. I doubt the poor girl will get much sleep this night, or any other night for the next year or so."

"His eyes are nearly black anyway," Victoria said, her hand lightly resting against her flat belly where their babe nestled. "You're being obtuse. Besides, you don't let me get much sleep even now, and you swore to me it wasn't just male lust. You swore you cherished me and adored me and were even building a pedestal upon which I would sit two nights a week so that you could bow and scrape and worship me—"

"That's nauseating, Victoria. Now, heed me. Naturally I felt and still feel lust for you. I understand lust, most men do. This other, well, it's all well and good and makes a man's life more happy than not, usually, if the wife is kept in her proper place, and naturally you've always known that place." He grinned down at her like a bandit.

"He's a beautiful man," she said. "North Nightingale, I mean."

"Passable, little more. He is nothing to me. You told me I was the most beautiful man in all of Cornwall, in all of Devon, too."

"Did I? My memory fails me. Ah, but North, just look at those white teeth of his, and how muscular he is, and so very lean and hard and—"

"Victoria Carstairs, would you like me to do something you will surely regret?"

She looked up at him, a siren's smile on her mouth, and said, "Yes."

He eyed her for a long moment, cursed, and took himself off to congratulate the bride and groom.

Caroline stared up at North, marveling that he was hers, all hers, and all because Owen had gotten ill and she'd gone into the taproom of the inn in Dorchester to find help and he'd been there. It was scary that one's life could be swayed and changed by such random chance. Ah, but in this case, it had been a wonderful random chance. He was hers at last. It had taken only eight and a half minutes.

She watched his profile, watched him smile at something Rafael Carstairs said. She wanted to touch his straight nose, his mouth that was so very beautiful she wanted to kiss it until she lost her breath. She wanted to touch his tongue with her fingertip and her own tongue, to feel his heat, to taste his taste and breathe in his scent. She saw herself standing on the beach, holding up her skirts and petticoats whilst he was on his knees, caressing her and touching her with his mouth. Oh dear. That had been something. She rather hoped he would be compelled to do that again. She shuddered, smiled like a fool, and continued her perusal of her new husband. His jaw was firm and stubborn, which was fine with her. He wasn't a man to back down. A good opponent always brightened her up.

"Caroline."

"Huh?"

"Where are you?"

"Oh, North. I was just looking at you and thinking that we will have wonderful fights. Actually I was thinking other things before that, but it wouldn't be at all proper to mention those other things here in the drawing room. Yes, we will have marvelous fights."

"So this is the future you envision for us? That pleases you?"

"You're strong and stubborn, just look at that jaw of yours. I wouldn't want a man I could kick into the dirt. You're just as I want you to be."

"Thank you, perhaps," he said, then leaned down and gave her a very light kiss on her mouth. "Oh damn," he said, and quickly drew back. "We have to wait until at least after luncheon. It isn't fair. I'm married to you, it's all legal, and I still have to wait. What were those other things?"

She giggled. "I will say only that they were beach sorts of activities. Now, if you're very good to me, I can perhaps have a stomach gripe, turn convincingly green, and beg to be excused. You, naturally, wouldn't want to leave me alone in my misery. You would want to nurture me, feed me soup, wipe my sweating brow. What do you think?"

He stared down at her, his eyes bright on her face. "Your mind is terrifying."

"It's a grand idea, isn't it?"

He laughed, a full, free laugh, and Tregeagle turned to his comrades and said in a depressed voice, "Did you hear that, Mr. Polgrain? Mr. Coombe? He's *laughing*. Nightingale men rarely laugh, particularly at something a female says." Tregeagle sighed deeply. "As far as I know, his lordship's father never laughed a day in his life. His lordship's father would have spat upon anyone who dared to laugh in his presence. He would have reviled such a thing. Ah, it's an unhappy day."

"She is a pernicious influence," said Polgrain.

Coombe shuddered, tugged at the thin edge of hair just above his ears, and dabbed the perspiration from the bald flesh just above. "Perhaps we could endure having her here at least for a little while, but more than just a little while? It is too much, gentlemen, far too much."

"We will endure," Tregeagle said. "Just look at those pregnant females, all lined up in a row. It hurts me to gaze at them."

"Mr. Owen will take them back to Scrilady Hall after luncheon, Mr. Tregeagle, don't worry," Polgrain said. "We can bear seeing them and their affliction for just a few more hours. Oh dear, I must get back to the kitchen. It galled me to do it, but I have made a champagne punch to rival the punch served by all the big nobs at their weddings in London."

"It's not what we're used to, Mr. Polgrain, no indeed," Tregeagle said, and sighed deeply again. "Feed everyone well and let's hear nice healthy belches. We don't want it said that the men of Mount Hawke can't carry off anything and carry it off well, despite their pain."

"I still can't believe he actually married her," Coombe said, looking hard at the young lady who was now the Countess of Chilton and mistress of Mount Hawke. "If he wanted to bed her there was no reason to marry her. He should have just taken her to bed and gotten her out of his system. Now we shall have to suffer her presence day in and day out."

"Ah, but she's a lady and thus all men's downfall," Tregeagle said. "To bed her, he had to marry her."

"She's a lady to begin with, perhaps most of them are, but she'll change," Polgrain said, "just like all the others. And she won't be here long, you'll see," he continued. "Don't you remember? His lordship's father brought his wife to visit here but once, before he understood the way of things and took her away again."

"Aye, but don't forget, *his* father was still alive and the master here. He wasn't about to let her stay. In fact, if his son hadn't disobeyed him, she never would have even visited here for a single day. But our lordship here, I don't know. He read the diaries, but he believes it's all nonsense."

"He will learn," Coombe said, patting his bald head yet again. "Poor young man, he will learn. I remember all the stories my father told me about the Nightingale men. I suppose we're lucky that there was enough vigilance in them so that a male child gets birthed and is indeed a Nightingale and not some other man's get."

"Barely in time," Polgrain said, "barely in time."

"We will get through this," Tregeagle said again. "We have much to do and we will do it with efficiency and graciousness. Goodness, all of them with child at once, even that child Alice is with child. It's dreadful and not to be borne."

"A remarkable *bon mot*, Mr. Tregeagle," Coombe said.

Owen stood close and all stiff beside his father in the corner of the drawing room in the late morning shadows. He'd been terrified his father would leap on North during the brief ceremony, but he hadn't budged from behind the large chair. He looked furious. Owen recognized the dark rage in his father's eyes; it had been directed at him enough during his life. But he'd held his tongue. He'd done nothing. He was, thankfully, still doing nothing. His hands weren't even fisted at his sides. Odd, but his father looked older, Owen thought, somehow he seemed to have shrunk. As Mr. Brogan approached, he closely watched his father for any signs of violence.

"Sir," Mr. Brogan said. "I am the solicitor for the former Miss Derwent-Jones, now Countess Chilton. His lordship asked me to speak plainly to you. He is, in short, now in complete control of her finances and her fortune."

"Not for long," Mr. Ffalkes said, and all but snarled. "No, not for bloody long, the damned poaching bounder."

"Father," Owen said.

"Be quiet, you little sod, you worthless, ungrateful piece of muck. As for you, sir, I will see you pay for what you've had the gall to do to me, why, you—"

Mr. Brogan continued easily, interrupting Mr. Ffalkes with the calm of Bishop Horton. "This envelope is for you, sir. It details all you have done to Countess Chilton, all your plots, your conspiracies that have, thankfully, all failed. It is attested to by Lord Chilton, Lady Chilton, and your son, Owen Ffalkes. Now, if anything were to happen to North Nightingale, then, sir, you would be immediately taken to gaol and then your neck would surely be stretched and you would shortly find yourself quite dead. So you see, it is to your advantage that Lord Chilton remain as healthy as a stoat. Also, if the remote possibility occurred that you weren't hanged, you would still gain nothing. Lord Chilton's estate isn't left to his wife, but rather to his friend, the Earl of Chase. Do you understand me, sir?"

"That's utter nonsense and you're lying. I am her relative. The estate couldn't be left away from her. I would contest it and I would win."

"Ah, but the viscountess wouldn't contest anything, sir, thus any action you would contemplate taking would result in you looking like a fool. I beg you to reassess your situation. I encourage you to leave Cornwall and forget the viscountess. It is all over. There is nothing here for you." Mr. Brogan merely nodded then to Mr. Ffalkes, turned, and left, a look of distaste clear on his pleasant face.

"Damned little cit," Mr. Ffalkes said. "As for you, Owen, you betrayed me?" He waved the thick envelope in front of his son's nose.

"No, sir, I did it primarily to protect you. You may not believe that, but it's true. There is something else Caroline asked me to consult you about."

"What does the little bitch have to say?"

"She wants you to return to Honeymead Manor and manage the property for her. She wants you to live there, if you wish. She also mentioned—and she did smile a bit—that Mrs. Tailstrop thought you were a grand fine gentleman."

"The old bag."

"Old!" Owen said, aghast. "Caroline said she was younger than you are, sir."

"There are differences in old when it's a man and when it's a woman."

"Well, there it is. You may go to Honeymead Manor or you may do as you please. I, sir, I will remain here and live at Scrilady Hall. I am now Caroline's manager. Soon I will be her partner, in fact."

Mr. Ffalkes cursed roundly. "You're nothing but a foolish, weak little boy."

Owen drew himself up. It was difficult with the scorn his father was heaping in bucketfuls on his head, but he did try. "I'm better, Father. Caroline and North both said so. I am very nearly my own man. Other men depend on me. Ladies depend on me. What I do counts for something. I rather like it."

Mr. Ffalkes roundly consigned his son to hell, picked up his valise, and without a backward look, took his leave.

"He's gone," Owen said.

"Yes," North said. "We saw him leave."

"I don't know what he'll do, Caroline."

"As long as he leaves the area I'll be content," Caroline said. "North has a man following him just so we can be certain he does leave Cornwall. Now, husband, it is nearly time to adjourn to the dining room. Polgrain says he and his staff have prepared a repast to bring tears to the most jaded eyes, of which there weren't many, he said, at least in this backwater group. I rather think it won't be possible for me to produce a stomach gripe. Your male minions would shoot me. Polgrain informed me, without really looking me in the eye, you understand, that no effort would be spared for the *event*."

Over a very grand luncheon of turkey and chestnut pasty, stuffed shoulder of lamb, pork with apples and sage, a delicious red-currant fool that was a lovely pink color—for the bride, Polgrain had muttered within her hearing—the talkative Mrs. Freely tendered an opinion on everything from Lady Carstairs's appetite, which wasn't enough to keep a bird alive, much less a poor little babe, to Mr. Brogan's glasses, which were, she pronounced, quite a handsome addition to his face, which, she fancied, would become even more handsome were he to procure himself a wife.

North looked at his wife and grinned. "What can one do?"

She drank more of her champagne.

21

Where was North?

Caroline stood there, her hands stroking over the fine lawn of her new nightgown—a soft peach with a row of Valenciennes sewn at the bodice and at the sleeves, all in all a wicked confection that she was certain would have North ogling over her with a good deal of interest. It was cut low over her breasts, and the band beneath pushed her breasts upward, giving them, she thought, a more arresting presentation.

Where the devil was he?

She wanted him to look at her and shake. Where his shaking would lead, she didn't know, but it was bound to bring infinite satisfaction to her. Perhaps she'd end up holding up her nightgown for him. She shook herself at the flood of quite interesting sensations that memory brought her. She moved to the small mirror and brushed her hair again, smoothing down the waves as best she could. Then she turned toward the door and frowned. This surely wasn't right.

Where was North?

This bedchamber, he'd told her, was the countess's bedchamber and adjoined the master's bedchamber through the single door she'd stared at on and off for the past hour. He had sounded uncertain about it being the countess's bedchamber, and she could see why. It was a dingy room, the paint a dull green that was faded and peeling, the cherubs that festooned the ceiling molding looked decidedly limp in the wings. The only furnishings were a narrow bed with a bleak gold brocade counterpane covering it that must have been at least fifty years old, a single chair that had unpadded wooden slats for the back—strongly resembling a painting of a punishment chair she'd seen at Chudleigh's Young Ladies' Academy—and a stool in front of the dressing table that looked older than the bed, which was saying something. There was antiquity in this bedchamber and it was very depressing.

Where the devil was her groom?

She frowned at herself in the mirror, tossed down the brush, and walked to the bank of narrow windows, five of them all set in thick lead, and stared out into the darkness. There was only a sliver of moon and a sprinkling of stars. The night was black, the only sound was the rustle of trees that were next to the house. She started to turn away, but something odd caught her eye and she turned back to the window.

She screamed at the top of her lungs, jumped back, tripped on her nightgown, and went down hard on her bottom.

North came flying through the adjoining door, nearly tripping himself. "My God, are you all right? What the hell is wrong?"

Her heart was pounding, she felt hysteria bubble inside her. She couldn't bring words out of her mouth, she was panting too hard, her throat was too constricted with sheer terror. She managed to point at the middle window as she picked herself up off the floor.

North ran to the window, unfastened the rusty latch, and after a few moments of frustration, managed to push the window outward. He leaned over, staring into the night. He didn't move, just looked and looked. Finally, he turned back to face her. "What did you see?"

She was shaking, suddenly colder than she'd ever been in her life, her arms wrapped around herself.

"Caroline, good God, what did you see?" He pulled her tightly against him, rubbing his large hands up and down her back, warming her, trying to calm her. After a few minutes, he said again, "It's all right now. I'm here. Tell me what you saw."

She burrowed her face in the crook of his neck.

"I've never seen you like this before. You become a wife and turn into a hysterical ninny?"

"You sod, you—"

He grinned down at her. "Good. You're back to normal. Kind of like having Alice kick old Bennett in his ribs, right? Now, talk to me."

She took a deep breath. "You're right, I shouldn't have become an idiot. It was a monster, North, but I'm not really sure what kind of monster, just that it was one. I was looking outside wondering where the devil you were, why the devil you hadn't come to me immediately since every time you've been near me in the past weeks you wanted only to kiss me and caress me, and then there was this monster." His arms tightened around her.

"No lust right now. Go on. What monster?"

She gulped, burrowed closer, and whispered into his shoulder, "It was a monster face, no body to go along with it, just a hideous face and it just suddenly appeared right in front of me. But it wasn't really a face, that's why I called it a monster. There was enough human about it, but it was terribly deformed and the mouth was grinning at me and it just kind of bobbed there in front of me."

He held her tighter if that was possible. "That would frighten the wits out of a virgin, which you are."

"You don't believe me?"

"Naturally I believe you're a virgin."

She poked him in the arm and he smiled down at her. "Better now? There's nothing there that I can see, Caroline. But it's so damned dark tonight. Maybe you ate some suspicious mushrooms that resulted in a dash of brain fever?"

She shook her head. "No mushrooms."

"Ah, then it was Mrs. Freely and her commentary on everything and everyone present today."

She tried to smile, but couldn't quite manage it. "Perhaps it was just a tree limb or something like that. I remember hearing the rustling of the trees when the wind pushed their branches against the house. It was just so unexpected and maybe I saw more than I normally would, and it scared the dickens out of me."

"No matter, I will still scour the area outside those windows on the morrow."

"North?"

"Hmmm?" He was kissing her neck, nuzzling her head back so he could have more of her.

"Where were you? What were you doing? I thought you were mad for me. I thought you wanted to toss up my skirts all throughout the afternoon, all during supper, all during the time you were sipping on brandy in the drawing room, even while Mrs. Freely was telling everyone that a groom shouldn't over-imbibe on his wedding night, that it led to disastrous results."

"I was reading in my bedchamber, studying, actually."

"Reading?" She leaned back in the circle of his arms to look up at him. "Studying *what?* How dare you? It's our wedding night!"

"An instruction book with pictures."

She just blinked at him.

"A book that tells a man what he's to do with a woman. A step-by-step instruction book. I was fairly certain all this lovemaking business had something to do with my manly parts and your womanly parts, but I wanted specificity. I wanted expert advice and explanations. I didn't want to be a clod on my wedding night."

She went up on her tiptoes and kissed him full on the mouth. She kept kissing him until he was kissing her back, parting her lips, running his tongue along her bottom lip, his hands going lower to cup her buttocks and lift her against him, molding her to him.

When she was nearly breathless, she leaned back just a bit. "You know, North, I'm not at all sure you're doing this properly. Perhaps you'd best go back and study that book more closely."

He stared down at her, his eyes glazed with lust, shook his head to clear it just a bit, then said, "My God, I need to study how to keep your mouth shut."

"Oh no, that's really quite easy. All you have to do is touch me and kiss me."

"I can do that," he said. He scooped her up in his arms, and nearly ran to her bed, paused a moment and stared at that narrow stingy mattress with its suspicious lumpy surface, then turned and did run into his own bedchamber. She wondered as he dropped her onto her back on the mattress of his bed that would easily hold six men side by side what exactly was going to happen. She felt herself flush, felt her heart speed up, felt her palms dampen. She cocked an eye toward him, watching him strip off his dressing gown. He was naked beneath it. His face was flushed and his eyes looked glazed.

She gasped. She'd never before seen a naked man, except for Mr. Ffalkes. He'd been disgusting. But goodness, North was something she couldn't have imagined.

"North, you—"

"Yes, Caroline?"

She didn't have time to answer because he was on her, jerking loose the ribbon tied in a bow beneath her breasts, pulling her nightgown over her head. "There," he said, throwing the gown to the floor in a heap atop his dressing gown. "Ah, Caroline," he said, then he was kissing her and he came down on top of her. All of him, all at once. The richness of his body, all its textures—from his flesh that was smooth and hot against her, to the crispy hair, thick and black as sin on his chest and legs, and the sheer size and heat of him, it froze her. She was engulfed by feelings she couldn't begin to understand. He was so different from her that she simply couldn't take it all in. There was too much of everything and it was hitting her too fast, and she gasped into his mouth, "North, do you think you could roll over on your back and not touch me?"

Her request was so unexpected it got through to him, breaking through the frantic urgency he felt, and he reared up on his hands, stared down at her, and said, "Very well."

He rolled onto his back, calmly crossed his arms over his chest, and closed his eyes. "Is this what you want? Shall I be holding a lily?"

"Oh no, please put your arms at your sides."

He did, only now he was watching her as she sat on her heels beside him.

Her hair was wild about her shoulders, spilling over to curl around her breasts.

"You are possibly the most beautiful woman I've ever seen," he said, lifted his hand to touch her breast, only to have her say, "No, please, North, keep your hands at your sides."

"Why?"

She looked mildly perplexed, then said, "It was too much at once, the differences between us were just too much for me. I couldn't take all of it in and it was frightening."

"I'll get that bloody book. Surely there must be a chapter about a bride losing her hold on things just because the groom disrobes and leaps on her."

"Oh no, just stay there, please. I want to look at you. I want to see what you're all about. I want to understand you before you, well, do all the things you want to do to me."

He laughed, his muscles so tense they were nearly cramping. He watched her study him, and her study was so thorough it took all his fortitude to lie there quietly and not fling her onto her back again.

She touched her fingertips lightly to his chest, then very slowly, she flattened her palms over him. She was leaning over him now, her breasts loose and very nearly touching him. He arched upward so he could feel her against his chest. It nearly sent him over the edge. He forced himself back flat against the mattress, groaned, and closed his eyes.

"You are very nice, North, just so very different from me. I like the way your hair is so very thick here on your chest, so crinkly beneath my fingers. And just look how it thins out over your stomach." She ran her warm palm down his chest over his navel, coming to a stop only at his groin. "It's not a thin line here," she said, and her hand stopped cold. He heard her suck in her breath. He couldn't help himself, he opened his eyes to look at her. She was silent, just staring down at him for a very long time, for far too long a time, he thought, and said, "Do I repulse you, Caroline? I'm not smooth and white and soft like you. Do you find all the hair and my rod and the rest of me distasteful?"

"Rod," she repeated, still just staring down at him. "That's an interesting word."

"There are many words for it, just as there are for your womanly parts."

She said nothing more, merely continued looking down at him. Then she was leaning down and her mouth touched his belly. Then she lightly rubbed her cheek, back and forth, across his belly. He nearly arched off the bed. He was panting like he'd just run up the cliff at St. Agnes Head. His chest was heaving like he'd just been in the boxing ring with Gentleman Jackson himself and had lost badly.

She immediately straightened and looked up his body—taking her time—until she met his glazed eyes. "Oh dear, I hurt you?"

"Don't be a fool. If you do that again, Caroline, you will be the one on your back and I won't be able to stop. No, don't touch me there, it's simply too much, it drives me over the brink. Oh, all right, kiss me some more, go lower, please, perhaps even touch me with your fingers or perhaps your mouth that's so soft and wet or—" He groaned and twisted as her fingers splayed through the thick hair at his groin until they finally closed around him. She stared down at her hands holding him. Then she smiled, giving him a sloe-eyed look, leaned over him, and touched her lips to his belly again.

Her hair fell in a thick curtain over his belly, hiding her from him. He wanted to see her killing him, see her holding him in her hands. He raised his hand and lifted the thick hair. She turned slightly so he could see her clearly. He nearly lost his hold on what little sanity he had left when she did, it was so incredibly provocative.

"You must stop that now," he said between his teeth. "I swear it, Caroline, I'll spill my seed if you don't stop. A groom spilling his seed in his bride's hand simply isn't done on a wedding night. I'd never be able to hold my head up again around other men. I would be cast out of the male fraternity. I would have been an inept clod on my wedding night and that I simply couldn't bear. Please."

She held him between her warm palms for just a moment longer, until just the point when he knew it was all over for him, when he wanted to throw back his head and yell, then she released him.

She stretched out on top of him, her belly against his, her breasts pressed against his chest. She held his face between her hands and looked down at him. "You're magnificent, North. I now understand a bit more about you and how you work. Perhaps you could take over things now?"

He laughed; it was the only thing a sane man who was on the edge of insanity could do. He didn't move, merely raised his own hands and cupped her face between them. "You're always a surprise, Caroline. You're also a tease. Oh, you don't know you're a tease, or perhaps you do. Perhaps all women know instinctively how to drive a man mad. Come here and open your mouth to me."

She leaned down and his mouth was hot on hers.

"Open your mouth. The good Lord knows I taught you how to do that the second time I saw you."

"Maybe it was the third time," she said, and opened her mouth. His tongue was inside her mouth, touching her own tongue, and it was quite splendid, she thought, until she felt his big hands on her bottom, kneading her flesh, pressing her hard against his man's sex. Then she stopped thinking. His fingers were between her thighs and he found her flesh and he was touching her, exploring, gently entering her and she was shaking now, moving against him, unable to help herself, all of her merging into him and what he was doing to her and what he was making her feel. In the next moment she was on her back and he was between her legs, pushing them apart with his hands and holding them steady and staring down at her.

"North, please," she said, not knowing what to do but knowing that something very wonderful and special was going to happen.

"Just hang on, Caroline." His voice was hoarse and deep and then his hot breath was touching her flesh and she arched upward, moaning, letting his hands lift her higher to his mouth, and soon, so very soon after that, she was crying, sobbing, twisting on the sheets, her hands fisted, hitting his shoulders, then clutching at him, wanting what was coming so badly she didn't think she could bear it, and then suddenly, heat spread through her, drawing her inward, and melded with the heat of his mouth and she yelled.

He held her there until he felt the complete giving of everything that was in her, and he knew that all her feeling had come to him and to herself and he wasted no more time. He came into her fully in the next instant, barred only a moment by her maidenhead, then he was through it, thrusting himself to her womb. He knew he was hurting her, that the haze of pleasure was falling away from her because of the pain of rending her maidenhead. He held himself still and pulled himself up on his elbows, a remarkable feat really, one he was pleased he'd managed to do.

"Hello," he said, looking down into her dazed eyes. "No, don't move. Let yourself get used to me, then I'll move, but not sooner, else it will hurt you some more. The book said I was to apologize abjectly at least ten times when I tore through your maidenhead. It's your badge of innocence and it's important to you and thus I must act appropriately sorry to be the one to rob you of it."

"All right," she said. "What you're saying is nonsense, but it's all right. This is all very strange, North, this business about you being inside me. I mean you're really inside me, not just your tongue in my mouth, but this part of you that's just for me and now you're doing what you're supposed to be doing, isn't that right?"

He grinned painfully. "I sure the hell hope so. I can't wait now, Caroline." He moved and it wasn't too bad. She clasped her arms around him and kissed him, letting his breath flow into her mouth, feeling his frenzy, his growing urgency, until he was arching up, his eyes closed, his head thrown back, and he moved and she felt his seed inside her.

He came down over her, panting hard, to rest his face beside hers on the pillow.

She whispered in his ear, "I don't think you missed any steps, North."

22

For several moments, he didn't know what she was talking about, his brain was too dead. He said then, "I should take my pleasure before giving you yours. Then I can twit you when you haven't any more of a functioning brain than a gnat. No, I didn't miss any steps. On the other hand, I could have made those steps much, much steeper and thus taken a much longer time to reach the summit. What do you think?"

"I think," she said, kissing his throat, "that you are entirely capable of finding us steps that are on side trails, very interesting, rarely stepped upon steps. Surely your book didn't cover every possibility. You're incredible, North. You're probably also very inventive."

"I am," he said, kissed her, then rolled over, pulling her against him. "Side trails, huh? I'll have one by tomorrow morning, all right?"

"I'll think about it too. I'm so glad I didn't have to marry Owen or Bennett," she said, then in the next moment she was asleep.

He kissed her hair, managed to lean over far enough to snuff the candles on the table beside the bed, then closed himself about her again. He hadn't slept with a woman in a very long time.

He'd never before slept with a wife. And that's what she was now, his bloody wife, and he'd given her a woman's pleasure. That was quite nice and well done of him. The male fraternity would approve. He was a damned fine man and a generous one. He hadn't been a clod, though it had been close.

Side trails with lots of individual steps. He only had time to smile about it before he too was deeply asleep.

North awoke the following morning to find himself alone. He thought of that monster's face she'd seen in the window the night before, jerked up in bed, and yelled, "Caroline!"

There was no answer. He turned to see the adjoining door open. He called her name again, but still no answer. He frowned and looked at the clock beside his bed. It wasn't even eight o'clock in the morning.

Damnation, he'd wanted to wake up, then kiss her awake and love her again until she was silly with it. He tossed off the covers and stood up to stretch.

He was in mid-stretch when the door opened and there was Tregeagle standing there, as stiff as a board, looking as horrified as a vicar in a den of iniquity.

North frowned at him. "What the hell do you want, Tregeagle? Where is my wife?"

"Your wife is with *them,* my lord, and *they* are here, all *three* of them, and it is unacceptable; it is not what we're used to. This is the Nightingale household, a household for men only, not some sort of inn for Mary Magdalenes."

North blinked through this bitter speech, then grinned. "Oh, I see, our three pregnant ladies are here. Caroline is with them?"

"Yes, my lord. She insisted that Mr. Polgrain prepare them a very generous breakfast because, she said, *they* had to keep *their* strength up. My lord, we allowed them to be present at your wedding ceremony, allowed them even to remain for the magnificent repast Mr. Polgrain prepared, but then, of course, they left to return where they belonged." Tregeagle drew a very audible breath. "My lord, what are the three pregnant ladies doing here at Mount Hawke, at a man's residence, at seven forty-five o'clock in the morning?"

"Why, Tregeagle, they're moving in. Didn't I tell you that yesterday?"

He thought Tregeagle would faint. He turned white, his limbs began to shake as if he were suffering from palsy. "Have Timmy the maid bring me bathwater, Tregeagle, and get a grip on yourself, man. It won't be so bad. I think the three of you will enjoy hearing feminine conversation and laughter, don't you?"

"No, my lord."

North laughed and laughed. He stopped, realizing what he was doing. This laughter business was becoming more natural. It had quite sneaked up on him and now he was doing it. It made him feel quite nice, when it didn't scare him to death.

When North strode into the small breakfast parlor a short time later, he drew up on the threshold, and just stared. There was Caroline seated unknowingly in his high-backed chair. To her left, right, and center were her three pregnant ladies all seated at the table, chatting gaily, all seemingly in very fine spirits. Well, Caroline should be in the best spirits possible, given how very wonderful he'd been to her on their wedding night. He wondered if in the near future he would have four pregnant ladies at the breakfast table. That made him smile. Then it made him frown, for oddly, it brought odd images to his mind of two very big people who were screaming at each other, then one of those big people was sobbing and cursing, and it was long ago in the past, he did realize that, but those terrifying scenes should have been long forgotten. He knew deep down it was his parents. He hated remembering. He firmly closed the door on those memories and walked forward.

"Good morning, ladies," he said, nodding to each of them. "Are you enjoying your breakfast?"

"Everything is delicious, North," Caroline said, and grinned shamelessly at him. "Polgrain has even presented himself three times to ensure that everything meets with our collective approval. Shall I pour you some coffee?"

He nodded and took his plate to the sideboard. He could but gawk at the lavish array of dishes presented. Polgrain had outdone himself and North wondered why. The kippers looked delicious, as did the bacon. The scrambled eggs looked fluffier than high summer clouds, the toast and muffins were golden brown, and the pots of butter and jam looked rich and creamy. Goodness, there were even nutty buns.

He turned to see Caroline giggling beside him. "You're wondering why everything looks so good, aren't you? You expected dog meat and pigeon droppings."

"How did you do it?"

"I told Coombe to tell Polgrain that if the breakfast wasn't worthy of a viscount's establishment, I would have the three pregnant ladies come help him in his kitchen because, obviously, he didn't know how to cook properly. I thought Coombe would smash me over the head with that hideous Chinese vase in the drawing room, but he contained himself."

"He is a man with self-control, thank God."

Suddenly, she lowered her eyes to the scrambled eggs. She scuffed the toe of her slipper against the edge of the Aubusson carpet.

He snaffled the biggest nutty bun on the well-polished silver tray, looking all the while at her from the corner of his eye, and said in a voice he'd hoped was seductive enough to melt the butter on his nutty bun, "I missed you this morning. I had definite very interesting plans for the use of your fair person when I woke up. There is so much of you that hasn't yet received a fair amount of my attention." He sighed deeply. "You shouldn't have left me. According to the book I was studying last night, Caroline, it simply isn't the done thing to leave your new spouse before he wakes up. It makes him feel inadequate, you see, as if he must have failed to please you on the wedding night, and thus you've left him alone to question his technique endlessly and wonder just how badly he performed."

Her head had snapped up and her mouth was open by the time he came to a polished halt.

"You're making that up, North Nightingale!"

"Not a bit of it. Have you eaten, Caroline?"

"Yes," she said. "Now, I must help my ladies move into their bedchambers. Oh dear, I sat in your chair. I'm sorry, I didn't realize." She was hauling away her plate and silverware, and he was just laughing at her, standing there, his plate in his hand, laughing.

"Hush," she said over her shoulder. "You're giving our guests a very poor opinion of me."

"Oh no, Miss Caroline," Alice said. "I couldn't have imagined a lady enjoying herself with a gentleman."

That was a stopper, but just for a moment. Miss Mary Patricia patted Alice's hand, and Caroline said briskly, "Now, let me show you to your rooms. They're really quite nice."

North called out to her, "It also said in my book that to leave the new spouse immediately after breakfast also puts him in danger of serious self-doubt."

She refused to let him dangle her about any longer, even though he did it splendidly. How could he ever have believed he was dour and dark and brooding? She moved closer to him, out of hearing of Miss Mary Patricia, Alice, and Evelyn. "Oh, I asked Tregeagle about the monster's face in my window last night. I looked him straight in the eye and put it to him."

"Ah."

"He didn't twitch a muscle, but still, he's had many years to perfect a show of innocence."

"Tell you what, let me check around and then I'll put it to Polgrain and Coombe."

"Good luck," she said in a gloomy voice. "They're very good, North, very good indeed."

"But you've thrown them, Caroline."

She cocked her head to one side.

"Aren't there now four ladies living at Mount Hawke?"

She gave him a wicked grin. "What will they say when the female maids arrive?"

"I don't know and I don't look forward to hearing it."

Two hours later, North was sitting in a huge wing chair in the library, Caroline on his lap, more or less, and he was playing with her toes. One silk stocking was lying discarded on her chest. "If you were in a more amenable position I could nibble on your toes. I'll bet they taste like lavender."

"I told Timmy the maid to pour lavender in my bathwater. He stood there and stared at me and then grinned this big toothy grin and poured out enough to bathe an elephant. You saw the bottle, didn't you?"

"It was nearly empty." He lowered her foot to his lap and examined it. "It looks as if your foot has healed all right. I was scared of that damned blister. You must be careful. I knew a boy in the army whose boots were too tight and he got a blister. He didn't pay any attention to it and not five days later he was dead."

"I'll be careful," she said. She'd been lolling over his right arm. Now she raised her hand to cup the side of his face. She loved to touch him, loved the feel of him, the myriad rich textures of him, the sheer differentness of him. He smiled at her. "I've got your left stocking off. I suppose it's time for me to pull down the right one. Then, I suppose, I should continue upward and finish the job, but slowly this time, very, very slowly."

She grabbed his face between her two hands and jerked him down to her, kissing him and not letting him up. When finally she did release him, he wasn't in any hurry to raise his head. "North," she said against his mouth. "Can you stop just a moment? I've an awful cramp in my leg. Perhaps you could rub it?"

He looked at how he'd twisted her about in his lap so he could get a better hold on her. "Sorry," he said, and began to massage her leg.

"The other one, but that feels good too. Up higher, North."

"Higher? You are a damned tease, Caroline Nightingale. Hmm, that doesn't sound bad, does it? Perhaps a wife isn't such a bad thing, particularly if her name fits so very nicely with her husband's."

"Higher, North."

His breathing hitched. "Is the cramp gone?"

"No, it's worse. It's even higher now, North. Oh dear, the dreadful pain of it."

He gave it up, slipped his hand beneath her skirt, and took the more direct route straight up to her bare thigh. "Ah," he said, kissing her nose. "There, Caroline? That nasty cramp that's nearly doubling you over in agony?"

She was staring up at him, her expression delightfully befuddled. She swallowed. "That's fine for a while."

"Let's just see." In the next moment, he was touching her woman's flesh, and she jumped. "North, perhaps that is too high, perhaps that isn't proper in the middle of the day, perhaps I was feeling too adventuresome and perhaps a bit too wicked, and now I'm admitting to cowardice—"

"It's two hours after breakfast, Caroline, and I'm in a bad way. If you were sensible, you would be in a bad way too. However, according to my book, after such a strenuous wedding night that wasn't really all that strenuous at all, I have quite a bit of catching up to do with you. I'm to be exquisitely attentive, not let you out of my sight for an instant, praise your eyebrows, and kiss you behind your knees and follow the trail of my fingers."

He cupped his hand over her and she just stared at him, unable to think of a thing to say, just staring at his mouth, wanting him to kiss her, and he finally gave her a crooked grin, leaned his head down, and—

"*Yoo-hoo?* My lord? Are you in the library, my lord? Perhaps you are beneath the desk over there in the corner searching for a bit of something? My lord?"

"Don't move even a toe, don't make a sound," North said into her mouth.

"My lord? Perhaps you are over there standing behind the curtains, but I don't see your boots. Ah, perhaps just here, right in front of me, seated in that very big wing chair that was surely too large for your great-grandfather who was, it is said, a man who did not extend himself very well vertically."

North eased his hand from beneath her skirt, smoothed down her clothes, gave her one last kiss, and said loudly, "Tregeagle, I am going to stand up now and set my bride beside me. Then I'm going to walk right up to you and smack you in your damned presumptuous mouth."

North was only three feet from Tregeagle, his arm already up, when his housekeeper said in the reproachful voice of a mother whose child has misbehaved, "My lord, I do not bother you apurpose."

"Ha!"

"My lord, please don't strike me just yet. Please lower your arm for just a moment. I am an old man, barely able to stand upright without assistance. Surely you are too much the gentleman to strike me, an ancient being who's also your housekeeper since well before you were born?"

"What the hell do you want, Tregeagle? Make it fast, my fist is fairly twitching to stroke your jaw."

"My lord, Mr. Bennett Penrose is here to see you."

"I see. Why don't you go tell him to wait. Say, for a good two hours?"

"He, er, is very offensive, my lord. He yelled at me. Actually yelled, demanded that I should bring down the little sluts. I told him the females were upstairs and that he could fetch them if he wished to—"

"That isn't at all amusing, Tregeagle," Caroline said, coming up to stand by North.

"Very well, miss, er, madam, I did not tell him where they were nor did I tell him he could fetch them himself. I am here to fetch you, my lord, so that you may deal with the young man. He isn't a very proper young man."

"No, he's a bloody sod," North said. "It would make more sense if he were Ffalkes's son and not poor Owen. Very well, I'll see him now. I'll come out. You stay here, Caroline. No need to put your stockings back on . . . Oh, you're still here, Tregeagle? Listening at full ear, are you? No, don't bother to answer."

Caroline planted her bare feet right in front of him. She wagged her finger in front of his nose. "Oh no you won't, North Nightingale. I am part of this and you won't lock me out by calling it some sort of man thing."

"Very well, Tregeagle. Show him in here."

"Yes, my lord, but I would prefer that you saw him in private. His language is deteriorating rapidly. I don't think that a female sort of person should have to listen—"

"Show him in, Tregeagle," Caroline said in a very loud voice. "This minute."

"Yes," he said, stiffer than a vicar at a bordello, and took himself from the library. He said over his shoulder, "Bare feet, it just isn't done, not in a gentleman's library, not in a gentleman's library at Mount Hawke."

"Go away, Tregeagle," North said.

North sighed. He was still feeling as randy as a goat with a new boot to chew, his fingers were still warm from her flesh, but now, given that Bennett Penrose was just on the verge of breaking up his peace entirely, his randiness was growing more distant by the moment. It just wasn't bloody fair.

"Caroline, your hair is a fright. Go straighten it. When are the new female staff arriving here?"

"After luncheon. They are all approved by Mrs. Trebaw, North."

"Does she also think they'll survive my three brave lads?"

"She didn't venture an opinion on that."

Scant minutes later, Bennett Penrose, looking like a male angel, strode into the library, primed for battle.

23

"What the hell are you doing here, Penrose?"

"I'm not happy," he yelled. "You, Caroline, you take away my pregnant pigeons—don't you recall that Aunt Eleanor made us *both* trustees of them?—and then that miserable man, Owen's father, Roland Ffalkes, stays the night, and we play whist. He's a rank cheater, do you hear? Rank! He took my last guinea, my very last one. He kept pouring me brandy, which was very good but it muddled my wits, and I wouldn't have drunk all that much if I had been the one deciding. And this morning he gives me this superior grin and tells me I should never drink when I gamble. Damned officious old man! He's gone now, but he's got all my money."

"Thank God," Caroline said. "I hope he went back to Honeymead Manor."

"Why are you thanking God, Caroline? You connived with him, didn't you? You told him to make me drink brandy and gamble recklessly."

"That's quite enough, Penrose," North said now, his voice very calm, very quiet, and it terrified Caroline to her bare toes. This was a voice she never wanted to hear directed at her. This was the dark, vicious, probably very dangerous North Nightingale.

"But—"

"No, be quiet. Now you will listen to me. The pregnant ladies are here at Mount Hawke because you can't be trusted not to try to rape them at Scrilady Hall. Yes, I know about your attempted rape of Alice, she being all of fourteen years old, which makes you something lower than a slug."

"She'll be fifteen shortly and that's a bloody lie. Why did you lie to him, Caroline? The little slut wanted me, she rubbed against me, she did everything but come out and beg me to come take her. I didn't really want to because she's got this brat in her belly, but at least I would be safe from having her accuse me of being the father. Damnation, I'm not a slug. And even though she isn't quite yet fifteen, she looks at least fifteen, maybe even sixteen."

"Bennett," Caroline said, her hand resting lightly on North's sleeve, "listen to me and listen very closely. I will pay you five thousand pounds to renounce your trusteeship of the pregnant ladies, those here now and any in the future. You will also renounce your residence at Scrilady Hall. In short, you will renounce everything, leave Cornwall, and stay gone. Remember, you wanted me to lend you five thousand pounds and you claimed you'd pay it back with interest. Very well, the money's yours, but in return, there's no payback to me and you renounce all your partnerships with me."

"Five thousand pounds?"

North was merely looking on now, as if he were an interested onlooker, but Caroline, knowing him better than she thought it possible to know another human being in such a short time, saw the tug of amusement on his mouth. It was there, she was sure of it. She couldn't let him down. She wouldn't.

"Yes, five thousand pounds. Mr. Brogan can be fetched to draw up the papers for you to sign."

"Ten thousand pounds, Caroline, not a guinea less. Surely my half is worth twice that amount, even more. You're just trying to take advantage of me because you made Mr. Ffalkes cheat me and pour brandy down my throat."

North said, giving his fingernails a study, never looking up, "Let me kill him, Caroline. He's surely not worth anything close to ten thousand pounds. Yes, I'll kill him. It will be quick and clean, and we won't have to see his bloody face again. I can bury him underneath one of the apple trees. I don't think anyone will care, do you?"

Bennett gulped and said quickly, "All right, seven thousand."

It went back and forth, in the most civilized fashion, until they both agreed to six thousand three hundred pounds.

"It's not enough to get an heiress," Bennett said.

"Perhaps not," North said, flicking an invisible speck off his sleeve, "but it's enough—if you use your brain and don't gamble—to live quite nicely for a very long time. Let me make it even more simple, Penrose. It will allow you to eat. Without it, you would starve, because I can't imagine a single soul who would give you any money or any free food."

"That's right," Caroline said, and walked to the library doors. "Besides, you told me five thousand would be enough. What's the matter, Bennett? Are you getting less charming by the minute? You don't think you'll succeed anymore?"

"No, naturally I'll succeed. It's just that I like knowing that I am still half-owner in everything here in Cornwall. It would make me sound more important, more steady to my future father-in-law, if I could claim residence at Scrilady Hall. By God, your feet are bare," Bennett said in a choked voice. "Good God, your feet have nothing on them."

"Penrose," North said in that soft voice, "Caroline has very nice feet. I enjoy looking at them."

She just shook her head and opened the library doors.

Tregeagle and Coombe were standing there, staring. Neither of them appeared at all embarrassed that they'd been caught eavesdropping.

"I didn't hear you, miss," Coombe said. "Ah, your feet are bare, just as I happened to hear Mr. Penrose say quite loudly. It isn't fitting. Now." He looked toward North. "My lord, what do you want us to do?"

Caroline cleared her throat. "I want you to have Mr. Brogan fetched here immediately, Coombe."

"My lord?"

"Do as her ladyship asks, Coombe," North said.

"I'm not certain I want to do this," Bennett said. "I'd be giving up everything forever."

North just turned and looked at him. He said nothing, just looked at him. Caroline saw that his hands weren't even fisted at his sides. He looked utterly calm and relaxed. She knew he was quite ready to smash Bennett. She hoped Bennett would give him provocation. She would like to see the greedy little bastard flat on his back on the library floor. But Bennett, with an animal's cunning, kept quiet. North took his arm and led him from the library. "You may sit in the hall, Penrose, and keep your mouth shut."

He came back into the library, shutting the door. Then he was examining it carefully. Caroline said, "What are you doing, North?"

"I'm wondering if there is still a key about to lock this door."

"We could put a chair back under the knob."

"No, I want a nice clean key. One that turns, one that couldn't be opened by Tregeagle or Coombe, even by Polgrain if he chances to wander out of his kitchen."

Caroline walked to the far windows that gave onto the east side of Mount Hawke. The slope was very steep here, with strewn rocks dotting the slope all the way to the bottom where a narrow length of stream ran. He said from behind her, "Now all we need is a visit from Roland Ffalkes, demanding the rest of your fortune, or here with a gun to shoot me and force you to marry him."

"I am getting gray hairs from all this," Caroline said, turning to face him. "Just look, North, right here over my right eye, a gray hair."

"Good God," he said. "It appears you've lied to me. I thought you were young and winsome when, in fact, you appear to have aged overnight, lying to me, a wolf in sheep's clothing, a crone in virgin wrappings."

She stared up at him. "You know, North, that was quite funny. You're a witty man, and when you laugh you truly seem to be enjoying yourself and life. So where is this dark brooding hero I expected to marry? You are the one who misrepresented himself. You told me you were a man who would give me somber looks, never speak, and act endlessly mysterious. You haven't walked your hounds even once to the moor."

"Damned if I know what happened to him, Caroline. Perhaps he finally realized that brooding wasn't all that exciting, that it was really a boring pastime."

By late afternoon Bennett Penrose was in possession of six thousand three hundred pounds and had signed away everything Mr. Brogan could think of to have him sign away. North, Caroline, Owen, and the three pregnant ladies all stood on the deep-cut front steps to wave him off. Mr. Brogan had dashed off to meet a friend, although Caroline suspected it was a female person who was much closer than just a friend. His eyes gave him away, she thought, as she'd thanked him. They were bright and distracted. Had her aunt Eleanor been more than just a friend with Mr. Brogan? Mrs. Freely was right. Mr. Brogan looked quite handsome; it had to be a woman.

Alice, Caroline noticed now, was still staying very close to Evelyn, now pressed firmly against her side. Evelyn patted her hand every so often.

"My lord."

North turned. "Yes, Tregeagle?"

"The three female servants aren't pleased with their bedchambers."

Caroline frowned. "But I selected their rooms myself, Tregeagle. The three rooms next to each other on the east side of the nursery. They're quite lovely rooms."

Tregeagle was mute as the great oak front doors.

"Tregeagle," North said in a very soft voice. "I think it wise that you speak to me."

"Er, very well, my lord. It's just that we didn't believe those rooms were fine enough for the female servants we don't want to be here and who aren't necessary in any case. We wanted them in more elaborate chambers."

"Where did you take the female servants, Tregeagle?"

"To the third floor."

"Where on the third floor?" North asked in that same soft, dangerous voice.

"Just beneath the attic, charming chamber, really, so warm during the winter."

To North's surprise, Caroline laughed. "It was a good try, Tregeagle, but surely you couldn't have believed you'd get away with it."

"One only hoped that they would take a disgust of us and leave without saying a word." Tregeagle sighed deeply, staring over Caroline's right shoulder. "The oldest one, Mrs. Mayhew, she threatened to speak to you and thus I thought it would be more prudent if I gave you my words first."

Caroline just shook her head at him. "Do see them all in the original chambers, Tregeagle. Do try to be patient. I know this is difficult, but you see, his lordship is now a married man and in the normal course of events, when this happens, females have to appear in the house."

"No more nonsense, Tregeagle," North said. "Do you quite understand me?"

"You are speaking so quietly, so grimly and darkly, it is impossible not to understand you, my lord. It is time for dinner. That is, Polgrain has prepared your dinner and *her* dinner. As for the rest of these people, I don't know."

North said in a perfectly pleasant voice, "Why don't you come with me, Tregeagle, and we will discuss it. Also, I want to talk about strange faces pressed against windowpanes." He winked at Caroline and took his house-keeper firmly by his arm and pulled him into the house. It occurred to Caroline that she should have been the one to pull Tregeagle's arm with his body hopefully following, into the house. She should be the one to curtail his male cronyism. She was now the mistress and she had ensured that breakfast this morning was delicious, not North. Ah, but there was lots and lots of time for that. Instead, she saw to her three new female servants, soothing upset nerves, trying to explain to them about this male household.

Whatever North said to his minion, it appeared to have been successful, for dinner was served to six of them, four ladies and two gentlemen, a wonderful diversity of concoctions, from chicken in cream of curry sauce to ducks boiled in the French fashion, that was to say, covered in a rich Bordeaux, to flounder dressed with garlic and mustard.

Owen said, "I wish I could have seen you bargaining with that sod Bennett. At least he's gone now, just like my father. You're sure he signed everything, Caroline?"

"Mr. Brogan stood over him, watching his every move," North said. "Don't worry, Owen."

"You see," Owen said to Alice, "I told you everything would be taken care of. There's no reason for you to ever be afraid again."

"Amen," Evelyn said. "Damned bloody sod."

"Now, now," Miss Mary Patricia said, "that isn't what ladies say, Evelyn, even when truly moved by a male's unpleasant behavior."

Evelyn grinned impudently. "Very well. Bennett Penrose isn't a very sterling human being."

"Sterling," Miss Mary Patricia said. "That's an excellent word, Evelyn."

"I heard his lordship say it to Miss Caroline. It had something to do with some performance of hers and his lordship sounded pleased, so I decided it must be something quite good."

"Oh?" Owen said. "I didn't know you played an instrument, Caroline."

Everything continued along quite nicely until Tregeagle glided across the dining room, chin high, eyes straight ahead, stopping only when he reached North. He leaned down and whispered in his ear, "Dr. Treath is here, my lord. It seems that another Female Person has been killed."

"*What!*" North reared out of his chair. "That's bloody impossible, Tregeagle, you're making it up."

24

Mrs. Nora Pelforth was lying facedown on the beach at St. Agnes Head, her body rolled in by the tide. Her hair was matted ropes of dark red, one wrapped around the knife sticking out of her back. Most of her clothing had been torn off by the sea and rocks, and the large patches of bloated white flesh were scored raw and deep.

North knelt beside Benjamin Treath. "Can you tell how long she's been in the water, sir?" There was no immediate answer, and North looked up at him. Dr. Treath's head was bowed, his eyes closed, and his mouth was a thin line of pain.

"She was my friend," Dr. Treath said, his voice as bowed as his shoulders. "Damn, North, she was my friend. She was so very kind to me after Eleanor was killed, listened to me, always welcomed me. She was always there whenever I couldn't bear the pain. Damnation, North, I'm so tired of death, so very tired of it. And now more violent death. It's too much, North, it's simply too much."

"Let's get her out of here, sir. Give me the blanket so we may wrap her in it."

It was as if he'd been in a trance. Dr. Treath raised his head and stared at

226

North, then shook his head. "Forgive me. Yes, you're right. She shouldn't have to lie here any longer. Such beautiful red hair she had, and she was so proud of her hair, and now it's all tangled in seaweed."

Caroline was standing at the cliff edge with Owen and a good half dozen men from Goonbell and St. Agnes when North came up the winding path, the dead woman over his shoulder, Dr. Treath following at his heels.

"Aye," a miner said, kicking his boot toe against a clod of earth. "Another one of our women, kilt dead."

"Fer wot?"

"Fer nuthin', that's fer wot," another man said. Caroline recognized the man who served ale in Mrs. Freely's taproom in Goonbell. "Miss Meg don't like this, I'll tell ye that. Who's killing our women?"

North gently laid Mrs. Pelforth in the back of the wagon and covered her with a wool blanket. She'd been a pretty woman, no older than thirty-five, he thought, her air sprightly, her eyes a deep blue and very calm. Her husband had been a draper in Trevellas; she'd been a widow for some years, her children grown, alone save for servants. He'd known her to say polite hellos, nothing more. He had no idea if his father had known her or her husband. And now she was dead, murdered, just like Eleanor Penrose. Jesus, what was going on here?

"Well liked were Nora," the miner said, and spat into the sharp wind rising from the north. "Niver 'ad 'er nose stuck in the air. Who kilt her? My lord," he continued, turning to North, "ye be the magistrate. Wot will ye do?"

North realized it was one of his miners from Wheal David, a man named Pillet. "All I can, Pillet, all I can. If any of you can tell me anything, please come to Mount Hawke." He turned to Owen. "See where Bennett Penrose is."

Owen nodded and slipped away.

The men spoke among themselves, shook their heads, and broke apart, heading to their homes.

It was near to midnight before North and Caroline walked into his bedchamber. He nearly tripped, looked down at the stool sitting in his path, kicked it out of the way, and said, "I wonder if Tregeagle put this stool here.

Maybe so. Maybe he hoped you'd trip over it and break your beautiful neck, the damned bugger."

He stopped, listening to the deep booming twelve strokes from the huge clock in the entrance hall, a monstrosity one of his distant ancestors had commissioned by a clockmaker in Brussels more years ago than he wanted to calculate. The damned thing didn't give up. At least two hundred years old and it wouldn't break down so it could be thrown in the kitchen midden.

"What are you thinking, North?"

"What? Oh, I was just listening to that bloody clock. It's always had the strangest sound to it."

"Yes, you're right. It sounds like a person with a very gravelly voice who's shouting but doesn't really want anyone to hear him."

"The way you think pleases me. I wish you hadn't come with me, Caroline."

"I had to. I just wish I understood any of this."

North walked to the fireplace, knelt, and lit the fire. He didn't rise, just turned on his heel to face her. "I sent Owen to check Bennett's whereabouts. He's probably gone now, but who knows? We know he didn't kill your aunt, but maybe, just maybe he killed Mrs. Pelforth."

"But why would he?"

"God knows. Perhaps she was giving him money. Perhaps he was her lover and she got tired of him or he got tired of her, what with his new windfall. In any case, we'll know about Bennett in the morning. Now, Caroline, it's gotten chilly. Do you want to stay in this bedchamber tonight?"

"It depends on where you will sleep. I only want to be with you."

He rose, walked to her, and clasped her face between his big hands. "Besides liking your mind, I also like you, Caroline Nightingale. You're a good sort."

And he began to kiss her. She'd believed herself beyond exhaustion, so tired she'd been leaning against the bedpost. But her weariness fell away from her like a bad dream. She felt energy bubbling up within her, buoying her up as high as the clouds, making her want to dance and kiss him until he moaned with the pleasure of it.

He turned her around, lifted her hair, and bent down to nibble and kiss and lick her neck and her ears. "Very nice, wife, quite nice, in fact." She jumped when his tongue lightly stroked her ear.

"I want to see you," she said, twisting back around to face him. "All of you, please."

He cocked a dark eyebrow. "You want me naked again? At your mercy? Like last night?"

She gave him a solemn nod. "I think it's good for me, not so overwhelming. Yes, let's go slowly so I won't be nervous and perhaps flee the bedchamber in terror. There's quite a lot of you, North, and even though you are splendid, you are nonetheless very different from me."

He patted her face, stepped back, and within three minutes he was naked and grinning at her. He flung his arms back. "Take me, Caroline. What would you have me do to please you?"

Her eyes were nearly crossed with anticipation and excitement. Her fingers itched to touch him. "Lie on the bed, North, on your back, please."

When he was sprawled in the middle of the huge bed, he said, "Do you want to tie my arms to the headboard?"

She cocked her head to one side in question. "Why ever for?"

He laughed at her, and she knew it was at her innocence. "So you can have complete control of me. So I can't suddenly fling you on your back and take over and overwhelm you, overpower you with my manly strength, and frighten you. I am stronger than you, you know, and as a man, I can be overcome with lust."

"So can I," she said. "I don't know about this, North. It sounds strange to me, perhaps something a new bride shouldn't consider doing. Perhaps it isn't all that discreet or modest or even chaste. Where are your cravats?"

She was laughing with him when she'd managed to loosely tie his wrists to the headboard.

"There, you're now at my mercy, North Nightingale."

"Yes," he said, looking up at her thoughtfully. "You sound quite pleased with yourself."

"What is it? You're regretting giving me control?"

"No, actually I was thinking I should write my own book for grooms.

229

Reassure them that if, on the second night, their brides want to tie them up, why then, it is just fine and they shouldn't be worried that she's gone over the garden wall or will begin trying to play Bach's French Suites in her bathtub. They should allow their lady anything she wishes."

"I like the sound of that." She climbed off the bed, lit several more candles, and began to undress, her eyes bright with excitement, teasing him now, and knowing exactly what she was doing and the effect it would have. By the time her chemise was pooled at her feet, he was so far gone he was panting.

"Caroline," he said. He started to yank his wrists free, then stopped himself. He realized he was quite enjoying himself. He was hard as the Carrara marble on the fireplace, his heart pounding so fast he couldn't stop his panting. He never imagined that a wife could be so very enthusiastic about matters of the marital bed, so filled with curiosity and eager to please him until he couldn't bear it.

"My hair," she said, and stood there, knowing she was making him mad with lust, just standing there, taking the pins out of her hair, combing her hands through her hair. Then she raised her arms, tossed her head, and said, "Now I am ready to give you attention, my lord."

He fell back on the pillow and closed his eyes. His entire body was pounding. He knew she was looking at him, studying him, and he wanted her hands on him, her mouth on him so badly he thought he'd cry.

Her hands splayed over his chest and he tensed; her hands splayed over his belly and he moaned deeply; her hands came around him and he arched off the bed.

He felt himself quickly spinning into oblivion. "Caroline, sweetheart, you've got to stop now, please."

Instead of stopping, she leaned down and kissed him. He gasped with the shock of it, the raw feelings that were roiling through him, and jerked upward.

He felt her palm splayed on his chest. "I'm very glad you're my husband, North."

His chest was heaving madly. He opened his eyes and stared up at her. Her eyes were wide and greener than the swamp grass at the base of the east slope. Her lips were slightly parted and he wanted to kiss her until they were both collapsed in a heap for want of breath.

"Will you let me go now, Caroline?"

"No, I don't think so. I want to kiss you and touch you. I fear I got my steps out of order. It's more exciting if one begins at the top of the mountain, it would seem, rather than starting at the, er, middle."

"Yes," he said. He felt her hands on him again and shuddered. "That's your delightful way of thinking at work again."

"Yes, but I should begin with your beautiful mouth, North." She was on her knees above him, her hair all pulled over her right shoulder. She leaned over him and kissed him, her tongue lightly touching his bottom lip, as if she wasn't certain exactly what to do. He didn't mind a bit. It took everything in him, but he didn't attack her or take the control from her. She kissed him more confidently and he thought he'd burst when her tongue slipped between his lips. She pulled away, looking down at him, then at his body. "Kissing you is very arousing, North. I must stop that for the moment else I'll skip all sorts of steps." She stopped, drew a deep breath that made his eyes fasten on her breasts. She said, "I like all the black hair on you. Here," she stroked and caressed his chest hair, "the hair's so soft and warm. I don't have anything like this."

"No," he said, wondering if there was a part of his body that could be considered unaware of her and what she was doing. He wanted her all over him. "Always your mouth," she said, and leaned over him again and kissed him. "I never thought kissing a man could be so very much fun." Her breasts were against his chest, moving, caressing his flesh, and he wanted more than anything to come inside her. He tugged on the cravats that tied his wrists and they immediately came apart. Slowly, he brought his arms down and closed them around her back.

"Forgive me, Caroline, but it's nearly too late for me. This might be fine for you, but for me it's simply too much." And he kissed her and stroked her and rolled her onto her back. He was nuzzling her ribs, trying to keep the meager control he had on himself, when he felt her hands sweep down his back.

He was over her then, staring down at her, thinking that surely she was the most beautiful woman he'd ever seen in his life or in any other life he'd chanced to live. He caressed her with his fingers, a deep rhythm that he knew excited her, then he simply couldn't wait a moment longer, and he was quickly part of her, pushing deeper and deeper and stroking her and kissing her, and when she gasped, stiffening, he smiled with satisfaction even as he kissed her deeply, taking her cries into his mouth. As for his own release, he thought he'd expire from the power of it.

"North?"

"Hmmm?" His head was beside hers on the pillow. How could she have recovered so quickly? He wanted to concentrate on breathing, nothing more, just breathing, so he would be able to live from one moment to the next, yet she'd been able to say his name clearly.

"Let's have a dozen children, all right?"

"Hmmm." He breathed in and out, slow, deep breaths. He felt her shifting beneath him, and to his chagrin and utter satisfaction he was swelling inside her. "Well, what the hell," he said, and reared up, leaning down to kiss her even as he felt her tight around him, and surely there could be nothing more miraculous than this.

"What?" He shuddered, stopping dead.

"Hmmm? Oh, that is so nice, North, please—"

He must have misunderstood her. He would think about that later. He brought her to pleasure and then let himself ease into that remarkable moment that seemed to crystallize everything important in a man's life. He was smiling, drained and sated and ready to sleep for a decade.

He tucked her against his side, felt her warm breath on his shoulder. "Children, North," she said against his flesh, and then kissed him and then nibbled at him. "Let's have lots and lots."

He groaned.

"I was the only child about when I was growing up. I didn't like it. Sometimes it was lonely. I remember my mother was pregnant two more times, but there weren't any children. I remember telling my father that I wanted lots of little sisters but he just shook his head and turned away from me. I remember when I was seven years old or perhaps even a bit younger I heard two maids talking about my mother nearly dying with that one and then they just sighed. I hope I'm not like my mother."

How could she think so coherently in order to speak like this? He wasn't up to it. He managed to kiss her hair, let her lavender scent fill his senses, then he was snoring lightly, sleeping the sleep of the sated man.

She hugged him to her. North had had a hard day. A man needed his rest. She pictured Mrs. Nora Pelforth in her mind and shuddered. What was going on here?

"What the hell do you mean you hope you're not like your mother? Of course you're nothing like your mother, damn you! Don't talk like that." He startled her so badly she jerked back away from him. He was up on his elbows, looking down at her angrily, his voice equally angry, but then, in the next instant, he was asleep again and she wondered if he'd ever really been fully awake.

She nestled close again, hugging him tight to her, realizing that she was glad he'd reacted so strongly. Surely that meant he must care for her a little bit, just a little something beyond his man's lust.

As for her woman's lust, well, surely that was just a natural part of things. She had uplifting feelings as well about him, warm human feelings, even spiritual feelings, lots of them that weren't the least bit corporeal, that were pure and wholesome, centering near her heart if not her brain. However, it was odd that these feelings didn't seem to make themselves known whilst North was making love to her.

She'd rather liked him lying there sprawled on his back, his arms pulled over his head.

25

"Er, miss? I mean, yer ladyship?"

Caroline looked up from her Nightingale memoirs on King Mark to see Timmy the maid standing in the bedchamber doorway.

"Good afternoon, Timmy. Did you manage to find more lavender for my baths?"

"Er, not yet, miss, I mean, yer ladyship. I thought Mrs. Mayhew would do yer bath fer ye now."

"I prefer you, Timmy."

"Thank ye, miss, yer ladyship. I see yer reading something that looks real important."

"I suppose to his lordship's male ancestors it was," she said. "Have you ever heard of King Mark, Timmy?" At his doleful shake of the head, she smiled, and said, "Well, people believe that he ruled Brittany and Cornwall in the middle of the sixth century, surely too long a time ago for anyone to really care. However, it seems that King Mark, who was also called Cunomorus, was betrayed by his wife, Iseult or Isolde, and he was—" She stopped. "It isn't really all that interesting, actually. What do you want, Timmy?"

"Well now, yer ladyship, I was wunnering if ye'd give me yer popper now that old Mr. Ffalkes be long gone and won't try to kidnap ye anymore."

"Ah," she said, and rose. She quickly forgot about King Mark, his faithless wife, and the possibility that Tristan wasn't his nephew, but rather his son. She fetched the small pistol, then turned to look thoughtfully at the boy. "You're sure your father wants this pistol because his is broken?"

"Oh aye, miss, er, yer ladyship."

"You see, I asked Coombe about your family and he said that your father had several guns, that he also had a blunderbuss the size of a barn."

"Oh," Timmy said, and looked down at his feet. "Then about this 'ere King Mark fellow—"

"Coombe also told me that your father isn't a nice man."

Timmy's head whipped up and he looked suddenly fierce, not at all like a little boy. "The bastid drinks until 'is liver is bloated at the taproom in Goonbell, even though Mrs. Freely makes him leave, says she won't have him ripping up her inn. Then he staggers home, still drinking his ale, and beats me ma and me sisters. When he comes after me, all puffed up and screaming, I jest run back 'ere to Mount Hawke, but me ma and me sisters can't go nowhere. I got to 'ave that gun, miss, er, yer ladyship. I got to protect 'em."

Caroline looked briefly at the pocket pistol in her hand. It had belonged to her father. She understood how Timmy felt; she understood the need to act to prove one was alive and capable and not damnably helpless. Her three pregnant ladies all had knives. Miss Mary Patricia even had a small pistol. Caroline's own knife was in a drawer in the armoire. She said, "You're right, Timmy. You need this pistol more than I do. Just promise me you'll be very careful. Don't shoot your father, do you promise me? If you have to stop him, then shoot over his head, very high over his head. This pistol makes so much noise it would frighten a cow out of its wits. I promise you it would get your father's attention. If the first shot doesn't, why then, you fire over his head again, all right?"

"I promise, miss, er, yer ladyship. I don't want to kill me pa, just scare the guts outta 'im so 'e'll keep 'is fists in 'is pockets. What do ye mean ye can fire it again?"

"Do you know how to shoot?"

His chest puffed out and he said, "No, I ain't niver fired a popper afore."

"Well then, let's go to the orchard and we'll practice. I'll show you how to clean it and load it. First of all, Timmy, this is a double-barreled pistol and it holds two bullets. These are the twin brass barrels here side by side. Keep the brass nice and shiny. This is iron and it's called a slider and it selects which barrel is connected with the flash pan. Now then, this is the flintlock mechanism . . ."

When North heard gunfire from the east slope an hour later he felt his hair stiffen on his neck. He broke into a run, and when the land sloped down suddenly, his legs ran faster than he could and he ran into an apple tree. He hung on to the damned tree, breathing hard and looking just beyond to see Caroline and Timmy the maid firing at a bottle some twenty feet distant from them. He heard her say, "That's right, Timmy, you've nearly got it. Hold the pistol very steady—I know it feels heavy, but you must hold it steady—and train your eyes to line up your target with the sights. That's it. Now, squeeze the trigger, very, very slowly."

There was a loud report. North watched the bottle spurt into the air and shatter into a hundred shards of glass.

What the devil was going on? He started to stride forward, the master of Mount Hawke, then he drew up short. No, he would find out later what she was doing with Timmy the maid.

He turned and walked back up the slope, snagging an apple from a low-lying branch on his way. He rubbed it on his thigh until it was shiny, then tossed it in the air, caught it again, and ate it in four bites.

Whatever she was doing with a gun and Timmy the maid, North knew it wouldn't bore him with the telling.

It wasn't the least boring. He stared at her, opened his mouth, then shut it and stared some more. He said slowly, all calm as the eye of a storm, "You told Timmy to be certain not to shoot his father when he was drunk and beating his mother or sisters, just to fire over his head and scare the devil and his pitchfork out of him."

"That's right. Timmy isn't stupid. Now he's a decent shot. I'll work with him until he's really confident and I am certain he won't shoot anyone if he gets suddenly scared. His father is in for a surprise the next time he lays onto his family, the drunken sod."

He just stared at her again, shook his head, and, knowing his duty, left Mount Hawke.

An hour later, Caroline was sitting with Miss Mary Patricia in the drawing room, helping her sew baby clothes, when Coombe entered and said directly to Caroline, ignoring Miss Mary Patricia, "Madam, Mr. Polgrain would like to discuss the week's menus with you at your convenience. It appears his lordship isn't here to do it."

"His lordship has never done menus with Polgrain, as you well know, Coombe."

"He should have, miss. It isn't appropriate that Mr. Tregeagle continue to do it."

Caroline set another several stitches, none of them very small or very straight, then set the small lawn shirt on the settee beside her and looked up in surprise. "Oh, Coombe, you're still there? Tell Polgrain I will meet him in the ladies' parlor in fifteen minutes."

"There is no ladies' parlor, miss."

"There is now. It's that bright sunny room just beyond the library."

"But—"

"Fifteen minutes, Coombe."

"Yes, miss."

When the door closed on Coombe's stiff back, Miss Mary Patricia giggled. It was an unexpected sound and really very nice. "He is a martinet, isn't he?" she said, and giggled again. "I was in Mount Hawke village yesterday and he was conducting a quite splendid flirtation with the woman who owns the small cake shop on High Street. He was saying something about the virility of bald men."

Caroline said, "Speaking of martinets, so is Tregeagle. Indeed, he's the biggest martinet of the trio. Both of them will be dancing about in rage when the draperers come tomorrow to do some decorating on the new ladies' parlor." She rubbed her hands together. "I can't wait."

"And other decorating as well?"

"Just one thing at a time. My Italian teacher at Chudleigh's Academy told me never to rub the nose continuously in the same dirt. It never led to peace, she said. I've never forgotten that. Yes, one step at a time." She laughed. "It's what North believes too. Our three male martinets are still reeling from the arrival of the female martinets. I don't think Mrs. Mayhew will allow them to tread on her toes even the slightest bit now."

"Why now?"

"Ah, after I took Mrs. Mayhew and her two assistants to their original bedchambers, I dropped a little hint or two in her ear. She remarked that everyone in the area knew about Mr. Coombe, Mr. Tregeagle, and Mr. Polgrain. They were women haters, she said, and all knew it and spoke about it and said it was all because of their masters. Indeed, she said she couldn't wait to come here and just see how they ran things. Yes, I fancy that our three male martinets will be learning a thing or two."

"Seven females in the house. They must be gnashing their teeth."

"Oh yes. Isn't it grand?"

Polgrain was not a happy man. He didn't want to be here, in this wonderful parlor that *she* had appropriated, and that she would *ruin,* he was quite certain that would happen, but it was obvious that his young, inexperienced, and innocent lordship, blind to what this female was doing in his own house, was lax in his lust for the female, and was allowing her *free rein.* What man stood a chance with a perfidious woman, and indeed, what other sort of female was there? And now there were three more of them here in addition to the other three who were with child and sewing small things that quite turned his blood cold. And now he had to wait upon this head female here in this charming room that shouldn't be hers.

Polgrain looked around the parlor and said, "It doesn't look like a ladies' parlor. It shouldn't ever look like a ladies' parlor."

"It will by tomorrow evening," Caroline said easily. "Light yellow draperies will make all the difference, don't you think so, Polgrain? Yes, lots of silks in lovely pastel shades, pale, just like ladies are pale. Oh yes, and soft cushions for the chairs and the settee."

He swallowed, but couldn't bring himself to nod agreement. She saw a spasm of pain cross his gaunt features. He was as old as Tregeagle, shorter, but just as lean, with grizzled dirty hair and a very sharp chin. There was a wide space between his front teeth. He didn't have any laugh lines at all. It made him look younger than he undoubtedly was, but not as human. Of the three of them, the butler Coombe was the youngest and quite dapper in his dress and manner. So he'd been flirting with the owner of the cake shop, had he? She wished she'd been with Miss Mary Patricia to have seen that. She supposed as long as the females weren't close to Mount Hawke, they could be tolerated, perhaps even liked and courted.

Caroline sat back in her chair, folded her hands in her lap, and said, "Tell me what you have in mind for our dinners, please."

When Polgrain left twenty-three minutes later, Caroline was shaking her head, trying to keep her hands from fisting up. She rolled her neck, feeling the knots in her shoulders. She had known she would have to do a lot of the suggesting because Polgrain would probably be perverse because she was female and not male and thus shouldn't even be here, much less giving orders to *him*.

When she'd asked him what he had in mind for their dinners, he'd merely stared at her blankly. She gave him one of her father's looks and said, "Very well, I am quite fond of potted venison."

"There is no venison available."

"You're resourceful, Polgrain. I'm certain you will manage."

"Resourcefulness is part of the Polgrain heritage. However, the managing of venison could be in doubt."

"Doubt is unacceptable, Polgrain, in the Derwent-Jones heritage. Now, Miss Mary Patricia is fond of pork with apples and sage, and Miss Evelyn told me her mouth watered for steak pie, you know the kind—with all the potatoes and fresh green peas. Miss Alice adores ox-tail soup."

"There is no sage. I do not make steak pie without sage."

"Ah, you will have someone fetch some from the village. Old Mrs.

Crimm grows all sorts of condiments in her garden. Didn't you know that, Polgrain?"

"I knew that. I merely don't understand how you could have discovered Mrs. Crimm in such a short time."

"I am a woman, Polgrain. I am very smart. It's very possible I see things you don't see."

"His lordship detests ox-tail soup."

"Then you can make him turtle soup. He is quite fond of that, isn't he?"

Polgrain chewed on his lip but remained silent as the faded dark wallpaper on the three walls, wallpaper he'd always admired with the dubious gray gobs that were probably clouds, that or dust swirls that Timmy the maid had missed or Robert the former footman hadn't even noticed. Oh yes, she doubtless saw things because she was female, curse her eyes. But now she was going to ruin this precious room. He did love that wallpaper that he knew would soon be on its way to the dustbin. It wasn't to be borne. Doubtless one of the females would clean it now and not Timmy the maid, who didn't see all the things that he should perhaps see, but it surely wasn't all that important that every single little dust mote be wafted away. Timmy was learning. He would have been the perfect maid if the females hadn't descended on Mount Hawke.

"Oh yes, some Italian bisket bread, cassia biscuits, and orange cake. Ah, and Shrewsbury cakes for Miss Alice. They're quite delightful, don't you think? It's the lemon and ginger, I think."

He shook his head, opened his mouth, but Caroline beat him to it. "I imagine it's difficult for you, being a man and being called upon also to cook. Perhaps cooking and being male don't go well together. Perhaps men simply aren't fashioned to be good cooks or learn new recipes easily. Perhaps I could speak to Mrs. Mayhew—"

"I assure you, miss, that I am quite the best cook in all the county! I can prepare anything using ingredients women don't even understand and I—"

"I'm pleased, Polgrain. Some baked cod and soaked mussels would also be a treat. You will please incorporate the other things you think will complement these dishes. Here's my list of requests. Thank you, Polgrain.

240

This time next week? If you need my assistance or advice or the actual help of any of the females in the house, do ask. All of us—all *seven* of us—are quite willing to help you. Oh yes, the new servants will, naturally, eat with you in the kitchen. They really didn't like having to take trays to their bedchambers. They say it makes them feel like outsiders. They want to be a part of the Nightingale family. No, they will eat with you." She gave him a smarmy smile and handed him the foolscap with her neat handwriting. "Oh yes, until further notice, there will always be six to meals." She patted his arm and left him to wonder what had befallen Mount Hawke.

At promptly six o'clock, Caroline was staring at the clock in the drawing room wondering where the devil North was. She listened with half an ear to Owen, who was speaking very quietly to Alice.

Then she heard him, his steps fast and solid on the stairs. Then the door opened and he strode in, his hair still wet from his bath, dressed in evening black, and looking more delicious than any meal she'd ever seen. There was no chance of Polgrain preparing something that could look better than North. She realized she was just staring at him when silence fell and she heard Evelyn snicker.

North was standing in front of her then, smiling in a satisfied way down at her, his knuckles lightly stroking over her cheek. "Good evening," he said, and he looked at her mouth. She swallowed, opened her mouth, aware that she was trembling here in front of all her pregnant ladies, and managed to say, "It was overcast today."

"Yes, and the clouds didn't move much in the sky, just hung there."

"I ate an apple in the orchard."

"I know. So did I."

"Where have you been?"

"In Goonbell. It was business, all business, and to be honest, I quite enjoyed it."

Owen said, "I say, North, did you discover anything more about Mrs. Pelforth?"

He stilled, the laughter gone momentarily from his face. He turned to Owen and said, "Nothing of import. Bennett was drinking at Mrs. Freely's inn, damn and blast. I'll tell you the rest of it later, though there's little to tell."

"I don't believe that for a minute," Caroline said.

"Later," North said. "I don't wish to upset anyone before dinner, or after it, as a matter of fact."

26

M iss Mary Patricia said, "Please, my lord, our ears are quite capable of taking in talk of this dreadful business. Indeed." She paused for a long, dramatic moment. "Indeed, my lord, Evelyn just might know something."

Over a magnificent serving dish of potted venison, which North praised to the heavens, Owen said, "The men in the villages are all up in arms. They say that everything was peaceful and quiet here until—" His voice fell into an abyss.

"It's quite all right," North said. "I found Caroline's aunt's body at St. Agnes Head. I am the stranger. I don't blame them for talking."

"Yes," Evelyn said quickly, "but that other lady who was killed. My lord, you were nowhere in the vicinity, and it was hoped that that toad Bennett Penrose was."

"However do you know that, Evelyn?" North said.

Evelyn blushed. It was fascinating, and Caroline could but stare at her. She finally said, "It was Mr. Savory who told me, my lord. A smart fellow he is and ever so nice. He told me he was assisting you in your investigations. He said you were ever such a smart gentleman."

He did, did he? North thought. He'd told Flash everything was confidential. He gave Evelyn a long look, saw the pitfalls for Flash, and gave it up. Even with her belly protruding, she was a remarkably fine-looking girl. Oh well, it was done.

"I'm sorry to tell you, Evelyn, but the toad Bennett wasn't here then either. It's a pity."

"There was something else, my lord," Evelyn added.

"Yes?"

"I know that Dr. Treath was a close friend of Mrs. Pelforth."

"Yes, I know that as well," North said. "When we found her washed up on the beach, Dr. Treath was very upset. He told me she had been very kind to him after your aunt was killed, Caroline. He was distraught."

Caroline's mind raced ahead and she opened her mouth to say something, saw North shake his head, and went back to the delicious buttered peas on her plate.

Owen, oblivious of any pitfalls at all, said, "I say, Dr. Treath was fond of your aunt, Caroline, and then he was fond of Nora Pelforth. Do you think perhaps he's mad, North? That he likes to jolly up to women and then kill them?"

"No," North said. "That's ridiculous. Eat your dinner, Owen. You're frightening Alice."

Owen immediately turned to her and patted her hand as if he were her uncle or her father confessor.

But Caroline was thinking: Did Dr. Treath know the woman who was killed some three years ago? What was her name? Oh yes, Elizabeth Godolphin.

North looked up to see Tregeagle, Coombe, and Polgrain all standing in the doorway. "Yes?" he said.

Tregeagle cleared his throat and said, "Er, my lord, we were just attending to what the Young Female was saying. We are telling all those buffoons that to believe you culpable of anything at all untoward is ridiculous."

"I thank you," North said. "Have you perhaps other duties that need your attention?"

"There are always duties in a dwelling this large, my lord. In addition, with so very many people now in residence, the duties have multiplied alarmingly."

Caroline said, "Shall I have Mrs. Mayhew—"

"Not at all," Coombe said quickly. "We will contrive. We always have, even under the most desperate and strained circumstances."

"My admiration for the three of you constantly assumes even more amazing proportions," North said. "Oh, Polgrain, the round of beef is excellent. The dumplings are tasty, as is the turtle soup."

"Since you are pleased, my lord, it is enough."

North merely nodded, caught his wife's eye, and smiled widely at his chef. "Actually, it seems that everything her ladyship requests is quite to my liking, Polgrain."

"One will assume then that the result is what we should prefer, my lord."

To everyone's surprise, Alice said, "I think the ox-tail soup be, er, *is* very good, Mr. Polgrain."

A spasm crossed Polgrain's face. He said, looking directly at the rather ugly epergne in the middle of the table, "It is the maturity of the cloves that makes the difference. His lordship isn't fond of ox-tail soup."

If anyone thought it odd to be discussing the dishes on the large table with the trio of male servants all lined up in a row, as stiff as Blücher's Prussian soldiers, no one remarked upon it until much later that evening, when Caroline eased off North's chest, up onto her elbows, saying, "I love the taste of you more than anything Polgrain could prepare."

"Is it the maturity of my flesh?"

She smiled as she kissed his shoulder, his throat, his chin, and finally his mouth. "A dash of salt overlaying the taste of damp exerted man," she said, and kissed him again. "Ah, North, are you already asleep?"

"Yes," he said, and pulled her down into his arms. "This business about talking after lovemaking, Caroline, it's difficult. You nearly kill me with your enthusiasm and then you want me to discuss philosophy with you."

"No, I just want to know where you went this afternoon. Was it about Mrs. Pelforth? And why didn't you tell me about Dr. Treath knowing her? Why didn't you tell me that our locals are wondering if you're some sort of madman?"

"No, it wasn't about Mrs. Pelforth. I went to see Timmy the maid's father."

She reared up, staring down at him, her thick hair dropping like a curtain on either side of his face. It was dark and erotic, the feel of her hair. "Why did you do that?"

"So Timmy wouldn't accidentally kill the drunken bugger."

"But I told you I'd teach him, work with him—"

"His father had just struck Timmy's mother when I walked into their cottage in Goonbell. I pulled him off her, dragged him by the scruff of his neck outside, and you won't believe this—Timmy's mother was running after me, shouting not to hurt her husband, all the while wiping the blood off her mouth. The three little girls were yelling their heads off.

"I told her to go back into the cottage and I sounded as mean as I could. Then I had a talk with Jeb Peckly."

"Peckly. Timmy the maid *Peckly?* That's quite an ugly name, North. Well, what happened? What did he say?"

"Not much of anything until I had his full attention." He unconsciously rubbed his knuckles.

She was smiling down at him as if he were the lord of the world. He'd never had someone look at him like that. He was suddenly embarrassed and mumbled, "I just made sure he understood what would happen if he ever hit anyone again. The thing was, Caroline, if old Jeb was really drunk and he went after them and Timmy got out that pistol, it would make his father go right over the edge. Someone could easily get killed. I couldn't let that happen."

"Oh, North, you're wonderful. There can't be another man as wonderful as you are in the whole of Cornwall or even the whole of Britain. I am the luckiest woman. Goodness, I love you so much." She was kissing him, laughing, stroking his shoulders and arms, the palm of her hand then on his belly, caressing him, and not a moment later, he came into her, moaning deeply into her mouth as she took him even deeper.

Then he stopped cold. He was balanced above her on his hands, panting like one of his old hounds, Cardaloo, after he'd run across Tyburth Moor. "What did you say?"

"I said you're wonderful, more than wonderful. Actually, you're quite the grandest man—"

"Then what?"

"I said 'goodness.' I don't remember anything else."

He realized then that she was afraid to tell him she loved him again because it would be like being the dangling white handkerchief in front of the enemy. No, no, surely he wasn't the enemy. Perhaps she'd just forgotten, or hadn't meant it. He took her mouth, tasting her, nipping her lower lip, all the while feeling the pleasure begin to flood through him. He pulled back, his back arching, his throat working madly, and he knew she was looking at him when his release hit him, holding him there for an endless moment of the most exquisite pleasure he'd ever felt in his life. She whispered into his neck again that she loved him. Then she whispered, "I love to see you in the throes of your release, North. It excites me and pleases me."

She drew him down on top of her, her hands stroking over his back as she lightly kissed his shoulders and arms. He fell asleep before he came out of her and that feeling was the sweetest he'd ever known in his life.

Caroline tried to be philosophical, she truly did. All right, so she'd blurted it right out there and all he'd ever said to her was that she was a good sort and he liked her. Actually she'd told him twice that she loved him. It was all right. There was nothing wrong with being a good sort. It was quite nice to be liked by the man she adored more than any other human being in the world. Surely a good sort was a fine thing to be for the next month or so, perhaps even for the next year or so.

She couldn't help it that she wanted to sing and dance and shout to the world that North Nightingale was a hero, that dour, dark, menacing—and all those odd things he'd believed himself to be—were nonsense. He was a hero and he was hers and she would do anything for him. It was that simple and that final. Caroline kissed his shoulder and he reared up just a bit, stared down at her with vague satisfied eyes. "That was very satisfactory," he said, leaned his head down, kissed her mouth, then rolled off her. She drew the covers over them, spooned herself against his back, and smiled into the darkness.

She wasn't smiling the following morning. Evelyn woke her up just after dawn. Alice was sick. She was vomiting in her chamber pot, her hair hanging in wet skinny ropes around her pale face.

She sent Timmy the maid for Dr. Treath.

She went back to her bedchamber and quickly dressed. When she returned to Alice's room, North was holding Alice, wiping her face with a wet cloth. She was shuddering with the force of the spasms racking her thin body. Caroline wondered if Alice even realized that a man was holding her.

Bess Treath was on her brother's heels as she always seemed to be. She shooed them all away as her brother examined Alice. Evelyn was standing in the shadows wringing her hands. "My poor baby, I heard her crying, then she cried out. When I got to her, she was vomiting, looking like death. My poor little Alice."

Owen came running into the bedchamber. "My God, what's going on here? Alice is sick? Oh no! I just knew something was wrong, I just knew it. When I saw Dr. Treath coming out of his house, I knew he was coming here."

North wondered what Owen had been doing in Goonbell, but now wasn't the time to ask.

Even Bess Treath didn't try to make Owen move away when Dr. Treath pulled up her nightgown and pressed on her child-swollen belly. Owen never even looked away from her face; he simply held her hand and whispered to her, telling her it would be all right, that she wasn't to worry, that he was here.

North said to Caroline, "This is very interesting."

"Yes," she said. "I hadn't realized. I pray she'll be all right."

Dr. Treath told Caroline and North some time later downstairs in the drawing room that he didn't believe she would miscarry the babe, which was his biggest concern.

Bess Treath said, "I don't know, Benjie. Perhaps it would be better for her. She's only a child herself and whatever will happen to her?"

Caroline smiled even though she wondered what kind of person Bess Treath thought she was. "Alice will be just fine, Miss Treath. Surely you never thought that my aunt Eleanor or that I would turn her out after she birthed the babe? No, there will be no problem. Tell me what to do, Dr. Treath."

Alice was asleep within moments of drinking the draught Dr. Treath had prepared for her. Caroline and North looked into her bedchamber before returning to their own to see Owen sitting beside her on the bed, holding her small thin hand. Owen was lightly stroking his thumb over her fingers.

He looked up at them. "She'll be fine," he said. "I'll take care of her. Dr. Treath thought it was something she ate, perhaps the ox-tail soup."

"No one else ate very much of it," North said. "It sounds like the culprit. Perhaps the mushrooms."

Caroline yawned widely. "I'm sorry, but I'm just so tired. It seems we don't ever have any quiet moments around here."

"Oh yes, Caroline," Owen said, "Mrs. Mayhew, Chloe, and Molly all came by. Mrs. Mayhew had more suggestions on Alice's care than I can even remember. She's very forceful. Sort of like my father."

"Yes," Caroline said, yawning again, but smiling with great satisfaction at the same time, "isn't she ever?"

Sunlight flooded into the bedchamber when North came into her slowly and gently all the while kissing her. She shuddered and moaned into his mouth when she reached her release.

"I like to see a smile on a woman's mouth when she's nearly asleep," he said, and pulled her tightly against him.

"Tell me I'm a good sort again, North."

He stared at her a moment, kissed her closed eyes, then her nose and her mouth. "You're one of the best sorts, Caroline," he said, then sighed softly when her hand stroked down his back. "All this badness, Caroline, we'll get through it."

"I know," she said, kissed him, and pressed her cheek against his shoulder.

27

It was very strange, the note he'd received that was right now crumpled in his breeches pocket, written by an unknown hand, given to Timmy the maid when he was out at the stables giving sugar to North's bay gelding, Treetop. "'Twere a young duffer with squirrelly talk," Timmy the maid had said, but he hadn't recognized him, which was odd because Timmy the maid knew everybody, or so he'd thought. What was squirrelly talk? North had asked. And Timmy the maid had said, "The little nit couldn't speak more than two words together without stammering hisself near out o' 'is boots."

North click-clicked Treetop toward the northeastern end of his property where the land softened and the gentle rolling hills were still green with lingering summer. There were about half a dozen of the hillocks, and learned men had said that beneath some of the hillocks, or barrows, as they called them, were tombs from long, long ago, even long before the Romans had lived here, even long before the Celts had swarmed over Cornwall. He remembered reading about Silbury Hill, a huge mound everyone had known was a burial mound, possibly hiding treasure. It had been the Duke of Northumberland who had launched a force of Cornish tin miners late in the last century to sink a shaft from top to bottom of the mound. They hadn't found anything, more's the pity, and most had stopped even remarking on the odd hills, so obviously placed there by man's hand and not God's.

Every once in a while villagers found strange things near these hills: pottery shards that looked to be older than the land itself, though on some of the pieces there were still spots of bright color, small bits of iron and steel that looked to be from long-ago weapons. And another mound would be dug into. Not long before, a mound had turned up a long, narrow burial chamber holding ancient skeletons, some pottery pieces, but nothing of value. He'd heard that in other parts of England, finding Roman coins and even Celt weapons was no great wonder.

Had King Mark been buried here, beneath one of those soft rolling hills? Had the gold armlet his great-grandfather claimed to have found come from near here? He sincerely doubted it.

He pulled Treetop to a halt atop one of the hills and looked around him. He forgot all about archaeology, forgot about King Mark and his lust-besotted nephew Tristan who'd betrayed him with the beautiful, treacherous Isolde.

The note said she would be meeting her lover close by to the northeastern boundary. Well, he was here. He looked toward the dense copse of oak trees older than the Druids, who had hung enemies in cages from the branches and then proceeded to roast them alive.

Where was she? It was a hoax, he had known that, he *knew* that, but still, he did expect to see Caroline here somewhere. Where was her mare, Regina?

When he saw her mare and another horse, a gelding, tethered behind a thick stand of trees, he felt his heart begin to pound, slow, heavy strokes. Her lover? Dear God, it was nonsense, that was all, just someone wanting to do them ill, probably one of his male martinets.

He wouldn't spy on his wife of three weeks, it was absurd. Caroline adored him. She loved him, she'd told him that whenever she'd crested her pleasure, kissing him, telling him over and over how much she loved him. He'd found that he wanted to hear those words from her, that he wallowed in the pleasure those simple words brought him.

But how could she come to love him in such a short time? Surely love didn't work with such dispatch. Was it just a woman's release that brought such words from her mouth, lust fulfilled and thus it was love?

North shook his head. He kicked Treetop in his muscled sides but he didn't gallop forward, announcing his arrival. No, he kept Treetop to a slow canter until he could see her and the man.

It was Benjamin Treath and he was standing close to Caroline, something in his outstretched hand. Ah, he was showing her something, nothing more, nothing less.

This was no clandestine tryst. But what was he showing her? And why here? She wasn't like all those former Nightingale wives who had betrayed their husbands, wives who had been faithful to the Nightingale men until they'd birthed the heir, then fallen into a whore's ways and birthed bastards, or were kicked out like North's mother was, and died. No, Caroline was loyal—to him and to no one else. He would wager everything he owned, all that he valued within himself, that she was loyal to him, only to him . . . yes, only to him.

Then Dr. Treath leaned toward Caroline and he placed his hand on her shoulder, a big hand, North saw, that covered a lot of her and he didn't like it. They seemed to be speaking very seriously about something. North felt himself freeze when Dr. Treath kissed Caroline's cheek, his big hand still on her shoulder, no, now it was moving down her arm. He watched him straighten finally and walk away from her, back to his gelding. He gave her a small wave and another smile as he settled into the saddle.

What the hell was going on here?

In that moment, every word North had read in those damned diaries Tregeagle had forced on him came back with raw clarity. Women weren't to be trusted. His mother had betrayed his father, had left him and died. His grandfather had also been betrayed and his father before him. Both his father and grandfather had written about the perfidy of women, the dishonor bred into them throughout the ages, the wit of Nightingale men not to trust them beyond the birthing of their heir.

No, he thought, he'd escaped Mount Hawke and his father, escaped this damning legacy because he couldn't bear the bitterness and emptiness of it, his father's continual ranting about his mother—a whore, a bitch—who had betrayed him; ah, and there was justice, for the damned trollop was dead. He remembered then that as a boy he'd had no idea what all those words meant, but he did now, and again he felt an instant of surprise that there were so many terrible words to describe a woman a man disapproved of. His hands clenched on Treetop's reins.

Thank God he'd had the good sense to leave ten years before as soon as he'd been able to make his own way. It had been difficult but he'd believed anything had to be better than remaining at Mount Hawke with his father. He knew in his bones that if he'd stayed, the next thing his father would have done would have been to force that damned diary down his throat and tell him it was his duty once he'd bred an heir off a likely female, to toss her out and begin his own entries about what sluts women were, wives in particular. And yet when Tregeagle had given him the diary, he'd read some of it, not all, certainly, for he wasn't that far gone, but still, some of the poison had seeped into him. And now he hated himself for it.

He wasn't like his father nor was he like his grandfather or his great-grandfather, and he would never accept that he was. The Nightingale legacy to its sons would end with him. As he rode Treetop straight to where Caroline was standing, he wondered what she was thinking. Surely she wasn't thinking of Benjamin Treath, surely not.

It was a lovely copse of trees, Caroline was thinking, and she much enjoyed the gently rolling hillocks, and the vastly romantic stone fence that stretched some hundred yards in either direction. The stones had been hand-placed, of course, and fitted together so tightly and with such care that there were still few places where they'd broken free and fallen to the rich earth. When had the stones been so carefully and skillfully made into this fence? Who had done it? And those hillocks, works of art, all of them, but why? What was the purpose? She looked up then and saw him.

She gave a shout and ran toward him. Her riding skirt was narrow, hampering her, so she simply jerked it to her knees, never slowing.

He pulled Treetop to a halt and jumped off his back to catch her in his arms just as she threw herself against him, lifting her high to twirl her around.

"Hello," he said, lowering her slowly, kissing her mouth as his hands molded her hips to him. "I missed you. It took you long enough to find me."

She kissed him again and yet again a third time for good measure. "By the by, how did you find me?"

He kissed her again and said, "Someone wrote me a note that you would be meeting your lover here."

She stared at him, so surprised she almost forgot to kiss him back, but then she did, loving the feel of him, the taste of him, and when she finally spoke, she was breathless. "You're jesting, aren't you?"

He set her back onto her feet and handed her the note. Caroline spread out the crumpled page and read it through once, then again. "Goodness," she said, looking up finally. "This is rather amazing."

"I thought it was."

"What nodcock could have penned it?" Before he could do more than shrug, she began to laugh. At first he drew back, wondering, a part of himself long buried, a part of himself that had been formed by his father's bitterness, his father's rage, that part was asking why she was laughing, was demanding to know if she was attempting to brazen it out.

She wiped her eyes on the back of her hand, then waved the crumpled letter about. "This idiot couldn't have known what an incredible lover you are, North. After all, who could possibly think I would have the energy to take another lover? And besides that, why would I want to when I've got the most wonderful man ever as my husband? Surely they couldn't know what you let me do to you, surely they couldn't believe I would want to tie another man's hands to the bedpost, could they?"

He could only stare down at her. He was all of that to her? She really believed what she said? "It is a puzzle, isn't it?" he said finally.

She snorted. "A puzzle? I'd call it bloody nonsense. We've been married less than a month. North, I'm sorry, but this smacks of your male martinets at work, just as I'm sure they did that monster in my window on our wedding night. Can't you just see Tregeagle or Coombe lying flat on his belly, hanging a wire down from the roof, with this monster face dangling off the end of it? I wish the sod had caught a bad chill. Perhaps I can see Tregeagle's style shining forth in this"—she waved the letter under his nose—"the damnable blockhead." She snorted again, and he felt a smile tugging at his mouth.

She was frowning now, waving that damned letter about. "But in this instance they misjudged their master's ardor. How could they possibly believe that I would let you out of my sight? Well, I did let you out of my sight just for a little while today, but you found me quickly enough. I won't ever again, you know, never. Now, kiss me."

He did, thinking there was no woman like Caroline in all of Cornwall and now she was his and all the duplicity of the past, the Nightingale legacy of betrayal, was ended, here and now.

But she had been out of his sight.

He raised his head and looked down at her, all his doubts, all his father's long-buried accusations about women making his eyes nearly black and opaque, his expression hard and frightening.

"Oh, North, is that your brooding look? Yes, it is, and I don't like it a bit. It is dark and menacing. You look dangerous and immensely fascinating. If you weren't my husband and I much preferred your laughter and jesting, because it's your laughter that makes me tingle all over, why, I'd probably think it vastly romantic. A silent strong man, yes, it would make a maiden shudder with mysterious delight, more fool the maiden. I'm glad I know as far down as my toes that you would never hurt me else I'd be frightened of you. I wouldn't ever want to be your enemy. You must have scared the French down to their shaking knees. They must have rejoiced when you sold out and returned to England."

"What were you doing here?"

She grinned up at him, locked her fingers behind his neck, pulled his head down, and kissed him again until he was caressing her back, pulling her so tightly against him he wondered if either of them would be breathing shortly.

"I was here because of an entry I found in the King Mark tome, made by your grandfather. He goes on and on about Queen Isolde, and how she betrayed poor Mark with his nephew Tristan, or maybe Tristan was even his son, and Isolde was a harlot, a slut, and any number of other nasty things, how the nunnery was too good for the likes of her—it gets quite boring really, all the same things your great-grandfather wrote—but then he breaks away from the same old stuff his father had written. He begins to speak about how Fowey used to be a very different place and how it was ripped apart in a huge natural upheaval way back even before the Vikings ruled most of England. And after the land heaved and twisted and formed itself anew, it became evident to this local monk that King Mark was nowhere to be found in that region, that everyone had been wrong, and the split-apart earth proved it. No King Mark in southern Cornwall. Your grandfather believed that this oak tree copse was where King Mark met his nephew Tristan to exile him from Cornwall, both him and Isolde. It was here he died, supposedly from a poisoned arrow from one of Tristan's supporters, and here he was buried—in one of these hillocks. Perhaps there is something here, who knows? Now, don't laugh, North, I'm trying to take your male ancestors a bit seriously."

"I'm not laughing just yet. But I must tell you, Caroline, that I've never heard of an earthquake down south of us. Did my grandfather write about which monk it was? His name? His order? Is there even a text in the library penned by this supposed monk claiming all this happened?"

She slumped down a bit. "No, of course not, but I didn't scour through every shelf and every volume, North. You know what really stymies me: that blasted gold armlet. Where did it come from exactly? Odd that your great-grandfather never gave its exact location. And what the devil happened to it? Why doesn't your father say a word about its suddenly disappearing? It doesn't make sense. Anyway, I came here just to see what I could find."

"And you've found nothing?"

"Not a single thing, not even a small piece of iron that could have belonged to a long-ago sword. All your ancestors seemed to live a very long time and all of them wrote not only about this King Mark business but about the perfidy of women as well. Do you know, North, that your great-grandfather actually wrote that women should be locked away, just like in those Moslem harems, and taken out only to be used to beget heirs? Did you know your grandfather, North? Did you know about his dislike of women?"

"I remember him, yes, too well. And yes, I know all about his dislike of females. It was an obsession, not only with him, but with his father and his own son. He looked like a Nightingale man, like me, in other words."

"All dark and hairy, and utterly exquisite?"

He grinned down at her, kissed the tip of her nose that was fast becoming sunburnt, and said, "Exquisite, am I?"

"Oh yes, and I think I'm in danger of becoming even more overwhelmed by you now than before. Yes, I think you should continue to let me have the upper hand for a while longer."

His eyes nearly crossed with lust. He pictured himself flat on his back, his legs sprawled, his wrists tied over his head, wondering how long he could bear what she was doing to him before he brought his hands down to her.

"North, your breathing is very fast and very uneven. Are you all right?"

"No."

"Well, in that case—" She shrugged out of her riding jacket. He froze, just staring at her. She grinned wickedly at him, tossed her jacket on the ground, and began to unpin her riding hat.

"Caroline, it's very open here—"

She grabbed his hand and tugged at it. "Then let's go to the copse. It will be cozy and warm and I can kiss you until I fall into a swoon."

Before they reached the copse, they were running, Caroline's bright, happy laughter warming his blood as much as his unbridled lust for her, a seemingly unending lust.

28

It was after midnight and still North lay awake, but he was careful to lie still because Caroline was pressed against him and her even breathing told him she was soundly asleep. He was frowning up at the dark ceiling for it had just occurred to him that he'd forgotten to ask her what Dr. Treath was doing there, what he was showing her, why he'd kissed her cheek. And she hadn't volunteered a thing.

He shook his head. Was he so much like the other Nightingale men that all his dealings with women—particularly his wife—were poisoned by distrust? Was it in his blood, this near obsession with betrayal?

Damnation.

He wouldn't think about it again.

Come to think of it, with each of his mistresses, he'd not questioned his possessiveness, his insistence that when in his keeping she keep herself only for him. One girl, of course, had taken another gentleman, and surely his reaction to it had been too ungoverned, his anger too cold and hard and deep, because she'd been naught but a mistress, after all, and life was life, carrying tears and laughter and disappointment, and men and women simply weren't saints. Ah, but when he thought about it now, he could remember the roiling fury that had torn through him when he found out she'd slept with another man, and it was at that moment his father's bitter diatribes came crashing through long-forgotten memories. Ah, they'd seemed to come from deep within him, from a place he hadn't even recognized as being a real part of him. Aye, he'd allowed this poison until he'd realized what he was doing, what he was thinking and remembering, and forced himself to think of other matters.

Had she distracted him with sex so he wouldn't ask her?

He couldn't stand himself. He wished he'd never read even a small part of that damned diary Tregeagle had given him before he'd married Caroline. It was filled with anger and rage; it was vicious and it was poison and there was a sickness to it that frightened him. And it went all the way back to his great-grandfather. Surely that was beyond coincidence, all those betrayals by Nightingale wives. Surely.

He kissed the top of Caroline's head, squeezed her against him, and nearly leaped off the bed when she said against his shoulder, "Why can't you sleep? What's wrong?"

"I suppose it's because I am in such dire need. You haven't done your wifely duty by me, Caroline. It's been a good six hours. I'm in a bad way. I probably won't sleep the rest of the night because you've not seen to my relief."

Had that easy flow of words really come from him? Why hadn't he simply just brooded out a single curt word to her? Why was he being amusing? He didn't begin to understand himself, this new self that bandied about words and mocked and teased and smiled a great deal too much, surely, and even laughed more than was necessary.

But then he forgot about being dark and melancholy. He forgot everything except her breasts against his chest, her hand stroking over his throat, his shoulders, down his arms until her fingers were clasped in his. Then she was between his legs, over him, and she was staring down at him in the darkness, and he blessed the fact that there was just a touch of moonlight coming into the bedchamber and he could see the shadows on her face and he saw that she was smiling down at him, and then he closed his eyes

259

because her palms were spread on his belly, going lower and lower, and he groaned.

"Forgive me, North, for not treating you as I should."

He felt the warmth of her breath and shuddered with the power of it. He sought for just a hint of melancholy, just the forgotten flavor of it. He sought for brooding, even for a dollop of wit, but there was nothing but a growing wildness in him, and there too, a vast space, always there but never recognized by him before, and this space was filled with her and with what she was doing to him and making him feel. And when her hands closed around him, he ceased worrying about anything at all, and managed to say, "Caroline, your mouth, put your mouth on me." She did and he thought he'd die from the glory of it.

When he was caressing her, letting her feel the heat of his body and the wet heat of his mouth, he knew that he moved her every bit as much as she did him. When she screamed, her back bowed off the bed. He smiled and held her close and dear in those moments of shattering pleasure.

"Ah, Caroline," he said, kissing her belly, his fingers still gently stroking over her, "you are more than a simple man deserves."

And she said, her fingers stroking through his hair, "You're the only simple man I want."

Caroline hadn't visited all the rooms in her new home. Since no one was demanding to speak to her just then, neither male nor female, she had some unaccustomed time to herself. She wore a wool shawl over her muslin gown, and stout warm boots. It was fall now, truly fall, with All Hallows' Eve not far away. The mornings were heavy with fog more often now, the afternoon air usually crisp and cool, the sharp smell of the sea stronger, wafting even to Mount Hawke on some days when the wind was high and the clouds dark and roiling low in the sky. Caroline loved Cornwall.

Miss Mary Patricia was giving Evelyn and Alice lessons in her bedchamber, saying that the nursery struck her as silly given the fact that all of them were grown women, carrying babes in their bellies. Owen was at Scrilady Hall, meeting with Mr. Peetree from the mines, a man Owen had told her knew what he was about, and he appeared to like Owen. North was with Flash Savory, the two of them questioning all the people who had known Nora Pelforth, searching for any clue, any hint of who had killed her. It was such a pity that Bennett couldn't have done it. He was such a rotten individual.

She also suspected North had Flash trying to find the boy who'd given Timmy the maid the note about her meeting her lover. Sir Rafael Carstairs was with them and Caroline imagined that the three men would end up in Goonbell at Mrs. Freely's inn, drinking her excellent local ale.

Caroline walked to the third floor of the east wing. It was so quiet here it was unearthly. It was a bit nerve-racking, all that silence. Dust motes hung in the air, shining in the spikes of sunlight that managed to penetrate the closed window shutters and aged draperies. No one had been up here in quite a while.

She sneezed as she opened the door to yet another room that was at the very end of the long corridor. It wasn't a bedchamber, rather it was some sort of storeroom. Heavy wooden-slatted shutters tightly covered the narrow windows. She unlatched them and let light flood into the room. There were very old wooden crates piled high against the walls. Also stacked against the walls were paintings. She pulled one of them toward her and took a step back.

It was a very stylized painting of a woman done early in the last century. She was very young, no older than Caroline was now. Despite the artist's deficits, she was also very pretty: dark eyes, dark hair, a wicked dimple deep in her right cheek. Beyond her stood a young man, proud and tall—no doubt he was a Nightingale man—his large hand resting lightly on her shoulder.

She pulled the other paintings out from the wall, turning them one by one so she could study each of them. They were all of ladies, going back well into the sixteenth century—one lady, older than most of the others, was pursing a very thin mouth and squinting too-small eyes. She wore a wide white ruff around her neck and three ropes of pearls. She looked like a harpy. Caroline wouldn't have wanted her for a mother-in-law.

There were at least two dozen paintings, all of them, obviously, former

Nightingale wives. All had been dumped here, removed entirely from the main living quarters of Mount Hawke and stacked in this out-of-the-way room to molder. At least they hadn't been burned or destroyed outright. She found a lady with her hair powdered and puffed high on her head in the style of the mid and late last century. North's grandmother, no doubt. Again, she was very young, no older than Caroline was now. But where was his mother? She couldn't find a more recent portrait.

Who had done away with the portrait? And then she knew. North's great-grandfather. He'd either destroyed it or refused to have her portrait done. After all, he'd been the one to teach all that bitterness to North's grandfather, who'd bored her endlessly with his whining and carping and his frankly despotic view of the world and his place in it, a place with women as slaves, possessed and kept under the man's thumb. It had been North's great-grandfather who had started the belief that King Mark was really buried here at Mount Hawke and not in Fowey or in Brittany. Given his endless diatribes against women that were liberally interspersed amongst his writings of King Mark, he had to be the one who'd had all the female portraits removed. She wondered now as she'd wondered several times before why the great-grandfather hadn't selected King Arthur—much more family and just as betrayed by his best friend and Guinevere. Why King Mark, who very few people even knew about? The perfidy of the woman was the same in both, after all. She shook away the thoughts. The Nightingale ancestors had been mad and their madness didn't have to recognize reason and it obviously hadn't.

She turned to study the portraits again. Most were in bad shape. They all needed some restoration except for the two painted in the last hundred years. She dusted her hands on her skirt. There was a militant look in her eye. Damn all those past Nightingale men. She managed to pick up the two portraits, one under each arm. She hauled them down to her bedchamber. She was still panting from her efforts when she rang for Mrs. Mayhew.

She then danced a jig, sending up clouds of billowing dust decades old from her filthy gown.

· · ·

North looked at his wife, at her soiled muslin gown, her dusty boots. She was filthy, smudges of the blackest dirt he'd ever seen on her cheeks, her hands grubby, but she was smiling at him. "Come here, my lord," she called out to him. "Do come here. I've a surprise for you."

He realized then that the other six female residents of Mount Hawke were standing behind his wife, all looking excited, hopeful, and, if he wasn't mistaken, a bit frightened. Of what? Of him? Off to the side were Polgrain, Tregeagle, and Coombe, and they looked ready to drag someone off to an *auto-da-fé*. He had no difficulty at all seeing them lighting the fires with eager dispatch.

He focused on Caroline. "You look like an urchin. What have you been doing?"

She grinned at him, said nothing, simply pointed up to the wall. He stood beside her and looked up. He stared; he couldn't look away. He felt his throat tighten. Beside the portrait of his great-grandfather was another portrait, one of that same long-ago Nightingale male painted when he was young, in his prime. He was standing behind a young lady who was obviously his bride and North's great-grandmother. North said nothing, just continued to stare. God, she was beautiful and so very young. His great-grandfather looked like a man blessed, happy, full of hope, and quite pleased with himself and the lovely young lady seated before him. North finally looked to see another single portrait of a lady, this one obviously his grandmother, this grandmother of his painted like his great-grandmother, when she was very young, newly wed. She looked gay and ever so filled with wicked humor. She looked ready to burst into laughter. She looked happy. There were no shadows in her lovely eyes, no hint of what was to come.

Suddenly he wanted very much to see his mother, wanted very much to see what she looked like, to try to remember, but there was no portrait beside his father's, just the old man's grim face, dark eyes narrowed, such anger and bitterness shining from them, and North quickly turned away. He said very quietly, "Where did you find them?"

"I was exploring in the east wing on the third floor. There are at least two dozen portraits, North, all of Nightingale women back to Queen Elizabeth's time. Most of those are in frightful shape, but I hope, I pray, they can be restored."

He said nothing, just stared hungrily up at his grandmother. "My mother," he said, then stopped. "She's dead, you know. You didn't find a portrait of her?"

"I'm sorry. There was no portrait more recent than this one of your grandmother."

"She looks so very young, so happy, as does my great-grandmother."

"I know. It's odd, but all the others—your ancestresses—are painted twice, once in their youth and again in their middle years. Yet your great-grandmother and your grandmother are painted only when they are surely newly wed."

"It's because they were booted out before they could have a chance to get old with their husbands. I just remembered. My mother's name was Cecilia. I wonder, if she'd been painted very early on, if she would have been smiling and happy like my grandmother and great-grandmother."

"My lord."

"Yes, Tregeagle?"

"May I speak with you, my lord?"

"Perhaps later, Tregeagle," North said absently. He turned to Caroline and smiled down at her. He rubbed the spot of dirt from her cheek.

"My lord."

"Yes, Coombe?"

"We would appreciate your attention to us, in private."

"Not now, Coombe."

"Very well, my lord. You force me to speak our mind in front of all and sundry and female. We didn't want these portraits brought down. Actually, even though we knew they existed and were in that room, we'd honestly forgotten about them. We tried to explain to *her* that your great-grandfather had had them all removed, that he forbade any female portraits ever to hang here at Mount Hawke, that the female portraits were meant to remain forgotten and locked away, only the door was open to *her* and we don't understand that, for Tregeagle swears it was locked."

"How do you know that, Coombe?"

"Your great-grandfather wrote of it, my lord. Didn't you read the diaries Mr. Tregeagle gave you before you brought this Female Person into Mount Hawke?"

To North's surprise, Caroline laughed. "Oh, do give it up, Coombe. Come, Tregeagle, this is a new and different time. The past is past, and all the unhappiness of the past is where it should be, behind us. It's no longer a part of us or of this house, nor should you continue harking back to it. Do welcome a return to what is right and just. These ladies are Nightingales just as much as are the men. All the men had to have mothers, you know, including his lordship here."

"We do not like it," Tregeagle said. "The Nightingale mothers weren't worthy. They were all, we regret to say, trollops. They were Nightingales only temporarily, only until the Nightingale men realized how very perfidious they were. It does lead one to generalize, my lord, and rightfully so." He paused apurpose, staring toward Caroline. "In the recent past there has been no Nightingale wife who was loyal and true to her husband. The Nightingale men carry this curse or this blessing, depending on how one regards it. It is their legacy—your legacy—my lord."

"I think that's quite enough, Tregeagle," North said, his voice low and smooth and quite deadly.

"But, my lord, we know she's already carrying on with Dr. Treath!" Coombe shouted. "Everyone knows!"

Tregeagle said, his voice earnest as a vicar's at a funeral, "It's true, my lord. She's just like all the others. It's the Nightingale men's burden to bear."

"I think," North said slowly, looking at each of his three male servants in turn. "I think I will just take you all out and shoot you. You'll not change. Caroline, may I borrow your pistol?"

"I'm sorry, North, but I gave it to Timmy the maid, remember?"

"Then a length of rope," he said. "I'll hang all the buggers from the apple tree branches in the orchard. When they rot they can hit the ground just like the apples."

29

"Now, my lord," Tregeagle began, a sheen of sweat on his brow. "That isn't exactly what I would call a playful jest on your part."

"I'm not jesting."

Coombe said, "It isn't something any of us enjoy contemplating."

"No, Mr. Coombe," Mrs. Mayhew said, stepping right up to him to stare him straight in the eye, "it isn't. Therefore, you'd best listen to me. His lordship has been more than patient with the three of you, but enough is enough. And you, Mr. Sniggledy-Piggledy," Mrs. Mayhew continued to Tregeagle, stepping even closer until she wasn't more than two inches from his nose, "her ladyship is quite right. Mount Hawke is no longer a male sanctuary, and it's about time things were put back to normal. Now, sir, why don't you and Mr. Coombe and Mr. Polgrain all go to the kitchen and have a nice restoring cup of brandy. It will soothe your nerves, perhaps grant you some proper perspective. It might also save you from his lordship, for he does indeed look ready to stretch your miserable necks."

"He doesn't have that particular look at all," said Polgrain. "He just looks a bit distracted, and no wonder, with all of you chattering about and doing things you shouldn't be doing."

"He wouldn't harm us," said Coombe. "It isn't civilized and all Nightingale men have been civilized."

"But he might if I helped him," Caroline said. "And I'll tell you, I'm close to the brink now. Just stop it. You must, gentlemen, accustom yourselves, for your attitudes will no longer be allowed here. This is a new day at Mount Hawke. Nightingale women are back again where they should be."

To her surprise, all six other females began to cheer. The three males of the Mount Hawke servant bastion stood there frozen. North looked from one side to the other and raised his hand. There was instant silence. He was the master, after all.

He looked quickly at Caroline, who just happened to be giving him the most adoring look he'd ever had directed upon him in his entire life, except for those other times when she'd been looking at him with that same adoring look. He forgot what he wanted to say. He wanted to kiss her dirty face and strip off her dirty gown. He wanted her filthy hands all over him. He wanted her legs wrapped around his waist with him carrying her, shoving into her as she threw back her head and screamed her pleasure, her hair falling free and thick. He cleared his throat. "Her ladyship is quite right. Whatever happened in the past here at Mount Hawke is over. Mrs. Mayhew is perfectly right as well. No longer will you refer to the Viscountess Chilton as *you* or as *miss* or as *madam*. She is your ladyship or my lady. The past will no longer taint the present. There will be a return to sanity now at Mount Hawke, and with God's blessing, there will be children, not just the obligatory Nightingale heir. I ask you to consider this carefully. Now, go away, all of you. Have a cup of brandy just as Mrs. Mayhew suggested. But know this: Mount Hawke is now going to be the way it was before my great-grandfather's time."

The three male martinets filed out of the great entrance hall, stiff and silent, and Caroline suddenly worried that the ox-tail soup that had made Alice ill had been done apurpose, just as had that monster face in her window. Oh, surely not. A monster's face dangling in her window was one thing, but poisoning soup was quite another. No, she wouldn't credit that. They were simply all old men who were faced with change none of them could accept, at least yet. Mrs. Mayhew wasn't, however, a gloater. She wouldn't tweak their noses; she wouldn't taunt them in their loss.

Mrs. Mayhew curtsied to Caroline and shooed Chloe and Molly away to get on with their duties. Miss Mary Patricia said, "Alice is feeling a bit peaked, Miss Caroline. Evelyn believes she should rest now. I'll see to it." She nodded to North and gave him a smile that bespoke a great deal of satisfaction. He didn't see it, Caroline noted. He was looking distracted again; he was staring again at the portraits.

"Caroline," he said finally, "why do you think my mother's portrait wasn't even painted when she was newly married to my father?" He closed his eyes a moment. "No, you don't have to ponder on that because I know. My grandfather was still alive when my father married my mother. She was allowed to come here to Mount Hawke only once, my father wrote in that damned diary. My grandfather kicked her out. After she birthed me, she, like the other Nightingale wives, cuckolded my father and he tossed her out on her ear. He told me again and again that she was a whore and I was to forget her. He told me she died and she deserved to die. I remember it more clearly now, just as I also remember their screaming at each other. I was very small, but I remember their being so big and so loud and I hated it and then suddenly she was gone forever. I don't remember living at Mount Hawke until after that day. But it was a miserable place and I hated it and wanted my mother. It didn't matter when my grandfather finally died, because my father had become just like him, maybe worse."

"I'm so sorry, North." She put her arms around him and held him tightly against her. "But things are different now; we will make them different. I'm so sorry."

"Why were you with Dr. Treath at that oak copse?"

She looked at him straightly, not blinking, not moving, and said calmly, "The note some idiot sent you to tell you I was meeting my lover—do you believe it, North?"

"No."

"You are not your father or your grandfather or your great-grandfather, nor am I any of those poor wretched Nightingale wives."

"I know."

"Dr. Treath said he'd wanted to speak to me alone and thus he followed me when I rode from Mount Hawke. He said he wanted to tell me about Nora Pelforth, that she had been his very good friend after my aunt Eleanor was killed, that he didn't understand any of this and he hated it. But foremost, he didn't want me to get the wrong idea if I heard he'd known Nora Pelforth from anyone else. He didn't want me to believe he was fickle and hadn't truly loved my aunt. He was distressed, North. I tried to comfort him, tried to assure him I quite understood, and he kissed me on the cheek and said he only wished that I could have become his step-niece."

"Thank you, Caroline, for telling me."

"I would have before, but I forgot all about everything when you began kissing me. You have great power over my mind, North Nightingale. Ah, that was lovely with you, in the copse, with those skinny slivers of sunlight coming through the oak leaves. I felt the heat of the sun on my face when you were over me. There could be nothing more wonderful than that."

He shook, but managed to say in a calm enough voice, "Yes, it was lovely. I remember the heat of the sun on my back. What did he show you?"

She looked up at him a moment, studying him closely, he knew, wondering why he was asking her, knowing it was distrust bred deep into him, yet accepting it, not getting angry with him, for he would change and he prayed she was right. She said simply, "It was a letter that Nora Pelforth had written to him after my aunt's death. In it she wrote that she knew how much he had loved my aunt and how very sorry she was. Would you like me to show it to you, North?"

He nodded and said, "No."

"Thank you for that, I think. Dr. Treath never gave it to me so I would have to ask him for it, and that would be a bit embarrassing. Ah, well, at least half of you believes me." She paused a moment, her fingers lightly stroking his upper arms, kneading him, and he knew it was unconscious on her part; she simply enjoyed touching him, having the physical contact with him. She said, "North, I'm so sorry about your mother. Perhaps one of the three male martinets can tell you more about her." He didn't say anything, but she could feel his pain, a pain from long ago that was vague now, but still there deep inside him. She placed her hand on his arm. "North, you said you remembered coming back here to Mount Hawke after that last horrible fight between your parents, when your mother left. Where were you living?"

He blinked, looked hungrily up at his grandmother's portrait, and said slowly, "I don't know, Caroline. I wasn't living here, thus it must have been at another property my father owned, another property that I now own."

"How many do you own?"

"There are three. A hunting box in the Cotswolds, near Lower Slaughter, a house on the Steyne in Brighton, and a country manor house in Yorkshire, near Northallerton." He paused a moment, then said, "Good God, I forgot all about that house when I was in Yorkshire just a month and a half ago."

"Why were you there?"

"I was visiting a very good army friend of mine, the Earl of Chase, and his new bride. You would like both Marcus and the Duchess."

"Duchess?"

"Yes, that is what Marcus named her when she was nine years old. She was his uncle's bastard."

"Goodness, North, I want to hear more about this."

"All right. Perhaps this winter when we're hunched close to the fireplace to keep warm, I'll tell you about their Wyndham legacy and all that happened."

Her eyes lit up and he kissed her quickly. "No, Caroline, later. I don't want to be rushed in the telling. Let me tell you about the houses. I haven't been to any of them in years and I just don't remember if I was raised those first five years in one of them."

"So you must have lived with your mother and father—when he wasn't back here at Mount Hawke being poisoned by your grandfather—in one of these houses. That seems the most likely, North."

"It's possible. I shall write to my man of business in London and ask him to give me a full accounting. It's something I must do in any case. He could tell me when my father and mother lived in one of those houses."

"Perhaps we could even go to the one in Yorkshire and see your friends. Now, there's something else I want to tell you, North. No, don't kiss me again just yet, just listen to me." She cupped his face between her palms. "You're my husband. I love you and I will always love you, even when you're old and haven't a tooth in your mouth, and all bent over. I'll still love you. Since I'll probably be in the same condition, it shouldn't prove too difficult. I will never, never betray you. I would kill anyone who tried to harm you. You are mine and what is mine I keep forever."

His breath hitched. "Caroline," he said, his hands coming up to clasp her.

Owen walked whistling into the entrance hall, saw them standing there, Caroline's arms around her husband's neck, and said, "What is so serious? Is something wrong? Oh, I say, who are those women? They weren't there before, were they? No, there weren't any portraits of women anywhere, and I thought that was quite odd."

"No, Owen," North said, dropping his hands as he turned to face Owen. "Caroline found all my ancestresses in a room on the third floor and brought these two down. We'll see that the others are restored and hung in their original places."

"Caroline always had her nose everywhere when we were growing up," Owen said, staring at the portraits. "You wouldn't believe the stories she told me about when she was at Chudleigh's Young Ladies' Academy. She was a terror, North, never kept her mouth closed and never minded her own business. She always wanted to fix things, even me. Oh, I got a letter from my father. You won't believe what he's done, or perhaps you would, given you know my father quite well."

It was very late. Caroline was reading in the library downstairs, a small branch of candles at her elbow. She was wrapped warmly in a scarlet dressing gown that she hoped North would admire excessively and wish to examine closely, then perhaps remove. She missed him and yet he'd been gone only three hours. He was visiting Sir Rafael Carstairs at Carstairs Manor. It had rained hard the past three days and there was a cave-in problem at one of the tin mines. They were meeting with other owners and managers to solve the cave-in and equipment problems in three of the mines.

It was odd, but she'd discovered that she hadn't wanted to stay in that big bed alone. It was cold and lonely and she hated it. No, she would wait for him to return, thus her presence in the library, reading Gottfried of Strasbourg's version of the Tristan and Isolde story, written back in the rein of King John, that mangy and cruel fellow who'd finally been forced by his barons to put ink and quill to the Magna Carta. Good for the barons.

This story was darker and uglier than Malory's later tale of doomed lovers, the only person worthy of compassion and respect being the dishonored King Mark. Ah, the patient and virtuous King Mark who only exiled his nephew Tristan and his own wife Isolde for their treachery, didn't cleave Tristan in two and stick a knife in his young wife's breast. Caroline knew that if she'd been King Mark, she would have gulleted the betrayers with great pleasure. Ah, but myth was more gentle and more lasting because it skillfully interwove all the classic themes of tragic love, betrayal, just a hint of triumph, but finally death.

This, then, was the portrait of all the Nightingale men since North's great-grandfather. How noble they must have believed themselves, and how utterly conceited, comparing themselves to the mythical King Mark of Cornwall, going so far as to claim he'd held court here and not on the southern coast near Fowey, as legend had it.

At least they hadn't touched King Arthur, leaving that richly magical king to live and die at Tintagel, a belief held fiercely by many Cornishmen. And, unlike King Arthur, whose legend lived on and on, few seemed to know or care about poor King Mark and his betraying wife and randy nephew. Caroline thought Arthur had been too strong a figure for the Nightingale men to take on, whereas the gracious King Mark, really a wilting ninny, was much easier prey, much more satisfying fodder for their fantasies.

She rather wished the Nightingale men had picked King Arthur for their idol, for he'd endured, unlike the weakly sweet King Mark. After all, he, too, had been betrayed by his queen Guinevere and his prize knight, Sir Lancelot. She shook her head. She realized they'd picked King Mark simply because he was the more forgettable, thus not many folk would care enough to bother disagreeing with them and their claims. Where people were impassioned about King Arthur, they were tepid at most when it came to poor old King Mark.

Caroline settled into the story. It was very difficult to decipher in the medieval French, but she did make out that Tristan, once exiled with Isolde, or Iseult, as the French wrote, swore to be with her "one heart, one troth, one body, one life." But good old Tristan proceeded to meet another Iseult and fall in love with her. So much for men and their constancy, she thought. Caroline yawned and went to search again through the references to Tristan, reverently collected by all those Nightingale men who had nothing better to do since they were such idiots with their wives.

Caroline read until the words blurred, her eyes felt gritty, and she yawned hugely. There was so much and it was all, she was certain, from the colorful imagination of Gottfried, whose work, however, was taken quite seriously back in medieval times, silly as it seemed to Caroline now. The book fell from her hands onto her lap, then slipped to the carpet.

She awoke to a scream that made her fall off the settee.

30

She was on her feet in an instant, her skirts yanked up to her knees, running into the entrance hall. She skittered to a stop and stared. Owen was straddling Bennett Penrose, his hands fisted in his shirt, shaking him hard, then pounding his head against the pale gold-and-white marble. Bennett was fighting him but he wasn't having much success. He was yelling like a man who knew he was in dire straits. Caroline felt immense pride in Owen at that moment.

"Owen! Goodness, I think you're splendid, but you must stop it, you'll kill him."

"He deserves it, the bloody bugger!" And Owen smacked Bennett's head again to the marble.

"Well, he does, true enough, but I don't want you to hang for killing him." She lightly touched her hand to Owen's fist. She saw his rigidity, his utter fury, and realized she'd never seen him so out of control in all his life.

"I gather it was Bennett who screeched?"

"Oh yes, and that was even before I hit him the first time, bloody little weasel." Owen looked down at Bennett Penrose, whose nose was bleeding profusely and who looked dazed and very pale in the dim candlelight cast by the wall sconces. He didn't yell again. Caroline thought he realized it would cast him into a very poor light to be yelling like a demented goat.

Caroline ripped off a strip from her petticoat. "Here, Bennett, wipe your nose. I don't want you bleeding on the beautiful marble. North wouldn't like it."

Owen got off him and stared down at the very handsome young man who was now struggling to sit up, dabbing his bloody nose. There was a wealth of dislike and, Caroline thought, of contempt in Owen's voice. Well, he had beaten Bennett very satisfactorily. "Now, Penrose, you'll tell us why you were sneaking about."

Bennett continued to rub at his nose, without much success.

"Oh, goodness, let's go to the kitchen and get some water," Caroline said, and led the way to the nether regions.

Owen shoved Bennett into one of the chairs around the huge kitchen table where, Caroline realized, the three male martinets ate their meals with the three females. She wished she could be present at one of those meals. They probably gave each other severe indigestion. She could just hear Chloe and Molly giggling at nothing in particular and see the pained look on Tregeagle's face.

Caroline wet a cloth and handed it to Bennett. She wanted to smash it against his nose herself. "Keep cleaning yourself up and tell us what you were doing here."

"Nothing, I wasn't doing anything," Bennett said finally. He sounded for the world like a sulky boy. "This stupid fool jumped me, caught me completely by surprise, and when I hit the floor the blow stunned me so this fool could gain the advantage on me, otherwise it would have been he with the bloody nose and the cracked skull."

Owen snorted and rubbed his bruised knuckles with satisfaction.

"No, Owen, don't hit him again," Caroline said. "He will, you know, Bennett, and so will I if you don't tell us what you were doing here. You and I made a bargain. You got money and I was free of you, forever, as were all my friends. Now here you are again, skulking around at Mount Hawke very late at night. I would say that you're extremely lucky that North isn't here. He would kill you."

"I knew he wasn't here," Bennett said behind the cloth, now dotted liberally with his blood. "I'm not stupid."

"Ah, so you thought that since it would just be Caroline, you damned bugger, you could do whatever you wanted."

Caroline wondered at that moment what Owen was doing here. Well, at least his purpose wouldn't be of a nefarious sort. "Why, Bennett?"

"You damned hound, you weren't coming after Alice again, were you?" It was close but Caroline managed to hold Owen's hands down until he calmed sufficiently.

"Good God, no," Bennett said. "Keep him away from me, Caroline, or I might be forced to hurt him. I wasn't after Alice. That little slut is probably so fat and ugly now I would puke to look at her. No, I lost the money. It wasn't my fault. This fellow cheated me out of it, the bastard."

"You lost the money gambling?"

Bennett nodded.

"You came here to steal something?"

"Well, not really, perhaps something small and not cumbersome, maybe Lord Chilton's strongbox from his estate room if I could have found it. But I didn't even find the estate room because this fool caught me by surprise."

"I find that remarkably interesting."

The three of them turned to see North standing in the kitchen door, leaning negligently against the door frame, his arms crossed over his chest. "You are the most miserable worm I have ever known in my life," he continued to Bennett in an utterly dispassionate voice. "Caroline, my dear, I trust the worm hasn't overset your nerves?"

"Yes, he did with his yelling. I fell off the settee in the library. You see, North, I'd fallen asleep waiting for you. I ran out like a demented dervish to see Owen sitting on his chest in the entrance hall. He was bashing his head quite nicely against the marble. I moved Bennett here when I realized his nose was bleeding. I didn't want him ruining that beautiful marble."

"Very thoughtful of you," North said, still not moving. He looked very dangerous in that moment, and Caroline shivered. It was his stillness that was so frightening, that outward calm that wouldn't give an enemy a clue that he was ready to kill.

"I shouldn't have stopped," Owen said, looking at North. "He's always going to be a problem, North. At least my father has settled things."

"Yes, he did, didn't he, and we never expected him to do it."

"If your father told the truth in his letter," Caroline said. "Mr. Ffalkes is a cunning fellow. I'm sorry, Owen, but it's true."

"I know from painful experience that you're right," Owen said. "But this time I believe him. He will marry Mrs. Tailstrop but I do think he'll snag her pug Lucy and drop the animal in a ditch. He quite hates it, you know."

"I've written to Mrs. Tailstrop," North said. "We'll see what she has to say."

"I didn't know you'd done that," Caroline said. "That was very smart of you, North, not that it surprises me." She sighed then, eyeing Bennett, who was suspiciously quiet, just dabbing his nose.

"What will we do with him?"

"Let me beat him to a pulp," Owen said, and massaged his knuckles vigorously.

"We could hang him with the three male martinets," Caroline said hopefully. "He could rot and fall to the ground with the rest of them and the apples we don't end up picking."

North just shook his head at them. "A nice thought, but not enough finesse, Caroline. It's such a pity we're certain he didn't kill your aunt or the other two women. That, I admit, does depress me." He paused a long moment, giving Bennett a very thorough look. Finally, he said, "Why not send him to your father, Owen?"

Owen gave a bark of laughter and Caroline grinned. "Oh goodness, he'd whip Bennett into shape, North—that or he'd kill him. What do you think, Caroline?"

"Hmmm, Bennett could work for your father, couldn't he, Owen? Either that or North could see that he was transported to the Colonies."

"It's either going to Honeymead Manor or starving," North said. "You don't have a sou, do you, Penrose?"

Bennett, still blotting at his nose, shook his head.

"Nor do you have my strongbox."

Again, Bennett, shuddering only slightly, shook his head.

"I don't suppose you want to be transported?"

Bennett put his face in his hands. He was silent as the clock that had stood in the corner of the kitchen that had stopped running the moment it was brought into Mount Hawke some seventy-five years before.

"Well?"

Bennett moaned and said behind his handkerchief, "I never heard of any heiresses in the Colonies."

"I've finally found our squirrelly lad," North said to Caroline a week later when they sat across from each other at the breakfast table. It was quite early and thus they were the only ones present.

"The one who couldn't put two words together without jumping out of his boots?"

"That's the one. Flash tracked him down in Trevellas. He's the son of a dairy farmer. He took Timmy the maid there before he took me just to make sure he had the right lad. Poor Timmy the maid couldn't imagine how he didn't know him. It upset him terribly that he'd let me down."

"All right, tell me. Who gave him the letter?"

"Coombe."

She felt both relief and depression. "Oh," she said. "Well, at least we know."

"Would you like to be with me when I confront Coombe with this?"

"Yes, I suppose it would be best. Oh dear, North, the three of them have been so quiet lately. I'd rather hoped they'd come to grips with things."

"Oh no, I never believed that for a moment," North said. He rose and tossed his napkin onto the white tablecloth. "More's the pity."

An hour later in the library, Coombe stood before his lordship, who was sitting behind the massive mahogany desk that dominated the entire corner. Coombe saw movement from the corner of his eye and felt a spasm of anger wash through him. It was that upstart girl who'd managed to snare his innocent noble lordship, the Female Person the master still doted on. What was going on?

"I met a young boy named Johnny Trilby, a lad who stutters and who does odd errands for people who pay him well because he's a cute little fellow and they feel sorry for him. His father approves, you see, lets him out of his chores on the dairy farm because the people pay him well and the father takes just about all of it."

Coombe stood straighter, saying nothing, looking over North's left shoulder.

"Young Johnny told me you paid him to give me that letter. Odd but I didn't recognize your handwriting, Coombe, but I haven't seen much of it, have I, since my return? And I was only sixteen when I left Mount Hawke."

"There is a mistake, my lord," Coombe said, his voice smooth as the bolt of crimson velvet that North had bought from a tinker near Oporto, Portugal, two years before and planned to give to Caroline at Christmas. He'd carried it around with him for so long it probably had moth holes in it. "Yes," Coombe said, "it's a mistake and not at all my fault. I venture to say it is all her fault, for everything has been topsy-turvy since she came here that first time, pretending she was in shock over her aunt's death."

Caroline said, "Your timing was excellent, Coombe, that or your luck. You had to have Johnny Trilby deliver that letter to his lordship when you knew that Dr. Treath was off to see me."

"No, Caroline," North said. "It wasn't difficult at all. I fancy if we question Dr. Treath, he too will have received a message purporting to be from you, Caroline, telling him you were concerned and wanted to see him. Doubtless you also wrote in your letter that you would be pleased if he wouldn't speak of it, to anyone, including you. Am I right, Coombe?"

Caroline said after the silence stretched on without Coombe filling it, "I'm very curious about something, Coombe. Do you really believe that all the Nightingale wives betrayed their husbands?"

"Dead sure," Coombe said, stiff as a nail, staring still over North's left shoulder. "Disloyal trollops, every one of them."

"Yet you lied to North, telling him that I was meeting my lover when in truth it was all a fabrication."

"You will betray him, it's just a matter of time. I only wanted him to get rid of you now before you really do cuckold him and make his life a misery."

"You want him rid of me even before I present him with an heir?"

"No, never! I—oh, dear."

"It appears you didn't think things through clearly, Coombe," North said. "It appears your dislike of her ladyship and all the changes she's brought to Mount Hawke clouded your reasoning. You mucked it up, didn't you?"

Coombe nodded now. "Yes, I suppose I didn't think things through, my lord. I wanted her gone from here so you could be happy again."

North could only stare at Coombe in utter astonishment. "Happy again? When the devil was I ever happy? Before I escaped my father and his utter lunacy? As happy as I was when my grandfather was still alive and ranting and screeching around here like a lunatic, not even allowing the vicar's wife to visit Mount Hawke, much less any person who happened to be female? As happy as I was in the army getting shot at in more battles than I care to remember? As happy as I was in my solitude, for a man alone I've been all my life, Coombe. Good God, man, I don't believe I've ever been quite so happy in my entire bloody life as I am now. With her. With my wife. Do you understand me, Coombe, she's my *wife*."

"No, no, yours is not the right kind of happy, my lord, and as a Nightingale man, you know it's only temporary. Also, we've all seen you laugh immoderately, exercise wit without sufficient restraint. You've even gone so far as to make people smile and laugh with your jests. It isn't proper for a Nightingale man to be so at ease with other people and with himself. A Nightingale man has more unplumbed depths, more richness of soul; a Nightingale man ponders profoundly the pitfalls of life and how best to avoid them. A Nightingale man lives more years than allotted to other less thoughtful, less discerning men. Well, at least some of them do."

Caroline stared at him. North could but shake his head. He said now, "Coombe, I can no longer trust you. You have lied to me, you have betrayed me. You are retired from service to the Nightingales as of today. There will be a sizable pension so that you may buy a cottage and remain in the area or, if you wish, you can travel elsewhere. I suppose you provided sterling service to my father and that this is what he would do. I'm sorry, Coombe, that it had to come to this. I truly am. I had hoped you would realize that your attitudes were not only outmoded, but just plain wrong."

"Your father wouldn't dream of doing this to me, your grandfather either. Both of them would have believed me had I told them she would be the cause of your downfall. Neither of them would ever have trusted a female more than they trusted me or any other man in their service. Both your grandfather and your father were saints, pious thoughtful men, they—"

"Both were bloody mean-spirited bastards," North said, and slammed his fist down on his desk. "Now, this is quite enough. I don't think I could tolerate you accusing me of making them spin in their grave."

"There's also your great-grandfather, doubtless a discerning, intelligent man, who—" North took a step toward him, so furious that Coombe finally realized he would soon be dead if he didn't shut his mouth. He managed to do just that, but he looked like he wanted to shout down the draperies. He looked pale and drawn and Caroline felt a stab of pity for him until he looked at her and she saw such fury writ on his face that she took a step back.

North said once Coombe had left the library, "Forgive me, Caroline. Had I simply acted immediately when he lowered the monster's head to scare you out of your wits on our wedding night, then this wouldn't have happened. I didn't know it was him, but I had a one-in-three chance of getting it right. Yes, I should have guessed, because he's the youngest of the three and thus the most agile. That roof is steep over your chamber. Too bad he didn't fall and bash in his damned head."

"I'm sorry too, North. I do wish it hadn't ended like this. I didn't want discord. I'd truly hoped they'd come to grips with things."

"I too," he said.

She walked to him, clasped her arms around his back, and kissed his chin. "I'm sorry about Coombe, but I'm frankly relieved that he won't be here to cause more mischief. You are an amazing man, North. You're compassionate, kind, funny, and the best lover in the whole of Britain."

"I must brood sometime, Caroline, surely it's in my black blood, else I might go mad and not ever slaver all over you again."

"Can I brood with you?" Her hand stroked down his chest to his belly. She felt him tremble and kissed his mouth. He lurched, pulling her hard against him. "The damned door," he said against her mouth. In a moment, he'd locked the door, then turned to look at her. "I want your legs around my waist, Caroline. I was thinking of that, picturing you with your back arched against my hands, your hair free and loose down your back. Yes, it's what I want."

She gave him the most radiant smile a man could dream about, and said, "All right, but I'm not quite certain how this will work."

"Don't worry. I'll take care of everything."

"You usually do unless you let me tie your wrists to the headboard and I got to do that only once."

His breathing hitched. "Now, Caroline."

He lifted her onto the desk, and his hands were beneath her skirt, going upward to the top of her stockings to stroke the skin of her inner thighs. "Oh goodness, that's quite nice," she said, then nipped his earlobe. When his fingers touched her she nearly fell off the desk.

"Easy," he said, freed himself, and lifted her onto him. He slid upward into her, felt her tight around him, felt her muscles clenching, and it was the finest feeling he could remember having in his life. He lifted her and she laughed, startled and excited, as he raised her legs to close around his waist.

"This is what I was thinking about," he said against her throat as he whirled her around, going even deeper inside her. "This is exactly what I wanted." She arched her back, pressing closer, and North thought he would go over the edge. "Hold still and that's an order."

She held perfectly still. "Is this all right, North?"

"No, but it will have to suffice. Jesus, Caroline, I couldn't have imagined anything like this and I did try to."

"This is very strange, North. You're walking around with me and you're inside me and it's very nice and—"

"Caroline, please keep still, at least about what we're doing. It drives me just as wild as you moving about."

"Then what can I do?"

He closed his eyes as he slowly withdrew, then pushed back into her, deep, very deep, and she moaned, her back arching again. "Just be you and it's too much," he said, and began to kiss her wildly. He laid her back on top of his desk, her legs dangling over. "No, this isn't the way I want it to be," he said, then shoved her legs up, bending her knees. "Yes, that's it." Then he very slowly withdrew from her, lifted his hands beneath her hips and brought her to his mouth.

There was a knock on the door. "Is anything wrong, my lady?" It was Mrs. Mayhew, and she didn't sound at all concerned.

Caroline's eyes were nearly crossed. She could scarcely draw a breath. She stared up at her husband, smiled at him, and said, "I am ready to expire now, North, quite ready."

"Oh no." He kissed the tip of her nose, rested his palm on her belly, and called out, "Mrs. Mayhew, everything is all right. Her ladyship merely slipped on the carpet. I'm seeing to her. Go away."

There was a long pause, then, if North wasn't mistaken, a very discreet giggle. Miss Mary Patricia? Oh no, surely not Miss Mary Patricia, not their resident pregnant governess.

He turned back to look down at his wife. Her eyes were closed, her lips roughened by his mouth, and parted. He saw the tip of her tongue. She looked utterly abandoned, her skirts tossed up about her waist, her legs bent, her hair free of its pins and tangled about her head. He said nothing, merely touched a finger to her soft flesh. She quivered.

"Shall we finish, Caroline?"

She opened her eyes and there it was again, that adoring look that made him feel like a king, a look so soft and warm it made him hard as a stone, a look that made him know there was something beyond what he knew was in this world and perhaps that something could be his. He came into her and she gasped with the pleasure of it.

A long time later, when Caroline sat in his lap on a huge wing chair in front of a fireplace that wasn't lit, when they were so sated with pleasure that they should have been quite content to just sit there and think about nothing at all, Caroline said, "There seem to be an awful lot of bad people around us, North. Understand, I haven't seen all that much of the world, or known many people, but most of the few I have met haven't been very nice."

"I know," he said. He raised her hair off her neck and kissed her. She tasted like salt and woman and Caroline. "I know and I'm sorry for it. At least you found me and I'm a nice person." He seemed surprised that he'd said that, but perhaps not as surprised as he would have been even two weeks ago.

"You're more than nice. You're the very best. You make up for all the others."

He hugged her, felt her breasts against his chest, felt the precious surge of lust wash through him, and wondered vaguely how he could possibly want her again so very soon after nearly killing himself two times before in far too short a time. He raised his hand and began to caress her breast.

She pushed forward, filling his hand, smiling at him, looking absolutely delighted. He made love to her yet again with her facing him in the chair and it was surely the finest moments he'd ever experienced in his life, if he didn't count the other finest moments he'd been with her, loved her, and caressed her.

Caroline's face was against his throat. She was panting, utterly limp. He very much liked her this way and knowing that he'd pleasured her so much she was ready to fall into a collapse. "I don't think I'm going to make it this time, North. It was too much."

"Yes, and I'll do it to you again just as soon as I've regained a modicum of vigor."

She giggled against his throat and bit his chin. "I love you, but I do need some reassurance. What do you think Polgrain and Tregeagle will do?"

He stilled, his hands now loose on her hips. Her gown was a mess, one of her stockings was hanging off the edge of the desk, the other lying like a white snake curled around the hearth sweep. Her slippers were at drunken angles by the chair. She looked well loved and it pleased him inordinately. "I don't want to think about them right now, but I know I must. I'll speak to them in a little while. This time I will be alone."

She was a coward, she realized, because she agreed with his plan immediately. "Not yet," she said, as she leaned down and kissed him. "Not just yet."

That night Caroline dreamed of Timmy the maid. He was pointing his pistol at North, and she was shrieking at him not to shoot, that North wasn't his father, that Timmy was confused. There was a loud report. Caroline jerked awake at the touch of a hand on her shoulder. She looked up to see Miss Mary Patricia's pale face in the dim early-morning light.

"It's time, Miss Caroline. Oh God, it's time."

31

D r. Treath and Bess Treath arrived at Mount Hawke within the hour. Miss Mary Patricia, efficient and stoic in giving birth as she was in conducting her everyday business, didn't lower herself to yelling or crying, and presented a squalling black-haired little girl at nearly noon the following day, the very picture of the master of the house who had raped her, she'd told Bess Treath, then hugged the tiny child to her breast.

Caroline hadn't been allowed in the room, Dr. Treath having said firmly, "You don't know about any of this, Caroline. You will learn all about it when you have your first child and not before."

It seemed strange to Caroline, but Bess Treath just laughed, saying, "My brother believes that if a girl saw another giving birth, she would never allow a man to touch her." She paused a moment, then added thoughtfully, "Perhaps he has a point. Giving birth isn't pleasant. I think it would have to be a very special man before I'd agree to it."

Caroline wanted to ask her why, then, she was allowed to witness the dreadful ordeal when she herself wasn't married and never had been, but she didn't. She supposed that Bess Treath's age, which was at least thirty, gave her more resistance for such unpleasantness, that and her experience assisting her brother for so many years. But what Bess Treath had said—it did sound frightening as the devil and Caroline said as much to North as they waited downstairs for Miss Mary Patricia to get on with it. "Is it so very dreadful then?" she asked. She kept her voice low. The last thing she wanted was for Alice or Evelyn to hear her. They were, at present, being distracted by Owen, who even managed to make Alice laugh once.

"Yes," he said, nothing more.

That diverted her instantly. She grabbed his arm and shook it. "Come on, North, how do you know about birthing babies?"

"I helped a woman deliver a babe in the hills of Portugal. Her husband had just been killed and it brought on her labor. My men set up a tent and I— well, I tried to help her."

"What happened?"

"The baby boy was dead. She died just moments later."

"Why did she die?"

"She was trying to birth the babe for nearly two days. She was exhausted. Her husband was dead. The baby was dead. She had no will to live." North realized then what he'd said, for Caroline's face was perfectly white.

He kissed her, hugged her. "Caroline, I was a fool to tell you about that. You are nothing like that poor woman. When you become pregnant, I'll be here to watch over you, to take care of you, and Dr. Treath will attend you. There can be tragedy in bringing life into the world, but not with you, Caroline. I won't allow it. I've felt your belly, you know, and even managed once or twice to look at you without undue lust. You've wide hips, surely wide enough to bear as many babes as you want to."

When Bess Treath came into the salon at nearly noon, holding the small babe in her arms, she smiled and announced, "She's a healthy little angel. Miss Mary Patricia wants to name her Eleanor. After your aunt, Caroline."

"Oh," Caroline said. To North's astonishment, she burst into tears.

Little Eleanor was sleeping soundly in her cradle next to Miss Mary Patricia's bed. Owen had returned to Scrilady Hall after assuring himself that Alice had drunk a warm glass of milk prepared for her by Mrs.

Mayhew. Bennett Penrose, in the company of Flash Savory, was now journeying to Honeymead Manor to Mr. Ffalkes, carrying with him a letter from North that requested he take Bennett in hand and make him into a man, a task North wasn't certain anyone could accomplish—he'd grinned then and told Caroline he believed, after his own dealings with Ffalkes, that the man considered himself above every other mortal in the land. It was a challenge he trusted Mr. Ffalkes wouldn't be able to refuse. Also, what more could Ffalkes want than a chance to pound another man into the ground after he himself had been so thoroughly pounded?

North was now standing against the mantel, his arms crossed over his chest. He said to Caroline, "I didn't have a chance to tell you all of it."

"Do you think Bennett will stay at Honeymead Manor with Mr. Ffalkes?"

"He doesn't have anywhere else to go. I asked Ffalkes to pay him for his labor. I also asked him to teach the fool how to gamble so he wouldn't lose all his wages. I also mentioned that Bennett's whining was rather annoying and he might also consider encouraging Bennett to stop it."

She laughed. "That's just perfect, North. You thought of everything."

Again, he felt as if something deep inside himself was unfurling, growing full and heady—her words and that lovely smile of hers making that something expand deeper and deeper still and making him want to smile and laugh and kiss her until his mouth was numb.

"We'll see," he said, trying to sound not at all touched, and probably failing. "Now, let me tell you about Polgrain and Tregeagle. They were at first very stiff in the collar, wouldn't meet my eyes, treated me like the hangman. I asked them if they wished to remain. Tregeagle said he hadn't realized what Coombe had done. He said the letter to me was beyond the line. However, he thought the monster's face on your wedding night hadn't been a bad idea, only he would have known it wouldn't work with you, for you're too bloody stubborn, too strong-willed. He said that argument and logic were the only weapons appropriate to men of good will. Polgrain then said he feared that Mr. Coombe had put something in the ox-tail soup.

"I then asked them if Coombe had felt so strongly when my father first married my mother. They looked at each other but refused to say it wasn't so, which leads me to wonder if perhaps Coombe, even as a very young man, took a hand in continuing with the Nightingale legacy of betrayal. I don't know, and I believe neither Polgrain nor Tregeagle knows either.

"So, I put it to them. They are to tell me tomorrow what they wish to do—either stay here and treat you as you should be treated, or retire to a quaint cottage down by Land's End and learn how to fish." He paused, expecting Caroline to say something. Indeed, he'd expected her to say something long before this, but she was utterly silent, just sitting there in the chair, very still, which was quite unlike her, not even moving her hands, which were always doing something, and when they were doing things to him, it invigorated him to his very toes.

"My God," he said at last, staring at her. "I do believe you're brooding. My Caroline is actually brooding. I must call the hounds and insist that you walk with them on the moor. I must fetch you a volume of poems from the library written to depress the spirit, to darken the soul, to question man's very existence on this pitiful earth. I must buy you a black billowing cloak and have you sit on those ancient pitted rocks by the sea and stare into infinity as a strong wind gusts around you."

She finally looked up at him and gave him a crooked grin. "I've never brooded before. Leave me alone, North. It's an experiment. I'm not certain I like it but I'm willing to give it a chance. A black cloak, did you say? Billowing in a nice high wind? I quite approve the gothic touch."

He laughed deeply, paused a moment, surprised that he'd laughed, then swooped down on her, hauled her up in his arms, and hugged her tightly against him. "Your laugh is wonderful, North," she said against his throat. "Just wonderful. I think I'd rather listen to you laugh than brood, all right?"

"All right. Don't worry about all the unpleasant folk. I have the feeling that Tregeagle and Polgrain just might surprise us."

"I shan't lay a wager on it, North."

Tregeagle and Polgrain decided to stay. They appeared chastened, they appeared resigned to all the changes at Mount Hawke. Polgrain even showed a modicum of politeness to Mrs. Mayhew, asking her opinion on an apricot sauce he was preparing for an evening's meal. Tregeagle even told Molly that she'd done a nice job polishing the silver. Both of them, when it was necessary, called Caroline "my lady."

Caroline didn't trust either of them.

It was becoming colder now that it was full into November. Not a bone-aching cold, but chilly enough to warrant fires in all the rooms.

Evelyn went into labor at noon on the twelfth of November and very quickly produced a little boy by dinnertime. She named him Frederic North. Eleanor squalled when she was introduced to the baby, which brought a smile even to Tregeagle's stiff face, or perhaps it was a grimace masquerading as a smile. Who ever knew with them?

Caroline said, "I suppose I should call you Big North as opposed to Little North."

"I do like the sound of Big North, makes me sound very important."

She laughed, punched his arm, then rubbed it, soon caressing not only his arm but his shoulder, his chest.

"Caroline, I just got a letter from Marcus Wyndham, the Earl of Chase. You remember, I told you about him. Well, he and the Duchess will be visiting us in a week. You will like them."

"Ah, good. I'll see that everything is in readiness for them. Oh, there's something else, North. I was thinking that Miss Mary Patricia is quite recovered now and seems a bit on the distracted side."

"What do you mean?"

"She's bored. She needs to be doing something. What do you think if we sent her to Scrilady Hall to be the female manager, so to speak, Evelyn with her, and they both could run the Hall for the purpose Aunt Eleanor originally intended?"

"Namely a refuge for girls who are pregnant and have no choices at all."

"Exactly. What do you think?"

"You're picturing Miss Mary Patricia as being teacher to the children born there? Perhaps Evelyn ensuring that everything the girls needed was provided, perhaps helping them find positions after their children are born?"

"Yes. I spoke to Mrs. Trebaw about it just the other day and she was—"

"Ah, so you've already seen to things, and here I thought you truly needed my superior advice."

"Sort of, but your opinion does mean a great deal to me, North. Now, stop jesting, this is important."

"What did Mrs. Trebaw say?"

"She was quite pleased. She said that Miss Eleanor had been a fine lady, if a bit eccentric, and she missed having laughter and fun in the house. She said little children added more warmth than a dozen fireplaces. She said Mr. Owen was a nice boy but he was still just a boy, rather almost a man, and that was very different, as in, I suppose, not enough jollity for her."

"No, probably not enough appreciation expressed for her fine house-keeping, how neat and clean she keeps everything, how nicely the plates sparkle on the dinner table. Speaking as a man, Caroline, we don't tend to notice the nicer things done for us. We're just oblivious, I guess."

"You mean when I wear a gown that is particularly fetching, you don't notice because of this obliviousness of yours?"

"No, a man is never oblivious of a woman's efforts to please him. Trust me. If you were to pull that gown of yours down just an inch, I would immediately go *en pointe* like the best of my hounds."

She laughed, hugged him tightly. He kissed her throat and said, "What about Alice?"

Caroline was silent for a moment. She wasn't feeling all that well and hadn't been for over a week now. When she'd first felt upset to her stomach, she thought of the ox-tail soup and paled, but the ill feeling had gone away. Now a wave of nausea swept through her and she closed her eyes.

"Caroline?"

"Oh, Alice. I don't know, North. I'm a bit worried about her and I know Dr. Treath is as well. She's so very thin and small. I would just as soon keep her here until after her babe is born. I don't want to take any chances."

"Then I think Miss Mary Patricia and Evelyn should remain as well. We don't want Alice to be lonely. Why don't you speak to Evelyn and Miss Mary Patricia and see what they think of your idea. Isn't Alice's babe due to arrive in a month or so?"

"I think so. That's a good idea, North. Ah, don't forget Owen. He's here more often than he's at Scrilady Hall."

"You don't think it's simply because of Polgrain's fine cooking?"

She smiled up at him. "No, I think he's smitten with Alice. I think Owen is growing up, and I also think he's growing up very well."

North pulled her against him, stroking his big hands up and down her back. He kissed her throat, lifted her heavy hair, and massaged her neck and shoulders. He said, his breath warm and soft against her ear, "When were you going to tell me about the baby, Caroline?"

She became utterly still beneath his hands. "Whose baby?"

"My baby. Our baby."

"Oh dear."

"It's the likely result of the activity you and I both enjoy to a rather immoderate extent."

"Oh dear, are you certain?"

He laughed. "No, I'm not absolutely certain, but you haven't felt well, indeed, yesterday at about three o'clock in the afternoon, your face turned quite green. When was your last monthly flow?"

She ducked her face into his shoulder. "A long time ago."

"Can you be a bit more precise?"

She shook her head. "So much has happened that I really didn't pay all that close attention. Well, perhaps it was about a month and a half ago."

"Yes, that's about right. Ah, well, there it is, then."

"I'm going to have a baby, truly?"

"Truly, I think."

"Are you pleased, North?"

"How is your belly feeling right now?"

"Fine."

He picked her up in his arms and swung her about, dancing the infamous waltz around the bedchamber.

Tregeagle heard their laughter from the corridor down in the west wing of Mount Hawke. He frowned even as he knocked on the master's bedchamber door to tell them that Flash Savory was here to see his lordship.

"Caroline," North said, "do you hear me? Now, why didn't you ask to speak to Dr. Treath when he was here?"

She shrugged but didn't meet his eyes.

He stared down at her, then suddenly hooted with laughter. "My God, you're embarrassed. My Caroline is embarrassed of a doctor."

She gave him one of her brilliant smiles. "That's the second time you've called me your Caroline."

"No, *my* Caroline. Now, why don't I ask Dr. Treath to come back and see you?"

"Not yet, North, please. I'm just not ready. You're the only man who's ever, well, you know very well what I mean."

"He's a doctor, Caroline. He helped both Miss Mary Patricia and Evelyn. Do you think he cared that they were both lovely young women?"

"No, probably not, but it doesn't matter. Give me a bit longer, North."

"Good grief, Caroline, he's nearly old enough to be your father. Surely you wouldn't mind him examining you if Bess Treath were with you?"

"Just give me a bit longer, to adjust myself to all this. It's very strange, North." She hugged her arms around herself, thinking that he'd called her his Caroline. No, she thought grinning, *my* Caroline.

She didn't think she'd ever been happier in her life.

She felt that way until the following afternoon.

Coombe had disappeared. He'd left Mount Hawke the day North had dismissed him. He accepted the sizable pension paid to him by Mr. Brogan, moved to Goonbell into Mrs. Freely's inn there, and brooded about, always silent, never speaking to anyone, North was told, never telling why he'd left Mount Hawke after more years than most of the locals could even remember. Then, he'd simply disappeared.

Mrs. Freely came to Mount Hawke to speak to North privately. North simply told Caroline that Mrs. Freely hadn't seen Coombe for two days. She'd gone to his room and found he'd left. No, he hadn't owed her any money, indeed, he'd paid her enough to hold the room for him for another month.

North went back to Goonbell with Mrs. Freely. When he finally returned to Mount Hawke, there was quite an audience awaiting him. All the female staff, Tregeagle, Polgrain, and, of course, Timmy the maid, and all the ladies, pregnant and otherwise, looking at him, waiting for the worst, only he knew they couldn't begin to imagine the worst that he had to tell them.

He stared at all of them, then said simply, "It's difficult, believe me, but it seems that Coombe might have been the man who murdered all the women. I'm sorry, Caroline."

"No," Mrs. Mayhew said, her voice surprisingly strident. "Mr. Coombe was in many ways a very strange man, sometimes downright nasty, but I can't believe he would have killed the women. I even liked him sometimes, not often, mind you, but two times I can remember. How many women were there?"

"Three women in as many years," said Polgrain. "All of them stabbed, as you know. My lord, she's right. Mr. Coombe wasn't a violent man." Then he shut his mouth, realizing what he'd said, for he too had wondered about the ox-tail soup.

North shook his head and said, "It appears that he simply left, but he didn't take everything with him. There were papers, some odd clothes, a pair of slippers." He drew a deep breath. "Amongst the papers we found a letter from Elizabeth Godolphin to Coombe—one supposes it was to Coombe; she was the woman who was killed some three years ago. It was of an amorous nature. Also, there was a knife wrapped in a shirt stuffed in the back of the armoire. There was dried blood on it. All three women were stabbed."

Caroline heard the words dinning in her mind, and for the first time in her entire life, she fainted. She heard North calling her name before the blackness closed over her.

32

Marcus Wyndham, the Earl of Chase, said to North, "I can't believe I let you come back to Cornwall and the first thing you do is get married and start laughing and jesting about like a man born to it. Why, you've given up your gloomy brooding entirely. It shocks the senses, North. What am I to think?"

North grinned, an engaging grin that held no melancholy, no gothic overtones at all. "What can I tell you, Marcus? I met Caroline and it seems that the damnable black cloud that always floated over my head wafted away, leaving only the sun. She smiles at me and I'm warm to my toes."

"Odd," the earl said, gazing over at his wife. "I've known the Duchess since we were children and I've never changed a bit. She's done nothing to improve my spirit or my character. Perhaps both were perfect to begin with, whereas you were too dour a fellow, North."

The countess said to Caroline, a slight smile playing around her mouth, "My lord counts himself a philosopher wit. It occasionally leads to quite unpleasant physical discomfort for him."

Caroline laughed. "Could you please be more specific?"

"No, not as yet," the Duchess said, but gave Caroline a small salute with her teacup. The earl looked as if he would demand to know the bit of specificity, but the Duchess continued quickly, "Ah, but you're having problems here, aren't you?" She set down her teacup, a particularly graceful gesture that made Caroline feel intense envy for a moment. The Duchess was, she thought, the most beautiful creature she'd ever seen. As for the earl, he and North looked like they'd been friends for years, at ease with each other, mocking each other with that familiar insulting humor that gentlemen seemed to enjoy so very much. They were both large men, athletic, confident, and to Caroline's fond eye, North was by far the more magnificent specimen. As for the earl, the Duchess did seem to find him satisfactory.

"Yes," North said. "Caroline fainted four days ago and scared all the sin out of me. I told her if she ever did it again I would strangle her."

"I agreed with him," Caroline said. "It was humiliating to be such a weak ninny."

"Why did you faint?" the Duchess asked.

"Ah, well you may ask," North said. He paused, as if uncertain, then said slowly, "We are having our share of problems, but there's something more important. Caroline is going to have a baby."

"Goodness," the Duchess said, "that's wonderful. You're entitled to faint at least once when you're pregnant, Caroline. Congratulations to both of you. Marcus is ever endeavoring to bring me up to the mark again, so to speak. And no, North, don't feel guilty about speaking of the child in front of me." She continued to Caroline, "I had a miscarriage a while ago, but I'm fine now. As I said, Marcus is a man of determination."

"I try my damnedest," Marcus said, interrupting his wife, rubbing his hand distractedly through his hair—an act, Caroline thought, an excellent act—"yes, I try daily to impregnate her, except when we're traveling, of course. The Duchess adores the huge carriage; it makes her positively lecherous with the way it sways and jostles about, and she won't leave me alone. After our first day of travel, I am forced to ride outside the carriage to regain my strength and my balance. It's odd though, I find that I even scarce think about a babe when I'm loving her, she—"

"That's quite enough, Marcus," the Duchess said, all smooth and serene and composed as a matron of six decades. "You're embarrassing me. I know you enjoy doing it and you do it very well, as I've told you many times, but you will hold back your wit or it will go badly for you later when I have you alone."

Caroline giggled—she couldn't help it—for the huge dark man who was the Earl of Chase was grinning at his wife like a gambler with a marked card and a winning hand. He was even rubbing those hands of his vigorously together. He said to Caroline, "I know you can't imagine her doing anything except sitting there with a delicate teacup in her dainty white hands. Yes, you look at her and see this calm creature who scarce ever hoists her voice above her hemline, who raises an eyebrow just the veriest bit and has all the servants scurrying about madly to make her happy, and yet she screamed at me, threw a Spanish saddle at me, knocked me unconscious with a bridle, beat me with her riding boot, and—"

"Marcus," the Duchess said, not so quietly this time, not so calmly or serenely, "you will hold your tongue, at least until I get to know Caroline better. You are certainly giving her a very strange opinion of me."

North shook his head and set down his brandy snifter. "Caroline, my dear, you will become used to Marcus soon enough. As for the Duchess, I have found her as good a friend as Marcus, though not as outrageous, which, naturally, is proper, since she is a lady and not a halfwit randy goat."

"Must I accept all three?" Marcus said, and punched North's shoulder. "All right, if it pleases you, just leave the randy."

"What do you think, Duchess?" the earl said to his wife.

"Goat isn't quite the animal I would have selected, but it isn't bad. It tells me that North knows you quite well."

Caroline said, "Well, I think North is a god. Since Marcus is his best friend, then we must elevate him above a goat. How about to a panther?"

"Rather he's the devil," the earl said, "and I'd have to become his familiar, according to your logic, Caroline."

"A man who's devilish sounds rather romantic," the Duchess said. "What is this, Caroline? No devil here. You believe North is a god?"

Caroline smiled up at her husband, every shred of feeling she had for him clear in her eyes. "He is the very best of men and I am the luckiest woman alive to have found him in that out-of-the-way inn in Dorchester."

"That is properly nauseating," the earl said. "I would rather hear more about the trouble you two are having than be an unwilling witness to this romantic drivel."

"He's right," North said. "Now, Caroline, I have told Marcus just a bit of our problems."

"You told him about my aunt and Coombe?"

North nodded. "I owe him my life, Caroline, thus I can trust him. Also, he has a fine mind—as devious as the devil's or the devil's familiar's—and perhaps he can see something we haven't. As for the Duchess, her mind is as sharp as a razor's edge."

Caroline nodded slowly. North saw the haunted look in her eyes and pulled her against him. He kissed her hair. "We will get through this," he said. "We will."

Caroline had a cold and she felt miserable. Her throat hurt, she was sweating like a stoat one minute and shivering the next, and every bone in her body pulled and ached. North poured one of Polgrain's remedies down her throat and then ordered her to rest. The Duchess was allowed to visit her as long as she kept her distance.

"I'm sorry you're ill, Caroline. I suppose it's the violent shift of weather, at least that's what Marcus told me. He said if I got ill he would beat me. I told him I would beat him as well if he came down with even one sneeze, and he just grinned at me in that wonderfully obnoxious way of his and told me he was never ill. He was too superior, you see. He's a sweetheart, my husband."

Caroline, less groggy now and feeling a bit more human since choking down Polgrain's vile-tasting potion, said, "I like your husband. He could be superior, Duchess, it's possible since he's North's best friend. But North is perfect and that's the truth of it."

The Duchess smiled, her fingers gently pleating and unpleating the folds in her soft burgundy wool gown. "I heard North mention something to Marcus about his male ancestors believing that King Mark was buried here and not in Fowey, with untold riches, naturally. And what of Tristan and Isolde, the lovers who betrayed him? Is it true you have a journal of sorts?"

And so Caroline told her of the Nightingale men and their two legacies— one that cursed the heir with a faithless wife, and the other a tale of King Mark's treasure, buried with him in the sixth century and mistakenly believed to be far from here on the south coast of Cornwall, but that wasn't true, for he was buried here, on Nightingale land, probably in one of those hillocks or barrows, and there were so many of them. Who could ever find the right one?

It was then that the Duchess told her about the Wyndham treasure. "King Henry the Eighth," Caroline said. "That's amazing, more amazing I think than finding proof that poor old King Mark is here."

"I don't know about that," the Duchess said. "Henry the Eighth is only three hundred years old, whereas King Mark is more than a thousand years old. That's impressive, Caroline, very impressive."

"I personally think it's all fancy woven from the tortured minds of North's male ancestors, misogynists, all of them, beginning with his great-grandfather."

"Tell me more," the Duchess said, and Caroline did.

"Hmmm," the Duchess said after an hour of talk and questions. "Let's put our heads together, Caroline. Two ladies, I believe, have a much better chance of figuring things out than two passionate gentlemen who would rather bust heads together than just think."

"That," the earl said from the doorway, "sounds very much like an insult to me."

"I agree," North said, coming into the bedchamber. "At least my wife still looks bright enough to give me a smile. That miserable potion is still working?"

Caroline was getting muzzy in her thinking, but North looked so very splendid, all windblown and tousled from riding in the chilly afternoon, as vibrant and as alive as a man could get, that she felt a leap of energy and smiled at him, she couldn't help it. "I feel wonderful."

"That look on your wife's face is all female besottedness, North. If you believe it, then you're more conceited than I had imagined."

The Duchess said, "We've been discussing King Mark and his treasure being here on Nightingale land. What do you think, North?"

"Hmmm? Oh, I'm sorry, Duchess. What did you say?"

Marcus poked him in the belly with his fist. "He's thinking about announcing to the world that he is a god above men, just ask his wife. So he pleases you, does he, Caroline?"

"Yes," she said simply, still smiling at her husband.

The Duchess rose and shook out her wool skirts. "I think it's time that Caroline had a nap. She looks like she's on the verge of a minor wilt. Marcus, I would like to speak to you now. Alone."

"Ah," the earl said, giving his wife his arm. "I fear she will order up our carriage and force me to—"

She punched him in the belly.

"I have found," Caroline said, "that North's cravats are very useful in gaining control. At least they were that one time he let me use them."

"How?" the Duchess said, an elegant black eyebrow arched upward.

Caroline turned crimson, her eyes nearly crossing with what had come unexpectedly out of her mouth. North laughed and said, "You see, there's no such thing as a private jest, sweetheart. Won't you tell the Duchess what you did with those cravats?"

"Yes, I will, when we're alone," Caroline said, then sneezed, a fake sneeze, North saw, but he let it alone. Her color was high. Damn and blast the miserable cold.

It was the Duchess who said to everyone the next afternoon at luncheon, "I read the entire journal last night."

"She told me to be quiet and repose myself," the earl said, and forked down a bit of Polgrain's delicious roasted wild duck garnished with watercress and small oranges.

"What truly surprised me," the Duchess said, "was that he did. He slept like a glutton who'd just eaten Christmas dinner. In any case, the journal was illuminating, Caroline."

Caroline, who was feeling much more the thing than the day before, said, "What did you find? I've skipped about in the journal and haven't read it all the way through. Have you, North?"

He shook his head. "What do you think, Duchess?"

"I think we should go to that spot where your great-grandfather said one of his men found that armlet. So strange that it just disappeared. Too, I'm afraid his directions aren't too specific."

"No, they're not," Caroline said. "I've been so frustrated trying to find something."

The earl looked at his wife with mild disbelief. "Surely you don't believe that pap? I'll wager my best Hessians that there never was an armlet save in your great-grandfather's head, North."

"I agree, unfortunately," North said. "I think he was already well over the edge when he began the journal. You read, certainly, Duchess, all the rantings and ravings of his about his miserable harlot of a wife. I think the selection of King Mark as his hero of choice is because King Mark was also betrayed by his wife, Isolde, with Tristan. I believe it pleased my great-grandfather to compare himself to the poor tortured king and transplant his remains and a boundless treasure closer, namely here on Nightingale land, thus aggrandizing himself in the process."

"I went there, Duchess," Caroline said. "There's a thick copse of oak trees, a long stone fence, and so many of those rolling hillocks. I looked and looked, but alas, I didn't find a thing, even a scrap of a pottery piece, nothing at all. I went there three or four times."

The earl said, "I tend to think there never was a golden armlet, else where is it? If it was stolen, then why didn't your grandfather or even your father write about it?"

There was no answer to that. North said, "Even the three male martinets don't know a thing."

"No matter," the Duchess said. "I want to go there." She said to her husband, "This reminds me of my searches at the abbey, Marcus. Remember, we neither of us believed in the Wyndham legacy and we were wrong. Just perhaps I'll find something. Actually I want to find something very badly."

"Treasure hunting is now in her blood," the earl said. "You should see her wearing that rope of pearls we found and nothing else, just the pearls—"

His wife's very white hand slammed over his mouth.

33

The Duchess had left Mount Hawke early to treasure-hunt, the gentlemen had ridden off to the tin mines, and thus Caroline rode into Goonbell. She wanted to see the chamber Coombe had stayed in before he'd disappeared.

Mrs. Freely was talking before she'd even taken Caroline's cloak and gloves. She learned all about how Jeb Peckly, that miserable sodden drunk, had become nearly a decent husband, drinking very little now, and she hadn't heard a thing about his beating his wife and daughters. Caroline smiled hugely at that. Mrs. Freely asked her questions about the Earl and Countess of Chase as she took her into her huge warm kitchen and gave her a mug of mulled wine, to ward off the piskey chill, she said, then patted Caroline's hair, and said, "Lovely hair you have, my lady. Rich-looking, not just a boring single color, but a multitude of interesting shades, just like the trees that surround the inn. I've always been fond of those elms and oaks and maples, yes I have. At least until they lose all their leaves, which I hope you won't ever do, in a manner of speaking."

Eventually, Mrs. Freely led her upstairs, wishing aloud that she could meet the Earl and Countess of Chase. Caroline thought about the Duchess dealing with the gossiping Mrs. Freely and thought it couldn't fail to be fascinating. She invited her to dinner.

"Now, my lady, no man has ever tried to tell me what to do," she said as they neared Coombe's chamber door.

"Huh?" Caroline said, at sea.

"No man who's around to tell about it in any case," Mrs. Freely added, nodding to herself. "There was one man who dared call me Meg and pat my bottom whenever I walked past him. I clouted him but good. Ah, here we are, poor Mr. Coombe's room." She opened the door. "I assure you there's nothing more to find. His lordship searched most thoroughly. Everyone hereabouts believes Coombe was a madman, and they're both relieved he's gone and worried that they don't know where he is. No one speaks of anything else, as you can expect."

"Yes, one would expect that," Caroline said.

It was actually a very nice room on the east side of the inn, on the second floor. There were four windows, all wide, all covered with lovely white lace curtains. The furnishings were plain but not at all unpleasant. Caroline stood in the middle of the room, just looking around her. Mrs. Freely was quiet for the first time since Caroline had met her. Then she just nodded, turned, and said over her shoulder, "That one man, the one who called me Meg, he was a lovely lad, he was." She nodded again and left Caroline alone.

"Did you kill my aunt, Coombe?" Caroline asked the still room. "Everyone is saying that you hate women, that the Nightingale legacy poisoned you. Everyone believes you killed the women because they rejected you or betrayed you. No one really knows. North doesn't know what to believe, truth be told, nor do I. He's wondered and wondered about that letter from Elizabeth Godolphin. He says he didn't know you had a nickname and neither did Tregeagle or Polgrain, and such an odd nickname. Did she really call you her *King of Diamonds?* Did she never use your real name? Did other women call you that as well? Why was there only one letter? And only from her? North is very disturbed, Coombe. He says you aren't stupid. He just doesn't understand why you would leave this bloody knife here in your room if you were guilty. Ah, I wish I knew what happened."

The chamber was utterly silent, not that she expected anything else. Caroline sighed, then turned to the armoire.

"Where did you go? If you escaped, why then would you leave all this evidence behind to be found?" Again, there was no answer, no sound at all. She opened the armoire. It was empty now, North had taken everything. There were drawers below that smelled of cedar. They were also empty. She rose and closed the armoire doors. There was a small desk with a quill and ink on top, nothing else, and three narrow drawers. She opened each of them. They were empty. North had found the letter in one of the drawers. Certainly he'd searched all of them carefully.

She straightened from the desk and looked around the chamber. It was chilly, for there was no fire in the small fireplace. Mrs. Freely had no one staying in this room at the moment. In fact, Mrs. Freely had told her that no one had stayed in this room since Mr. Coombe had disappeared. Too many flapping jaws, she'd said to Caroline, everyone telling strangers about the bloody knife, and how the room was now haunted. "Your ladyship knows how we Cornish love our ghosts. If there isn't a ghost for every cottage, for every inn, for every twisted tree, then you simply aren't in Cornwall. Aye, you're in Devon or Dorset, no imagination in any of those folk. They sit around and boast about their silly Devon cream, which doesn't hold a candle to Cornish cream, let me tell you. Still, I do hate to lose money with this room empty."

Caroline felt no strange lurking feelings standing in the middle of the room. Perhaps since she wasn't Cornish she wasn't able to scent the ghosts or feel them or perhaps even hear them. "Where did you go, Coombe?" she asked the silent room. "Didn't you think Mrs. Freely would notice that you weren't here? Didn't you think she and North would search your room?"

She jumped. She heard a rustling, slapping sound, then drew a deep breath, realizing it was a tree branch lightly sliding against a window.

"Maybe I was a Cornish woman a long time ago," she said. It helped to speak out loud. It made her feel less alone.

She felt depressed that she hadn't discovered anything, but then again, she really hadn't expected North to overlook anything. She was on the point of leaving when she noticed the beautifully carved wooden poles on the Hepplewhite bed that had once been much taller, supporting a canopy. Obviously someone had cut them off, for now the four poles ended in rather roughly carved pineapples. She walked slowly to the bed, her eyes on those carved pineapples. She lightly touched one of the poles at the foot of the bed. It didn't move. She tugged at it. It still didn't budge.

She went to the other one at the foot of the bed. It too didn't move. It was the third one at the head of the bed that turned easily in her hand. Her heart speeded up. Slowly, she pulled the pineapple off the pole. There was a hole beneath, not solid wood. She reached her fingers into the cavity and touched paper. She managed to hook her fingers around the paper and pull it out. It was a single sheet and it had been folded into a square and then into a smaller square until now it was no larger than an inch square and very thick.

She stared at the folded paper in the palm of her hand. It was yellow and crisp with age. Very gently, she eased the paper from its stiff folds.

She didn't know what she expected the folded paper to be. Perhaps a long-ago love letter written by one lover to another upon leaving early in the morning fog. She shook herself. She was being quite silly.

She carefully spread the paper out atop the bed counterpane. It wasn't a love letter. It wasn't an old tradesman's bill or a simple list of household linens.

It was a letter threatening murder. It had been written in May 1726 by Viscount Chilton, North's great-grandfather, to a man named Griffin. The black ink was spidery and difficult to read in many places, but the letter itself was straightforward enough. "'Griffin,'" she read. "'You will keep away from my wife or I will thrust my sword through your black heart.'" And it was signed "D. Nightingale, Viscount Chilton."

D. was Donniger. Yes, it was certainly North's great-grandfather. Donniger Nightingale, an odd name, one she hadn't forgotten.

Who was Griffin? What was the letter doing stuffed down into one of the sawed-off, pineapple-carved bedposts?

She smoothed the paper over her hand and dashed downstairs to the taproom. She was breathing hard and Mrs. Freely said, "My goodness, child, whatever do you have there?"

"You'll not believe it, Mrs. Freely. I found it hidden in one of the bedposts. Just look, it's rather amazing, and this, I fancy, is the beginning of the Nightingale legacy of betrayal."

Mrs. Freely ushered her into the kitchen and the two of them spread the paper on the kitchen table.

"Ah, Griffin," Mrs. Freely said. "My granny told me about him."

Caroline found herself again marveling at the tenacity of the Cornish memory. If she asked, doubtless Mrs. Freely could easily discover Griffin's middle name. "Who was he?"

"A wild rogue, from what is still said around these parts, a handsome young man too, with scarce a worry on his shoulders, and too much money from his pa. He seduced more ladies than old Casanova himself. This letter makes it seem like he was the one who cuckolded his lordship's great-grandfather. You know, if I remember aright, he didn't stay around here, left, he did, and never came back to Cornwall. He probably went to London to seduce his way through those ladies of the *ton*. So he left her to face her husband and then she died. Interesting, isn't it, but I don't know why that old letter would be stuck down in a bedpost."

"Where did the bed come from?"

"Ah," Mrs. Freely said. "That I can find out, my lady. Just you sip on the tea and I'll look through my ma's journals. My ma recorded every purchase she ever made for this inn. Sure enough she'll have written down where she got this bed."

Caroline was both excited and depressed because it did seem true that North's great-grandmother, that smiling happy young lady whose portrait now graced the huge white wall at the foot of the stairs, did indeed betray her husband. Caroline supposed she'd wished it wasn't true.

When Mrs. Freely told her that the bed had belonged to the Griffin family, Caroline wasn't surprised. It seemed the family had fallen onto hard times, what with all the sons gambling and wenching, and had left England to go to the Colonies, selling off their furnishings before they'd left, way back in the 1780s. "Aye, my ma wrote in her housekeeping book that they went off to Boston to stay with their kin."

Well, that was indeed one Nightingale wife who had betrayed her husband. Caroline was depressed. She'd started the whole thing.

She told North that night as they snuggled together, "I read all your great-grandfather's part of the journal. He never wrote Griffin by name. Also, it appears he didn't kill him, or if he did, he buried him deep because no one ever found his body. Then your great-grandmother died only a month or so after he left. It's all so tragic."

North was silent for a very long time. "You know, I think I'll write a letter to the Griffins in the Colonies. You say Mrs. Freely heard they'd moved to Boston?"

She nodded against his shoulder, breathed in the scent of him, and was lost.

"My God," North said some time later when he was able again to put two words together, "you surely give me glimpses of heaven, Caroline."

"Don't you ever forget that, North Nightingale," she said. She nipped his chin, then sighed deeply. "I wish our King Mark legacy could be real, like the Wyndhams' legacy. Just think, the Wyndhams found old books and strange clues and they managed to weave their way through it all and discovered it was real."

"Sorry, sweetheart, but it won't ever be more than the meanderings of bruised male hearts."

"What a nice way to speak of your male ancestors. I had really hoped that your great-grandmother hadn't betrayed your great-grandfather. Now there doesn't seem to be any doubt."

"No, no doubt at all. But perhaps there were reasons. Who knows?"

Caroline just shut her eyes and clamped her mouth closed. "Now, Caroline, just relax. I won't hurt you, but I do have to poke about just a little bit. North, please step back, unless you want to do the poking."

North stepped back and watched Dr. Treath examine his wife. He didn't lift her nightgown, merely slipped his hands beneath the covers and the gown. He pulled his hands free then and said to North, "Her belly is smooth and malleable but I need to examine her internally."

Before North could even begin to sputter, Dr. Treath stood and said to his sister, "I need some hot water and soap. Yes, Bess, it's important, and must be done."

"I don't like this at all," Caroline said to Dr. Treath.

"I wouldn't either, my dear, but as I told Bess, it must be done. I do it on every one of my female patients who is with child. I'll be careful not to hurt you, but I must examine you."

Before he did that, he felt her breasts, and she tried to think of other things. His fingers were long and dry and she hated the way they felt on her flesh. When he eased two fingers inside her, he was careful and gentle, she'd give him that, but it was mortifying. His fingers were large and that hurt and he pushed, and with his other hand pressed down on her belly until finally she gasped with pain.

"Done," Dr. Treath said, and eased his fingers out of her. "Well, my dear, it appears that you're just fine, quite healthy, actually. We won't have to do that again until you're much farther along. Now, North, let's go downstairs whilst Bess helps your wife get dressed."

"That was awful," Caroline said when the men had left the bedchamber.

Bess Treath was frowning as she assisted Caroline to rise from the bed. "You're not feeling nauseous, are you?"

"Oh no, just horribly embarrassed. I know it's silly since he's a doctor, but true nonetheless. Thank you for helping me, Miss Treath."

"Yes, he is a doctor." Bess Treath smiled down at Caroline, who was still very flushed in the face, and handed her her chemise and stockings.

The Duchess was depressed. She'd searched every single foot of that area Caroline had told her about, she said, and not a thing, not even a clue to be found anywhere. She then sighed, forked down a bite of blancmange, and said, "Of course, it's been over a thousand years. Doubtless many feet have walked over that entire area and many eyes looked to see what they could find. If only your great-grandfather could have been more precise about that wretched armlet, North."

"Sorry, Duchess, but believe me, that wretched armlet never existed, or if it did, it didn't have a thing to do with King Mark."

The earl patted his wife's hand. "You tried, sweetheart."

The large clock that sounded like it had swallowed a frog began chiming seven strokes.

Alice shivered. "How I hate the sound that clock makes. Has it always done that, my lord?"

"As long as I can remember. I was telling Caroline that if only the bloody thing would stop, I'd dump it in the kitchen midden."

"I rather like the sound of it," Owen said. "Rather like a king with a very bad cold."

Caroline laughed and shook her head. "All of you are vastly romantic and far too imaginative. It just sounds to me like it needs a good oiling."

After a sumptuous dinner of carbonnade of beef, baked anchovy pie, roasted lamb with white beans, innumerable side dishes, and blancmange and macaroons for dessert, the earl and countess announced that they would be leaving for London on Wednesday.

Caroline was down in the mouth. She liked the Duchess and was finally at her ease with her and her outrageous husband, who said exactly what he wanted to say, teased his wife mercilessly, then kissed her hard, and was very amusing, not as amusing as North, but nonetheless, he did occasionally make her smile.

"Come, sweetheart," North said to her later that night in their bedchamber, "and climb on my lap. I don't like to see you depressed. That's right, face me, ah, yes, the feel of you, how much I love the feel of you." He kissed her then even as his hands were pulling up her dressing gown and nightgown, his fingers on her bare flesh, stroking her and caressing upward.

"Goodness, North," she said into his mouth and promptly moaned when his warm fingers touched her. When they slipped inside her, she suddenly stiffened.

"Whatever is wrong?"

"That's what Dr. Treath did. It was awful."

"Well, I didn't like it either, but if it had to be done, then so be it. Now, just relax. It's me, not Dr. Treath, and I have scarce a thought about the babe, just its mother and making her scream with pleasure. That's right, Caroline, you're becoming softer. I like it. Kiss me some more."

When he lifted her onto him, she sighed with the pleasure of it. When his fingers wove their magic, she screamed. North felt the wet of her tears against his neck when she was slack against him.

He froze. "What the hell is wrong? Did I hurt you?"

"Oh no, it's just that I love you so very much, it's sometimes too much, that's all."

"I see," he said slowly, "nothing more than that. Good, that relieves my mind. Let's go to bed, Caroline."

He didn't sleep for a very long time, but he didn't let her away from him, holding her close the entire night. He knew he'd give anything to keep Caroline with him. He knew he'd give his life for her.

But it wasn't North who saved Caroline's life the following day. It was the Duchess.

34

Caroline and the Duchess were riding close to the sea, high above on the narrow cliff road, before cutting inland to search about the series of hillocks and in the midst of the oak tree copse again. Ah, and there was that long stone fence with perhaps some crevices between the stones that held something, a clue perhaps, another armlet like the one North's great-grandfather had claimed he'd found. At the moment, though, the wind whipped at their riding hats and they were discussing why Coombe would leave evidence behind that surely proved his guilt.

They pulled up their horses a moment to look over the Irish Sea. "It makes no sense," Caroline said, tucking her hair up beneath her hat.

"And that relative of yours, Caroline, Bennett Penrose?" the Duchess said. "No chance at all that he was responsible, at least for your aunt's death?"

"No," Caroline said. "North looked into everything, probably even checked Bennett's teeth. Unfortunately he just wasn't here when Aunt Eleanor was killed. As for poor Nora Pelforth, Bennett had many witnesses to claim he was at Mrs. Freely's inn in Goonbell until he had to be carried back to Scrilady Hall, so drunk he couldn't even crawl."

"A pity."

"Yes indeed, the little worm. Did I tell you that North got a letter from Mr. Ffalkes and he sounds horribly pleased about having Bennett dropped on him, just like North guessed he would. He is probably torturing Bennett, rubbing his hands together in glee the whole time. He also wrote that he's giving the lackwit gambling lessons. They wager for chores, of all things. He said Bennett might even have an arm muscle by the end of next week."

"From what you've told me about both gentlemen, they deserve each other."

"At the very least. I must admit that I do feel just a dollop of pity for Mrs. Tailstrop—rather, Mrs. Ffalkes now. I imagine she has to protect that ratty little pug of hers from her husband's hands. Owen said his father hated Lucy."

The Duchess laughed, threw back her head, closing her eyes a moment, and Caroline knew she felt the beauty of the crisp autumn wind to her very bones.

"I've never been to Cornwall before. It is so very different from any other place I've ever seen. It's wild and fierce and magnificent. And the smell of the sea, with you all the time, and you can fancy you hear the waves no matter where you are. I used to live near Dover, but it isn't the same thing at all. There's a pull to it, isn't there?"

"I think it's magic."

"All right, enough rhapsodizing. Now, who else is there who could have killed the women? You know, the question Marcus and I should have kept asking ourselves when I kept getting hurt: Who would gain the most if I died?"

"Marcus would."

The Duchess laughed, then looked surprised that she had actually laughed about that time at Chase Park. "Let's not tell him that, all right? I can see him completely go over the edge. He's very possessive, you know."

Caroline grinned and click-clicked Reggie forward. "I had guessed that."

"Just as is North."

"North? No, not really. He just feels great responsibility for me and—"

"Bosh."

"What?"

"I said bosh. He is tail over tip in love with you. Don't be a fool, Caroline, you can't begin to imagine how he looks at you. You come into a room, you giggle, you just sit there and drink tea, you even yawn, and he looks utterly hungry and at the same time, content. He is a very happy man."

Caroline didn't say a thing, but she was wondering if the Duchess could possibly be right. The trick would be to catch him looking at her lovingly.

"Now, I've gotten us off track. Back to Coombe. Everyone believes he's mad, clearly and completely mad, that the women rejected him and he killed them, that he perhaps even believed that they betrayed him, that he wanted to perhaps avenge all the Nightingale men by killing women he saw as faithless. But your aunt, Caroline? Didn't you tell me that she and Dr. Treath were in love? How could she possibly fit into any madness of Coombe's?"

"She couldn't."

"And where did Coombe go? I know everyone local is saying that he went off to kill himself, and left the knife so everyone would know—a sort of expiation—but still—"

Regina stumbled forward onto her knees, sending Caroline flying over her head to fall in a huddle on the ground beyond.

The Duchess leaped off her mare's back, tripped flat on her face, pulled herself up, and ran to Caroline's side. She was unconscious, lying on her back, her royal blue velvet riding hat smashed, the feather broken in half. Her riding skirt was askew, showing her white petticoats and white stockings and her soft black leather riding boots.

She felt Caroline's pulse and heaved a sigh of relief. It was strong and steady. She gently began to feel her head, unceremoniously pulling off her riding hat and smoothing out her thick hair. She'd struck her head on a very small rock, just behind her right ear. She felt her arms, her legs, nothing broken. All she could do now was wait. She pulled off her own gold velvet riding jacket and tucked it around Caroline's chest and neck. She sat beside her to block the breeze coming from the sea.

Caroline moaned, opened her eyes, saw the Duchess looking down at her, and said, "I'm all right. I just feel stupid, letting Reggie throw me so easily. Oh goodness, my head does hurt, only not as bad as it did when Mr. Ffalkes struck me."

"Just lie still for a while longer. You struck your head and I want to make certain you're not going to fall unconscious again."

"What was it, Duchess? A rabbit hole? How could I have been so careless? I hope Reggie is all right."

"You hold still and I'll go look. Reggie seems to be just fine. Hold still now, Caroline."

When the Duchess came back to her some minutes later, she was pale and there was anger and something else in those beautiful calm eyes of hers. "It wasn't a rabbit hole."

North blinked when he saw his wife riding bareback in front of the Duchess, the sidesaddle gone, the Duchess's hands securely around Caroline, holding her steady. Reggie was trailing behind them.

Oh God. He was racing to them, yelling as he ran, "Marcus, get out here now!"

His heart didn't cease its frantic pounding until Caroline was lying on a puce brocade settee in the drawing room, a pale blue knitted blanket pulled over her.

"Tell me again you have no pain in your belly."

"No, North, just in my head."

"All right. Tregeagle has gone to fetch Dr. Treath. He'll be here very soon now. Here, drink this tea Polgrain made for you. Alice, I swear to you she's all right. Please don't worry. You sit down and drink a cup of tea yourself. Duchess, please see that Alice sits down and drinks."

Dr. Treath and Bess Treath arrived just as the clock was painfully grinding out its four afternoon strokes, sounding like a king with an awful sore throat bellowing at his subjects.

Dr. Treath smiled at her even as she knew he was studying her, then pulled

315

over a chair and sat down. "Now, let me see this lump on your head." His fingers were gentle, probing very lightly, feeling the outline of the bump that was rising. Then he sat back and just looked at her.

"Hold still now," he said, slipped his hands beneath the cover and her clothes. Caroline tensed up, she couldn't help it. North took her hand and held it.

"Do you need anything, Benjie?" Bess Treath said.

He didn't immediately answer.

"Benjie?"

"What? Oh no, Bess. She's all right." He smiled down at Caroline. "I do want you to rest, no strenuous exercise. If you have any bleeding, any cramping at all, you send for me. Tregeagle thought it was a rabbit hole?"

"Yes," the Duchess said.

When at last the Treaths had left, Alice was finally convinced Caroline wasn't going to die and had retired to her room to nap, the Duchess cleared her throat and said, "Please close the door, Marcus."

He cocked his head at her, but did as she asked.

"What is it, Duchess?" North said.

It was Caroline who answered. "It wasn't a rabbit hole like we'd first thought."

"No," the Duchess continued. "It was a wire stretched taut between an oak tree and the stone fence. It's narrow in that stretch. I didn't want to tell anyone, best keep it amongst ourselves for now."

"She rides that way most every day," North said, and felt pain and fury knot his guts.

"Which means," the earl said, "that the wire was meant for her, no one else. But you were with her, Duchess. How did you miss that wire?"

"Caroline was riding a bit in front of me there, since it is so narrow. When she went over I immediately pulled up my horse. I tripped over the wire when I was running to her, though, and landed flat on my nose."

"Then," the earl said slowly, "both of you could have been hurt. Damnation, North, I don't like this at all."

North was remembering when both the earl and the Duchess had been shot, the fear, the utter rage he'd felt, that he'd seen in Marcus's eyes. He shook his head. He remembered telling Marcus that he had to stay calm, rage wouldn't help his wife. He wondered if Marcus would tell him the same thing now. He drew a deep breath.

"I have spent four months now with death and mystery and tragedy sitting on my right shoulder, never far from my thoughts or my mind. I hadn't been home two weeks before I found Caroline's aunt, dead on that ledge beneath St. Agnes Head. I couldn't find out who'd killed her. Then that poor woman, Nora Pelforth, and I've been unsuccessful there as well. Then Coombe disappears and there's the bloody knife in his room. All of it is madness. It must be aimed at me, it must. I simply can't figure out who's doing it and why. I can't figure out who would hate me so much."

Caroline said even as she lifted herself onto her elbows, "You're forgetting about Elizabeth Godolphin, who was killed three years ago, North. You weren't here then. No, you're wrong about this."

North cursed rather fluently, then said abruptly, "Then it must be revenge against my father or my grandfather. Marcus, I want you and the Duchess to leave. The thought that the Duchess could have been hurt again curdles my blood. Yes, I want you gone tomorrow."

"No," the Duchess said slowly, "I don't think so, North."

Tregeagle cleared his throat from the doorway. "My lord."

"Yes, dammit, what is it, Tregeagle?"

"It's the Young Person, Alice, my lord. She informs Miss Mary Patricia, who rightfully informs me since I wouldn't allow her to come in here and disturb you, that Alice believes her time has arrived."

"Oh no," Caroline said, struggling to get to her feet. "The babe is too early. He was getting really big, but it's too early. Oh no, North."

It was the Duchess who remembered that Owen should be fetched immediately. Caroline sent Timmy the maid to Scrilady Hall.

It was soon clear that it wouldn't be an easy labor. Dr. Treath and Bess Treath rarely left Alice's side even when Alice fell into a stupor, so weak even the contractions couldn't break through her exhaustion.

Owen paced outside the bedchamber like an expectant father, pale and drawn.

A pall fell over the house during the second day. Caroline, who'd flinched whenever she'd heard Alice cry out, now flinched because she couldn't hear a thing. Alice was too weak and getting weaker.

North found her in the east wing on the top floor in the storage room where she'd found all the Nightingale women's portraits. She was furiously cleaning the frames, afraid to touch the canvas, but the frames were shining.

He gently squeezed her shoulder. She stopped her frantic activity, looking up at him.

"I'm sorry, Caroline."

"She's dead?"

"No, not yet, but Dr. Treath sees no hope for her now. She birthed the baby, a little boy. He's not as small as Dr. Treath had thought he would be. Indeed, he was simply too big for Alice to birth him."

"Then how did she manage to birth him?"

"Dr. Treath pulled him out of her, there was no other choice, otherwise both of them would die. Do you want to make your good-byes?"

She closed her eyes, saying with such hopelessness that he wanted to howl with it, "Those men who raped her. They killed a young girl . . . just killed her and went on their drunken way. Dear God, I hope they rot in Hell."

Alice opened her eyes a few moments after Caroline sat down beside her. Caroline smiled down at her, saying, "You have a fine little boy, Alice. What do you want to name him?"

"He's Owen," Alice whispered, her voice hoarse and raw. Suddenly, with surprising strength, Alice clutched Caroline's wrist, pulling her close. "Take care of him, Miss Caroline. Please."

"Of course I will," Caroline said as she wiped Alice's forehead with a damp cloth. "And so will you. You will rest and get well again, Alice."

"No, Miss Caroline, I won't and you know it. Would you tell my son about me? That I loved him and I didn't want to leave him, but—" She stopped and gave Caroline a heart-wrenching smile.

"Your son will never forget you, Alice, I swear it. You must see Owen now, he's right here, just waiting to kiss you. What do you think about that?"

"Oh no, don't let him see me like this, Miss Caroline. Make him go away. Oh, I never told him, but he was so nice to me, so nice. There was no time for us ever to be more than what we were, but he was so nice to me. No man was ever so nice to me as Owen was."

"Then you should tell him right now. He cares mightily for you. He rarely left you, Alice—in fact, he's here right now, here to see you. Would you like a drink of warm milk that Polgrain just fetched here for you?"

"Alice?" Owen eased himself down beside her. "Come, love, you're going to drink the warm milk, all right?"

There was a very soft whisper that sounded like *love.*

Then there was nothing. Alice's head was turned slightly away from Caroline and Owen. Her eyes were closed.

"It's over," Dr. Treath said, and gently moved Caroline and Owen out of the way.

"No!" Owen just stood there by the bed, staring down at Alice, shaking his head back and forth. "No," he said again, "no, she's so sweet, so innocent, God, it isn't fair . . . isn't fair."

Caroline said, "Owen, come and kiss her good-bye. Let her go." But even as she said the words, she felt something deep inside her turn cold and hard, then just as quickly she felt herself crumbling inward, sinking down into darkness that she welcomed, oh yes, she wanted that darkness and its deep shadows that hid the pain from her, that hid Alice's young face, so calm in death, so very sweet, without life.

Caroline had never worn black in her life and she had no intention of doing it now. "Alice wasn't quite fifteen years old. I will not honor her young life with black. I will wear white, white as pure and innocent as she was." And Mrs. Mayhew simply nodded.

All the women from Mount Hawke wore white. When the vicar arrived with Mrs. Plumberry—uninvited—he looked from Caroline to Miss Mary Patricia, then at the rest of them, and said, "This is not right. Even though Alice was not worthy to continue her life of sin, still our black trappings are God's idea, meant to honor Him, to show Him our respect, more than the one deceased."

Caroline just stared at him for a very long moment.

"I suppose these others"—he jerked his head toward Evelyn and Miss Mary Patricia—"talked you into it, didn't they? No piety, those two, just cheap little sluts with no sense of what is right and proper, and they've fooled you, my lady, and made you forget—"

Caroline drew back her fist and sent it right into Mr. Plumberry's jaw. He dropped like a stone. Caroline stood there rubbing her knuckles.

His wife howled, dropped to her knees, and shrieked up at Caroline, "How dare you! You don't deserve that my fine Plumberry lowered himself to come here for that little trollop's—"

Caroline was shivering with anger, not with cold. She called out, "Tregeagle, Polgrain, do come here and assist the Plumberrys from Mount Hawke land."

"Don't you dare touch me!" Mrs. Plumberry yelled. "You miserable—" She was shrieking now constantly, but it was better than the horrible words that had spewed out of her mouth.

Caroline called out, "North, thank you for carrying Mr. Plumberry into his coach. Could you please dump him on the floor?"

North did just that, indeed he dumped him on his wife's feet. Mrs. Plumberry leaned out the window, screaming, "All of you will pay for this! Horrid sinners! Look at all of you—just standing there, doing nothing! All of you impious females, wearing white like heathens. My Horace will send all of you to everlasting Hell, you will see!"

Bishop Horton from Truro, who thankfully arrived after the Plumberrys' coach had rolled down the hill, read the words over Alice's grave that Caroline and Owen had written together. His voice was deep and rich, reaching even to Mr. Dumbarton's smallest child, who stood at the very edge of the Nightingale cemetery, unwilling to come closer.

"Alice would like that," Owen said. "The bishop of Truro here, for her. I always wished my voice was deeper and richer, just like the bishop's."

The morning was cloudy, windy, the air cold and damp, a perfect day for misery, Caroline thought, standing close to North, her arm through his. Her knuckles hurt, which was wonderful. There were nearly fifty people at Alice's funeral. Alice would have liked that too, Caroline thought. Alice probably would have flushed scarlet with embarrassment, lost her nearly excellent English grammar, and said, "Lawks, Miss Caroline, would ye jest look at all the toffs? And jest plain ordinary folk too. It pleases me, Miss Caroline, it surely does."

Caroline didn't feel the tears slipping down her face until she tasted the salt and felt North's gloved finger wiping her cheek.

35

I t took Caroline a good three days to realize she was being followed. She was visiting the seamstress in Goonbell, fetching small blankets and wrappers for the babes, when she made her move.

She quickly slipped into an alley between two buildings and waited. Sure enough, not two minutes later, she saw the long shadow of her follower. Her heart pounded. She pulled the pistol from her pocket and waited. She was ready. No more fear, damn the wretched person.

It was Timmy the maid and he nearly dropped to his knees with fright when she grabbed his arm, whirled him around, and stuck the pistol in his face and shouted, "What are you doing? Why are—"

She stared down at the boy, whose mouth was unbecomingly open, eyes terrified. "Timmy, whatever are you doing following me?"

"Er, my lady, ye done scart the stuffing out o' me. Could ye move the popper from me puss?"

"What? Oh yes, I'm sorry for scaring you."

"Aye, and wit' me own popper, leastways it were mine until after ye took it back from me."

She slipped the pistol back into the large pocket of her thick brown wool cloak. "Why are you following me? Oh goodness, I hadn't even considered . . . You're my shadow, my protection. His lordship set you after me, didn't he?"

"Aye, I suppose there ain't no 'iding it now that ye caught me fair and proper."

"Very well. Do you have any idea who tried to hurt me? Remember when we went back to find that wire and it was gone? Have you heard anything about any wire, Timmy, anything at all?"

"Nay, not a bloody thing, beggin' yer ladyship's pardon, and that's wot's drivin' 'is lordship 'round the bend, so to speak. The way 'e thinks is if it were old Mr. Coombe what popped the ladies, then who's trying to pop ye?"

"Your choice of words could use some improvement, Timmy," she said, then pulled him from the alley.

"Ye know, yer ladyship, Flash Savory an' Cap'n Carstairs don't know a thing either, can't figure out who's doing all these evil things. Then there's 'is lordship, the Earl of Chase. Now, 'e's got a bonny brain, 'e 'as, but even 'e don't know who's doing naught."

She only sighed. "I know, even the Duchess is stymied, and that's something. Now that you're here, you can help me fetch the parcels for all our babes."

He looked horrified.

"Come along, Timmy, I did catch you fair and square, you said so yourself."

"No, ma'am, I said it was fair an' proper."

"Come along, Timmy."

That evening at dinner, there were only four at the table, the Nightingales and the Wyndhams. Miss Mary Patricia, Evelyn, and Owen were all upstairs fussing with the babies. Little Owen was eating like a stoat, and the good Lord knew, Tregeagle was heard to say on a deep sigh, that the little blighter's lungs were just dandy.

Caroline told them about Timmy the maid.

North looked at her, smiled, then cursed. "I wish you hadn't seen him, Caroline. He's little, but he's fast. Damnation. You've got good eyesight."

"I do like the notion of a twelve-year-old bodyguard, North, but perhaps he could just accompany me instead."

"No," the Duchess said, "that's not the point. You would be endangering Timmy were he to simply be with you. No, he must follow you, out of sight, so that if anyone tries anything, he would be on the spot."

Caroline sighed as deeply as Tregeagle ever did when awakened in the middle of the night by Little Owen screeching his head off for milk. Both Evelyn and Miss Mary Patricia took turns feeding him, and both agreed that he was a proper little glutton, even as they kissed the soft blond down on his head.

Thank God, Caroline thought. Alice, your son will grow up big and strong and he won't be hurt ever, not if I can help it, not like you were.

She shook her head, hating the tears that always seemed so very close to trickling out of her eyes.

North said to the earl and countess, "Dr. Treath came to see Caroline today, even asked to see her alone, so he could talk to her. Miss Treath and I were consigned to the corridor. Did he tell you that all your roving about wasn't all that good for you right now?"

She tried to smile, but it was so difficult. "Yes, he told me to rest more, but, North, there's so much to be done. I wrote a letter to this man in London that Marcus told me about. He just might come here and begin restoration on all the Nightingale women's portraits. I do hope it's soon."

"At least all the frames are spotless," the earl said. "Oh yes, the Duchess told me how you'd scrubbed them down to their gold."

"Yes, I did. I do hope we can have the fellow who will restore the paintings here right after Christmas."

"Only two weeks away now," the Duchess said. She sat forward, laying her fork down on her plate of spiced pears. "Marcus and I have decided we'll remain here at Mount Hawke until four days before Christmas, then we must return to Yorkshire to Chase Park to be with our own family. We'll return here around the first of the year and we'll stay until all the mystery is cleared up."

North was shaking his head. "Oh no, Duchess. You could have been hurt that day. I can't allow it. Marcus, take her to London, take her home, and keep her there. I don't want either of you coming back after Christmas. Besides," he added, seeing the stubborn set of the earl's jaw, "there could be no resolution for months and months. As much as I think both of you are excellent houseguests, I must tell you that I am beginning to tire of you and even a respite at Christmas won't help. It's true, I'm not lying. Isn't that right, Caroline?"

"Yes," she said quickly, right on his heels. "Already I'm bored, just like North. It's all I can do to stay awake in your company. I already wish you were well gone from here."

"You didn't have to go that far," North said to his wife. "And you're laughing at me, aren't you?"

She wished she weren't seated ten feet away from him at the other end of the table. She wished she were seated in his lap, his palm gently smoothing up her stocking to her thigh whilst she was nipping at his earlobe, lightly licking his jaw, kissing his bottom lip. She wished . . . "No, North," she said, "it's just that you don't know your friends. They will be back after Christmas and then, I dare say, they won't budge until everything is resolved. And that means that we must determine who was behind that wire business else they'll be living with us forever, and I can't imagine anyone happy with that arrangement."

North cursed and said to Tregeagle, "I would like a bottle of port. I would also like the ladies to excuse themselves so that the earl and I could drink ourselves under the Aubusson carpet."

Caroline laughed. It felt good, but life being what it was, memories flooded through her, and the laughter died.

"I know," North said, then turned back to speak to the earl. Caroline rose and said, "Duchess, shall you and I go to the drawing room and drink our own port? There's rather a large carpet in there as well."

"You won't, Duchess," the earl shouted, the pulse pounding in his neck. "I forbid it. You won't get tipsy without me to entertain you."

"I told you he was a sweetheart," the Duchess said to Caroline. She turned back to her furious husband and said, "Try not to bore North, my dear. He just might eject both of us from Mount Hawke this very minute." She then grinned at her husband and followed Caroline from the formal dining room.

. . .

Every Mount Hawke denizen, including old Pa-Dou, who was toothless and hard of hearing, argued, yelled, poked, and insulted one another, all in all having a fine time before the yule log was finally agreed upon and dragged behind two dray horses to the castle, there to be lit and remain burning in the cavernous fireplace in the great entrance hall until after Boxing Day.

Polgrain prepared a delicious hot mulled wine and all toasted North when he finally managed to get the log lighted. The laughter was sweet, poignant, with a bittersweet edge to it when Little Owen waved a tiny arm toward Miss Mary Patricia, whose turn it was to feed him, pumped his legs, and yelled.

If Caroline wondered why there were always at least three people with her except when she had to relieve herself, even when she'd wandered off to look at some rather pretty moss growing in the rocks, she didn't let on.

Everyone cared about her and that felt wonderful. She tired easily but any nausea was gone. North said to her as she sat on his lap in front of their fireplace later that night, "Your breasts are larger. Are they sore?"

"No," she said, nodding, and kissed him.

"Don't lie to me, Caroline. Dr. Treath told me that—"

She reared back in his arms, so embarrassed she nearly sputtered. "You and Dr. Treath talked about my breasts?"

"Yes, don't be silly. He just warned me to be careful when I touched you. Just like Rafael and Victoria Carstairs."

She closed her eyes and flopped against his shoulder. "I can't believe it. This is awful. Oh goodness."

He laughed. "I also asked him when your belly was going to get round. He said every woman was different, that the babe would grow at its own pace. He then assured me that I could love you until April the fourteenth. What do you think?"

She bit his chin hard.

Then she licked his chin and began to kiss him. "I think," she whispered into his mouth, "that we'd best get on with it. I want you to have wonderful memories when the time comes to keep your hands and other parts to yourself."

North agreed with that.

Caroline whisked into her bedchamber to brush her hair. She'd been walking about outdoors with the Duchess and now looked a fright. Her cheeks were ruddy from the cold breeze and she felt marvelous. She was humming to herself when she chanced to see a folded piece of paper slipped under her jewelry box. She frowned as she slipped it out and unfolded it.

Then she turned cold. She read the few words again and again.

You may think you're well protected but you're not. My little note is here, isn't it? You're a slut like all the others and you will die, just like they did, just like your aunt did.

She refolded the single sheet of foolscap, slipped it into her pocket, and slowly walked downstairs. Only North was in the library, reviewing the final papers with Mr. Brogan on Caroline's inheritance. He looked up to see her standing there, utterly without color, utterly motionless, and quickly rose as he excused himself. He gently took Caroline's arm and led her from the library. "What the hell is wrong? Are you ill? Caroline, what's going on?"

She simply gave him the foolscap.

It was Christmas afternoon. The three babes were on a large blanket in front of the fireplace in the drawing room. The sideboard was weighted down with a large punch bowl of hot mulled wine and a huge silver tray filled with cakes, biscuits, and candies. Everyone at Mount Hawke was there, with Caroline and North dispensing gifts and well wishes. Caroline imagined that the Duchess and Marcus were more than likely performing the same functions at Chase Park. They'd been gone four days and Caroline continually found herself starting to say something to the Duchess, then realizing she wasn't here. She was torn. She missed them, yet having North completely to herself was entirely to her liking. She grinned at Polgrain and handed him his present, a pocket watch made in Belgium with his initials engraved on its back in gold. It was a handsome piece and she wasn't at all certain he deserved it.

Earlier in the day there had been another huge affair for the farmers, the servants from Scrilady Hall, and the miners, who were ushered to Mount Hawke by Mr. Peetree. Polgrain had been in his element. He'd hired six helpers and terrorized them witless, all in all, being in a manner very similar to that of Mr. Ffalkes, but the result was delicious; even Mrs. Trebaw from Scrilady Hall voiced her approval. She scolded Dumpling, the scullery maid from Scrilady Hall, only once for being a glutton.

Caroline gave both Miss Mary Patricia and Evelyn rectangular wrapped packages. "Happy Christmas," she said, and kissed their cheeks.

Everyone turned to watch. Miss Mary Patricia very carefully unfastened the paper, rolled the ribbon, and opened a small wooden box. Inside was a key. She looked up at Caroline, confused. Evelyn held up her own key, dangling it at the end of its black velvet ribbon.

North said, "It's your key to Scrilady Hall, Miss Mary Patricia, Evelyn. Caroline and I would like you, Miss Mary Patricia, to become the director of the Hall, which will be a refuge for young women who have been abused and have found themselves with child and in a hopeless situation. You, Evelyn, we would ask that you be in charge of the children, that you also work with Miss Mary Patricia with the young women to see what they would like to do."

"There's so much to do," Caroline said. "Amongst all of us, we should be able to see that everything is done properly. What do you say?"

Miss Mary Patricia simply stared at the key, then at Caroline and North. "I think Eleanor Penrose would be very, very proud of you, Miss Caroline."

"Oh bosh," Evelyn said, and shouted with laughter, then began to dance around the room, waking Little Owen, who promptly decided it was time for him to eat, and yelled.

"It's wonderful! Just wonderful. Oh, Miss Caroline, your lordship, Miss Mary Patricia and I will make Scrilady Hall the finest place in all of England. Aye, Miss Mary Patricia will see that everyone speaks proper good English and I will see that everyone is clothed suitably and looked after until they burst with health."

Suddenly, Evelyn stopped, looked down at Little Owen, who was now red in the face, and burst into tears. "Oh God, how I wish that Alice could be here. She would watch all the little ones. She loved little Eleanor and Little North so much. She never had the chance to know her own son. It's not fair, just not fair."

"Little Owen is here and he will grow up knowing his mother was a fine, fine girl," North said.

"Her English was getting better and better," Miss Mary Patricia said. "She was so proud when she spoke a complete sentence with no mistakes."

Evelyn dashed her hand across her eyes. "No, this is a happy day. Alice would want us to be jolly, and just look what we're going to do. We're going to make a bloody difference." She leaned down then and scooped Little Owen into her arms. "Let me feed the little master before he yells the bricks off the castle walls."

Owen looked at Evelyn, who was patting Little Owen's back. He said, "This is Christmas. It is a day for giving and laughter and obviously eating. I want to adopt Owen. I want him to be my son. He will live at Scrilady Hall, but he will be mine."

"Oh, Owen," Caroline said. "I think Alice would be so pleased. I also think you've grown a very strong chin."

Little Owen shrieked. Evelyn laughed and carried him from the drawing room.

Later that evening, North and Caroline were finally alone, exhausted, sated with too much food, namely, Polgrain's Christmas boned beef ribs with parsnips and oysters, prepared as he sang at the top of his lungs:

A wife, a steak, and a walnut tree—
The more you beat 'em, better they be.

She leaned back against him as they stood together in front of the fireplace in their bedchamber.

"I think I drank too much of that wonderful sweet wine," Caroline said.

"Does that mean I can tie your wrists with my cravats and have my way with you?"

"That sounds interesting. Could you be a bit more specific, North?"

He kissed the nape of her neck, then let her hair fall again. He cupped her breasts in his hands and gently caressed them as he whispered in her ear, "It's Christmas night. It's a night of magic and a night when the unexpected just might leap into your lap. I shan't tell you a thing. Just be tipsy and let me make you yell with pleasure."

"All right," she said, turned in his arms, stood on her tiptoes, and kissed his mouth, running her tongue over his bottom lip. "You may do as you please, but then it's my turn. Oh, North, I do love you so." The sweet warmth of her breath mingled with his.

"I think I rather love you too," he said, and she became as still as a statue. "Don't faint, love, it's true. Do you believe me?"

She looked up at him, her eyes wide and questioning. She didn't say anything, just stood there, pressed against him, her arms around his back.

"I didn't give you your Christmas present. Just a moment." He left her to go into his small dressing room. When he handed her a small box wrapped with bright red tissue, she again remained silent, taking the box, slowly unwrapping it. She opened the box. She could only stare.

"My God," she said, then looked up at North. Slowly, she lifted out an armlet so old that she was afraid it would crumble in her hand. On it were etched the letters *REX*. "My God," she said again. "Where did you find it? It isn't fair, North. The Duchess and I searched and searched those damned barrows and didn't find a single shard of pottery, a single bit of a tool, or a single sliver of a weapon. Where did you get it?"

"Actually, it was Marcus who walked by that wretched clock in the entrance hall when it was chiming. He stared at the thing, put his hands over his ears, and when it was done, he pried open the front casing. The reason the thing has sounded so bloody hideous for all these years is because someone hid the armlet inside. It's been brushing against the mechanism for God knows how many decades. I thought you'd like it, Caroline. You know, of course, that *REX* stands for king."

"I don't believe it," she said again. She gently touched her fingertip over the faint letters scored deeply into the gold by a deft hand. "My God, this means that your great-grandfather wasn't lying after all about finding it. But who the devil hid the thing in the clock? Why didn't anyone say anything about it when it disappeared?"

"Good questions. I haven't any answers. Both Marcus and the Duchess thought it would be a nice present for you since you've spent so much time trying to prove that King Mark just could possibly be buried here."

"But I never believed it, not really. Like you, I decided they'd woven the betrayal myth in with their own personal betrayal, mixing them together until they couldn't tell one from the other."

"Well, now perhaps all of us will have to believe it."

Caroline's present to her husband wasn't at all serious until he looked into her eyes, saw the sparkling, utterly wicked excitement there, drew a deep breath, and said, "Forget what I said earlier about my cravats. You go first. How do you fasten these things?"

North was flat on his back, his arms tied over his head with the satin-lined leather wrist cuffs, fashioned, Caroline told him, by Pa-Dou. The old man had never uttered a word, never let on that he knew what the cuffs were for. North just lay there, grinning like a fool, until Caroline kissed his belly. He heaved at the cuffs, his blood pounding through his body, and just before he felt himself explode, he heard Caroline whisper against his hot flesh, "Happy Christmas, North."

36

The next morning, everyone, including Tregeagle and Polgrain, simply sat about not doing much of anything. North was walking across the entrance hall to the library. He grinned at the sight of Tregeagle slumped down in a very old chair with a high lattice back, his shoes off, massaging his left foot. When there was a loud knocking at the front doors, Tregeagle looked toward the door with loathing. North just laughed, waved him away, and said, "Don't bother, Tregeagle, I will see who's here to see us. Perhaps it's only the Prince Regent, here to see if there are any scraps left from Polgrain's delicious Christmas dinner."

He pulled the great doors open.

A tall woman stood on the steps in front of him, big-bosomed, as fair as he was dark. She was staring at him, just standing there, staring at him as if she couldn't believe he was there, a flesh-and-blood man, then she said, and he noticed that her eyes were nearly as dark as his, "Frederic?"

He shook his head, frowning at her, and he couldn't look away, odd, but true. He said slowly, "No, my name is North."

"I named you Frederic. I called you Frederic after Frederic the Great of Prussia, you know. I admired him, as did your father. Your father must have changed your name after he brought you back to this house. No, it was probably your grandfather who changed your name to North."

North felt his heart begin to pound deep, fast strokes. She was older, this woman who was standing there in the cold morning air. There were lines on her face, but still, he saw the sweetness in her dark eyes, the humor in her mouth, that firm jaw that denoted a very strong will.

She said now, "I know this will come as a shock to you, but I'm Cecilia Nightingale. I'm your mother."

He shook his head even as he said, "There's no portrait of you."

"Your grandfather refused to allow it done," she said, still not moving, still standing there, the dyed green feather in her bonnet fluttering in the stiff winter breeze.

North heard a gasp behind him, then Tregeagle said, "Madam! Oh good lord, you're here!"

"Hello, Tregeagle. You continue to age well. I suppose you will age well even when you're dead."

Caroline was there then, her head cocked to one side in curiosity. "Who is it, North?"

"This is your wife, Frederic?"

"Yes, this is my wife, Caroline. She's going to have a baby."

Cecilia Nightingale smiled. "You're lovely, Caroline. Congratulations."

"Thank you, ma'am." She looked toward North. He said simply, his hand outstretched to the woman, "Caroline, this is my mother, Cecilia Nightingale."

"Oh goodness," Caroline said. "Oh my goodness. North thought you were dead. Oh my. It's Christmas and this is the most wonderful gift North could ever have. Do come in, ma'am. Please, come in."

North stepped back when his wife tugged on his sleeve. It was then he saw the female who had been standing behind his mother. She was young, not older than Caroline. He could but stare at her.

"Yes, Frederic, this is Marie. She's your sister."

Caroline stared from one to the other. They could have been twins. She blurted out, "You didn't betray North's father! I knew it."

"Oh no," Cecilia said. "Indeed I didn't."

"But how did you come now?" North said, trying to grasp what was happening, what was real, and the consequences of this meeting.

"I brought her, my lord."

It was Coombe. He stepped forward, his shoulders thrown back, looking brave and defiant and scared.

Caroline threw herself at him, hugging him close. "I knew you couldn't have killed those women, I just knew it, and we were all sure when someone tried to kill me after you left and then there was that note left in my bedchamber calling me a slut and saying I would die. And do you know that some people still said you were in hiding and still doing all those awful things and—"

"My lord," Coombe said. "I gather there has been some excitement since I left?"

"A bit, Coombe. How would you feel to know that someone left a bloody knife in your room at Mrs. Freely's inn?"

Tregeagle said quickly, "None of us believed it, Mr. Coombe. However, we were greatly relieved that her ladyship was thrown when someone stretched a wire between a tree and the old stone fence. Then there was that nasty note left in her bedchamber and we knew it couldn't be you, unless, naturally, you were in hiding, and everyone knew you could get into Mount Hawke with no trouble at all."

"This is all well and good," Caroline said, "but North, your mother is here and your sister."

North turned slowly to face the woman who hadn't said a word once she'd stepped into the vast entrance hall at Mount Hawke. She said now, "How I wanted to belong here, but your grandfather wouldn't allow it. I was allowed to stay only three days, and every hour of every one of those three days I listened to your father argue with your grandfather. Then your father took me away."

"But I wrote to my father's solicitor in London, asking him where I spent the first five years of my life. He wrote back to tell me it was the house on the Steyne in Brighton. He wrote that my father had told him that you died and thus he was bringing me back to Mount Hawke."

"No, no, I didn't die, North. I've been living in Surrey for twenty years.

Actually, your father sent me a yearly stipend, I suppose you would call it. It didn't arrive this year, so I knew he must have died."

North just looked at her, then at his sister, who hadn't said a word, who just stood behind her mother, silent and still. "I don't understand."

Caroline said quickly, "Why don't we all go into the drawing room. Tregeagle, please have Polgrain prepare tea and cakes. There must be lots of good food left from yesterday." She turned to her mother-in-law. "Please, won't you and Marie come with me. It's chilly today. You can warm yourselves by the fire."

It was an uneasy silence until everyone held a cup of tea in his hand. Then Caroline said, "My mother died when I was eleven years old. I missed her dreadfully. I still miss her. North has believed you were dead since he was five years old. He has missed you dreadfully as well."

Cecilia Nightingale gently laid her cup on its saucer. "It's stopped, hasn't it?"

"What?" North said.

"The legacy of betrayal to Nightingale men. Coombe merely told me that you'd run away from Mount Hawke when you were sixteen. He said you couldn't bear your father's bitterness and the rage. He said you didn't turn out like your father or your grandfather wanted you to."

"That's right, I didn't, thank God. My father had been poisoned utterly by Grandfather. But that isn't important now. Why didn't you write my father to tell him of Marie? For God's sake, she's the very picture of him; she's my twin. He couldn't believe that you betrayed him once he saw her."

"He never saw her," Cecilia Nightingale said quietly. She reached for her daughter's hand and held it tightly. "I didn't want to give up, for I loved your father, despite everything. In those early years, he was so torn, so uncertain, wanting to believe in my love for him, in my loyalty, then hearing his father carry on and on about how I would betray him and I would hurt him dreadfully. Your grandfather did poison your father—that is a good word for it—not just against me, for it would have been any woman who'd married him, any woman who had already birthed the precious Nightingale heir. I begged your father to come and see Marie. He didn't come, but your grandfather did, when she was five years old, the image of him, the image of your father, the image of you when you were five years old. He looked at her, then at me, and said, 'You are a lying slut. Never again write to my son. He didn't want to see you. He asked that I take care of this for him.' And that was that. Until Coombe came to see me."

"But she is obviously North's sister," Caroline said. "Why would he have said that?"

Cecilia said as she looked at her son, "I think he couldn't bear to end the legacy of mistrust. It was such a part of him, after a while, perhaps it was the main part, the only part he understood and accepted. It made him what he was, I suppose. And to be shown wrong in front of his son, I suppose it was too much for him. I felt sorry for him for a little while. Then I came to hate him and your father, Frederic. Oh, I'm sorry. It's North. I shall have to adjust my thinking. During the past twenty years, you've always been Frederic to me, always. Oh, dear." She lowered her face into her hands and began to cry.

Marie gave her brother a vicious look, then pulled her mother into her arms. She patted her mother's shoulder, light little taps that brought Cecilia's head back up. She sniffed. "I'm sorry. It's just that—"

North rose and walked to her. He held out his hand. To his surprise, his sister pushed his hand away. She rose, standing in front of their mother, and then pushed at his chest. She looked fierce and strangely confused and quite ready to kill him to protect her mother.

"No, Marie," Cecilia Nightingale said very calmly, drawing her daughter's hand away. "No, little love. It's not North's fault. Look at me, that's right. I never lie to you, you know that, don't you? Of course you do. It's not his fault. Do you understand?"

Marie looked perplexed, very worried really, then suddenly she turned away and sat down, her hands in her lap, her eyes on her hands.

"What's wrong with her?" North said.

"When she was born, the local doctor was nowhere to be found. The midwife, an old, half-blind woman, did her best, but she hurt Marie's head. Marie was damaged. She is simple, North, but ever so sweet and, as you just saw, very protective of me. All of this is strange to her, indeed, she doesn't really understand what is happening. Actually, I believe that is the second reason your grandfather didn't want to recognize her. She was defective, and you weren't. You were the Nightingale heir. You were whole. She would have just been an embarrassment to him. Also, if your father had ever seen her, he would have known your grandfather had lied to him. Perhaps your grandfather would have lost him. I don't know. Maybe it didn't matter by then. Maybe your father would have detested her for her simpleness. They're dead so we'll never know the truth."

"That god-awful bastard," North said. "Oh Jesus, and now I've frightened her as well." He dropped to his haunches in front of his sister. Very slowly, very gently, he laid his hand atop her folded ones. "Marie," he said. "Won't you look at me?"

Slowly she raised her head and he stared into his own dark eyes, his nose that was sculpted more delicately, his firm jaw that was softer and more rounded. "You're beautiful," he said. "You're my sister and you're beautiful."

She cocked her head to one side, as if considering what he'd said, then, suddenly, without warning, she smiled, a wide dazzling smile that made North suck in his breath.

Cecilia said quietly, "No man has ever before told her that. She does know the word, as you can see. Actually, she's learned a lot. I'm very proud of her."

North remained on his knees, holding his sister's hands, and said, looking up at his mother, "Why didn't you come to me sooner? It's been nearly two years since my father died. Why didn't you come?"

"I had no idea that you were any different. When no money came I just assumed that you felt as your father had. I knew they began to fill you with hate from the moment you came to Mount Hawke. Your grandfather didn't die until you were nearly twelve. I didn't know until Coombe told me that you'd run away and joined the army."

"I hated both my grandfather and my father," North said simply. "I couldn't bear my father's venom, his bitterness, his rages. It is odd though. When I was nineteen, he bought my commission. I became a captain, eventually a major. I sold out just last July. I never wrote to him, never thanked him, never acknowledged what he'd done."

Caroline said loudly, "North, you know the man who is coming to restore all the paintings? I shall write him today and ask for his recommendation for the most prominent portrait painter in London so that your mother's portrait can be done quickly. Yes, I'll do that right now." She jumped to her feet, then stopped suddenly at North's burst of laughter. He rose and walked leisurely to her. He grasped her shoulders and pulled her against him. He kissed the tip of her nose. "Caroline Nightingale, come and sit down. Now that Mother and Marie are here, we have all the time in the world."

"North, can she be my mother too?"

"I don't know. Let's ask her." The two of them turned to face Cecilia Nightingale.

Her face was careworn; there were deep lines about her eyes and mouth. There were streaks of gray in her light brown hair. Then, quite suddenly, she smiled, a smile as beautiful as her daughter's. She looked young again and happy.

"Can she, Mother? Can you accept another daughter? I must warn you that she can occasionally get herself into devilish fixes, but she makes me laugh and she loves me."

Cecilia said, "I cannot imagine a woman not loving you. And to hear you laugh, North—ah, once your father laughed, but it didn't last long. Now I'm being foolish. Another daughter. It is a wonderful notion. And soon I will be a grandmother. But I must ask you, Freder—North. What is it you wish to do?"

"I want you to live here at Mount Hawke because it is your home. I want you and Marie to be a part of this family again. I want my mother back."

Marie sat on the blanket surrounded by the three babes in front of the drawing room fireplace. She was holding Eleanor, then tossing her very carefully into the air, cooing to her, shrieking with laughter when the baby yelled happily.

Cecilia said, "Marie adores the babes and she is so careful with them."

"Yes, she is," Miss Mary Patricia said as she set another stitch in a small woolen shirt for Little North. "I hadn't believed his lordship could be happier than he was with Miss Caroline, but he is, my lady, now that you're here. He is lit up with happiness. Mr. Tregeagle told me once that his lordship wasn't meant for laughter and jests, that he was a Nightingale man and he was to brood and think deeply and never, never smile immoderately."

Cecilia laughed and clapped her hands, making Marie turn quickly. "No, no, love, I was just enjoying Miss Mary Patricia's conversation. Ah, here you are, Caroline. You're looking very well, my dear. How do you feel?"

"Wonderful, ma'am. Did you know that our three male martinets knew you were still alive, or at least they assumed you were? Evidently North's grandfather told them and gave them strict orders never to tell North. He was to grow up believing you were dead."

"And a harlot and slut and goodness knows what else," Cecilia said, the bitterness faded now, and soon it just might be gone altogether.

"True. Actually the three martinets believed you had betrayed North's father. Goodness, you wouldn't believe how they ran Mount Hawke."

Miss Mary Patricia chuckled as she smoothed out Little North's shirt on her lap. "You should have seen the look on their collective faces when three pregnant girls arrived on Mount Hawke's doorstep the day after Miss Caroline and his lordship were married."

"The changes you've wrought are astounding," Cecilia said. "I even saw Tregeagle speaking amiably to Mrs. Mayhew. Chloe giggled in front of Polgrain. I begin to think you a miracle worker, Caroline."

North strolled into the drawing room. He kissed his mother's cheek, hugged his wife, and went down on his haunches next to his sister.

"So soft," Marie said to him, never taking her eyes off the baby, then kissed Eleanor and rubbed her cheek against hers. "So soft."

"Yes, she is." He turned to his wife. "That's what I tell you, Caroline. Here, let me see." He lightly ran his fingertip over Eleanor's cheek. "I don't know. It's really not the same sort of softness. Oh, and Mother, she does work miracles, but they're only temporary ones, minor ones really."

"I suggest that you moderate your speech, North, else your mother just might think you a rogue and a reprobate." But she was smiling when she said it, for her mother-in-law was looking so blissfully content to be called Mother by a son she hadn't seen in twenty years.

North said, "Just wait until she hears Marcus speak to the Duchess.

That's the Earl of Chase, Mama, and his wife. They're coming back on the first of January, and they refuse to leave until we discover who is out to hurt Caroline."

"At least we know it isn't Coombe," Caroline said. "He couldn't have been hiding out here doing bad things and off fetching you at the same time. Mrs. Freely told me that no one believes him guilty now. Indeed, everyone is up in arms that someone local would try to make him look like a murderer. Yes, everyone admits now that it is someone in our midst, and that someone purposefully left that knife in his room in Mrs. Freely's inn and that person was the killer."

"It offends deeply that the villain tried to blame me," Coombe said from the doorway where he'd been standing silently, a platter of cakes and sandwiches in his hands.

"Just don't thank God again," Caroline said, craning around to look at Coombe, "that someone tried to kill me, thus clearing you of suspicion."

"It is, however, an unexpected event that can't help but raise my lowered spirits, my lady. I might add that from reading that letter left in your bedchamber that the person is really quite insane."

"I would agree," North said slowly. "I hadn't really believed the killer sane, but the letter, it showed such imbalance. Also," he continued to his mother, "we've tried to remember everyone who came to Mount Hawke that day because one of those people managed to leave that note in Caroline's dressing table. There were many people in and out. There are very few local people we can eliminate."

"I vote for the vicar, Mr. Plumberry," Miss Mary Patricia said. "He is a dreadful man."

"He hasn't the guts," Coombe said.

"He wasn't here either, more's the pity," Caroline said as she took a cucumber sandwich from Coombe.

"Goodness sake," Miss Mary Patricia said, her sandwich in midair to her mouth. "I do believe that the Plumberry servant was here, speaking to Mr. Polgrain in the kitchen."

"No, no," North said. "That's quite impossible."

"The vicar hasn't the guts," Coombe said again. "However, I will ask Mr.

Polgrain about this visiting Plumberry servant. You won't worry about it, my lord."

"Thank you, Coombe. Do tell me what Polgrain says."

Caroline said, "Before you do that, Coombe, tell us why you simply left without a word to fetch North's mother."

"I wouldn't have felt right about saying anything," Coombe said simply. "I didn't know for certain that she was alive. I didn't wish to raise his lordship's hopes, then just to have them dashed. Thus I went off to see for myself. She was well, thank the good Lord, and there was Marie as well, all grown up and looking the spitting image of his lordship. Understand that his lordship's grandfather told us that the little girl looked like a friend of your husband's and thus another Nightingale wife had betrayed her husband. It was then he made us swear never to tell his lordship here that you were alive."

"What changed your mind, Coombe?" North asked, looking up. He was seated cross-legged, now holding Eleanor on his knee.

"You were so bloody happy," Coombe said. "As much as I wanted to despise her, to believe that she would hurt you as did all the other Nightingale wives, I ended up thinking perhaps that I'd been wrong. I said nothing of what I was going to do to either Mr. Polgrain or to Mr. Tregeagle. I just went to Surrey, to Hollywell Cottage in Chiddingfold. Thank the good Lord that Lady Chilton was there. Thank the good Lord she didn't slam the door in my face."

"I was only tempted to for a brief moment, Coombe. I was so surprised to see you. Actually, truth be told, I would have had to write you, North, for the money was quite low. I was giving deportment and music lessons to the local children, but still it was difficult. Then here is Mr. Coombe, standing on my doorstep, hat in hand, and looking ever so pleased with himself and scared to death at the same time."

"When I saw Miss Marie," Coombe said, "I knew it had all been a lie. I knew that all of us had been wickedly wrong all those twenty years. I begged her to come back to Mount Hawke with me to allow me to make things right."

"You're rehired, Coombe." North handed Miss Mary Patricia her little daughter, rose, and stretched out his hand. "All you have to do is promise you won't dangle any more monster masks in front of her ladyship's window and you'll stay here as long as you want to."

Coombe drew himself up as high as his five feet, five inches could carry him. "I must admit that was beneath my dignity."

"Well beneath it," Caroline said. "But I imagine it was fun if you weren't too afraid of falling off the roof."

"Yes, well, I suppose I was a bit nervous. Everything is different now, that is, I see different things now. It is now my quest to discover this awful creature who killed her ladyship's aunt and those other two women, that creature who had the gall to try to blame it on me. Yes, Mr. Tregeagle and Mr. Polgrain and I have our heads together. The three of us—with perhaps a tiny bit of help from Mrs. Mayhew—will solve this mystery and all will be well again. There will be laughter at Mount Hawke and all of us will accustom ourselves to it. Perhaps we will even trade about a jest upon occasion."

"If you and Tregeagle and Polgrain will allow her ladyship and me to be of minor assistance," North said, "we would be most grateful. Now, give me one of those lemon seed cakes."

37

It was the coldest night of the year, that twenty-ninth day of December, at least that's what Caroline thought as she waited downstairs in the drawing room for North to come home, listening to the wind howl. The windows were clouded over and the wind whipping off the sea was harsh and brittle, sending naked branches slapping against the glass, each time making her jump. North and Sir Rafael Carstairs had ridden with Flash Savory to Goonbell because Flash had heard from Mrs. Freely that a man, deep in his cups, was shooting his mouth off in her taproom about stabbing faithless bitches.

Caroline shivered and moved her chair closer to the roaring fire. But it wasn't really that she was cold from the frigid weather. Rather she was cold from the inside out, as with a fever, only this fever was made of fear and she hated it, hated it not just because she was afraid for herself, but also for North, more for North, which was silly because he was strong and smart and with Flash and Rafael. Still, none of that mattered. If only he'd let her go with them to Goonbell.

"No," he'd said, and kissed away her arguments. "It's cold and you're carrying a babe. You must take care of our babe, Caroline."

That old clock stroked eleven times, only it wasn't ugly and raw and gravelly and hoarse-sounding anymore, not since Marcus Wyndham had found the gold armlet. Now the clock stroked deep and true. Now that the miserable thing sounded like a clock again, she thought, twisting her wedding ring about on her finger, it would probably very soon give one final stroke, gurgle, and die.

She looked over at the armlet. Just this evening she'd placed it on a bed of deep crimson velvet atop a stand that had previously held a hideous Chinese vase. Now everyone could see it and marvel at it. She thought most of the time, as she did now, that it was likely the armlet would be the only small bit of evidence that King Mark was buried here.

More than likely, she thought, with her luck and the luck of the Nightingale male ancestors, the armlet had probably been found down near Fowey, where King Mark was really buried, and some tinker had brought it here and sold it to North's great-grandfather. If something like that were true, what a scheme that first Viscount Chilton, old Donniger Nightingale, had perpetrated on his progeny.

She sighed, leaned her head back in her chair, and closed her eyes. North had been gone for three hours. She hated waiting, she always had. She wanted to be *doing,* not sitting here twiddling her fingers or sighing. She wondered if Victoria Carstairs was sitting waiting for her husband. Being a woman, she thought, wasn't that wonderful all the time, like now, when she couldn't take charge and make her own decisions and make certain that North was all right.

She looked up when Coombe came quietly into the drawing room. He was carrying a tea tray with a beautifully polished early-eighteenth-century silver service. "From old George the First's beginning years," he'd told her when she'd first arrived, and it hadn't been quite so beautifully polished then. "Aye, way back in 1722, I believe, purchased by his lordship's great-grandfather, our first viscount."

Caroline had hated the service from the moment of hearing that tidbit.

"It's cold," she said to him as he gently placed the service on a table and carried it next to her chair.

"It's beginning to rain now. I dislike his lordship being out in such weather."

"So do I. I should be with him. I would keep him dry. I don't wish him to become ill."

If Coombe thought that was rather illogical, he kept it to himself.

She sipped at her tea, then said, "Don't go just yet, Coombe, if you don't mind. Tell me, do you have any idea about who would have hidden the gold armlet in that old clock?"

"Not a clue, my lady. I asked both Mr. Tregeagle and Mr. Polgrain, but they are as mystified as I am, a circumstance none of us relishes."

"If it was North's great-grandfather, then why did he do it? Surely it would prove his theory about King Mark, at least an actual, quite tangible golden armlet with *REX* engraved on it would make his theory a bit more palatable. No, it makes no sense at all. It must have been inside the clock for years and years. None of the Nightingale men wrote about it, just North's great-grandfather. I do hate mysteries."

"Actually, my lady, there are more important things on my mind at present. I told his lordship, and now I will tell you, that the Plumberry servant was indeed here that fateful day when the vicious note was left in your bedchamber. However, to the best of Polgrain's memory, the servant never left the kitchen. Indeed, the servant is a female sort of servant, a spinster named Ida, and enamored with Mr. Polgrain, thus causing him acute embarrassment as well as making him quite distracted."

"In short, the female sort of Plumberry servant could have enjoyed tea in the drawing room and Polgrain wouldn't have noticed."

"I fear it is possible."

"Oh, all right. As best as I can remember, the only people who didn't visit us that day were the Carstairses."

"Ah, but that fellow Flash Savory did. I don't trust him, my lady. He's too handsome, altogether too cocky, if you know what I mean."

"That's a theory I hadn't thought of. I think Flash is safe, Coombe, but then again, who knows? He was here to see his lordship, and probably Miss Evelyn."

"So the wind blows in that direction, does it?"

"The wind is always blowing. Thank God it blew his lordship to Dorchester to find me."

"Once I would have said it was a foul wind, my lady, that blew him anywhere near you, but perhaps now, the wind that is responsible for you being here isn't all that noxious, just a bit irregular."

"Thank you, I think." Caroline took a final sip of tea and rose. "I think I'll snuggle under all those wonderful blankets Tregeagle spread on his lordship's bed. You should retire as well, Coombe. We have no idea when his lordship will return, curse his hide."

Coombe drew himself to his fullest height, which was still below Caroline's eye level. "I am not carrying the Nightingale heir, my lady, thus, I will await his lordship's return and have a brandy snifter warmed for him."

She rather fancied a snifter of good smuggled French brandy rather than the bitter tea she'd just consumed, but she could just imagine Coombe's reaction to a pregnant lady drinking spirits.

"Is Miss Marie feeling more the thing?"

"Aye, it's just a little stuffy nose and a mite of a cough. Lady Cecilia, however, won't leave her, as you know. She did tell me to bid you good night for her. I imagine she and Miss Marie both will be downstairs tomorrow."

She was whistling as she walked up the staircase. She looked once at the empty wall space she'd cleared of one of North's father's paintings, the one where he'd looked so sour, so malevolent, he could have been the Devil's right hand. It would one day soon hold Cecilia Nightingale's portrait. And also a portrait of Marie, with North. Yes, it would be proof for all eternity that a Nightingale wife was faithful and loyal to her husband.

She felt exhaustion weigh her down. She felt as heavy as the statue of the god Mercury that stood in a deep niche at the head of the stairs standing on the toes of his winged feet. Each step she took became more of a chore. She shook her head and frowned at herself. The babe was making her tire more easily. She didn't like it a bit.

She was nearly trembling with the immense fatigue when she reached the master bedchamber. Even turning the doorknob was a mighty effort. She thought about calling one of the maids to help her undress, but decided it was too late. There was a nice fire set in the bedchamber, blazing brightly, casting shadows in the dim corners of the huge room, and she managed to make herself walk to it. She stretched out her hands to warm them. She looked at her hands. They seemed to fade even as she watched them. Lighter and lighter they became, the pale blue lines beneath her flesh brightening, then they too became vague and insubstantial as her hands themselves, like the shadows flickering in the corners, or maybe it was simply the firelight that was making her hands look so very strange to her.

Something wasn't right. She turned slowly at the very soft sound coming from behind her. She saw nothing, but she was so tired, her legs so weak, she could barely stand, much less investigate the likely mouse that was scurrying about in the far corner of the room. She took the two steps to the wing chair and clung to its back. Again, there was a soft rustling noise and it was coming closer now, just over there, next to the Chinese screen she never used because when she bathed North invariably turned up, all wicked smiles and wandering hands.

She stilled, trying to make herself pay attention. She was so bloody tired. There it was again, that silly sound that probably wasn't anything really, just something out of her imagination, woven there by her fatigue. Yes, that was it.

She slowly turned back to face the fireplace. The flames were dancing like the Cornish piskeys now, scampering and waving to and fro, always changing, shifting, their heat reaching out to her but she couldn't feel it. She raised her hand to her face, or she tried to. Her arm dropped to her side. She was too overwhelmed by fatigue to move.

The noise came again, but she didn't have the strength to turn. It was closer now and she knew it. She was now just simply waiting for it. Like a rabbit looking down a hunter's gun, she thought, just standing here, waiting for that noise to come and get her.

How could a noise hurt her?

There was a soft murmuring beside her. She whispered, "What is happening? What is it?"

Soft sibilant murmurs came close to her ear, meaningless sounds, just nothing, really. She would have sworn that fingertips lightly brushed her hair. "You're a whore," that sweet dreamlike voice said. "A whore and you'll die now, just like the other whores."

"No," she said. Her mouth was dry; it hurt to say that simple word. "No," she said again. She felt arms close about her. She breathed in an elusive scent, then ever so gently, she was lowered to the floor. At last, for an instant, she felt the blessed heat of the fireplace, then it was gone and there was only coldness.

"North," she said, then her head fell to the side and she said nothing more.

The wind was howling. There were swirling grains of sand in the air; the taste of salt was strong.

Without really realizing what she was doing, Caroline huddled down into the velvet cloak, then wondered why she was wearing it. Surely she hadn't come for a walk without wearing something, but she couldn't remember, couldn't seem to grasp preparing to come for a walk.

It was dark. There was a quarter moon high in the sky to her left. Dear God, it hurt to open her eyes, but she did and she saw that moon, tasted the salt from the sea on her dry lips, and felt the bone-deep cold. She shivered then and came fully awake. She was tucked as far as possible underneath the jutting ledge of a large black rock. She knew where that rock was. It was very close to the cliff at St. Agnes Head. She knew too how she'd gotten there. Someone had drugged the tea. Someone had come to the bedchamber and made those odd rustling noises, then whispered in her ear that she was a whore and she was going to die, and then that someone had carried her away from Mount Hawke and brought her here.

What someone?

She stretched about, realizing her hands were bound behind her back, her ankles bound as well. She was leaning back, the main force of the wind off her, but the cold was hard and deep.

Where was that someone?

She was quite alone.

She knew terror that froze her brain and numbed her body. She saw her mother then, quite clearly: her beloved face, her green eyes bright with laughter, eyes just the same color green as Caroline's, but then her mother's face faded away and left only the memory of it. She'd not remembered that her mother's eyes were green. "Mother," she whispered. "Mother."

She was alone in the dark of the night, the howling wind dinning around her. Surely it was a man who had brought her here, a man who had access to Mount Hawke.

Coombe? He'd come back, all smiles and sheepish looks, bringing with him North's mother and sister, all to make him look like a saint, a reformed character, a man of conscience, to make all of them forget that he'd lied about Caroline meeting her supposed lover, Dr. Treath, that he'd possibly poisoned the ox-tail soup that had made poor Alice so ill.

She heard a low moaning sound, close, too close. She huddled in on herself, wanting to escape it, knowing it was frightening, and then she realized it was coming from her, from deep within her, and the terror was now a part of her. It was over for her. She'd found North, but now after only months he would be alone again. No, no, he had his mother now and his sister. He wouldn't become a brooding dark man again who didn't laugh or jest.

She didn't want North to laugh without her. She was selfish, but there it was. She didn't want to just sit here and wait for the someone to come and stab her and push her off the cliff. She didn't want to die.

She felt clearheaded for the first time. She didn't feel much hope but she didn't feel like rolling over and simply waiting for the someone to come and kill her. She tested the rope wrapped around her wrists. It was secure. She tried to pull her ankles apart. There was only about six inches leeway, not enough to run, barely enough to hobble along.

All right then, if she wasn't just going to give up, she had to do something. She felt the edges of the huge black outcropping rock. Ah, yes, there was nothing but sharp edges; she just prayed they were sharp enough.

She realized then that her hands were bare and they were cold, almost too cold now, and soon they would be numb. So her attacker had wrapped her cloak around her, but pulled no mittens on her hands. That wouldn't be so bad, she thought, as she began to rub the rope vigorously against a sharp edge. Then she wouldn't feel the pain, and she knew that was coming.

She gritted her teeth and sawed back and forth.

A black roiling cloud crashed against another, and the two of them covered the moon. It was terrifying, that complete, utter blackness. It seemed colder, the wind seemed louder. She could clearly hear the maddened waves crashing against the rocks at the base of St. Agnes Head, sending their freezing spray upward nearly halfway to the top of the cliff.

Move, dammit. She sawed faster. She felt stickiness and knew it was her blood. At least she felt it. That was something. She was breathless, with the pain from her hands, with the cold, piercing sharpness in her lungs. It hurt to breathe. She stopped a moment, drew a deep breath, and gently tugged at the rope.

It was loose.

She wanted to weep with the relief of it, the hope of it.

She went back to work. Soon the rope snapped and she was free. She brought her hands in front of her and stared down at them. They were red, abraded, and the outline of the rope was clear on her wrists. It didn't matter. She was free and she was still alive. She quickly freed her ankles. When she scrambled to her feet she promptly collapsed.

Weak, she thought, she was too cold and too weak. She frantically rubbed her legs, her feet. Sharp stabs of pain shot through her legs. She ignored it as best she could.

She rose again, more slowly this time, hanging on to the rock. She didn't fall this time. She took a step, then another, and another.

It was then she heard a horse coming. Actually, she felt the pounding of the horse's hooves rather than heard it. He'd come for her. She wouldn't just stand here and watch him come.

The cliffs were barren. What to do?

The beach, she thought, and picked up her cloak and skirts and ran northward along the cliff edge toward the beach path, only another fifty or so feet ahead. She would find a weapon on the beach, a rock or a piece of heavy driftwood. She would be able to hide against the base of the cliff at the back of the beach. The killer would have to walk down the steep path and that would give her time to plan, time to find a weapon, the chance to see who he was. Perhaps she would be able to take him by surprise.

She heard a shout. She heard a cry of sheer fury, then a string of curses, wafted away in the wind, that same wind that was deep inside her now, for she was gasping for breath, a stitch in her side, doubling her over. But she was nearly there, nearly to the cliff path.

The horse was coming closer. She could hear the shouts now, the curses, hear them blur and become indistinct. The wind was becoming stronger. No wonder there were no trees here. They would never survive this wind.

Her babe. Her hands went to her belly, as if holding her hands there would protect the child. She nearly lost her balance, flung her arms out to steady herself, then nearly plummeted down the cliff path. She caught herself, skidding to a stop sideways, sending a spay of rocks and dirt flying from beneath her feet.

She righted herself, stood there a moment, panting, listening. The horse was coming closer. Soon the man would be just above her, looking down, then climbing down after her. She had to hurry.

She skidded, ran, several times nearly going headfirst, but she had to be reckless, she had to or she could just sit down on the path and wait to die. Who was the man?

She stumbled and flew forward. She flung her arms out, breaking her fall, then rolled to the bottom of the path. She lay there just an instant, hoping she hadn't broken a leg, then she rose. She looked back to see the cloaked man at the top of the path, looking down at her. Then he was coming down, as fast and recklessly as she had, his black cloak billowing about him, making him look like he was flying, looking like the Devil himself.

She ran as fast as she could over the wet clinging sand, looking wildly for a weapon, anything really, and she saw it then, a thick branch, but not too thick for her to grasp firmly. She grabbed it up, never breaking stride, and headed for the back of the beach. There were overhanging layers of shale sandstone, thick slabs of it, the porous rock cut away over the centuries deeply back under the cliff.

She would be trapped, she thought, stopping just a moment, her breath harsh in her ears, ripping pain through her chest. What to do? Then she knew that it was dark under that cutaway cliff and that would give her protection. But he would come for her and he was stronger. She would have to surprise him.

The black clouds suddenly cleared overhead and the moon shone down. She even heard a lone kestrel as it hovered. It was then she saw the vague indentations going upward beside the overhang. North had never mentioned this, nor had she noticed the outlines that surely would allow a person to climb upward. She didn't question why the outlines, which were really actual footholds and handholds, were there or who fashioned them there. She didn't think further, but raced to the first outline and hoisted herself upward.

Her foot fit quite nicely into the foothold. She grabbed a rock, surely a handhold there to aid the climber, and pulled herself up to the next foothold when she realized she couldn't climb and carry the branch at the same time. She turned, saw the man below her, and threw the branch down at him with all her strength. She didn't have much leverage, but she did the best she could. No, her chance lay in getting up there, before he did, perhaps she could get to his horse.

She heard him curse when the branch struck him, not hard enough, but it slowed him for just a moment.

She found a handhold and dragged herself upward to each foothold. Up and up she went until she was a good thirty feet above the beach. If she fell from here she'd surely die.

She stopped just a moment to catch her breath. She looked down to see him coming, sure and fast. She had to hurry. She looked up. Only about twenty more feet to the top. She just had to keep climbing and she would beat him. She'd have time to get his horse and ride away.

Suddenly there were no more handholds, no more footholds. They simply disappeared, or they'd never been there in the first place. She felt betrayed by the ancient people who had carved this upward climb. Why had they stopped? It made no sense. She looked about frantically, her bloody hands digging into the dirt around the jagged rocks, searching, searching.

To her right, yes, just to her right and straight beside her there was a foothold, but it would take all her strength to drag herself over to it.

Suddenly she heard a shout from above her, a man's shout and it was familiar. She felt a wild spurt of hope. Then she heard the report of a gun from below her. There was nothing else from above, not a whimper, nothing.

The man below her had shot her rescuer. North? Oh God, she couldn't bear to think about that. She stretched as far as she could to her right, then heaved herself sideways, her hands frantically clutching at jagged rocks that seemed just beyond her reach, pulling herself until her feet found a hold. Then there was another, and it too was going sideways, back in nearly a straight line across the cliff edge. It made no sense, but she didn't care. She just kept going, not thinking now, just making herself move.

She heard the man beneath her. She knew that he'd reached the end of the vertical handholds and footholds, knew that he wouldn't have to take the time to discover they turned sharply sideways, going back along the face of the cliff.

Then, without warning, her foot slipped and she was hanging there, clinging to the rocks above her head, her legs dangling now, trying desperately to get a foothold but not finding one. Then he was there beside her, not more than six feet away from her, and she knew he was laughing because she would fall and she would die. Her hand slipped. She was flailing wildly but it was no use. She lost her remaining grip and fell, her scream of failure hurtling into the howling wind.

38

She grabbed wildly at a gorse bush growing out of the cliff, and caught it. It slowed her but nothing more, then when it ripped out, she rocked hard sideways, her hip slamming against the cliff. It seemed to tremble beneath her weight. Then it gave, collapsing beneath her. She felt herself falling sideways, down, down, into dry musty air now, for the cliff had simply crumbled under her. She landed on her side on an incline and rolled another six feet to a smooth sandy flat ground. She lay there, panting hard, not wanting to know what had happened, not yet, simply because it had happened too quickly, a cliff collapsing beneath her and now she was inside the cliff itself, and she couldn't seem to bring herself to accept it, much less understand it.

Her breathing finally slowed. The stitch in her side lessened. She felt her belly, but there was no pain there, no hint of cramping. The babe was all right, at least for the moment. Very slowly, she turned and sat up. The only light was from the moon high above the jagged opening her body had made when she'd burst through the earth.

She looked around, wondering what the devil this place was, then realized it had to be a cave, but it didn't really look like any cave she'd ever seen before, not that she'd seen many, just one, and it had been small and dark and very damp. This cave was dry, the earth beneath her feet sandy and flat. She stood there, just looking around, querying her body, but all was well. Her hands were bloody and raw, but that didn't matter. In fact, she welcomed the stinging pain. It meant she was alive.

The man would somehow get down here, then he would kill her, for she was now indeed trapped. If only she had a light. She walked away from the cliff face, inward, and she could still make out shapes. Perhaps the cave twisted back onto itself and gave out again onto the cliff and there was another opening. Of course there really hadn't been an opening here, it had simply given way beneath her weight.

But surely the handholds and footholds had been planned apurpose just to get to this cave. But what had happened? It struck her then that there simply had to be another way out of here and maybe that way was upward.

She just had to find it. She kept walking slowly, looking, listening for the man, because she knew it wouldn't be long before he found a way to climb down and get into the opening of the cave.

Whom had he shot atop the cliff? No, she just knew it hadn't been North. But whom?

Suddenly she tripped. She didn't fall, just stumbled and caught herself. By her foot there was something shiny sticking up out of the smooth, dry, sandy earth. She knelt down and freed it. It seemed to be circular and very smooth. It was shiny, a piece of jewelry of some kind. She wished she could go back to see what she had, but she had no intention of taking such a chance.

She slipped the jewelry into her cloak pocket and kept walking into the darkness.

From behind her, she heard an eerie call, like a ghost's taunt on All Hallows' Eve, a specter's cry, all muffled and distorted by the cave walls. It echoed deep and dark, that voice that called like a beguiling siren, "Caroline, Caroline, you might as well stop now. I will have you soon enough and I will make you die very, very slowly. That damned brat in your belly, that little bastard, will die with you."

She began to shiver. She wrapped her arms around herself, felt the keening cries from deep within her bubble up, choking her, making her wheeze with fear. She forced herself through sheer strength of will to remain silent as the rocks on all sides of her. The voice came again, echoing and threading through the darkness, closer now, "Come here, Caroline. You're more resourceful than the others, or perhaps you're just luckier. Let me tell you about that pathetic woman, Elizabeth Godolphin. She whimpered, she was on her knees to me, begging me not to kill her, but I did, of course. She was even a worse slut than your aunt. I'll tell you all about how your dear aunt died once I have you, Caroline. I want to see your face while I tell you how she tried to save herself, but she didn't stand a chance. But her death was justice, she deserved it. No more about her now, not until I have you. Come out now, Caroline. You don't want to make me angry."

She shivered more violently. There was madness in that echoing eerie call. Madness and determination.

A weapon. She had to find something. She kept walking back into the cliff. The ceiling lowered, but it was still at least ten feet high. She turned a corner to the left. Suddenly it wasn't quite so dark. She could make out shadows. Another opening, she knew it, there had to be another way, and she'd found it. She hurried now, running toward the vague glittery light, then stopped so fast she nearly fell over her own feet.

There, in front of her, on a long, very wide flat rock lay piles of gold— coins, jewelry, many armlets, bracelets, necklaces, so many of them, and there were loose jewels as well, spilling out of several gold chalices. And in the middle of all these jewels a mighty sword rose at an angle a good foot and a half into the air, its handle encrusted with diamonds, rubies, and emeralds. It seemed to be embedded in the rock at least half its length. Good God, the sword must be at least four feet long. She just stared, her terror at bay for a brief second, realizing what she'd found.

It was King Mark's treasure trove, it had to be. The Nightingale men had been right. His treasure was here, buried a thousand years before, more treasure than a single mortal man deserved.

She walked closer, her hand stretched out to touch the sword. But she held back. She was afraid of it, it was that simple. What was it doing here, buried in that stone? She knew it was something beyond what a human should know, beyond what a human should see and experience. It wasn't of this earth, of this time, yet it was here, as if it was waiting. It glittered like gold but it was made of steel. It was magnificent: hard and long, ferocious. Its blade was a glittering silver in its sharpness, the brilliant edge glittering. It still looked deadly after one thousand years.

She stared at that sword. There was something about it that drew her. Without really thinking, she clasped her hands around the hilt and tugged. To her absolute astonishment, the sword moved. She pulled harder now and the sword simply slipped out of the stone, and she realized that the stone couldn't be solid as it appeared. There had to be a chamber built within it for the sword, a scabbard for it, a place of honor for it, to display it as she'd displayed the armlet. But for whom?

She'd pulled it free, and now just stared at it lying there atop the stone amid all those incredible gems, those piles of gold. How could she lift it? It was at least four feet long, perfectly straight, its top so pointed, so deadly, that just looking at it made her shiver.

But it was a weapon.

She gingerly tried to raise it with both hands wrapped around the handle. Again, to her astonishment, she discovered she could lift it easily. She brought it up with but one hand clutching about the jewel-encrusted handle. It fit well into her palm. Her fingers closed easily around it. But it had looked so big, so foreboding thrust into the rock. She swung it. It weighed so little, but that didn't make sense, simply couldn't be real. She didn't care. She swung it again. It seemed an extension of her arm, flowing and smooth. She felt powerful; she felt the strength of it, or she fancied she did. She felt as if it had been fashioned for her and only her.

She smiled. Now she had a chance. Then she remembered the shot. The man had a gun. Even this wonderful sword would have no chance against a gun. She turned again toward the light, the other opening. She could escape him.

She followed the shadow light. To her despair, not six feet behind the stone slab she stood beneath the light. It was not more than a small circular opening, more a narrow tunnel that seemed to twist back on itself, back toward the edge of the cliff. There was nothing else.

She felt bowed by defeat. Then, very carefully she eased the sword behind her back and walked forward again, back toward her killer. The sword felt so light. It lay so easily pressed against her legs, her single hand holding it without effort. Odd that the handle had looked so massive, but it wasn't. It didn't strain her arms at all to keep it from dragging on the ground.

She walked now toward the light from where she'd crashed through the cliff, back toward the man who wanted to kill her, the man who was insane, the man whose voice terrified her, drew at her confidence, her strength.

She heard him call again, his voice soft now, echoing deep and dark, forming and reforming like shadows off the rock walls. "Caroline, how much longer can you hide from me? Come to me now and I will slip my knife quickly into your heart. You won't suffer, Caroline, and Lord Chilton will be free of you, all of us will be free of you, me most of all."

She was closer to the man now and his voice sounded that much more frightening, more inhuman, more like a specter's than a human being's. She pulled back close to the wall, becoming part of the darkness, and sang out softly in a voice that made her shiver herself, "Why has a madman come into my burial chamber? It is forbidden. You are not one of the chosen. That girl who dared enter now lies dead, as will you very soon now."

She heard a yelp, she was certain of it. She heard a quickening of breath, she heard no more movement. She pressed herself even closer against the wall.

"Well? Who are you? Why do you come here?"

The killer's voice now, coming like a thread of fear, low and hoarse, fright filling it: "I will leave but I must have the girl's body. She is an abomination. If I leave her here, she will be a scourge to this chamber. Her very presence will curse you. I will take her."

"You will take no one! I will kill you now just as I killed her. Prepare to die."

There was utter silence. It seemed to grow even darker. The air was so dry she wanted to cough, but she didn't dare to. She held herself perfectly still. It was then Caroline felt the warm dry breath against her cheek. "That was a good show, but not good enough. Couldn't you tell I was coming toward you even as I spoke? No? The echoes in this chamber distort everything, more's the pity for you. Hold still now, Caroline, I want you to know who will kill you before you spend eternity in hell."

Caroline didn't move. She clasped the sword more firmly behind her back and readied herself. She couldn't do anything yet. The man was holding the gun against her ribs.

"Come, Caroline, you can't see me here. Come."

Slowly, the man's hand around her arm, she walked back toward the opening in the cliff wall.

It took only a moment or two. So close she'd been. Then the man shoved her away. She struck a wall, but managed to keep hold of the sword behind her, and her balance. She watched the cloaked and booted man walk until he stood directly beneath the collapsed opening. Then he straightened and threw back the hood of his black cloak.

She looked into the face of Bess Treath, and she said, "I thought you were a man."

"Yes, I know. I deepened my voice for you. I knew it terrified you even more to think a madman was chasing you. But I'm not a man and I don't have to pretend with you any further. You've given me a good chase, Caroline, but it's over now. You even found a treasure trove for me."

"Bess Treath," Caroline said aloud, wondering if saying the woman's name would make any of this any more real. She stared at her now, still unable to grasp what she was seeing, what she'd heard. "But why? Why did you call me a slut? Why do you want to kill me? And my aunt? Why Aunt Eleanor? She loved to laugh, there was no one to betray, she wasn't married."

"She would have, though . . ."

"Yes, she would have married your brother, she—" Caroline's voice fell like a rock from the cliff wall just beyond her.

"Yes, I see you understand now. I couldn't allow my brother to marry Eleanor. He would have left me and that I couldn't have borne. He was mine, Benjie was, all mine. I was only eleven years old when our parents died and he became both mother and father to me, and eventually lover, but that was just for one night when he was drunk, when he'd lost his sweet little wife, that slut, who dared believe she could keep him to herself."

"But you told me she died in childbirth."

"Yes, she did, and let's say that I helped her along. Poor Benjie was so exhausted, for the weak little ninny couldn't even birth the babe easily, not like I could have if only I'd ever had a chance. No, she screamed and struggled, and I finally told him he had to rest, that I would watch her, that I would call him if anything happened. Ah, but she knew when she opened her eyes and saw me smiling down at her, she knew that she was going to die and I didn't disappoint her. I stuck my hand inside her body and I tore her. That was all, just those few seconds and she died so quickly then, with Benjie weeping over her, begging her not to leave him, and I just stood there and watched, and when he chanced to look at me, I found tears and I shed them but I still smiled inside and I knew that I'd won."

The sword seemed to tingle in her palms. It was all the gems, she thought, the gems were growing warm, even hot, against her flesh.

Bess Treath leaned back against the stone wall, the gun still pointed at Caroline. "Don't you want to know more? Don't you want to know everything, about those other women, about your dear aunt, who died really very easily, too easily, for I wanted her to suffer more?"

Caroline raised her chin and smiled. "Why? You're nothing but a madwoman. Whatever you have to say is a lie, and if it's not an outright lie, then it's so distorted because you're distorted, you're twisted, just as everything you could say is twisted."

"Shut up! Damn you, you miserable slut, just shut up."

Caroline shrugged, the smile still on her mouth. "It sounds to me like you're the slut and the evil one. You seduced your brother? How old were you, all of thirteen?"

"No, I was the same age as that miserable little Alice." Her eyes narrowed and there was regret there. "No, I didn't have the chance to dispatch that one, and I fancy she deserved it. Benjie wouldn't leave her, nor would that damned Owen Ffalkes. But then she croaked herself. I was pleased, but I missed smiling at her, stroking her child's cheek even as I told her that I was killing her."

"So you were the slut. You seduced your brother? And you were fourteen?"

"You're stupid, Caroline. You keep repeating yourself. Do you hope to rattle me, make me shriek then hurl myself to the beach below because you twist my mind through your manipulations? You are stupid. Do you know that Benjie didn't remember? He never knew that when he was so drunk from the brandy and the whiskey that his damned sex so shrank that I had to take him in my mouth and when he finally became part of me, he became mine that night and I vowed that he would remain mine. No, he didn't remember, or if he did, he kept it to himself.

"No matter. He was mine and I vowed he would remain mine, no other woman would ever have him. There were other women after him, but none serious until that whore Elizabeth Godolphin. She got him into her bed before I realized what was happening. He was all smiles, all distracted, going about humming and grinning. He fancied himself in love with the trollop, but I took care of her, yes I did, as soon as I had the opportunity. I waited until he was off at a tin-mine accident, then I went to her and I stabbed her and hurled her off the cliff near Perranporth. She blubbered and wept and swore to me she'd release him, but she'd already sullied him, already put her mouth and her hands on him, already opened her legs to him and offered him her womb."

It was simply too much. Caroline leaned over and vomited. It was the drugged tea mainly, for she'd eaten none of the cakes Coombe had brought her. Then she stood there, bent over, head down, and her body heaved in upon itself, but she didn't bring her right hand forward, she held onto that sword handle with all her will and all her strength. Suddenly the sword seemed even lighter, and she didn't even consider it, not really, just held it there behind her back with one hand. With her left hand, she lifted her skirt and wiped her mouth. Then she looked up at Bess Treath. She even managed a smile as she said, "You know, old Miss Bess, this turns my stomach, as you've just seen. Now, if you've killed a goodly number of women, I'd just as soon not hear you bray about all of them. Do you want to kill me? Well, you may certainly try. Yes, come on, you withered mad old crone, come try to kill me. You might as well let me kill you, for your brother will look at you after this and he will vomit just as I did. He will revile you. He would kill you himself were he here. Come, you pathetic old woman."

Caroline beckoned to her with her left hand, taunting her, knowing that she wanted it to end, one way or the other. She just couldn't stand here, listening to that madness, that filth. She knew she couldn't bear to hear about her aunt Eleanor's death at this woman's hands.

"Well? Are you a coward as well as old and quite mad?"

"Shut up, damn you! You want to die, Caroline? Now? That's fine with me."

"Before you try to dispatch me, why don't you tell me how I've tried to seduce your brother, who, if you hadn't noticed, is old enough to be my father. Besides being mad, evidently you can't even understand what's right before your nose. I love my husband very much. Not your damned brother."

"But you will come to want him. You see, he wants you, I've seen the lust for you in his eyes. He can't hide his feelings from me anymore. I know him, have known him all my life. I have wondered, though, what it would feel like to have him touch my belly and my breasts as he did you. Ah, and he put his fingers inside you. Did you enjoy it? Did he caress you?"

"No, he didn't. He's a doctor. I was horribly embarrassed."

"You're lying. Every woman wants Benjie. I've seen it over and over again."

"He's old, even older than you are. But you know, Bess, when they put you in Bedlam, you're not so old that you won't survive another twenty years or so. I do hope you will enjoy telling all your stories to others as mad as you are. Do you think they'll listen or just start scratching their lice?"

Bess Treath yelled her fury, threw the gun to the ground, drew a knife from her cloak pocket, and ran at Caroline.

"No, damn you, no! Stop!"

Caroline whipped the sword from behind her back at the same moment Coombe dropped through the opening, yelling, "No, Bess Treath, leave her alone!"

Bess Treath whirled about, immobile for just an instant. "I shot you, you mangy little bastard. I shot you! You damned little pest, you left Goonbell, and I knew you'd run away in your shame, in your mortification. That's why I left the bloody knife in your room, so everyone would know you'd killed all those women. Why did you come back?"

362

"I always planned to come back. I brought his lordship's mother back with me, and his sister."

"A lie, you little bastard. His mother is dead. She betrayed his father, like all the lying sluts. I'll bet he even killed her. I wasn't told about her so I know you're lying to me. No, he didn't tell me and he would have. Aye, that lying slut would have wanted Benjie just like all of them did and then I would have killed her too.

"You were supposed to stay gone, then when Caroline died, all would think you'd sneaked back and done it. Damn you to hell!"

She lunged toward him, the knife arched high, ready to come down into his chest.

Caroline raised her own sword, so light it was, and its steel blade glittered silver and sharp in that dim moonlight, and she screamed, "Here, Bess! Here, come to me! Coombe is wounded, he's no worry to you, leave him be."

Bess Treath turned and stared. "That sword, where did you get it?"

"Why, it was here, just for me, here for me to kill you. Come here, Bess, yes, that's right, come here." Again, Caroline held the mighty sword easily in the grip of her right hand, and beckoned with her left hand to Bess Treath. From the corner of her eye, she saw Coombe easing toward the gun Bess Treath had flung to the ground. She saw the blood dripping from his shoulder. He looked weak and pale. Suddenly she knew she didn't need him to get that gun, she just knew it.

Bess Treath screamed, a scream filled with madness and fury and perhaps even of acceptance, and lunged at Caroline.

Caroline lifted the sword, swung it back and forth in front of her, the fine steel hissing cleanly in the air. Bess Treath stopped suddenly so that glittering sharp blade tip wouldn't slash through her. She was heaving with madness, with fury, and again she raised that knife, but she couldn't get past that long swinging blade.

Caroline jumped forward, that magnificent sword extended its full length. Bess Treath managed to leap to the side, and the sword only slashed through her cloak over her right shoulder. She yelled in pain and rage.

"I'll stick this knife in your belly and kill that bastard of yours first!" She ran straight at Caroline, straight into that high swinging sword.

The blade slid cleanly into Bess Treath's chest.

Bess Treath just stood there a moment, hanging on that massive sword, a good foot of it protruding from her back, and she just looked down at it, then back at Caroline, who stood so close to her now, holding the handle, just holding it there as it drained her life away. "I knew it would have to end someday," Bess Treath said. "But this sword, how do you hold it so easily? It's huge. It must weigh as much as you do. You're but a weak woman. It's not possible."

"It seems you're wrong," Caroline said. She watched Bess Treath weave there, silent now, then she fell hard sideways.

Caroline pulled the sword from her body. She looked at Coombe, who now held the gun in his hand, standing there, staring at her, down at Bess Treath, pale and sweating, and Caroline said, "I'm so glad you weren't the one to drug my tea. Your shoulder is bleeding. We must get you back to the top of the cliff, Coombe."

"It isn't really all that bad," he said, trying to keep a grip on himself. "I managed to climb down, but I feared I would be too late. She was strong, so very strong. What is this chamber?"

"It is King Mark's treasure chamber."

Coombe just stared at her.

"Come," Caroline said. "I'll show you."

"But I must tell you first—" Coombe gave her an oddly helpless look, took one step, sighed, then slowly crumpled to the sandy floor.

"Tell me what, Coombe?"

He opened his eyes for just a brief instant and she could see the pain it was costing him. "Tregeagle," he whispered. "Tregeagle."

39

Caroline found Coombe's dangling rope as she eased herself out of the collapsed cliff wall. She hadn't had time to wonder how he'd gotten down to her, but now she knew. Where had he gotten the rope? Then she recognized it. It was the rope that had bound her wrist and ankles. He'd knotted the ends together.

She grasped it firmly and pulled herself out against the cliff face. She didn't look down. The wind was strong, tearing at her cloak and her hair. She drew a deep breath and began to climb. She had to save Coombe now. She'd wrapped his shoulder in strips of material she'd torn from Bess Treath's cloak and wrapped him against the cold as best she could. He'd remained unconscious after he'd managed to say Tregeagle's name.

Tregeagle. He'd drugged her? Evidently so. Evidently he'd been the one to put the note in her bedchamber. Had he tried to kill her by stringing the wire that felled her mare?

She began to climb, slowly, dragging herself upward, fighting the tug of the wind, the sting of the sea spray it hurled against her face. She looked up. It was more than a mile, it was farther away than it had been just a moment before.

Her arms trembled with pain. At least the blood on her hands made it easier for her to grip the rope. She stopped just a moment to catch her breath, and found that she was smiling, her face pressed inward against the barren cliff wall. She'd won. She'd won. It was then she heard his shout.

"Caroline!"

She felt a spurt of energy and pulled herself hand over hand, not hesitating, not resting, not feeling the pain, only wanting to see him, to hold him.

She felt his hands clasp her shoulders. He pulled her over the edge of the cliff. He lifted her up and stood her in front of him, his hands on her shoulders. He looked down at her, just looked, saying nothing.

"I thought you were dead," he said at last. "I couldn't have borne that, Caroline. When I read the note Coombe had left me, I didn't know what to think. He just said to come to St. Agnes Head as soon as I could."

She threw herself against him, burying her face in his chest. "We must get Coombe. He tried to save me and he's wounded."

"Where?"

"I don't think you're going to want to believe this, North. I found King Mark's treasure trove." She paused, shook her head, and said, "But that's not important right now. There's something else first. Before Coombe lost consciousness he said Tregeagle's name."

"Oh no. Bloody hell, I don't want to believe that."

Suddenly Tregeagle's voice was there right behind them and it was low, very tense, and filled with fury. "You damned bitch, you're luckier than any human has a right to be. Well, it's almost over now, and then we'll be at peace again."

He was walking toward them. Caroline saw Rafael Carstairs unconscious on the ground some six feet away.

North very calmly moved to stand in front of Caroline. "Listen to me, Tregeagle, you're right. It is over now."

Caroline said very slowly, knowing she was speaking not only to Tregeagle but to North as well, "I killed Bess Treath. Did you know Bess Treath was mad, Tregeagle? Did you know she very nearly killed Coombe?

Did you know she'd killed all those other women? Did you know she's obsessed with her brother, Dr. Treath?"

North was staring at her, disbelieving as she'd been when she first saw Bess Treath's face, disbelieving in that instant before she knew the woman was there to kill her.

Tregeagle ignored her, saying, "Coombe deserved it, tried to interfere when he realized what had happened, wouldn't listen to me. I would have killed him had I been here. I wish she had killed him, the miserable traitor. Yes, I told him what was happening, begged him to join me to rid this place of her, but he looked shocked that I would say such a thing. Shocked! He called me mad, just as you believe Bess Treath was mad. She was as sane as I am. She killed all those miserable sluts, but she failed with you. And I will finish it." His thick white hair was plastered to his head by the raging wind. He stood tall and proud, his black cloak billowing out behind him, looking like an avenging angel.

"Why?" Caroline said, stepping around to stand beside North. She felt him stiffen, but didn't look at him. "Why do you want to kill me, Tregeagle? What did I do to you?"

He said simply, "You took my precious little boy and you changed him." It took her a moment to realize he was talking about North. "Yes, you changed him and now his trollop of a mother is here—all your doing—and that simpleton daughter of hers. What a disgrace that one is, staring about like a vacant puppet, and her mother trying to claim Nightingale blood in her. It's disgusting, and I'll see soon enough that she's away from here again."

"But she's the very image of North," Caroline said, aware that North was very slowly trying to ease in front of her again. But she wouldn't allow it. "It was an accident that she is simple, nothing more, just an accident."

"No accident. It was her blood that did it, and her lover's, not Nightingale blood. When his grandfather visited her, he knew she'd betrayed her husband, cuckolded him like all the other Nightingale wives had betrayed their husbands, and that's when he made certain she'd stay away forever, hiding her disgrace, her perfidy, from the world."

North said very gently, his voice barely heard over the blustering wind, "Tregeagle, did you help Bess Treath kill all those women?"

"Certainly not, my lord! I am not like that. She is perhaps a bit mad, I'll grant you that, but only at times, only when it's warranted. Her deep and abiding love for her brother brought her to this pass."

"How did you discover she was the murderess?"

"I saw her go into Coombe's room at Mrs. Freely's inn. I followed her. I saw her with the bloody knife wrapped in the shirt. I told her I wanted you dead, *my lady,* and she said it was nearly time for you, that soon you would be in love with her brother, like all those other foolish women. I was willing to assist her. But we had to bide our time. You managed to survive the wire stretched across the narrow course, more's the pity. If you'd just died then like you were supposed to, then this wouldn't have been necessary. Coombe wouldn't have had to know. He wouldn't have had to be killed. Or mayhap, he would have, for he is a soft fool.

"Yes, we had to wait to get to you, because his lordship kept people around you, always people about to guard you. I asked Timmy the maid, and the little bugger lied to me. To me!

"Except for tonight. Tonight was just perfect. She and I together wrapped you in the cloak and brought you here, but she had to leave because her beloved brother was waiting for her, so I tied you tightly, but not tightly enough. I had no reason to stay here because she wanted to be the one to kill you, she alone. She told me it was her privilege, her duty, so I returned to Mount Hawke and there was Coombe and I realized that he suspected. I didn't say anything, and there the old fool was, wringing his hands, incoherent with worry after he discovered you were gone from Mount Hawke. I told him all about it then, tried to make him understand, but he wouldn't. I even told him about Bess Treath and how she would take care of you. He turned white, the cowardly old man, but then he struck me. When I came to my senses, he was gone, come here to help you. I knew it just as I knew I would have to make him pay for it."

North said, "Did you know that her ladyship just found King Mark's treasure trove? Down there, in a chamber behind the cliff."

"That's a bloody lie, my lord. *She's* taught you how to lie. Now you won't try to distract me again. I've got to kill her and then I don't know what I'll do because you'll be here and know that I killed her, and perhaps you'll be angry with me and want revenge."

He raised the pistol. North lunged at him, grabbing his raised arm, bending it back. The two men went down, North tangling in the folds of Tregeagle's cloak.

Caroline jumped forward, tripped over the rope, and went to her hands and knees. She quickly grabbed the rope and looped it even as she ran to where North and Tregeagle were rolling about on the ground, closer and closer to the cliff.

"North!"

He was straddling Tregeagle now, pounding his fist into the man's mouth. Tregeagle, with one final spurt of strength, whipped up his legs, striking North in the back. He went over Tregeagle's head, toward the edge of the cliff, rolling, rolling, faster and faster. Caroline ran after him, jumping over Tregeagle, who was lying there, huge breaths wheezing out of his chest, and she grabbed at North. She caught his ankle, managing to hold him long enough to slide the looped rope over his foot and pull tightly. She sat back, digging in her heels, trying to gain leverage, but still he slid toward the edge of the cliff. She yelled at the top of her lungs, "Rafael! Help me! Rafael!"

But it wasn't Rafael Carstairs who pulled North back. It was Tregeagle. Once he'd secured his master, he looked down at him, then over at Caroline.

"I couldn't beat you," he said very slowly. "You took my boy and I couldn't beat you. I nearly killed him and you saved him." Then he turned and simply stepped off the cliff. There was only the sound of the howling wind.

North was on his hands and knees, looking over the edge of the cliff. He saw Tregeagle spread on his back, looking for the world like a fallen angel, on the beach below.

He rose slowly and turned to face Caroline.

"It is too much," he said, more to himself than to her. "I take it back. He doesn't look like a fallen angel lying down there, he looks like a pathetic old man."

"Yes, but you're alive. Nothing else matters."

He pulled her to her feet and into his arms. He held her close, rocking her. "My God, are the two of you all right?"

It was Rafael Carstairs and he was still none too steady on his feet. "We're all right."

"I saw Tregeagle jump. Why did he do it? What the hell happened? Caroline, where were you? He sneaked up on me and struck me. I'm sorry."

"We're alive," North said. "We'll explain everything later. Actually, nothing else is all that important."

"Well," Caroline said, drawing a deep breath. "Actually there is. As I already told North, I found King Mark's treasure trove. There's a chamber some twenty feet down the face of the cliff. I fell through it and into the chamber. Come, I'll show you."

North clutched her arms in his hands. "You think you're climbing down that cliff face again?"

"Why, certainly. I found the treasure. It's my right, North, my right."

"Like hell it is. I don't believe you, Caroline. You're pregnant—oh God, is the babe all right?"

He was pressing his palms against her belly, trying to cradle her in his arms.

"The babe is fine. Now, listen. Rafael, after you let us down with the rope, you'll have to pull up Coombe. He's been wounded. Then you must take him to Dr. Treath."

"I still can't believe that Bess Treath is the one who murdered all the women. It boggles the mind, even now that I can glimpse some understanding." She knew he was trying to grasp the reality of it, the truth of it.

"She loved him in her mad way, and any woman she fancied he loved or she fancied wanted him, she killed. She planted the bloody knife in Coombe's chamber at the inn, just as Tregeagle told us. She hoped he'd left for good and thus could be blamed for my murder as well."

North's hands tightened on her shoulders. "But Coombe saved you?"

"No, I saved myself."

"But how?"

"Let's go back down and I'll show you everything, including the sword. It was magic, North. It's true, Rafael, it was made just for me, just for my

370

hand. It's huge, all strong glittering steel, at least four feet long, and its handle is covered with jewels, and it was embedded in this huge slab of rock but I pulled it out easily. I could lift it just as easily with one hand."

"Sword?" North shook his head. "Listen to me, Caroline. You're not going anywhere. I want you to stay here and try to keep warm. Rafael and I will—"

She just smiled up at him. "No," she said very calmly, very gently, and he looked at her long and hard. There was something different about her, perhaps it was the quiet look of determination in her eyes that he'd never seen there before, perhaps it was the vibrant intensity he felt coming from her, a new sense of strength, of knowledge. It was deep and full, this new force in her, and he realized it was now a part of her. It was her right to see this to the end.

A magic sword?

It was Rafael Carstairs who eased both North and Caroline back down the cliff wall, a rope tied beneath their arms.

When North eased down through the collapsed opening into the chamber, he couldn't at first believe his eyes. Then he strode quickly to where Coombe lay, shivering with shock and cold, but awake.

"My lord, she fetched you, didn't she?"

"I told you I would, Coombe. You should learn to believe me."

"She saved me, my lord."

"You will tell me all about it very soon now. I'm going to ease this rope beneath your arms and Rafael Carstairs will haul you to the top. Then he'll take you to see Dr. Treath."

Coombe shivered at the name. Caroline didn't blame him.

Both North and Caroline leaned out of the collapsed cliff wall to watch Rafael pull Coombe to the top. When he eased Coombe over the edge, they both breathed more easily.

North looked down at Bess Treath, lying there in a pool of blood, her face smoothed out and calm. She didn't look like a madwoman. "It is ridiculous, you know," he said.

"Yes. She told me many things, North, how she loved her brother, how she killed his first wife, then seduced him. Do you think he knows?"

"How could he not have suspected? We will see."

Caroline pulled up short. "Oh goodness, where is the sword? I pulled it out of her and carefully laid it on the ground beside her. What happened to it? No one could have taken it."

He was right on her heels as she ran back into the cliff. When he saw the flat stone that looked like some sort of ancient shrine, its top piled with jewels and gold and chalices, he sucked in his breath.

"King Mark," he said.

"Yes, but he doesn't seem to be buried here. This just seems to be some sort of hidden shrine. There's just his treasure, just like your great-grandfather and grandfather believed, North, just like your father believed." Suddenly, she gasped and took a step back.

"What is it? Are you all right, Caroline?"

She raised her arm and pointed. "No, it can't be." But there it was, the sword, embedded deeply just as it had been in the stone once again, its steel blade shimmering in the dim light, the jewel-encrusted handle glittering with mad color. She walked forward, her voice vague, utterly blank. "But how did it get back here? I don't understand, North. I left the sword beside Bess Treath's body. Where's the blood on the blade? It looks as though it's been polished. It looks just like it looked when I first saw it."

She reached out her hand and tentatively touched the handle. She tried to fit her hand around it but couldn't. It was massive, much too large for her woman's hand. She wrapped both hands around the handle and pulled. The sword didn't move. It was firmly planted in the stone. She pulled again, harder, with all her strength. Nothing happened.

North gently placed his hands over hers and pulled them away from the handle. He wanted to tell her it didn't matter, that somehow it had been Coombe who saved her, that her fear, her terror had changed things about in her mind, but he said nothing. What was there to say? Even though Coombe had said she'd saved him, how could that be? Was he to believe that the damned sword was magic? He saw the bewilderment in her eyes, saw the myriad questions squirreling through her mind.

He just held her hands, remaining still. Then she shook herself and there was this strange smile on her mouth. She turned from him then and once again touched the massive sword. She said, "North, there's something written on it here, just where the handle fits to the blade. Can you make it out?"

He stepped closer and squinted at the vague lettering. He said aloud, "I believe it says something like *Excalibur.*" He stared at the sword and said again, "*Excalibur.* No, my God, that's legend, ancient myth. It's not real, it can't be real. It's simply not possible. I won't believe it. We're in this strange buried chamber and our minds aren't functioning properly. No, I won't believe it."

"King Arthur's sword," Caroline said slowly. She traced her fingertips over the etched lettering. "His sword. Malory wrote all about it. King Mark has nothing to do with anything here. He never did. All along, it was King Arthur and the magic sword that came loose from the stone only for him. But it came loose for me as well. That sword came free in my hand so easily, why, I lifted it effortlessly and swung it. Why? Because I was in danger? I don't know, but what other explanation could there be? And now it's back where it belongs again. The sword must remain here, North, it must."

"I don't believe we could pull it out in any case." But North nonetheless, simply because he had to try, grasped the sword between his hands and pulled with all his strength. It didn't even quiver.

"It will stay here," he said, "since no one could pull it free, except for you."

"When I desperately needed it or I would have died."

North disliked the thought of magic, thoroughly disliked anything he couldn't eventually explain, but he couldn't deny the presence of the sword in front of him or the etching clear and fine on its shining steel. Had she really pulled it free? Rather, had the sword come free in her hands because it was magic?

He smiled down at his wife. "Those jewels aren't embedded in the stone. What do you want to do with them, Caroline?"

She leaned forward to pick up one of the golden chalices and bumped her hip against the stone. She felt the gold piece of jewelry she'd tripped over when she was trying to escape from Bess Treath. Slowly she withdrew it. It was an armlet. It seemed to match the one that sat in its place of honor on the crimson bed of velvet in the drawing room with the etched letters *REX* on it.

"Where did you get that? It looks just like the other one."

"It does look like the other one's twin. I tripped over it when I was running away from Bess Treath and stuffed it in my cloak pocket. There's etching on this one, North. Can you make it out in this dim light?"

He squinted at the etching, turned the armlet this way and that, then very slowly lowered it. He looked very pale in the shadowy light. His hand holding the armlet was none too steady.

"I don't believe this," he said.

"What is it?" she said, clutching at his arm.

"I really hate to have to say this. This armlet shouldn't exist, shouldn't feel warm and alive in my hand, as if it was worn around her neck just moments ago." He handed her the armlet. "Here, Caroline. Read it."

She turned it over and over in her palms, just feeling it, not looking closely at it. He said, "Are you reading it with your fingers?"

She gave him a smile. "Actually, I really don't have to. It's the mate to the other one, and since the other one says *REX,* I have no doubt that this one says *REGINA.*"

"Oh no, it's much more specific than that," North said. "It says *Guinevere.*"

40

The Earl and Countess of Wyndham were seated in the drawing room, the Duchess frowning sadly into her teacup. "To think, Marcus, we missed all the excitement, every drop of it, and only by three days. It's not fair."

"You must have just missed my messenger," North said.

"Your messenger," the earl said, "is right this minute very likely enjoying himself greatly. My servants will feed him and cosset him and will no doubt wring every scrap of information out of him, count on it, then they'll probably send him back with advice, the bloody meddlers."

"Now, Duchess, it is fair," Caroline said. "It was our adventure, not yours. Now, since you and Marcus just might have been the ones to save the day, North and I wish to thank you both very much and to give you this." Caroline handed the Duchess a beautiful gold necklace, thick and rich-looking, so very old, yet shining and vibrant, warm to the touch.

"You can wear it with your pearls," the earl said, lightly touching his fingertips to the rich gold links.

"As for the remaining jewels and gold coins and jewelry, like you and the Duchess, Caroline and I are sending some to the British Museum, giving the chalices to the Salisbury Cathedral, and displaying the remainder here at Mount Hawke so all can come and see them."

"If we ever lose all our groats, we can always sell a bracelet or two and save ourselves," Caroline said.

"Ha, you'd send me to work in the tin mines before you'd part with a single piece of jewelry we found," North said, lightly stroking his fingertips over her arm.

She smiled, and for a brief moment it was a faraway smile, one that severed her from all of them completely, but then she was back again, and her smile was warm and filled with mischief and happiness. She looked over at the bed of crimson velvet. In it now were two armlets, touching each other, together again for as long a time as the Nightingales existed. As for the sword, she and North had agreed that it be left where it was and that no one else should know about it, not even their family, not even the Earl and Countess of Chase. He'd told her that same night, "The fewer who know, the better. Rafael Carstairs won't say a thing, I've already spoken to him, and naturally Coombe won't."

Caroline had frowned, saying, "It still isn't enough, North. We don't want anyone accidentally stumbling upon it. Indeed, from the beach you can see the shadows there in the middle of the cliff, see there's something strange. Anyone with a whit of curiosity would investigate. I know I would. The last thing we want is scavengers going in there and trying to steal it. No, what we need is a nice explosion of some kind. The good Lord knows there are enough of them at the damned tin mines."

"We need a bloody miracle," North said. "God, I'm so tired I can't think anymore. We'll worry about it in the morning."

Both of them had indeed considered it a miracle. Near to dawn that same night, when they'd finally fallen into their bed, so exhausted they could barely think, the wind had risen to gale force, the rain had pounded the earth and uprooted trees, sending even huge rocks tumbling over the cliffs and into the water, and the cliff had collapsed in on itself, sealing away forever that chamber and the sword *Excalibur* embedded in that slab of stone.

Caroline said now to her mother-in-law, "You refused to tell me what you wanted of the treasure. Please, you must have whatever it is you desire. Marie, too."

Cecilia Nightingale said, "I'll ask Marie. Doubtless she would enjoy one of the armlets. As for me, my dear, I would just as soon never touch any of those things again for as long as I live."

"Why ever not, Mother?" North said, his head cocked to one side in question.

"Er, it's rather difficult, North," she said, looking down at her hands, which were whiter and softer now since she'd come to Mount Hawke. "I saw the armlet Caroline placed over there on that crimson velvet, the one your great-grandfather supposedly found here on Mount Hawke land. And the one beside it that you found, Caroline, in the cliff."

"Yes," Marcus Wyndham said. "I found the first one in that croaking old clock. It was the reason the thing sounded so bloody ugly, like a sick person trying to cough."

Caroline said, "I guess it will remain a mystery. Who put it there and why? When was it done? Why didn't any of the Nightingale men ever say anything about it?"

"It's not a mystery, Caroline," Cecilia Nightingale said.

"What do you mean, Mother? Do you know anything about the damned thing?"

"Ah, well, I did it, you know."

"Did what, Mother?"

Cecilia Nightingale looked at her son and said, "I overheard your grandfather speaking to your father. It was one of the very few times your grandfather wasn't screaming at your father to rid himself of me. Anyway, I eavesdropped. Your grandfather was showing your father the armlet. He was stroking it as if it was alive, as if it was the most precious thing in the world. He said that the Nightingale men kept it close, never showing anyone else. You see, North, your great-grandfather, who had found the wretched thing, had nearly had it stolen, and thus he hid it away. He didn't tell your grandfather about it until he was dying. Your grandfather, who'd been ill the previous winter, decided it was time to pass the armlet down to his son, your father. I'll never forget how he stroked the thing, caressed it as one would a man or a woman. It was obscene, and rather pathetic. I watched when your grandfather placed the armlet reverently back into the safe. I saw the combination. Late that night, I opened the safe and took the armlet. I wanted to get back at your grandfather, North, as simple as that. He loved the armlet as much if not more than a human being loves another human being. I hated it and I hated him, so I took the damned armlet and hid it in the clock. Paltry of me, I know, but I wanted him to suffer, to lose something he valued above all else. No one said a word. It was as if the thing had never existed, but I knew the pain he must have felt, knowing someone had stolen it and not knowing who had done it. His own son? I do wonder if he blamed his son, your father, if he even accused him of taking it. Or perhaps he believed it was one of the male martinets. And I was pleased because I knew he'd never know. He would listen to that bloody clock for the rest of his days and never realize what was inside it. And now you found its mate."

"Where the devil do you think that first armlet came from?" North asked no one in particular.

"Well," Caroline said slowly, eyeing the armlet, "it must have been accidentally dropped by those people who were carving the chamber into the cliff. Good Lord, at least a thousand years ago, don't you think? There was no reason for your great-grandfather to lie about where it was found."

"Near the barrows and that stone fence and the copse of trees," North said. "It's the only explanation, I guess."

"And to think," the Duchess said, "all this time everyone believed that if any king were here, it was King Mark."

"But King Arthur isn't buried there."

"Just the treasure and the s—"

"The what, Caroline?" the Duchess said, raising a graceful dark eyebrow.

"Nothing. My mind is just meandering. Goodness, here's Miss Mary Patricia with two babes!"

The cooing and laughter, the pats, the kisses, the pained looks from Coombe, and the occasional yells for food from Little North and Eleanor became the focus for the remainder of the afternoon.

Coombe came into the drawing room that evening, his arm resting in an interesting sling, cleared his throat, and announced, "Dinner is served, my lady."

"Ah, Coombe, thank you," North said. "You're looking quite the romantic hero. How are you and Polgrain doing?"

"We will survive, my lord, we will survive, but it is difficult. One thinks that one knows another, but in this case, it wasn't true. Poor Mr. Polgrain deeply regrets that he wasn't conscious enough to aid you that night, my lady, but Mr. Tregeagle had drugged him as well as her ladyship, as you know. It was only me he believed would succumb to his plot. It has depressed us profoundly."

Perhaps disappointing and depressing for him, Caroline thought, eyeing the very neat sling he wore around his shoulder and under his elbow. It made him look very dapper. The memory of that night was clear and sharp. All that had happened, the terror, the grinding pain, and finally the triumph, all of it was there deep inside her, and would be with her always. But most of all what would remain with her until she died was the image of herself easily drawing *Excalibur* from the stone, feeling how it had been made just for her, that it was part of her. It would always be with her, that aura of being touched by something beyond herself, beyond this modern world. She'd been touched by magic, by ancient magic that had no explanation, but it did have reality, it did have meaning. It had saved her life. No, it had given her the gift of enabling her to save her own life.

"You're looking deep and thoughtful," North said to her as he placed her hand over his forearm to lead her into dinner. "Are you perhaps considering the use of those wrist cuffs on me tonight?"

She grinned up at him. "Yes, that just might please both of us mightily."

It did please both of them, North in particular, who lay sprawled on his back, staring up at his wife's flushed face, wondering how she could look more beautiful than she had just that morning. Her breasts were larger, and he gently pulled his hands from the cuffs and cupped them in his palms. "I love you," he said, and she leaned down so he could kiss her.

"Come lie next to me," he said, and pulled her down, gently pressing her cheek against his shoulder. "Now, let me tell you about Dr. Treath. He is leaving next week. I spoke to him this afternoon. He blames himself, which perhaps he should do, I don't know. I don't understand how he could be so blind to what happened to every woman who ever came into his orbit, but there it was. I didn't ask him if he remembered taking his own fourteen-year-old sister to bed. I didn't think it mattered. Everyone knows about his sister now, just as everyone knows that Tregeagle drugged you and helped her take you away to St. Agnes Head. Thank God she had to leave for a while to go back to her brother, for he would have missed her. But it gave you the time you needed." He leaned over and kissed her forehead. "You're still damp from our lovemaking. I like that. Also, let me tell you that I admire you, Caroline. You're brave and loyal and inventive, but then again, it was those qualities that drew me to you in the first place, those qualities, your beautiful self, and that mess of problems you carried on your back. But, you know, there's something new about you, something that happened that night—" He paused, and she felt his shrug.

"Perhaps it's a new strength I sense in you, a deeper understanding of why we mortals are here, why it's important for us to be decent, to cherish those important to us. Ah, I'm making no sense at all."

She kissed his shoulder. "I received a letter today. The painter will be coming with the man who will restore all the Nightingale women's portraits. Can we be painted together, North, after he paints your mother and Marie and you with both of them?"

"So we'll be hanging about forever and ever?"

"Yes. I want our great-great-grandchildren to know that we were together always and we loved each other and there was nothing that ever set us apart. Just as those two armlets are together again."

"Shall I be painted with my wrist cuffs on?"

She laughed into his shoulder, licked his warm flesh, then began to caress him with her mouth and hands. And she thought, *I'll be touched by magic every day of my life.*

Epilogue

Mount Hawke, Cornwall
March 1815

North walked into the drawing room, several pieces of folded paper in his right hand, an odd look on his face.

Caroline looked up from her embroidery and said, "Look at this, North. Even Miss Mary Patricia approves. I've managed to stitch a Nightingale bird here on the corner of your handkerchief." She picked up the piece of fine linen and stared closely at it. "Yes, you can tell it's a bird. I know that Nightingale men detest the thought of also being birds, but what can you do? I say flaunt it. I say learn how to warble. North? What's wrong?"

He looked distracted. He sat down then and put his hand on her belly and began to caress her. It was an automatic gesture. He'd told her it helped him think, to solve problems. The babe obligingly kicked his palm, and North blinked and grinned.

"Hello."

"What have you got there?"

"A letter from Boston." He drew a deep breath. "Remember when we discovered that my great-grandmother had had an affair with that rogue named Griffin? And then they both disappeared, my great-grandfather putting it about that she'd died, even going so far as to bury her? Then we found out that the rest of the Griffin family left Cornwall for Boston in the 1780s?"

She nodded, leaned over, kissed him, and said, "You've found her, haven't you?"

"Yes. It appears that she and Griffin ran away together to Boston. My God, Caroline, I have lots and lots of family over in the Colonies. Cousins by the score. It also appears that both my great-grandmother and Griffin outlived my great-grandfather. When Griffin's family wrote him of my great-grandfather's death, the two of them got married and legitimized all their children."

"She was happy."

"It would appear that Griffin was indeed a rogue, but he fell in love with my great-grandmother and became constant. How would you like to visit Boston? The blasted war ended last fall."

The babe kicked North's palm again. He grinned, leaned down, and put his cheek to her belly. "He wants to go meet all his cousins," he said.

Caroline laughed, grabbed her husband's ear, and pulled him up. She kissed him. "I think it's a wonderful idea. At least they're not named Nightingale so I don't have to stitch a lot more silly birds on handkerchiefs. Now, I have something to tell you as well, North."

He cocked a dark eyebrow.

"Coombe is marrying Mrs. Mayhew."

He choked, stared at her, dropped the papers on the floor, then threw his head back and laughed and laughed.

"I thought you had all the magical experiences in this family," he said at last, "but it appears that Mrs. Mayhew has performed the greatest magic of all time."

Author's Note

King Mark, if he really did exist, was most likely buried near Fowey, in the south of Cornwall, as most legend believers claim. As for King Arthur, everyone wants to lay claim to him and insist he was as real and as powerful and as noble as Malory's book painted him way back in the fifteenth century in his *Le Morte d'Arthur.* The Scots, the Welsh, the Cornish, the English, all want him to be of their soil, of their blood, of their character. All of them want him buried in a hidden cave on their land.

If by chance Arthur did live and die in Cornwall, I choose to believe it was near Tintagel, which lies only about forty miles northeast of Mount Hawke. It certainly makes a romantic setting for Camelot.

Did either of these kings really live, or were they just the stuff of legends and myths, stories to be added to, like squares of a quilt, many hands making it grow and change continually, making it more and more complex, destined to enrich the minds and dreams of generation after generation?

Mark, that duped nitwit of a king, wasn't ever real to me. As for King Arthur, he was always more than real. Indeed, he is legend, an epic spirit. He can't be allowed to pass into the mists of time. He will always be here with us, to inspire us, to ennoble us, to touch our souls with his special magic, to show us greatness tempered with failure, to show us grace and humility in the face of devastation and loss.

As for Arthur's sword, *Excalibur*, I know deep down that it exists somewhere. It's as real as King Arthur.